TELL THEM YOU LIED

TELL THEM YOU LIED

A Novel

LAURA LEFFLER

HYPERION
AVENUE
LOS ANGELES · NEW YORK

Copyright © 2025 by Laura Leffler

All rights reserved. Published by Hyperion Avenue, an imprint of Buena Vista Books, Inc. No part of this book may be reproduced or transmitted in any form or by any means, electronic or mechanical, including photocopying, recording, or by any information storage and retrieval system, without written permission from the publisher. For information address Hyperion Avenue, 7 Hudson Square, New York, New York 10013.

First Edition, May 2025
10 9 8 7 6 5 4 3 2 1
FAC-004510-24318
Printed in the United States of America

This book is set in Railroad and Chronicle
Designed by Amy C. King

Library of Congress Cataloging-in-Publication Data

Names: Leffler, Laura, author.
Title: Tell them you lied : a novel / by Laura Leffler.
Description: [New York] : Hyperion Avenue, 2025. • Summary: "Two New York artists' tumultuous friendship takes a dangerous turn when a prank goes wrong and one of them goes missing"—Provided by publisher.
Identifiers: LCCN 2024013003 • ISBN 9781368102469 (hardback) • ISBN 9781368103763 (paperback) • ISBN 9781368103312 (ebook)
Subjects: LCGFT: Thrillers (Fiction) • Novels. Classification: LCC PS3612. E349698 T45 2025 • DDC 813/.6—dc23/eng/20240325
LC record available at https://lccn.loc.gov/2024013003

Reinforced binding for hardcover edition

www.HyperionAvenueBooks.com

Logo Applies to Text Stock Only

For Jordan

*Art is whatever
you can get away with.*

—ANDY WARHOL

PART
1

One

YOUR MESS WAS EVERYWHERE. Coffee grounds marched like ants across the counter, a carton of milk left out to spoil. There were toast crumbs, empty Sweet'N Low packets, and two dirty mugs near the sink. I picked up one of the mugs, a graduation gift from my little brother, and turned it in my hand. *World's Best Sister.* I'd taken so much care when I'd packed it three months before, swaddling it in Bubble Wrap and thick blankets for the U-Haul trip to New York. Now there was a sharp nick in the lip and the handle had cracked off completely. That was the whole problem, wasn't it, Willow? You thought everything was yours, and it made you careless.

My grip tightened until I felt the mug might go to pieces in my hand. Then I let go. I dropped it into the garbage along with the milk and the rest of your trash and wiped down the counter. I wouldn't let you get to me anymore, especially not on the day everything between us would change.

I allowed myself to imagine it the way I had a hundred times before—you, crossing Tenth Avenue on your way to the gallery, platinum hair glinting in the sun, a slice of stomach peeking out between your skirt and top. We had become so accustomed to the city's eyes on us, the ogling and catcalling and sweaty faces, the tongues flicked between split fingers, the scurrilous shouts from passing cars. It meant nothing to us, and, because of that, I knew you wouldn't sense the danger in just another man. In another impotent pair of eyes.

But the danger was there, Willow—because this man wasn't just watching, he was waiting. He was holding a knife.

I knew that because I'd paid him to be there.

<hr>

The buzzer rang. I froze, sponge in hand, before making my way to the intercom. "Hello?"

"It's me."

Milo. I pictured him on the stoop—frayed T-shirt over bony, hunched shoulders, those paint-flecked work boots he always wore. I never thought Milo was handsome, not the way you did, but there was something about him that tugged at me, like the pull toward sleep. I could almost feel his fingertips on my skin, my tiny hairs standing at attention, skin goose bumped.

"Let me in," he said.

I pushed the button to unlock the door, then waited for him to climb the four flights of stairs to our apartment. When he got there, his face was crooked. Sweat circled the neck of his shirt. My scalp tingled, cold, because I knew. Right away, I knew. Something had gone wrong.

"Have you heard from her?" he said, boots planted wide on the landing.

I glanced back at the little red numbers on the microwave—9:55 a.m. *A half an hour,* I thought. *We still have thirty-five minutes.* That's when you were supposed to call from the police station and tell me about the man with the knife, how he'd pulled you into an abandoned warehouse and taken your wallet. Milo knew that. He was the one who'd hired Tyler, who had told him where to wait for you, and when.

"It's not even ten o'clock," I said.

Milo put his palm flat on the door, trying to push past me, but I blocked him. It was a reflex, something deep in my subconscious warning me that he was carrying danger with him, an unpinned grenade.

"Jesus, Anna." He gripped my shoulders with both hands and guided me backward. It was like we were dancing, until my back thumped against the door. He dropped his hands, brushed past me. "Turn on the TV."

The screen was the size of a cereal box, but I saw what was happening all the same. The World Trade Center was on fire, red gashes cut into both buildings, smoke billowing. I looked to the open kitchen window. Nothing but brightness, blue sky.

Milo clicked up the volume. Newscasters were talking about the Pentagon, an explosion, maybe a bomb, maybe another plane. The White House was being evacuated, the Capitol Building too. Words rolled along the bottom of the screen, indecipherable as runes.

"This can't be real," I said. I couldn't have slept through something like this. The birds wouldn't be singing. The sky wouldn't be so blue.

And then, on the screen, a magic trick—a tower turned to smoke.

It happened in slow motion but also fast, and the enormity of it, the sheer scale, crashed over me, filling my ears and muffling every sound except my own thundering heartbeat. The collapse replayed on screen, slower and slower, the building falling straight down, through the middle, inside itself. A black cloud took shape in its place.

How many people did I just watch die?

It was impossible. *Impossible.*

That building had seemed as permanent as the sun.

I found myself sitting on the bare wood floor, hands stacked over my mouth. People on TV were running and bleeding and covered in ash, and despite those real people in our new city on that ordinary workday, moving along, not questioning their lives or their jobs or the buildings that held them up, I was thinking of only one person.

Only you.

The C train went right under the financial district, but—*no*—it was ten o'clock. You'd be well past the World Trade Center by then, off the subway entirely, making your way to your position behind Roche Gallery's huge front desk. *To Tyler and his knife.* The footage flapped like a filmstrip through my mind—his face covered in a bandanna, his hand over your mouth, the tip of his blade pressed into your neck. It was all wrong now, absurd. That fallen building had changed everything.

"Milo . . ."

He faced me, eyebrows stretched apart like wings. A million questions twisted through my head, but I couldn't articulate any of them. My hands were in fists against my cheeks, and my voice came out strangled. Unrecognizable.

"What did we do?"

He blinked. He shook his head. "This is terrorists, A. This has nothing to do with us."

On the screen, that enormous, churning gray-black cloud. If I could have thought logically, I would have known Milo was right—there was no way that what we had done, our stupid little prank, could have wreaked so much havoc. This was outside us. Beyond us. Bigger than us. But logic wasn't working that morning, and the disaster across the bridge didn't feel like a coincidence. It felt like one of your tricks.

Abracadabra, I thought. *Poof.*

Milo grabbed the cordless phone off its charging dock and held it out to me. "Call her."

I stepped back. "You do it."

"You know she won't talk to me." He wagged the phone. "Come on, Anna. *Please.*"

I grabbed it and dialed your cell. A recorded operator whined in my ear, telling me the number was out of the service area. That wasn't right. That couldn't be right. I dialed again. Milo hovered, watching me, biting the skin on his thumb. That same loud, nasal voice in the receiver. Out of the service area. I pulled back, looking at the phone like it might come alive in my hand. It didn't make sense. I dialed again, and again, and again.

"It isn't working," I said. "It's a weird message."

The people on TV were talking about the FAA, the PLO, Flight 11. So many words and letters and numbers I didn't understand. My heart swam inside my chest, my palms grew slick. I wiped them on my robe, the cheap fabric only making me sweatier.

Milo snatched back the phone. He dialed and listened and frowned. "What the hell is going *on*?"

He shifted from foot to foot, biting his thumb and staring at the phone. He was cracking. Doubting himself, doubting me. Our plan had been a small thing, a joke, a *lark*. We wanted to scare you, to mess up your plans, a little revenge for all the shit you'd put us through. Milo thought making you afraid would soften you, which is what he always wanted—for you to be soft enough to mold. But I knew better. You were made of glass, not clay; to be free, we'd have to shatter you completely.

Milo flung the phone against the wall. I covered my ears as it bounced off the floor and broke into two pieces, the battery pack hanging by thin red wires. Milo's head was in his hands. I could almost hear his nails scratching his scalp. I could almost feel his fingers tugging through my own tangles.

Another bulletin. Pennsylvania. Missing planes. Newscasters saying names I had never heard before, all of it sounding like fables, like fantasy. Everything was so foreign and far away. I thought of my family back home in Bexley. They were probably watching the same news, huddled around the living room TV, *Good Morning America* so rudely cut away to *this*. I pictured my mother nervously folding laundry, Henry curled on the couch in tears.

I picked up the cordless phone, snapped the pieces together, and replaced the battery pack. Another news bulletin. All the city's subways were shut down—the bridges and airports, too. I blinked at the screen, then at the walls around me, your photographs, my paintings, our framed exhibition posters. Everything felt too small. Too tight.

We were trapped.

I pressed the talk button on the phone with a cold, nearly numb finger. There was no dial tone.

"You broke it," I said.

Milo dragged his fingers down his face, pulling his skin until the flesh under his eyes turned inside out. "I cannot be here right now."

I glanced back at the television, the smoke, the sirens. A minute passed, maybe two. It took that long for it to click: *This is an emergency. The normal rules do not apply.* I needed to call my family, to hear my brother's voice—no matter how much the stupid daytime minutes cost. I ran into my bedroom, snatched my cell phone from my nightstand, and dialed the numbers to the little yellow house in Ohio. Instead of ringing, the phone let out an angry cranking noise, then went dead.

I rushed out to tell Milo, the tumble of words leaving my mouth before I even made it into the living room. "My cell's not working, either. I don't understand—"

But the room was empty.

Milo was already gone.

I didn't know it yet, Willow, but so were you.

FOUR YEARS BEFORE

IT WAS SEPTEMBER when they met—the first Wednesday in their first week of college classes, still hot enough for frat guys to tarzan into Wabash Lake, and for their girlfriends, in near-matching tans and J.Crew bikinis, to cheer them on from its rocky banks. But it was in an entirely different part of the Balwin University campus that freshman Anna Vaughn situated herself—neatly, quietly, at a battered two-person drafting table in a second-floor studio of the Highsmith Art Building. The stool next to hers remained empty, which wasn't unexpected, and didn't yet matter. Anna laid her notebook and sharpened pencils on the table, then traced a finger over the graffiti cut into it like a frieze, feeling herself *there,* in the studio, *finally.*

It wasn't the freedom of college that excited her. Not the keg parties or the hookups, not the soft green lawns or century-old brick dormitories. Anna didn't care about any of that. It was Highsmith, this ugly hunk of '70s Brutalism on the corner of Ash and Asbury, discrepant amid the rest of campus's Gothic Revival architecture. It was Highsmith that called her here,

Highsmith that held the illustrious professors and cutthroat crit sessions that she'd read about and thought about and yearned for since her high school art teacher first told her about the place. Highsmith was the reason Anna had come to this otherwise conservative, middle-of-nowhere Ohio college. It was the first step in her plan to becoming an artist—a real, gallery-represented, world-renowned *Artist*.

Professor Anthony Kape walked into the room, and a hush fell over the students. Kape was more than campus famous—he was art-world famous, too. He had a New York City gallery, several *Artforum* reviews, and a nomination for the first Guggenheim Hugo Boss Prize, and there were rumors he could actually win the second. He'd been teaching at Balwin University for ten years, and three of his students had already gone on to be famous painters in their own right. One of them, post MFA and age twenty-six, had been included in a Whitney Biennial a few years before, and when asked about his influences said, "Only one—Tony Kape."

That's exactly what Anna wanted—to shoot from Balwin into the best MFA painting program in the States, Yale, where the top gallerists scouted fresh talent the same way Goldman Sachs did the school's MBA program. She could get there. She was good enough, she knew. She just needed a way in. She needed Anthony Kape's recommendation.

Now, inside the room with the man himself, Anna found him disappointingly average—bulky and middle-aged, with a salt-and-pepper goatee and work boots and an apron smeared with black paint.

"Welcome to Two Dimensions—" he started, but he was cut off by the clang of the steel door behind him.

It was a girl. The final student. She entered the room like an explosion, loud and diverting, wearing a black tank top cut off under her ribs, clearly braless, and low-rise faded jeans that flared so absurdly over her feet that Anna couldn't see her shoes. She was small but curvy, and a tiny diamond flashed in her belly button, another in her nose. Her hair was so long and tangled it verged on rangy. She should have been repulsive, but she wasn't. Not at all. She was beautiful. Anna felt a strange tug in her stomach, like there was something metal inside her lurching toward a magnet.

"Sorry," the girl said to Kape, brushing back her wild brown hair and smiling. She faced the class, the twelve students who had each fought as hard as Anna to be there—who had sent portfolios to the Balwin BFA program admissions a year ago, who had endured the snaking registration line last week and paid the studio fee to get here, to this particular classroom at this particular time with this particular professor. All of them were pent-up and excited, and they had all frozen at the sight of this new girl.

"Sorry," she said again, this time to the class. "I couldn't find the building."

Kape gestured for her to find a seat. "It happens."

Nobody moved as she crossed the room. Nobody spoke. She walked by the empty stool at Anna's table, trailing the scent of cigarette smoke and something green—blooming honeysuckle, cut summer grass. She sat behind Anna, next to a girl with her hair clipped into little plastic butterflies. She saw Anna watching her and smiled.

Anna felt caught. Blood rushed to her cheeks. She turned back to the front of the room.

Kape blinked a few times, as if to clear smoke from his eyes. "Does everyone have the text?"

Anna had the book on her table. *The Visual Experience.* She'd bought it in the bookstore, used, for twenty-one dollars, and had already thumbed through most of it. She flattened a palm against the cover, waiting for instructions.

"Close your eyes," Kape said.

Anna, confused, looked around. Her classmates hadn't hesitated. They were doing what Kape had told them to do.

Anna shut her eyes, too.

"Now picture *art*," Kape said. "Any art. Whatever comes to you."

Anna saw herself daubing paint on a stretched canvas, making a landscape in a huge, sunlit studio. Serious as O'Keeffe. Skilled as Canaletto.

"What do you see?" Kape's voice floated by. Anna sensed him walking past her, toward the back of the room. "There are eight main principles to consider here—texture, line, gesture, value, shape, color, space, perspective. As you look at the work in your mind's eye, I want you to consider each."

There was a sound beyond the purr of the fans—a rustling. Anna's eyes twitched. She wanted to open them, to see what was happening, but she didn't dare. There was a click, a low whir.

"Now," Kape said from behind her. "Open your eyes."

Anna blinked. The studio lights were off and the blinds were down, flapping gently in the warm breeze. At the front of the room, there was a projected image of a painting. A portrait of a woman, distorted, disturbed, fingers clawed in her mouth, face broken into shards. A Picasso, Anna knew, probably from the 1930s. A portrait of one of the master's many muses.

"What do you see?" Kape asked the class.

"Picasso," Anna said.

"Yes, that's a given."

Anna's face went hot, and she gripped the sides of her stool. She did not like being wrong.

"I want you to remember the principles," Kape went on. "Texture, line, gesture, value, shape, color, space, perspective."

"Space."

Anna turned to see who had spoken—the girl with the wild hair. Her face was calm, and she was twisting a pencil between her fingers.

"All three dimensions at once," the girl continued. "Every angle of the face at the same time."

"Very good." Kape pressed a button, and the slide changed. Another portrait of a woman, this time a work by Matisse. The woman was sallow and unnatural, and the painting was ugly, Anna thought, its colors too intense.

"Here?" Kape said.

"Color," someone said.

Kape flicked the image. Leonardo da Vinci's *Mona Lisa*. But Anna understood that it wasn't the answer. The model wasn't what mattered—she was only a means to an end. It was how the artist had handled her face and figure that Kape wanted his class to see.

Anna knew the answer. She forced her mouth to open. "Perspective."

Kape nodded and changed the image again.

Toward the end of class, Kape put a fishbowl on a table.

"Everyone," he said, as the students gathered around. "Pick two papers from the bowl."

The students took turns pulling out small, folded scraps and reading them. Anna reached her hand in cautiously. She had no idea what was inside, and ignorance made her nervous. She unfolded the first paper to see *pride* written in Kape's floppy cursive. On the second, *envy*.

"The seven deadly sins, right?" someone said.

Kape nodded and explained the assignment: Each student was to make a work that reflected both themes they had received. "Broaden your minds," he said over the zipping backpacks and rustling papers. "Think Northern Renaissance. Bosch and Bruegel. Think Serrano or Mapplethorpe, even Mallarmé. But mostly, I want you to remember the principles we discussed today. Texture, line, gesture, value, shape, color, space, perspective."

Anna watched her classmates clump together into groups of two or three to make their way back to the dorms or the dining halls or wherever groups of kids went, but she stayed on her stool, bent over her notebook, writing down Serrano and Mapplethorpe and Mallarmé to look up later. There were so many names to know, especially the modern and contemporary artists. Anna had studied as much as she could on her own, and she knew the biggest names, but the canon felt slippery, like she was trying to catch fish with her hands. When she finished making her notes, everyone was gone, even Professor Kape. She had nowhere to be, no one to meet, so she stayed where she was and calligraphed the eight principles, and then the words she'd chosen—*pride* and *envy*—and stared at them for a moment, trying to solidify flimsy notions into an image. Into something she could paint.

Eventually Anna made her way out of the studio, walking slowly down the perforated metal steps, her fingertips grazing the bumpy white wall as she tried not to tread too hard or make too much noise, though that seemed impossible. Everything in Highsmith banged and echoed around her. At the bottom of the staircase, she pressed against a push-bar exit and found herself blinking into the late-summer haze. There was a low brick wall on Ash Street, a remnant of the building torn down in the 1970s when an endowment had funded the new art department, Brutalist building and all. Now the students used the wall as a bench, a place to meet and complain about the crits they'd gotten, to gossip and sketch and stub out cigarettes in the words etched in the concrete—HIGHSMITH ART STUDIOS EST. 1974.

Perched on that wall was the girl with the mangy hair, cigarette loose in one hand, a set of keys with a kitschy little Eiffel Tower in the other. Anna stopped short. The steel door caught the heel of her sneaker and bumped her forward. She let out a small yelp.

The girl watched Anna placidly, then blew a line of smoke over her shoulder. "You were in Kape's class just now," she said, her voice so low and lazy she sounded bored.

"Yeah." Anna tucked her straight, thick hair behind her ears. Her hair was something she'd always been proud of—glossy and clean and well-tended—but at that moment, it felt provincial, embarrassing.

The girl held out a hand, and Anna saw her eyes for the first time—ice blue. Gamblin Radiant Blue, actually, mixed with two parts white.

"I'm Willow," she said.

"Anna."

Their hands clasped. Willow's skin was cashmere-soft, so atypical for artists who worked with caustic materials all day, who cut themselves on X-Acto knives and washed their hands raw with Masters soap.

"Freshman?" Willow asked.

Anna nodded.

"Same. Where are you from?"

"Bexley." Anna gestured vaguely behind her. "It's right outside Columbus."

"Oh, cool," someone else said. Anna saw the other girl then, the one with the butterfly clips, and was startled.

"Nice to be so close to home, right?" The other girl stuck out her hand. "Hey. I'm Lizzie Stone. And before you ask, I'm from Louisville."

Anna turned back to Willow. "You too?"

"Oh, no." Willow dropped her cigarette on the sidewalk and lifted a bell-bottom—combat boots, Anna noted, not dissimilar to the ones Professor Kape had been wearing—and ground the butt into the cement with her lug sole. "We met in the dorms. I'm from Chicago."

A city girl. That was it—it was starting to click. Willow projected the laconic glamor and confidence that Anna associated with big cities. She'd never been to Chicago, but she'd been to New York, once, on an art club trip when she was sixteen, and it had opened her eyes: the style, the creativity, the hyper-ordered chaos. She'd always loved to draw and paint, but at that first visit to MoMA, spellbound in front of a sixteen-foot Helen Frankenthaler stain painting, she realized she wanted more than a sketchbook and ribbons from school shows. She wanted *that*. She wanted to be on *those* walls. She wanted to be a Real Artist.

"So, what'd you get?" Willow said, and, when Anna didn't respond, went on. "Lust, greed, pride?"

"Oh," Anna said. "Pride and envy."

Willow raised her eyebrows. "Trade me?" she said. "I really wanted pride."

Anna slipped her backpack off her shoulder and pulled the scraps of paper from the inside pocket where she'd stashed them. Her actions were automatic, like she was in a dream. She didn't know why she handed the paper to Willow, only that she wanted to please her.

Willow put her own in Anna's hand.

Anna looked down.

Wrath.

———

There was a week before the next 2D class, and in the meantime, Anna surprised herself looking for Willow everywhere—in every classroom, dormitory, dining hall, and bathroom, on every lawn and sidewalk. Growing up, Anna didn't have any friends. The people in Bexley acted almost *afraid* of her, keeping their distance from the entire Vaughn family, as if Henry's illness made them contagious. Henry and his seizures, Henry and disabilities, Henry and his appointments, Henry, Henry, Henry. Her family's little yellow house had been closed off to the outside world. Anna never had sleepovers or birthday parties. There were no team sports or after-school clubs or dances.

Not even babysitters. Her parents spent all their time tending to Henry and had nothing left for other adults. There were no family friends or neighborhood parties, and because of that, Anna never learned how to socialize. At home, she had her paints and her brushes and the art books she checked out from the library to keep her company, and at school, she had art class, where her talent could shine and the teachers encouraged her with praise and attention. For years, it felt like enough. It felt like all she deserved.

But something about Willow had jolted her. Anna kept Kape's scraps of paper with her and watched for Willow as she went to her other classes—Intro to Art History, where she saw Lizzie; English Lit, where she was meant to decipher *Beowulf*; Spanish, because a foreign language was mandatory; and Intro to Geology, because science was, too. She couldn't force herself to pay attention in these classes—not even in Art History, since they were beginning with the cave paintings at Lascaux, and Anna didn't care about prehistory. She was here to learn how to make work that mattered *now*.

She thought instead about the studio and the deadly sins project, the two little words in her backpack: *envy* and *wrath*. Envy was easy—she felt envy all the time, she was envious of every artist she'd ever seen represented in a textbook. But wrath? She thought about Henry, but shut that down hard. *No.* Anna had no experience with wrath.

Geology met from seven to ten on Monday night, and it was dark when Anna left the science building. She'd only been on campus for eleven days and was still learning to orient herself among its lawns and libraries and quads. Balwin was a small school, only two thousand students, but it sprawled over seven hundred acres. It seemed to Anna that there were never enough people around, especially at night. For most of the walk, she stuck to the lit sidewalks, but as soon as she glimpsed the gray-shingled roof of her dorm through the trees, she felt brave enough to cut across North Lawn.

Midway, there was movement near the hedges.

Anna turned. *Nothing*.

She sped up, a prickle of fear across her shoulders. A few steps later, she sensed something approaching from behind— something was coming at her. She spun.

There was a pop—a bright flash of light in her eyes.

Anna put her hands up and let out an involuntary sound from the back of her throat. Her eyes squeezed tight. She braced for a rough grip on her shoulders, an act of violence or violation, a punishment, but it didn't come. What she heard was laughter—light, easy, female laughter.

She opened her eyes.

Willow.

The girl Anna had been thinking about all week was right in front of her, like Anna had finally conjured her, smiling and glowing and holding a clunky Canon Rebel near her face.

"You scared me," Anna said.

"Sorry." Willow replaced her lens cap and fixed the camera strap around her shoulder. "You looked so beautiful walking out here, I just had to capture you."

Anna's chest swelled. She cast her eyes down to the cuffs of her jeans, damp and dirty from the grass, her ugly Jesus sandals and oversize T-shirt.

Beautiful, she thought. *I'm beautiful.*

She wasn't dressed nicely at all, but maybe that was a good thing in this new place, with this new girl.

"Anne, right?" Willow said. "From Kape's 2D?"

"Anna. Yes."

"Willow," Willow said, as if Anna could have forgotten.

"You're a photographer?"

Willow smiled wryly. "Among other things."

What other things? Anna wanted to ask, but she didn't let herself. She didn't want to betray the naivete she was carrying around. But she wasn't ready to let Willow go, either.

"What are you doing out here?"

"Just walking," Willow said. "Taking some snaps."

From the high corner of a building, a light flickered on, cutting across Willow's face. Anna was reminded of Picasso's portrait from class—a face in shards.

Willow pulled a silver flask from the back pocket of her jeans, unscrewed the top, took a swig, and handed it to Anna. "Here."

Anna held her hands at her sides. "What is it?"

"Vodka and a little cranberry juice."

Anna had never had vodka. She'd once snuck a beer in her bedroom, all alone, to see what it was like, but it tasted bitter and sour, and after she'd forced it down, she fell directly to sleep.

She shook her head. "I'm okay."

Willow lowered the flask. "Have you done your assignment yet?"

"Not yet." Anna still hadn't figured out wrath, and she was starting to think she never would. "You?"

That half smile again. "Oh, yeah, mine's all finished."

Anna felt something rotten in the pit of her stomach and almost laughed. It was envy, how apt. "Lucky you."

Willow shrugged, took a swig from her flask, then put it back into her pocket. She had a funny expression on her face. She held up her camera again. "Can I take another picture? You're so skinny, like Kate Moss or something. You're, like, my perfect model."

Anna felt the swell of pride again. "Sure."

"Here," Willow said, slipping Anna's backpack off her shoulder, setting it in the grass. She took Anna's wrists in her hands and led her toward a huge oak tree. "Stand here."

Willow stepped back, holding the camera in front of her face. "Okay, walk toward me. Look at the camera. Look right into the camera."

Anna walked, feeling calmness wash over her as she smiled into Willow's big lens.

"Wait," Willow said, lowering the camera. "Go back. This time don't smile. Make your face blank. Go—*empty*."

Anna did as she was told. She floated atop the grass like an automaton, a machine, a ghost. She heard the fast click of Willow's shutter, and she did not react.

"Yes!" Willow said, and when Anna was almost on top of her, Willow put the camera down. "Those are going to be so good. I'll show you as soon as I develop them."

Anna felt her senses return. She smiled. "Okay, cool."

Willow put the cap back on the lens. "Well, see you in class," she said and turned in the opposite direction of Anna's dorm.

Anna stood still and silent for a moment, so glad to have been of service to Willow's art, so *flattered*, so newly unafraid, it almost paralyzed her.

"See ya!" she called, when she remembered to speak.

TUESDAY AFTERNOON

I WAS ALONE when the second building fell. You hadn't called from the police station like you were meant to, but by then I understood that you couldn't. Milo had broken our cordless phone, and my cell was useless. They all were. The downtown Verizon tower had been destroyed in the attacks, the trunk cables between Manhattan and Brooklyn had been cut, and all the attempted calls had short-circuited the lines that were still intact. Nothing was going through.

Three full miles from the World Trade Center, but still the smell of disaster, acrid and ozone, had already seeped into Carroll Gardens. Our apartment door was latched and locked, a thick slab of metal cutting me off from the rest of the city, but I kept the kitchen window open—unsure if I'd need to climb down the fire escape or barricade myself behind the furniture in my room. In those first hours, war felt imminent. Actual war, and *here*. It was suddenly so easy to imagine tanks rolling across the Brooklyn Bridge, soldiers shooting each other on Fifth Avenue, missiles bombing Broadway. Museums and shops and playhouses deserted. Postcard-pictured buildings turned to dust. The only wars our generation knew were those we'd read about, in jungles or in the black-and-white past, so far away they couldn't touch us. And yet, here it was. *Our turn*, I thought, the inevitability of it clicking into place. *Of course.* Our generation wasn't immune to disaster, it had only felt that way.

I logged into AOL, biting my lips through the slow screech of the modem, the pages loading with intolerable slowness, much slower than normal, as if the screen itself were pushing against a tide. When my inbox finally opened, I emailed my family to let them know I was safe, that my phone wasn't working, that I couldn't get through. The message I got back from my father, minutes later, was brief and flustered: *We're watching the news and trying to call. Be careful, Anna! Don't go outside! We don't know what's happening.*

A tick of annoyance. My parents didn't understand why I had sacrificed the security and comfort of the Midwest to struggle here, why I had given up my dream of a Yale MFA, where *at least there's a chance of finding a suitable husband.* They didn't understand that art was a religion in New York. This was the only place in the world as ambitious as we were. They didn't understand the city, and they didn't understand us.

OK, I wrote back. *But I'm all the way in Brooklyn. I'm fine.*

I shut my computer, itchy with anxiety. I had to *do* something. Anything. I dragged the hatbox that held all my supplies from under my bed into the living room, along with a bouquet of nylon bristle brushes. I didn't have a blank canvas, so I tore a discarded cardboard box into a wide, flat sheet and sat on the floor with it. The news circling above me, I unscrewed the tops of my Gamblin tubes, taking big, comforting inhales of the unctuous scent, and squeezed as much color as I could onto the melamine plate I used as a palette. The tubes were nearly empty, as I knew they would be. I'd already used up so much.

Somehow, despite everything, it hadn't fully registered how huge that day would be. How it would cleave time itself. How the things that had brought me to New York had already been destroyed. I was still thinking about the Andrews Foundation Young Artist Award. If I won—and I had to win, I had to beat you—people would see what I was capable of. I'd get press and gallery representation. My career would be launched. I'd make my dreams come true, and I didn't need you to do it.

The promise of the award, its ten-thousand-dollar prize and the solo exhibition, had kept me going through the summer's endless shifts at La Soeurette, taking orders, dropping picked-over plates in bus bins, and stuffing dirty tips in my apron so I could afford rent and basic art supplies. It was all okay. I was paying my dues. Working toward something. I was surviving. I was going to survive. And to do that, I needed to paint. Even that day. I needed to find a way into the hypnotic calm that let me lose myself in my art for hours without the need to eat or drink or go to the bathroom. I needed to stop thinking—about the buildings, about the city, about you and Milo and what we had done.

Let me have this, I thought, pressing bristles into the last of my India Red. *Let me disappear.*

Sometime later, a roar came from the kitchen window, and I froze, face inches away from the cardboard, brush in hand, a wave of red and black paint rising in front of my eyes. Terror stabbed through me: *This is it.* The end. I dropped my brush and ran to the window in time to see a trio of military planes fly overhead in a *V.* They had been the only thing besides birds in the sky for hours.

Below the window, a group of people had converged on Congress Street, squinting up as if the sky were about to crack open and rain down something biblical, frogs or locusts. Someone was waving at me. I ducked, stupidly. When I looked back out the window, I saw that it was only Lizzie, gesturing for me to come outside.

I left the apartment door cracked, the bolt extended to stop it from shutting all the way. I didn't want to be caught fumbling for my keys if something happened out there and I needed to rush back inside. I ran down the four flights of stairs, stepping outside for the first time that day. The wind was already blowing smoke and debris toward Brooklyn, and the air smelled thick, smoldering and oily, like the welding studio at Highsmith. Like a thousand trucks had slammed on their breaks and skidded at the same time.

I edged out through a cluster of people who must have been my neighbors—blank, unfamiliar faces—to meet Lizzie, standing in the middle of the street. She wrapped her arms around me. Her shirt was damp with sweat, and she smelled like a hangover. I pulled away.

"I was coming to get you guys," she said. "Tom's talking to his parents. He's on his way." Her hair looked greasy and slept on. Face bare except the gold ring in her septum. "Are you okay?"

I nodded. "You?"

"I guess. I tried to call, but nothing's going through. We're going to Happiness."

I glanced down Court Street. It seemed impossible that our favorite bar was still standing, still serving beer, its kitschy chili-pepper lights still flickering, the jukebox still blasting.

"Is Wills upstairs?" Lizzie asked.

I held my face still, that filmstrip again flying though my head—Tyler's knife, the abandoned warehouse, a hand over your mouth. I shook it away. It was still early; only three hours had passed since the second tower fell.

"She went to work," I said, as calmly as I could. "I keep trying to call."

"I know, me too. She's probably walking. Did you see all those people on the bridge, covered in ashes?"

Before I could answer, Tom appeared, already talking. "Boomer's on his way. He's gonna walk from Midtown."

Lizzie turned sharply. "He got through?"

"He was still at work. Seems like office phones are okay." Tom hesitated. "Should we go?"

I glanced up at our kitchen window and thought of my paints on the floor, uncapped and drying out, and the red painting on cardboard that I hadn't looked at properly yet.

"Let me leave Wills a note," I said. "Wait for me."

I flew up the stairs and went to my painting. It was nothing, a wasted smudge of rust, devoid of meaning. I folded the cardboard and jammed it into the trash, dropped the empty paint tubes on top, then put the lid on the hat box and the melamine plate in the sink. I found an old receipt and a Sharpie in the junk drawer and tried to write, but the ink had dried out. I threw it away and dug around for something usable.

Meet us at Happiness, I wrote, using a little heart to dot the *i*, because I needed to pretend that everything was okay. I left the note next to the coffeemaker, then grabbed my keys from the hook, locked the door, and left.

Even in the light of the afternoon, Happiness was dark. We sat in a booth with a clear view of the TV—the news still spitting out its bolus of half facts and hypotheticals. Across from me, Lizzie smoked a cigarette and Tom carved the date into the wood table with a pocketknife: *9-11-01.* All our cell phones were in front of us, a little bonfire, ringers on high.

Finally, after a few hours, the bartender shouted over at us: "Call for you." He was holding the receiver aloft, white T-shirt pulling up to reveal sleeve tattoos.

Tom looked up. "Who?"

The bartender shook the phone. "Any of you."

You, I thought. *The police station. Finally.* I hopped up before anyone else could. "I'll take it."

But it wasn't you. It was Milo. "I tried calling your place," he said.

I snorted. "You broke my phone, dummy. Where are you?"

"At a pay phone on Tenth. I walked." His voice cracked. "I walked right by it. The whole thing's still on fucking fire. And it smells so bad. It's like—it's like—"

"I can smell it here," I said, but I wasn't thinking about the rubble. I was thinking about Tenth Avenue. Chelsea, the heart of the art world—and where you should have been until six p.m. when Roche Gallery closed that night. Milo had gone to find you. It shouldn't have stung, but it did.

"Is she there?"

"No," Milo said. "The gate's down. Everything's locked up. No one's there."

I imagined you at the police station then, filing a report. Then something worse: Tyler's bandanna slipping off his face. A fight. A slash in your blouse. Blood on your cheek. My heart hammered in my chest. *No*, I thought, and pushed the image out of my mind. That wasn't what was supposed to happen.

"I don't know what to do," Milo said, and it sounded like he might cry.

"She's probably walking. It'll take a while." I kept my voice calm. I had to. Lizzie was watching me from across the bar, and even though there was no way she could hear me, I lowered my voice. "Are you still going?"

A moment passed before Milo answered. "Where?"

I cupped a hand over my mouth. "Arcadia," I said, annoyed. I shouldn't have had to say it. This was the plan. It had always been the plan. Milo was supposed to meet Tyler at the bar at five o'clock for a postmortem on the mugging.

Milo blew out a breath. "I haven't even thought about it."

"We need to know what happened. Before we see her. You need to talk to Tyler."

Milo didn't say anything.

"You have to go," I said. "Now. And come here after. I'll wait for you."

He still didn't respond, and I went hot with anger.

"Bye, then," I spat, and punched the end call button, then handed the phone back to the bartender.

"Everything okay?" he asked.

"Yeah," I said. "I mean, I think so. You?"

He tossed a washcloth over his shoulder. "Okay as can be." He set four shot glasses on the bar and sloshed the cheapest, yellowest Cuervo into each of them. He slammed one of them back, wiped his mouth with the back of his hand, and waved me away.

Lizzie eyed me as I set the shots on the table. "Who was it?"

"Milo." I downed the tequila, cringed, and chased it with a gulp of beer. "He's coming, but he has to walk."

Lizzie watched me, her expression pinched.

"What?" I said.

"Are you still hooking up with him?"

Lizzie thought she understood what was happening with us, but she didn't. You'd only told her one side of the story. Your side.

I slipped my hands under my thighs. "He wasn't calling for *me*, Lizzie. He asked for any of us."

She tutted.

I opened my mouth to lie or to explain, but there was no point. Lizzie, with her trust fund and live-in boyfriend and wishy-washy ambitions, would never understand what was going on with you and Milo and me.

Another tray of shots landed on the table. "Ladies."

Ugh, I thought. *Boomer*. I forced myself to smile, my fakeness inflating my anxiety like a parade balloon, swelling me to insane proportions. The truth was that I hated Boomer. I had hated him since our bad hookup four years before, back at

Balwin, when I was desperate to stay in the little club you had built. I still relived the embarrassment of that night each time I saw him. But he was as much a part of the group as I was. There was no guarantee that if I made you choose between us, you'd pick me.

He sank into the seat next to me and set a beefy hand atop mine. I slipped it out, then shifted down in the booth. He held up a shot glass of frosty liquor. Lizzie perched her cigarette in the ashtray and took a glass. I took the last one.

Lemon drops, sweet and easy, like the old days.

"Where are Wills and Milo?"

I bristled at the way Boomer said it—*Wills and Milo*—as if the two of you were still a couple. Tom slid back into the booth, draping an arm around Lizzie's shoulders. His fingers hung limply, big and pale and clean, with auburn knuckle hairs, patches of dry pink skin, and a couple of cheap silver rings he'd picked up on St. Mark's. I thought of Milo that morning, running away from me to find you. I thought of my family, far away. I almost wanted Boomer's hand on mine again.

"Milo's on his way back," Lizzie said.

"And Wills?" Boomer asked.

"Nothing yet."

I caught Lizzie's eye and saw it flash with something. Fear, maybe. Or judgment.

"She'll be back," I said. You'd been gone before, and for much longer. At least this time, you actually had an excuse.

Four

FOUR YEARS BEFORE

ANNA PINNED HER PROJECT to the studio corkboard and sat at the same desk she had the week before. After Willow had taken her picture on North Lawn on Monday night, she'd been inspired to finish her deadly sins project. It was Willow's flash that had broken through. It reminded Anna of the Brad Pitt movie *Se7en* and the Weegee-esque crime scene photographer who turned out to be the killer. Anna fashioned a cardboard box from a brown paper bag, complete with a top flap and a round-head fastener latch. Inside were the decapitated heads of actresses, which she'd cut from an old *US Weekly*.

It was not technically 2D, but she was trying to be brave—she was used to painting pretty pictures, not making collages, not breaking the rules. It seemed to be paying off. At the corkboard, her classmates were opening and closing her box and laughing. They understood what she'd done, and they liked it. Which meant they liked *her*.

When Willow entered, carrying a Styrofoam cup and a plain manila folder, she didn't make eye contact with Anna, despite

Anna's readiness, this time, to smile. Willow went straight to the corkboard and slipped an eight-by-ten sheet from the envelope, a color photograph, and pinned it to the corner. A typical yearbook senior photo—Willow herself, Anna realized with a jolt. In it, Willow was smiling brightly, looking shiny and clear-eyed and glossy-haired as any cheerleader. Anna was confused at first, then disappointed. Willow hadn't altered the photo in any way. She hadn't *done* anything.

Professor Kape walked in, and the room hushed. He stood at the head of the studio, contemplating the projects for several moments, then pointed to Willow's picture and turned.

"Let me guess," he said, smiling. "Pride."

Willow smiled back. She had a scarf tied kerchief-like over her hair that day, yellow-and-blue silk. Half the girl in the photograph, half the girl Anna had met last week.

"Yep," she said.

"What's the other one?"

"Isn't it obvious?" Willow asked. "I didn't do anything."

"Aha." Kape cupped his chin and smiled. *"Sloth."*

The class erupted in laughter. When Anna caught on, she forced herself to smile along, but she couldn't help being infuriated. Willow had made a joke out of the assignment, but there was nothing funny about art to Anna.

"A readymade," Kape said approvingly. "I take it you're all familiar with Duchamp?"

There were murmurs and nods all around the room, closing in on Anna, tightening against her edges. She had heard of Marcel Duchamp, but she didn't know much about him. There had been no art history classes at Anna's high school. She was self-taught, which meant she was behind. Always behind.

"Elle a chaud au cul," Willow said.

Kape let out a bark of laughter. But he was the only one. The other students looked around blankly, as confused as Anna.

Someone from the back called out, "Sorry, *who* has a hot ass?"

Kape, still smiling, shook his head. "*El—ash—oo—oo—coo*. Spelled *L.H.O.O.Q.* It's Duchamp's *Mona Lisa*. Worth looking into." He walked over and knocked on Willow's table. "Very good. Very clever."

Anna scribbled the letters in her notebook—*L.H.O.O.Q.*—to look up later.

"Let's do the little box next," said Kape. "Whose is it?"

Anna raised her hand, a pounding excitement in her chest.

"It's not exactly 2D, is it?"

Heat rose to her face as she shook her head.

"It's week one, so I'll let it slide." Kape turned to the class. "Who can talk about this?"

"Heads in a box," said a girl with curly hair from Anna's dorm floor. She had a boy's name, but Anna couldn't remember it. "Like in that movie."

Kape nodded. "Okay, what else?"

The room was silent. Anna sensed the students looking at one another. She glanced at Willow, who was doodling in her notebook.

Kape pointed to the box. "Who can guess the sins the artist chose?"

"Envy!" shouted a boy from the front.

The professor dropped his hand. "Why?"

Quiet. Then: "Kevin Spacey's character." It was the same girl from her floor. *Ryan.* Her name was Ryan.

"Exactly," Professor Kape said. "This is procedural. It's very clever—but referential. The image itself is actually quite cliché."

Anna sucked in a breath, pushing down the urge to flee. All she wanted was to be an artist—to be told, *Yes, you're special and talented and we see it and we care about what happens to you.* Art was the only thing she had. It was all she could count on. She had mapped out her life, and this class was the starting gun—Kape advisee, Balwin BFA, Yale MFA, gallery representation, until, finally, she'd spend eternity hanging on the walls at MoMA. But if she failed this, the very first step, her whole plan was ruined. Anna's eyes stung. She held her body very still.

"You're wrong, Professor."

Willow. Every head in the room turned. Even Kape raised his eyebrows, his forehead creased in surprise.

"Am I?"

"It's topical," Willow said, pencil twirling. "Not cliché. The artist is pointing to misogynistic violence in Hollywood. She's totally subverting Hollywood's power by using its own images against itself."

Anna's mouth slackened. She'd never heard anyone her age talk like that. The rest of the class was silent; the only sound was the whirling of the huge metal fans. Kape turned back to the corkboard and tapped his chin.

Anna swallowed and waited, feeling her heartbeat thud out the seconds.

Finally, the professor laughed. "You know, Miss Whitman, you might be right."

Anna turned. Willow sipped her coffee as if nothing had happened. Then she lowered her cup and winked.

At the end of crit, Professor Kape announced the second assignment. "You have one week to make anything you want. As long as it remains in two dimensions." He looked right at Anna and smiled. "Okay with you, Miss Hollywood?"

Anna blushed again, nodding. Her chest fluttered, and even though she was being scolded, it felt good to have Kape's attention.

One of the guys in the back called out, "Anything?"

"Absolutely anything," Kape said. "As long as it has a length and a height and no width, and it highlights at least one of the principles we discussed last class."

Anna slipped her notebook into her backpack, already planning her redemption from the dreaded cliché. Painting was her thing, and she never should have stepped outside her comfort zone. Give her a canvas, a brush, and a few tubes of paint, and she could do anything—turn primary blue into the most sublime shades of lapis and turquoise, mulberry and plum. With red and black she could make blood, fire, rubies, or skin. Whatever anyone wanted.

She wasn't about to waste time. From a bin in the corner, she found an abandoned piece of unstretched canvas. Everyone else had left the studio, but Anna got some wood and nails and hammered together a stretcher. She went back to her stool and stapled the canvas to it. There was no rush to return to the dorms, to stare at her walls and listen to CDs by herself, to slog through *Beowulf*. Instead, she got to work blending colors—sky blue, sheer yellow, a tropical pink, the darkest black. A few people came and went while Anna painted on and on. Her canvas came together in less than three hours. A cityscape sunset, it had color, perspective, and shape, and it was a stunner.

—

It was six o'clock by the time Anna finished cleaning her brushes and putting away her materials. The dining halls were open, and her stomach was rumbling, but she decided to stop in the library first, to look up Duchamp and *L.H.O.O.Q.*

She found it in the first monograph she pulled out. It was a work from 1919 and, according to the text, emblematic of Dadaism. A postcard reproduction of the *Mona Lisa*, but with a mustache drawn on her face and the letters *L.H.O.O.Q.* penned at the bottom. In French, Anna read, the title was meant to sound like the phrase *Elle a chaud au cul*, which was what Willow had said in class, what had made Kape laugh so loudly. It was old French slang for, basically, *horny*. The mustache was a wink-wink to Leonardo's homosexuality. The mass-produced postcard, an objet trouvé, with its written defacement, was what Duchamp called a "rectified readymade."

Anna slammed the book shut, as if the whole thing offended her. It hadn't—she didn't care about sexuality or bawdiness—but Duchamp's work ripped apart her ideas about successful art, what it required. She thought about her cityscape, now tucked away in a rack at Highsmith. Yes, it was beautiful. Yes, technically, it was a successful painting, and clearly Anna was deft with her brush. But Anna saw now that skill wasn't the point. Skill didn't mean anything. It didn't say anything. Anna had made *another pretty picture*—exactly what Duchamp had rebelled against almost eighty years before.

Anna took the book to the checkout desk, scanned her student ID card, and stuffed it in her backpack. She wasn't hungry anymore, not for food, at least. She made her way to her room, got under her quilt, and read the monograph from cover to cover, until she figured out what to do.

One of Duchamp's most famous works, *The Bride Stripped Bare by Her Bachelors, Even*, was a window of glass that had shattered in transport. Rather than throw it away or fix it, Duchamp embraced its brokenness. The cracks, he had said, were an improvement.

That was it. Anna had her solution.

The next morning, she woke well before nine a.m. English Lit. She ran-walked all the way to Highsmith and found her canvas in the rack. She ripped it from its stretcher, rolled it up, and stuffed it into her backpack. She made her way to the humanities building, through the *Beowulf* lecture, nearly vibrating with impatience until she could be alone with her painting again.

By Wednesday, her cityscape had become a woven assemblage. Anna had ripped the canvas into strips, which she then latticed together so the vivid colors were slashed apart by the black lines of buildings. She'd kept the edges raw. It was chaos, but beautiful chaos. It reminded Anna more of New York City than the actual skyline she'd painted. She pinned it to the corkboard and waited.

Willow and Lizzie arrived together. Lizzie pinned up her picture first. It was a drawing in black Sharpie, a comic strip panel with a female superhero standing with her arms raised heavenward. Anna had no thoughts about it—try as she might, she had no interest in comics or anime. She knew there were some popular contemporary artists who worked in this style, but Anna ignored them, believing their work slapstick, one-note.

Willow pulled another piece of 8x10 photo paper from her knapsack. Anna craned her neck, trying to glimpse the image through the mass of bodies. When Willow turned, her eyes landed right on Anna. She smiled and stepped away to reveal the print.

Anna's own face. It stared back at her from the front of the studio. Her eyes were huge and dark, her brow slightly furrowed, her lips parted just enough that a finger could slide between them.

The real Anna, the one atop the metal stool, shivered.

Willow sat in the empty seat next to Anna's for the first time that day. "Told ya they'd be good."

Anna dipped her chin to hide her pleasure.

Professor Kape motioned for the rest of the class to sit, and they did. Kape stared at the board for such a long time that the class began making faces at each other.

Finally, he pointed to Anna's cityscape.

"Who did this?" It sounded almost like an accusation.

"I did," Anna said.

Kape nodded once, brusquely, then addressed the class. "Who has thoughts?"

A boy across the aisle spoke up first. "Sweet colors—looks like fire."

"But, like, what is it?" asked Ryan.

"Does it matter?" Kape crossed his arms. "Couldn't it be abstract?"

"It's not, though," Ryan said, pointing. "You can see that those black shapes are buildings."

"What about the canvas?" Kape asked.

"It's torn."

"So?"

No one said anything. No one had an answer. Even Willow's head was down. Anna crossed her arms and held her elbows, resisting the urge to nudge Willow into action.

"Texture, anyone?" Kape's brows arched. "To me, this is a work about destruction. Cataclysm. From the fiery colors to the broken buildings to the ripped canvas. It's quite impressive, I think, and playing with many elements. Color, texture, line, shape, perspective. It's all there, and it's quite moving."

Anna met his gaze and felt a dart stick into her chest.

"Thank you for this," he said. "Miss Hollywood."

There were some stifled giggles around the room, but Anna felt warm. None of the other students had been given a nickname. It seemed meaningful to her, weighty, as if she had already achieved a special rapport with Kape. As if she had already catapulted herself over her peers.

Kape tapped Willow's photograph next. "What about this?"

Anna glanced at Willow, but she stared straight ahead.

"Dope," someone said. "Corinne Day meets Wolfgang Tillmans."

Anna scribbled the names down in her sketchbook and kept her eyes down. She didn't know those photographers. She didn't know what it meant.

"Maybe a little *too* much, though?" Ryan said. "It's more like *Seventeen* trying to play subversive."

Willow snorted.

Kape put out a hand. "Let her finish. What would improve the photo in your opinion, Miss Zimmerman? Be specific. Think of the principles."

Ryan held up her hands, as if to block out the rest of the room. Her head tilted to the side, and her eyes narrowed. As she focused on the image, something happened to the edges of Anna's physical body—a tingling, a disintegration.

"Color," Ryan said finally. "If I have to be formal about it, I'd say *color* is what's missing."

"No," Lizzie said. "I love the black and white. That's what separates it from a lot of the mainstream photography right now. It *elevates* it."

"A valid discussion here," Kape said. "I will posit one more theory. It is easy, Miss Whitman, to take a beautiful picture of a beautiful girl."

Beautiful—again, Anna felt the word wrap around her like a hug.

"What *isn't* easy," Kape went on, "is capturing a zeitgeist in a singular image. I think you're close. Keep going. Keep pushing. You'll get there."

Willow nodded, a small, unreadable smile on her lips.

TUESDAY NIGHT

WHEN I SPOTTED Milo coming through the door at Happiness, my whole body tensed. He beelined toward me, our eyes locked from half a room away. It was dark by then, and I was drunk. The mood in the bar had transformed—fear had morphed into a strange and belligerent kind of patriotism. Someone had muted the TV, and the jukebox was blasting Bruce Springsteen. Boomer, Tom, and Lizzie were in the middle of the bar with the tatted bartender, their arms around each other, scream-singing along, "Born in the USA!" The song was an anthem, a rallying call, and as meaningless to me as the college football games last year. *We win or they do*—it didn't matter, just another reason to drink and dance. I couldn't bring myself to join in.

Milo scooted into the booth next to me, and my stomach fluttered. He was yours, I knew that—he'd always been yours, and maybe that's why I wanted to possess him so badly, why I wanted him to possess me. I wanted the three of us to crash together so violently that in the aftermath, no one would be able to tell who was who.

"What did he say?"

Milo glanced at me, then swiped my beer and took a gulp. "He didn't show."

"What?" My heart skidded. "Did you call him?"

"I can't. I only have his cell."

My mouth went dry—that sick, guilty feeling crawling up my throat. The feeling that somehow, our prank—our childish, twisted lark—had caused the entire world to crack open.

"We have to go to Arcadia, then. We have to find him."

Milo's brow creased. "Don't be crazy."

"Crazy?" I repeated, but my heart was thumping too hard for me to go on. We didn't know anything about Tyler, not really. He was a bartender we ordered drinks from sometimes. Beyond that, we didn't have a clue. Anything could have happened. His knife could have slipped. You could have fought back. His bandanna could have fallen from his face. "Oh shit." I put my head into my hands. "Oh my god, Milo. Oh shit. What if she—"

"Stop," he said.

But I couldn't stop. I was already seeing it all. "What if she recognized him?"

"No," Milo said, but from the way he tented his fingers over his nose and mouth and avoided my eyes, I knew that he could see it, too.

I put my hand on his chin and pulled his face toward mine. "She could have pulled his bandanna off. Or his hat. He could have freaked out. He could have hurt her."

Milo pulled away from me. "Stop. Seriously. Nothing happened. There's no way. He wouldn't do that. He's not like that."

He's not like that. I couldn't make my eyes see straight. They flitted from Milo's stoic profile to the bar to the wavy crowd of dancers. *He's not like that*—this man who had agreed to hold a knife against a young woman's neck for a couple hundred bucks.

It had been hours now. How many? Twelve? A wave of adrenaline rushed through my chest. I swallowed hard, tightened my jaw. The bar had grown louder—it was the exult of survival, the randomness of it, amped up with booze and music and all the possibilities the city still held, even now, even in the shadow of those fallen buildings. Or maybe because of it. I gritted my teeth harder, tucked my hands under my thighs, palms up, so I could wipe the damp onto my cutoffs. I couldn't fake it. I couldn't do anything until we knew what happened. The music in the bar was too loud. There were too many people.

She's fine, I told myself. *She's fine.* You'd been fine so many times that you shouldn't have been. You never got caught. It was just the way things were for you. You always survived.

Every time someone opened the door, I looked up, thinking it must be you. *Now*, it must be you. Each time I heard laughter—the short, sharp, head-back guffaws you elicited in people—I searched for you. But you weren't there. You didn't come.

Everything started to spin. The Cuervo, the lemon drops, the beer—it was too much. I was going to be sick.

I nudged Milo with my knee. "I need some air."

He didn't move. My panic swelled. I pushed him with both hands. "Move!"

He looked at me, eyes wide with surprise, and slid out of the booth. I scooted out and ran past Lizzie and Tom, still dancing, past Boomer talking to the bartender. I yanked open the metal door. The cool, contaminated air rushed up, surrounding me. It was noxious. I coughed and shivered in my hoodie and cutoffs and plastic flip-flops. My teeth chattered. That smell. That awful, awful smell.

I bent over, gagging over the sewer grate. There was something malignant inside me—something awful and poisonous burrowing itself into the lining of my stomach. Shaking, I stuck my fingers down my throat. It would be so much better if I could get it out, but it wouldn't budge, no matter how I tried.

The door crashed open. Milo wrapped me in a bear hug from behind and whispered into my ear, "You have to calm down."

His arms were like metal bars, penning me in. I couldn't move. I knew this feeling, this claustrophobia and guilt and confusion and fear, the malignancy inside me. It brought me back in time. *I didn't mean to hurt anyone.* My mind knotted, a tangle of bad memories. I couldn't breathe. I tucked my chin and sank my teeth into Milo's forearm, biting down hard.

"Jesus Christ!" He dropped me.

We stood on the sidewalk, staring at each other. My heartbeat was in my ears, my shoulders hiked up like a street cat. I looked at my hands, trembling, the fear and the guilt trapped there, right under my skin. *Don't be crazy.*

Was Milo right? Was I overreacting? It hadn't even been a full day. It didn't mean that Tyler had hurt you. It didn't mean that it was my fault. It didn't mean anything yet.

"I'm sorry," I said. "I'm freaking out."

Milo took my hand, pulled me to him. He smelled sticky, like candy and wet metal, like an amusement park after a rainstorm—and underneath all that, somewhere on his shirt or his skin or his hair, I caught a whiff of you, too. Honeysuckle and cigarettes and Angel perfume. I leaned in. The music from the other side of the bar door sounded hollow and far away. Milo's arms were around me. I nuzzled deeper into him.

He pulled back and I looked up at his face, expecting the inevitable, the warm crush of his mouth on mine. He brushed a lock of hair from my lips.

"Anna," he said.

I waited, face tilted up, open and ready, but the kiss didn't come. Not this time. He dropped his hands and backed away. My belly hollowed, embarrassed to have exposed my desire to him. He had been so hungry for me before—his eyes slick and strained with lust—but not any longer. There was no force in the way he looked at me. It was empty.

The door clanged open again. It was only Lizzie. She gave Milo a questioning look, then put a hand on my shoulder. "You okay, babe?"

"I'm fine." It was late, dark and chilly and quiet. "Really, I just need to pass out."

"I'll take her home," Milo said.

Lizzie scowled. "Seriously?"

"What?" I said.

"Not my business," Lizzie said, "but Willow's going to kill both y'all."

Milo started to speak, and I was so afraid he'd agree with her, that he would change his mind and make me spend the night on my own, that I cut him off.

"We're only going to wait for her."

"Right." Lizzie turned back to the door, pushed it open. "Whatever."

An idea came to me. I turned to Milo. "Let's go to yours." I'd only been to his place that one time, when we had our taxi stop for him on our way to the Brooklyn Museum, but I'd never been inside.

"Nah, my roommate is there," he said. "And your place is closer."

"'Kay." I turned away from him. It had been a test, and he had failed. He didn't want to be with me at his place, only at ours. I only meant something to him when you could see.

We walked in silence, him matching my pace like a big dog on a leash, but by the time we got to our stoop, whatever sadness I had felt bloomed into anger. The same anger that had been simmering in my gut all summer.

I was digging for my keys when Milo spoke.

"I hope she's home."

It landed like a punch. I took the stairs two at a time and was out of breath by the top. There was no sign of you. No mess. No half-full Diet Coke can. No Parliament stinking up the air. I turned on the TV again, a distraction, and let Milo check your bedroom by himself.

There was nothing new on the news.

There was nothing new at all.

FOUR YEARS BEFORE

AFTER THE SECOND WEEK of 2D, Willow lagged behind after class as Anna did. "Okay, *Hollywood*." She had a coy smile on her face as she handed Anna a manila envelope. "Check it."

When Anna opened the package, she saw a photo of herself, black-and-white, hand printed in a darkroom, almost identical to the one Willow had chosen for crit, except a wisp of hair that had blown over her parted lips. Underneath, there were more. Anna counted five.

"Look at your arm," Willow said, finger tracing down the length of Anna's skin in the top photo. "You're so like one of those waif models. Tragic beautiful."

Anna didn't know how to respond. She didn't have the words for the way she felt—flattered and warm and awake and shy at the same time.

"These are for you." Willow flipped over the top print, showing off a little squiggle. "I signed them so when I'm famous you'll be rich."

"I'll be famous by then, too," Anna said, and laughed. It was the first time she had admitted her ambition aloud.

Willow tilted her head down and lifted her brows. "Paint me something, then. And sign it."

The two girls mirrored each other, eyes locked and smiling the same smiles, and Anna understood that this moment was a handshake, a pact. They were equals, and they could lift each other up, rise into the canon together. They would be stars in the same sky.

Weeks passed. Lizzie began to join them in the studio, and together, the three of them made art and talked until eventually it was understood that they were a unit. They ate together in the dining hall and walked to classes and met in the library and posed for Willow's camera. It was Anna's first real friendship, after years of loneliness, and she felt it profoundly. She fused so tightly to Willow and Lizzie that they were often confused for lovers. Willow seemed to enjoy this, encouraging rumors by taking Anna's hand on North Lawn or resting her head in Lizzie's lap on the bench outside Highsmith, letting Lizzie try to detangle her wild hair. It baffled Anna at first, but she didn't question it—she was too afraid to disturb it, to muck it up. Soon enough it felt natural to have Willow's small, soft hand clasped in hers. It felt powerful.

As autumn settled on campus, and the leaves changed and the grass browned and the wind blew colder, Anna mixed palettes and blotted paint onto hand-stretched canvases, tearing and slashing when she felt the urge. Lizzie sketched comics in

Sharpie, filling notebook after notebook with her space character, a "badass alien avenger" named Poet. By then, Anna knew about artists like Roy Lichtenstein and Takashi Murakami and Yoshitomo Nara, artists who legitimized contemporary cartoon-making by calling it Neo-Pop or Superflat, but that didn't mean she liked it. Lizzie's work was simple, she thought, and if she were honest, not even *technically* good.

Meanwhile, Willow hardly made anything at all. Instead, she read. She brought so many books to the studio—piles of artists' monographs, tomes on postmodern theory, manifestos and journals and letters and articles. Most often, she lay on the cement floor, head on her messenger bag, feet propped on a stool, highlighter uncapped in her mouth, book in her hands.

One Friday afternoon in late October, Willow tossed a slim volume called *The Life and Art of Dora Maar* across the room and sat up.

"I'm bored," she said. "Let's go shopping."

Anna deflated. She'd been so happy in the past six weeks—and she knew it had been too good to be true. It was only a matter of time before a problem came and pushed her back into her place. And here it was: Willow and Lizzie had more money than she did. They both had real diamond earrings and monogrammed bedding and department-store makeup and endless art books. Anna had a university meal plan and a small monthly stipend from her parents, just enough for studio fees and a few treats each week. There was no room for shopping.

"I can't," she said without looking away from her canvas. A wash of white and pale yellow. It had only just begun.

Willow ignored her. "Can we take the Rover?"

Lizzie shrugged. "Sure. You want to go to Columbus?"

"I *can't*," Anna said again, this time more forcefully. She couldn't go shopping, but the idea of driving two hours to Columbus, right around the corner from Henry and her parents, was actually nauseating. She wasn't ready to tell Willow and Lizzie about Henry. It would change their perception of her—she'd be the *tragic girl* once again.

Willow brushed off her thin corduroys. "We don't have to go that far."

"Where, then?" Lizzie asked, nose scrunched. There were no shops around the Balwin campus beyond Walmart.

Willow put her hands on her hips and smirked. "Have you bitches ever been thrifting?"

Lizzie laughed, but Anna didn't say anything. Her mother bought most of her clothes for her at Lazarus. On rare occasions, she was allowed to go to the outlet mall and pick out a few discounted things from chain stores like J.Crew and Banana Republic. Thrift shopping had never come up. It seemed poor to Anna, and Anna didn't want to be poor. But as she took Willow in now, the diamonds in her ears and nose, the tigereye in her belly button, the cords that looked rubbed raw, the T-shirt that read *MYRTLE BEACH '84*, she realized something.

"Is that where you get your clothes?"

Willow nodded. "You can find the sweetest shit for like a dollar, if you know what you're doing."

Anna looked down at her own outfit—a preppy red-and-white-striped sweater and jeans that never quite fit her right. Willow's clothes may have been weird and old, but they were a choice. They were a *style*.

"I barely have an extra dollar," Anna said.

"Come on." Willow smirked at her. "How much money have

you wasted on the vending machine? You don't need that shit. Look at you. You can eat art."

"Oh god," Lizzie said, laughing.

But to Anna, it made complete sense. She *didn't* need that shit.

"Let's do it," she said.

Lizzie's old hunter-green Range Rover was parked in the freshman lot behind Rector Hall. Anna walked around back, glimpsing a BALWIN ALUMNI bumper sticker on the fender. They all got in, and Lizzie handed Willow a thick black binder full of CDs.

Anna slammed her door. "Did your parents go to Balwin or something?"

Lizzie glanced at her in the rearview. "Yeah, my grandparents, too, on my mom's side. I'm a legacy."

"What's that?"

Willow turned, grinning wickedly. "It means Daddy's on the board."

Lizzie pushed Willow's shoulder. "Oh, stop. It means my parents went here so they had to let me in."

"And?" Willow said.

Lizzie laughed. "It's actually *Mommy* who's on the board, thanks so much."

Anna laughed with them, everything finally making sense. Lizzie wasn't talented, just rich. Anna felt oddly bolstered by this—she'd gotten into Highsmith based on her talent alone. Like Willow had.

Lizzie pointed at the glove compartment. "Grab the black pouch in there, Wills."

Willow dug around and pulled out a quilted leather makeup bag, then unzipped the top and squealed with delight. "Where'd you get these?"

"In Louisville, last weekend. But I have a lead on someone who can get stuff at Balwin, if you want." She merged onto Main Street, then glanced at Willow. "I wasn't sure if you'd be interested."

"Ha," said Willow. "I'm *always* interested."

Anna clicked her seat belt. She had an idea of what was in the pouch, and she didn't know what to do about it. She'd never gotten high before—not because she hadn't wanted to, but because it had never been offered.

Willow turned. "What about you, Hollywood? Interested?"

Anna didn't want to admit to her inexperience. Willow and Lizzie were different from her. They'd had boyfriends in high school; they'd been to parties and gotten drunk and probably had sex, though their friendship was new enough that they hadn't talked about that yet. Willow and Lizzie were experienced in a way Anna was not.

She hadn't expected this when she came to Balwin—these girls were not part of her plan—but she could already tell that they were improving her. They were improving her art. There was no choice. She had to hold on to them.

"Always," she said, her pulse quick.

Willow squealed again and lit the joint. The smoke was sweet and pungent and familiar—Anna had smelled it in the dorms many times, she realized, but hadn't known what it was. Willow passed it to Lizzie, who took a hit and passed it over her shoulder to Anna. She inhaled and coughed a little, embarrassed, but Willow and Lizzie didn't seem to notice or care. The three of them took turns, passing the joint around the car until the thing was burned to a nub and Lizzie flicked it out the window.

Anna's hair flew in the breeze. Her skin felt cool and soft. She closed her eyes and still saw all the colors of the sun. She was featherlight. Giggling. She felt a hand on her leg and opened her eyes. Willow's arctic stare. Willow's red lips.

"I'm so glad I found you," those red lips said. "Both of you."

Anna closed her eyes again, letting her head loll back and her lips spread into a smile, relishing the moment. Because there, in Lizzie's Range Rover, on a flat, two-lane highway in the middle of Ohio, with the wind blowing cold and Beastie Boys playing too loud, she was the happiest she'd ever been in her life.

Twenty minutes later, still giggling, they were inside the Salvation Army, which smelled of mothballs and shoe polish. Willow led them to the men's section, where they dug through all sorts of things—pleather trench coats and wool slacks and seventies-era corduroys like the ones Willow was wearing. In the boys' department they found Fair Isle sweaters and old raglan tees with strangers' names ironed onto the backs. They found long patchwork skirts and oxford shirts, scarves, fedoras, flannels, more bell-bottoms.

Anna was surprised that they were allowed to try things on—but they were, in a big communal fitting room with one wall entirely made of mirrors. Willow pulled off her T-shirt, not seeming to notice Anna's wide eyes on her bare chest. Willow's figure was so different from Anna's—her breasts were full and her hips were round, but her waist was tiny, like her body had been shaped by a corset. Willow pulled on a cable-knit sweater, and Anna snaked out of her own clothes.

It was like being another person, she thought, as she slipped into someone else's jeans and a thin white sweater meant for a child. She'd been wary of the freshman fifteen, but it hadn't happened to her. Despite the vending machine treats, she had actually lost weight in the past two months. She looked at herself, skinny and tall and brand-new, between her friends.

"Oh, Hollywood," Willow said, turning to her. "You look so fly. But chuck the bra. You have the best tits."

"I don't have *any* tits," Anna said, without blushing.

It was okay—she had used the word *tits* for the first time, and she hadn't stuttered and her voice hadn't cracked. She studied herself as she unhooked her bra, tossed it on the floor. The jeans cinched her waist and the sweater was cropped slightly above the belt loops. Her nipples were conspicuous, outrageous. She stood on her tiptoes and wetted her lips.

Willow was right. She had never looked better.

"We're getting it all," Willow said. "And then we're going *out.*"

They got ready in Willow's room, spraying her Angel perfume on the clothes to mask the mothball smell. Anna pulled on the bell-bottoms and little girl's sweater, slipped into a pair of Willow's platform loafers. They shrugged men's oversize, ankle-length wool coats onto their shoulders, linked arms, and marched across campus—past the frat houses booming hip-hop, past the sorority girls stumbling in their regulation Nine West heels, past Highsmith and Wabash Lake. They marched right off campus, to a place only Willow had heard of.

The Bar Car was a townie dive that had baskets of peanuts and a pool table and line dancing on Tuesdays. None of the girls had fake IDs, but they were pretty enough that nobody asked. They sat at the brass-plated bar and drank cheap beer out of cans. The bliss Anna had felt after getting high had faded, and she wanted it back. She felt almost *nostalgic* for it, that was the only word she could think of, though it had only just happened.

The girls huddled together and talked, mostly about themselves and what they would do with their lives. "New York City is the only option," Willow said. "The only place."

"I don't know." Anna dipped her finger in a puddle of condensation on the bar. "I've always wanted to get an MFA." She didn't want to tell them about Yale, how she'd dreamed of going there since she knew it existed. She was afraid naming her desire out loud would ruin it, jinx it.

"Just go to NYU," Lizzie said. "Maybe we all should. Or Columbia."

"Waste of time," Willow said, waving her fingers. "We have to strike when the iron is hot."

Anna was smiling, but felt something tighten around her neck. "What does that mean?"

"I mean." Willow cupped Anna's face in her hands. "Look at you."

Anna's mouth opened, but before she could conjure a response, Willow dropped her hands, gesturing to Lizzie, then herself. "Look at *us*. The iron is fucking hot right now, girls. We'll get a big loft in SoHo. Kape will get us into his gallery. We'll date aristocrats. Or rock stars. *Artforum* will eat us up. *Page* fucking *Six* will want us." She raised her arms up and wide open. "The whole city will fall to its knees for us!"

"You don't need an MFA to date a rock star," Lizzie said, laughing.

"We are too *good* for MFAs," Willow said.

Anna was smiling, too. She still felt Willow's hands on her cheeks. She would have said yes to anything Willow asked.

"Hey, look," Lizzie said, nodding her head to the door. Two guys around their age, likely Balwin students, had walked in. One was short and stocky with chin-length auburn hair. He was scruffy, but in a new way, as if the preppy version of himself lay underneath. A pentimento. The other guy was tall and thin, a sock hat pulled over long dark hair. The bartender carded them, and they showed IDs and, in turn, had full pint glasses slipped into their hands.

Anna watched Lizzie and Willow watch them. Anna saw her friends' lips pucker and their shoulders roll back, settling into poses. Her heart sank.

These boys were going to wreck everything.

They hadn't even finished their beers when the guys approached with a small tray of shots. The dark-haired one leaned over Anna to stub out his cigarette.

"Lemon drops," he said, and held Anna's gaze. He was not objectively handsome, his forehead was too large and made his chin look small, almost dainty, but he had lush black eyelashes and full lips, and there was a confidence in him that hit Anna in the gut.

"For *us*?" Willow gave a look of mock surprise. She had always had things given to her, Anna knew. Doors opened. Drinks purchased. Cigarettes lit. On top of being pretty, she was smart and decadent and weird, and it made her glow. Willow was used to attention. She accepted it as if it were nothing. As if it weren't everything.

Willow and Lizzie picked up shot glasses, so Anna did, too. They smiled and thanked the guys, so Anna did, too. They clinked glasses and threw back their shots, so Anna did the same. It was easy to swallow, like lemonade.

"Yum," Willow said, licking her lips.

"Yum," Anna said.

"Let me guess." The redhead flicked a Zippo. "You ladies are in the art school?"

Willow rolled her eyes and smirked, as if it was the most obvious assumption she'd ever heard. "How'd you guess?"

They introduced themselves, and it turned out that the guys were freshmen, too, with fake IDs and cash and never-ending cigarettes, but only the redhead, Tom, was in the art school. He and Lizzie bonded over comics and manga, both chain-smoking and gesturing emphatically. The dark-haired guy, Milo Arvanitis, was studying philosophy, liking, he said, the "mind fuck of it all."

He was looking at Anna as he said this, and despite herself, she was intrigued. Milo seemed different from the guys she'd grown up with. Older, even though they were the same age. Comfortable with himself. Confident. She liked his name and the way his jeans hung on his hips. She liked the way he leaned into the bar, and his sharp nose, and how his big brown eyes lingered on her. She liked that he didn't know about Henry or what had happened to him. He saw her only for herself, and from the way his gaze lingered, it seemed he liked what he saw.

Anna wanted to keep him there, to keep his eyes on her, so she asked the first question she could think of. "What kind of name is that—Arvanitis?"

He smiled, and Anna felt something stir in her stomach. He threaded his fingers through his thick black hair. "My family's Greek."

"A Greek philosopher." Anna was smiling, too.

Willow snorted. "Okay, *Socrates*."

Milo rolled his eyes, but Anna could tell he was pleased with the nickname.

"I'm into art, too," he said. "It's a big reason I came here. I want to take some classes at Highsmith. Painting, photography."

"That's my major," Willow said. "I've been obsessed with photography since seventh grade."

Milo lifted his brows at her. "Where's your camera, then? Don't you always have to be ready for the *decisive moment*?"

Willow framed him with her fingers. "Click."

Milo's gaze caught on Willow then and didn't move for the rest of the night. Something moved through Anna—fear, loneliness. Was it so easy to lose a man's attention? Was Willow really that special?

Anna wanted to step between them, spread her arms wide to push them apart, but she knew that she could not.

She could only watch.

The next day, Anna was in the Highsmith library dissecting the *Ghent Altarpiece* when a tight square of folded paper landed on her table, like the origami notes she saw passed in middle school. She looked around but didn't see the person who'd tossed it. She unfolded it.

Unfamiliar print, unsigned: *It's time to do something about this mess.*

Anna frowned at the paper. She flipped it over and looked around the library again. Maybe it wasn't meant for her. Maybe it fell from someone's bag when they weren't paying attention. She carefully returned it to its square and set it aside, taking up her red pencil again. She was recreating the van Eyck brothers' sacrificial lamb, its blood dripping into a chalice. Anna liked to copy the works they were studying in art history; it helped her hold on to them. It helped her understand the artist's technique, his use of color and texture. As she got deeper into her drawing, everything else fell away. Anna forgot the strange note. She ignored the people around her, the flipping pages, the coughing and whispering. She heard nothing. She felt nothing. She was in another place. She was inside her work.

Until cold fingers grazed her bare neck. A whisper: "Boo."

Anna startled, the skin on her arms prickling. But it was only Willow, and she was laughing, pulling a chair closer to Anna's.

"Get my note?" she said, smiling, eyes wide, pupils yawning. Her hair had been brutally chopped into an uneven pixie. With the wild glint in her eyes, she looked like Peter Pan on drugs.

"*What* did you do to your hair?" Anna said.

Willow ignored her, peering at Anna's drawing. She traced a finger on an angel's black wings. "This is beautiful," she said. "Why don't you make figurative work in class?"

Anna closed her notebook. "It's just a copy." She liked realism and figuration, but for skills practice only. She never made her own anymore. It was too *pretty*. Serious contemporary work existed on a different plane, a higher level. It was, almost to a fault, abstract. Just look at that huge Frankenthaler at MoMA. If Anna painted faces, she might end up making work like Lizzie's, work that would end up in the funny pages of a newspaper, or worse—nowhere.

"What mess do we need to do something about?" Anna said.

Willow fashioned her fingers into guns and shot both sides of her head. "This."

Anna laughed. "Why did you do that to yourself?"

"I was bored."

"Jesus." Anna brushed the jagged ends of Willow's hair with her fingers. "What can I do?"

Willow pulled a box of grocery-store hair dye from her bag, thumped it on the table. *Platinum Ice*, it was called. *Maximum-strength bleach kit.*

Anna looked at Willow, her brows high. "Are you serious?"

Willow rolled her eyes, then smiled. "It's just hair, Hollywood. Don't be so scared."

That night, everything shifted. Lizzie and Tom went first, ducking out of the Bar Car in the damp, dark cold to kiss, then, drunker and caring less, kissing inside the bar in front of everyone else, zipped together side by side, not able to stop touching each other's hands, arms, belt loops.

Anna was not surprised. She and Willow made faces at each other—pouting and miming tongue kisses. Willow's new cropped white hair had changed her face, accentuating her icy blue eyes and sharp cheekbones. She smudged her thick black eyeliner and wore red lipstick and looked luminous, Anna thought, nymphlike, even more beautiful than she'd been before.

Milo stood in front of them, legs wide, arms crossed. "I might switch majors."

"What now?" Willow said, eyeing his beer. "Fermentation science?"

Milo smiled. "Painting."

Anna tried to catch his eye, but he wasn't looking at her. His chin was tilted down and his gaze was trained on Willow. *Only* on Willow.

Willow licked her lips. "That's rad, Socrates."

"I'd be in some of your classes, I bet. You think I should?"

In the murk of the bar, Willow's hair glinted. She smiled at Milo, red lips open wide like a trap. "Abso-fuckin-lutely."

It almost made a sound, the way they clicked together. She watched Willow pull Milo to the dance floor, that Jewel song crooning, too loud, too familiar, too desperate. Milo's hands were all over Willow, his face a grotesque mask of pleasure. He looked ready to eat her, Anna thought, disgusted.

An iron weight pressed into her chest, pressed down into the pit of her stomach, anchoring her to the stool. The bartender asked her if she wanted another beer. She could only shake her head, unable to even finish the one in front of her. She couldn't swallow another goddamned thing. Anna wanted to grab Willow, pull her away from everyone else, out the door.

Instead, she jumped off the stool. She needed to get out of the bar before she made a fool of herself. Their wool coats were piled in the corner of the bar. She pulled her own loose, then stopped. Willow's was right underneath. Maybe it was the alcohol, loosening the vise grip she'd had on herself since she was seven years old, but in that moment, Anna didn't care about consequences. She yanked both coats from the heap, letting the rest tumble to the dirty floor.

Outside it was cold and dark and she felt stupid for what she'd done, knowing she'd have to walk two miles back to campus alone. She wrapped Willow's coat over her own, two layers of wool to protect her from whatever was lurking in the shadows. She thought about her art as she walked, about her sublime colors and slashed canvases and the meaning she could pull from threads. Maybe she would shred Willow's coat, paint it, plait it, make a piece out of it. She put her hands in the pockets and felt something cold and hard.

She pulled it out, looked down. Willow's keys. The Eiffel Tower key chain. *Shit.* Anna felt ridiculous for taking the coat then—reactive, juvenile. She stopped walking, glanced over her shoulder at the bar behind her. What could she do about it now?

She made a fist around the keys, stuffed them into her own pocket, and dumped Willow's coat on the sidewalk.

WEDNESDAY MORNING

I BLINKED OPEN MY EYES to see the TV mutely cycling through footage of cars and streets gray with ash, bombed-out windows, snapped metal poking out of rubble like the skeleton of some absurd prehistoric creature. From the couch, I fumbled for the remote—*enough!*—and the screen snapped to black.

My mouth was pasty, rancid. Milo lay curled on the floor, my old quilt only half covering him. He was still wearing his baggy cords and T-shirt, a pair of old white tube socks with a hole in the heel. His hands were tucked under his face, using a couch cushion as a pillow. His eyes were closed. Next to him lay his beaten-up paperback of Kafka's *The Trial* and a pair of boots. Inside were his keys, wallet, smokes, and a lighter—everything he needed, neatly tucked together.

I stood slowly, afraid I'd throw up or wake him, and put an ear to your door. *Nothing.* I opened it slowly, sure I'd find some evidence of you—stereo on, *Artforum* splayed on the bed, even you yourself, lazily blowing smoke through a cracked window.

There was nothing in that room but the smell of you.

I tiptoed into my own room to check my cell phone. I dialed my parents' house, but nothing happened. Cell phones still weren't working. I'd have to buy a new cordless later, I thought—fifty dollars at least, which meant it'd be even longer until I could replace my canvases and paints. *Screw it.* I'd make Milo pay for it. I was so sick of cleaning up after everyone.

I plugged my computer into the phone jack and logged into AOL, biting my lips as the homepage loaded, scanning my inbox for your name. If you'd gone to the police after the mugging like you were supposed to, they at least would have gotten you someplace with a computer, someplace where you could have emailed me. But again, there was nothing, only five new messages from my family, including one from my brother that simply said *Come home!* Henry was seventeen but had always seemed much younger than he was, being delayed in everything from speech to sports. We'd gotten the epilepsy diagnosis years before, and the medications and the appointments Scotch-taped him together, but he would always be different. I loved him in a fierce way, protective and cautious and guilty of the life I had, all the freedoms that he didn't.

I wrote back: *I can't, Henry. The airports are closed. My phone isn't working, but I am safe, I promise. I'm with my friends. I will call you as soon as I can! Tell mom and dad. I love you so much!*

I clicked send, imagined my parents reading over his shoulder, their arms crossed and faces sour, and pushed it out of my head. I thought instead about trying to email La Soeurette—but I didn't know anyone's information. I wasn't supposed to go in until dinner service the next day anyway. I pulled up the Andrews Foundation website, waiting for the page to load. I did this often since I'd found out about the competition, reading and rereading the rules for the AFYAA, to soothe myself, to make plans, to make sure I was on the right track:

- Artist's statement *(done)*
- Portfolio of images *(done)*
- One work to represent applicant's oeuvre *(not done)*

That phrase, *one work*—it was code. It meant *masterpiece*. It's what I'd been digging for all summer. Nothing I'd made in school, not even *Swell*, was good enough. It wasn't explosive enough. It didn't say enough. Kape was right—it was too soft, too crafty, too *feminine*. I needed something new to encapsulate everything I stood for as an artist, while also sending waves through the art world. If I made it through the first round of cuts, that one work would go from slide or JPEG to actuality, transported to the Foundation to be judged and evaluated in person. It had to be provocative. Gutting. Spectacular. The kind of thing no one could look away from.

All materials due by midnight on December 31, 2001.

Two and a half months. I closed my laptop and leaned back in my chair. Yesterday's stink punched me—the acrid stench of fear, the metal and rubber fug of disaster, Happiness's marinade of stale smoke and cheap beer. I stripped off my T-shirt and cutoffs and stretched in the mirror, palpating my ribs as if they were piano keys, then touching the soft spots between the bones, where a knife could slip so easily. I pressed into my flesh until it hurt.

In the shower, my thoughts circled round and round like vultures. *Where is she? Why hasn't she found a pay phone? Borrowed a computer?* I scrubbed my scalp with shampoo, and a sour dread filled my stomach. *She recognized Tyler and tried to fight back. He panicked. He fucked up.*

I squeezed my eyes shut. *Don't be crazy.* I knew you, Willow. You walked through fire for the fun of it. You knew how to take care of yourself. You were fine. You were always fine. Your boss had a place in the West Village, walkable from Chelsea. He probably closed the gallery and took his whole staff there and you were probably in some fat, fluffy bed right now, sleeping in. You wouldn't be worrying about us. You wouldn't care that we were worried about you. It had only been a day. Any other day, and I wouldn't have thought twice about not seeing you. None of us would have.

I ran a razor along my armpits and bikini line, and my thoughts skidded again—*but.* You should have called Lizzie, at least. And why hadn't Tyler shown up to meet Milo last night? We didn't *really* know him, the kind of person he was outside of tending bar at Arcadia. He could have been anyone underneath that smile. He could have been a monster.

My stomach plummeted, and my razor with it, taking a sliver of skin off my shin. Blood ran down my leg, between my toes. I held my calf out in the running water, my heart thumping, my mouth dry and sick, as the blood circled the drain. Lizzie's disappointed face outside the bar last night came back to me, her *Willow's going to kill both y'all.*

Oh Lizzie, I thought. *You have no idea.*

I hopped out of the shower, drying off quickly, sticking a dot of toilet paper on the cut to stop the blood. I flipped my hair over and used the towel to twist it off my shoulders. Your white silk robe hung on its hook, draped and angelic as wings. I pulled out a sleeve—at first just to touch it, to feel its soft coolness on my fingers. It was so delicious. I slipped it from the hook and wrapped myself in it.

I went back to your room, certain I could figure it out, that where you were was written on your calendar, or a note on your desk. I ran my fingers along the binders of your developed negatives, safe in their plastic sleeves. It was the only thing you kept organized in your entire room. I touched your balled-up sheets, resisting the urge to look for your comforter and make your bed, standing instead in front of your wall of black-and-white self-portraits—thirty-nine photos, framed and hung salon-style. I stared at your face in the center photograph, your white hair piled high like a crown, the shadow line of your small nose, your pillowy lips moonlit, adumbral. You were beautiful, of course, but there was something wrong with you, too, something tight and angry and mean right below the surface.

I pulled open the top drawer of your desk. Inside was your mother's Hermès scarf. I picked it up, ran my fingers against the yellow-and-blue silk, and glimpsed a photograph tucked underneath. I flipped the picture over. It was black-and-white, hand-printed in 5x8 and slightly overexposed, and it was of me, sitting on the wall outside Highsmith. Old—from freshman year, maybe sophomore, I was still wearing those ridiculous bell-bottom corduroys and my blue beanie. I picked it up to examine it, to determine when you'd taken it, but as I brought it to my face I caught the figure in the background. *Jon Potts.*

He was leaning against the building, talking to Professor Kape.

"What are you doing?"

I dropped the photo and slammed the drawer shut. Milo gawked at me from the doorway, arms crossed. His eyes were puffy, but everything else about him—his nose, his cheeks, his elbows, his hips, even the black hair that fell in his face—was sharp.

"Nothing."

"Is that her robe?"

I pulled my shoulders back. "Mine was dirty."

He stared at me for a moment, and I shifted my eyes.

"Anything?" he asked finally.

I shook my head. "I bet she went to Philip Roche's place with her gallery people. They could have walked there. It's only like thirty blocks."

Milo stepped inside the room, gazing at your bookshelves, gently running a finger along the spines, then turning to your wall of self-portraits as I had done. Already, the place felt like a shrine.

He didn't face me as he spoke. "Have you checked your email?"

"Yeah," I said. "There's nothing."

"We should go to Lizzie's," he said. "She may have called them."

Or maybe, I thought again, *Tyler slit her throat*. Maybe he bashed your head in. Maybe you were lying dead in that warehouse, and the cops would never find you because they were all in the financial district, digging for survivors in a two-acre pile of burning rubble.

My armpits went wet. I was jittery. I felt the urge to climb something.

"Should we . . ." Milo said. "Do you think we should call the police?"

I stopped, glared at him. "You tell me, Milo. I don't know shit about Tyler."

He shook his head fast, back and forth, back and forth, like he had some kind of tremor. "Not because of Tyler. I'm just worried that she . . ." He ran his palms on his dirty corduroys. Then his fingernails, making a zipping noise that made my stomach turn.

"That she what?"

Milo didn't respond, but it didn't matter.

I could picture everything without his help.

THREE AND A HALF YEARS BEFORE

WILLOW POUNDED on Anna's door.

"Babe, it's me. *Open up!*"

Anna was still in the old T-shirt and boxer shorts she'd slept in, her eyes spider-legged with last night's mascara, playing with paint on her floor. Immediately, she thought of Willow's coat, abandoned on the sidewalk, and Willow's keys, which were still stuffed in Anna's own coat pocket.

"Hey."

She tried to read Willow's face, to see if she knew, somehow, what Anna had done. But Willow danced into the room wearing a black leotard and black tights, her bleached pixie slicked into a side part, twirling two full spins before plopping herself on the rough wood floor. Legs crisscrossed beneath her, she rustled through a shoebox of acrylic paints Anna had been experimenting with. A flap of cardboard held neat circles of oranges and yellows, still wet from mixing.

Willow ran a finger along a row of tubes. "Jesus, you keep this shit so organized." She laughed. "I can't even find my keys."

Anna's heart flipped over. "You lost your keys?" Everything moved in slow motion—the alcohol and partying was still new to her, and Anna's body often felt this way in the mornings—sluggish, slightly stupid. She closed the door. "Where did you sleep?"

Willow struck a match and let it burn in her fingers. "Milo's."

Anna turned away. She'd messed up, she realized, taking those keys. She'd given Willow and Milo the perfect opportunity to hook up. *Stupid.* Anna's stomach roiled; her mouth tasted sour. She fiddled with the bottles on her dresser.

Willow blew out the match, leaving a sulfur smell in the room. "I borrowed the master key from the RA this morning." She lit another match. "He said if I don't find mine, I'll have to pay fifty bucks for a new one."

Anna didn't have to look at Willow to know that she was smiling. Willow didn't care about fifty dollars. Fifty dollars was nothing to her.

Anna spritzed a cheap vanilla perfume onto her wrists, rubbed them together. "Well, how was the night? How was *he*?"

Willow said nothing. Her silence struck Anna with hope. Maybe it had been bad. Maybe something awful happened between them.

Anna turned. "Not good?"

Willow shook her head, her expression fuzzy. She touched the dead match on the floor. "It's not that."

"What, then?"

"He said . . ." Willow paused, then looked up. "He said he was actually into you."

Anna leaned forward, surprised. *"Me?"*

Willow lit another match. "He wanted me to ask if you'd go out with him."

Anna stared at her, thinking about the way Milo's eyes had lingered on her before Willow snatched them away. "I thought you liked him?"

"Well." Willow let the match burn down to her fingertips, then blew it out and set it next to the other one. "What am I gonna do? *He* likes *you*."

Anna tried to think of something to say. A moment passed.

"So, would you?" Willow asked. "Go out with him?"

Anna shrugged. "I guess so."

"Ha!" Willow dropped the matchbook and jumped to her feet. "I *knew* you were into him."

Anna grimaced, stunned, not understanding the shift the conversation had just taken. "I didn't say that. I'm not into him."

Willow crossed her arms and jutted out a leg, the black tights shrinking her figure into something childlike. "I'm messing with you, Anna."

Anna licked her lips. She said nothing.

"I saw the way you were watching us last night. And now I know I need to watch my back." Willow was smirking, and her voice was treacly with amusement. "You little bitch."

Anna fumbled for a response, but nothing came. She went on the offensive instead. "What's with the matches? And what are you wearing?"

"I'm Edie Sedgwick."

Anna drew a blank.

"One of Warhol's superstars," Willow explained. "I'm super into her right now." Willow pulled a hardback out of her bag and dropped it on Anna's bed. *Andy Warhol: The Factory Years.* "Look at the bookmarked pages."

The girl in the photos was pale and pretty, with short, bleached hair like Willow's. She had dark, heavily lined eyes, as big as planets.

"Look at that face," Willow said. "She looks like you."

Anna furrowed her brow. "No way. She looks like you."

"Ignore the hair. You could change *this,*" Willow took a handful of Anna's dark hair and tugged gently, "and totally be her."

Their eyes locked, and for a moment, Anna thought Willow was going to suggest cutting her hair, too, dyeing it platinum so they could be twins. Anna would have said yes. She would have loved to see herself looking more like Willow, less like everyone else. But Willow smiled, letting Anna's hair fall through her fingers.

"She was Warhol's muse," Willow went on. "A socialite. She was in his movies. She wanted to be a film star for real, but never made it. She was the original it girl."

"She's dead?"

Willow nodded. "OD'd before we were born." She grabbed the book back. "But that's not why I'm here, Hollywood."

That evening, Willow twisted Anna's hair into knots, pinning here and there, leaving flyaways just so around her face. She tweezed Anna's brows into arches and circled her eyelids in thick black shadow, like Edie's. She sprayed Anna with Mugler's Angel. And she talked. She told Anna about the guy who would be waiting for her at the Bar Car. Willow had met him in Figure Drawing. He was a high school football star, tall and hot, but with an artist's mind. Good old Midwestern boy, but with an edge. His name was Boomer.

"Boomer?" Anna said. "Like the Bengals player?"

Willow frowned. "Who?"

Anna shook her head. "Never mind. It's a football nickname, I guess."

"This Boomer is not just a jock, I promise. He's cool."

Anna returned her friend's smile, but she was not looking forward to the setup. She hadn't had sex—she hadn't even kissed a boy—and didn't really want to, afraid it would change some essential part of her. But everyone was coupling up around her, and Willow vetting and offering Boomer to her seemed to be a declaration of their friendship. A promise, from Willow to Anna: *I will not leave you behind.*

"His parents are super religious," Willow said. "Same bullshit as me."

Anna followed Willow with her eyes. "Your parents are religious?"

"My dad is." Something came over Willow's face—a scrim. Everything went to shadows. "My mom's just sick."

Anna thought of Henry, at home, prey to seizures, mood swings, stigma. "Sick how?"

"Close your eyes," Willow said, and Anna did as she was told. Willow's brush tapped her skin gently.

Three months of friendship, and she still felt like she only knew the basic facts of Willow's life. She was from Chicago and had no siblings. She'd gone to an all-girls private school. She lived alone with her dad, an old-fashioned, suit-and-tie kind of man who cared more about stocks and bonds than art and culture. Her dad indulged her, though, buying her photo equipment and a new car and any clothes she wanted. The thrift store love, it had occurred to Anna, was an act. A way for Willow to break from under her father's conservative ideology. But Willow never talked about her mom, where she was or how often she saw her.

"You mean *sick* sick?" Anna asked.

The brush stopped moving. Anna opened her eyes. Willow had turned away.

"What is it?"

Willow wasn't looking at her. "I haven't told anyone at school. I don't like to talk about it."

"Hey." Anna reached her hand to Willow's wrist. So tiny. Anna could circle the bones with her fingers. She probably could have snapped them, if she wanted to. "You can tell me anything."

"You wouldn't understand," Willow said. "Your parents are still together. Your family's so *normal.*"

Anna laughed, then shook her head at Willow's confused face.

"Not laughing at you," she said. "It's just—my family's not normal at all."

No one at Balwin knew about Henry. No one tiptoed around Anna like she was a human land mine. She was a new person there, unfettered by tragedy and stigma, and she had every intention of keeping it that way. But Anna also understood that Willow was on the verge of sharing something big, something that would tie them together, bond them, no matter who or what might try to pull them apart.

Anna could give Henry to Willow. She could use him like a blade to open her up.

She took Willow's hand, their fingers twisted together. Anna felt a great swell of emotion. This was what it meant to have a best friend. It was only since she'd met Willow that she understood what she'd been missing. What Henry had taken from her. It was only right that she used him to get back what she'd lost.

"Tell me," Anna said. "And I'll tell you."

Willow closed her eyes. "My mom," she said. "She has MS. Multiple sclerosis. She's been in and out of the hospital my whole life. It's really advanced now. She can't walk." Willow looked up at the ceiling, eyes wet and reflective like an El Greco painting. "She can't do much. We had to move her into a special home."

A missing piece, Anna thought. "I'm so sorry."

"That's why I live with my dad."

"Oh, Wills." Anna had so many questions, but she held back. If she demanded too much, Willow would shut down. "I understand. I really do."

"Your turn."

Anna closed her eyes. Willow's fingers were soft and warm in hers.

"My brother, Henry," Anna said. "He's fourteen now, but when he was little . . ." Anna had never actually had to explain it before—everyone in Bexley already knew what had happened to Henry.

"It's okay," Willow said. "You can tell me."

"When he was little . . ." Anna shook her head. She couldn't get it all out, it was too deep inside her, like the skin had grown over it.

Willow squeezed her hands, encouraging her to go on.

Anna let out a quivering sigh. "He got sick," she said finally. "He lost consciousness and got brain damage. He started having seizures after that."

Anna felt tears prick her eyes. It was hard to talk about Henry, and not for the reasons anyone might think. Seeing Willow's sympathy, her sadness—it made Anna feel like a traitor to her brother. There had been so many words used to describe him, the way his brain worked, and Anna had heard them all: *damaged, delayed, slow, retarded*. None of them fit. Anna would never say any of them.

"He's just *different*," she said.

It was such a relief that Willow didn't ask questions, only leaned in and wrapped her arms around her. It was all Anna needed. The girls stayed there like that, holding each other for a full minute, breathing in each other's secrets, each other's sadness.

When Willow pulled away, she wiped her eyes and smiled. "Don't cry, Hollywood. Your makeup looks too good."

Anna tipped her head back and laughed.

They held hands on the walk to the Bar Car, and everyone was waiting for them, including Boomer. He was tall and thick as a mattress with short brown hair, and a broad, class-president smile. He wore a navy hoodie and smiled at Anna with large white teeth. Even if Willow hadn't prepared her, it would have been obvious what everyone had in mind that night, nudging Boomer closer and closer to Anna's barstool.

He ordered boilermakers. Anna batted her black-smudged eyes and arched her chest in his direction, as she'd seen Willow do with Milo. After her conversation with Willow, she felt lighter and more rooted, like she was growing in two directions at once. She understood now that the boys didn't matter, that no one could ever come between their friendship.

The bartender set the boilermakers in front of them—two half-pints of beer, two shots of whiskey. Boomer held his shot glass, tapped it against hers, then dropped it into the beer glass. It fizzed violently. He brought it to his mouth, downing the whole thing in a single, bobbing gulp. Anna did the same with her own set, but it tasted like poison. It took her half a dozen sips to get it all down.

Boomer watched Anna struggle, brows pulled in and raised, lips in a wry smile. "Lightweight," he said when she finally finished.

Anna shuddered, pushed the foamy glasses away from her, and reached for the plastic basket of peanuts. She sucked salt from several shells to rid her mouth of the taste. He ordered a couple beers.

"Willow says you play football," Anna said.

"I'm retiring."

Anna raised an eyebrow. "You're quitting?"

"I don't want to do the camps this summer." He looked sad for a moment, then reassembled himself, smiling and holding up his can. His teeth were white, and very large—too large, Anna thought, too perfect. His smile looked fake, like one of those old Ronald Reagan masks. "College has more to offer than just football, right?"

He was looking in Anna's direction, but not quite *at* her. His eyes focused somewhere on her edges. She touched her ear to make sure there wasn't something gross hanging there. She smiled back at him, or the corner of him, and nodded.

"What's your major?"

"Design." He held his beer to his cheek, like he was hot. "I do mostly robotics, some industrial stuff. I like architecture, but I'm terrible at math. You?"

"Painting," Anna said.

Boomer smiled. "I bet you want to be one of Tony Kape's advisees, then."

She nodded, smiled back. "Sure do."

Anna looked across the room and saw Willow squeezed into a booth next to Milo. Willow winked and raised her eyebrows a few times, fast and silly, a slapstick expression. Anna understood the message. She could almost hear Willow's voice in her head.

Go for it, Hollywood.

Later that night in Boomer's dorm room, under a bright red comforter that smelled like cinnamon gum and drugstore cologne, they made out. Boomer's tongue was sharp and surprising in Anna's mouth, and his knee grinded between her legs and against her jeans so hard that the thick seam started to tear her skin. Anna's lip curled in discomfort, and she stared at the ceiling, conjuring Willow, her voice—*Go for it, Hollywood.*

Boomer sat up, fussing with the comforter, and Anna could

sense his interest in her waning. It was her fault, she knew. She wasn't doing enough to make him want her. She had to get it together. She had to make it work. *For the group*, she told herself. *For Willow.* She put her hand on his arm and pulled him back. She did not let her body flinch at his touch; she would not allow herself to jerk away. Anna forced her gaze on him—his bulk and chin stubble and half-open eyes. He fumbled around with the button on her jeans, but when it was clear that he couldn't manage it, Anna peeled them off herself. She took him in her hand. The surprise of his flesh was like the touch pool at the aquarium, a sea creature squirming in her fingers.

Boomer pulled away again and Anna propped herself on elbows, afraid, but he was rustling around in his jeans. A condom. She dropped onto her back again. Then the shock of it: a sharp, searing pain. Anna clenched her teeth. She didn't make a sound as he thrust. She held herself steady, wanting it to be easy for him, wanting to get it over with. He slowed after a few pumps, drunk and heavy on top of her, and soon he passed out, his dick limp, snoring over the covers.

Anna's first time was over.

She sat there, horrified, staring at him. *Get up*, she told herself. *Get out.* She patted around for her jeans and yanked them on, her heart banging, and took herself back outside into the night. The campus was as quiet as a snowstorm, the few streetlamps yellow and gauzy. She knew she ought to be afraid—out here in the middle of the night—there could be drunk frat boys, or rowdy townies, or some new, unthinkable menace.

But she wasn't afraid. Her insides were sore and her ego was bruised, her head hammered, but she was sober again, *too* sober, and she couldn't force herself to care what happened next. Whatever brutality would come rushing up from behind the bushes, whatever pain would come from punches or weapons or fingers around her neck, from broken bones or torn skin or contusions—it would feel like relief now.

WEDNESDAY MORNING

LIZZIE'S HOUSE was old and narrow, a three-story red brick on 2nd Place. In the Midwest it would have been considered shabby, but in New York, where even most grown-ups lived in boxes stacked on top of each other like mink pens, her place was a prize. A wedge of stone propped open the door, and Nina Simone crooned from deep inside. I never admitted this to you—you were so sure Lizzie's turntable was *affected*—but I cherished the warbly sound of those records. Their quaint fragility.

Lizzie stood under the arch in the front hall, cigarette smoldering between her fingers. "Shit," she said, taking in the sight of us. "Nothing?"

I shook my head, knowing exactly what she was asking, and answering my own question before I could ask.

Tom sat on the living room sofa—that huge, ornate thing with burgundy velvet and lacquered feet that one of Lizzie's yard boys had driven up from Kentucky. Of all the things pinned to the walls—my drawings and Lizzie's cartoons and Nuyorican posters—it was your photos that I saw first that morning, the twenty or so pictures you'd taken at Lizzie's spoken-word performances at Arcadia over the summer. I couldn't escape them. I couldn't escape *you.*

Lizzie padded across the rug and sank next to Tom on the sofa. His eyes were narrow as sheets of paper, his body a slab of rock. Stoned out of his mind. I walked past the tufted chairs and brocaded cushions and settled into a cheap, plush beanbag chair.

Lizzie tightened her arms around her chest. She was glaring at me and Milo. She thought the worst of us, of *me,* that I was stealing your boyfriend while you were away. I didn't meet her eyes. I didn't feel like explaining anything to her. And anyway, I couldn't. Not then. Not when the enormous, sweltering fear that had been set over the city like a cloche had gotten closer and hotter by the hour. It was just us under that silver dome now. Just us, waiting for you.

Milo pushed through the swinging door to the kitchen. "I need a beer."

Tom turned slowly to watch him leave. It wasn't even noon on a Wednesday, but drinking seemed like the right thing to do. Drinking or getting high or dancing or painting or disappearing. Whatever it took to get through it.

Lizzie twisted her legs under her, tapping her cigarette against a giant glass ashtray. She was stoned, too, tense and buzzing, barely blinking, panic bulging her eyes out like marbles. "I heard there are people trapped underground," she said. "In the subways. They said the whole Cortlandt station is crushed."

Tom and I spoke at the same time.

"That's speculation, baby."

"She wasn't on the subway."

Lizzie cut her eyes to me. They were bloodshot, shadowed. "You don't know that, A. We don't know *anything*. She could have been running late. She could have stopped somewhere. She could have gotten trapped. She could be unconscious in some hospital. She could be *dead*."

I bit the inside of my cheek and glanced back at your photos on the wall. Lizzie was right, I knew. No matter what Milo believed about Tyler, I knew the truth: Men were capable of violence. *All* men.

Lizzie flapped her hands. "We need to call her dad, guys."

I opened my mouth, but a sound came from the front door. A slam. Everyone froze. My heart swan-dived in my chest. *You.*

But it was Boomer. Boomer barreling into the living room, too loudly, too *happily*, for the moment. I looked him up and down, really *looked* at him for the first time in months, and realized he'd lost weight this summer. He looked healthy. Clean. Something about him was changing. *He must like his work*, I thought, *doing whatever it is he's doing at the advertising firm*.

"What's wrong?" he said.

Lizzie lit another cigarette. Her voice was high-pitched, near frantic. "We still haven't heard from Willow."

"Shit, really?" he said. Then: "Has anyone tried Mason yet?"

As soon as he said it, it seemed so obvious. You and Mason had been partying together all summer. I should have thought of him ages ago.

"We don't have his number," I said.

Boomer pulled a bottle of Absolut from his bag. "I do."

I blinked at him. "You do?"

"We hung out at that rave," he said. "You were there."

The way he looked at me felt like an accusation. I put my palms on my chest, ready to defend myself. But he shook his head. "They weren't hooking up, though, if that's what you're getting at."

"No," Lizzie said. "We know that."

"He's . . ." Tom flopped his hand around. "You know."

Boomer's lip curled. "*Gay*, you mean?"

"Yeah, man, just saying."

"She could still be with him," I said, suddenly hopeful that *I* wasn't responsible after all. "Even if they aren't hooking up. She could be with him or her other gallery people. At her boss's place. Or she could be someplace we couldn't even *conceive of*, because she doesn't tell us shit, and no one really knows what she does or where she goes."

"Anna," Lizzie started.

I smacked my hands on my jeans. God, how I wanted this to be your fault. "I'm serious. This just *screams* Willow. You know it does. She's not thinking about us. She doesn't care that we're worried. Not even with . . ." I waved my hands over my shoulders, indicating the door, the outside, the city, the burning hole near Wall Street.

"Oh, come on," Lizzie said.

I was being defensive and weird, and I had to stop myself. I stood and stomped my way to the kitchen, a shiver rolling over my shoulders when the door swung closed behind me. I wasn't sure what was working me up—your inconsideration or my guilt—but it didn't matter. I didn't want to drink, but I popped open a Red Stripe with the bottle opener tied to the fridge and took a gulp anyway. I forced my breaths to even out. I had to calm down before I said something stupid.

When I pushed the door back into the living room everyone was just as I left them. Silent, and watching Boomer. He had Lizzie's house phone to his ear.

"Nothing. I can't even leave a message."

"Call again," Lizzie said.

"Who is it?" I asked.

Boomer pushed some buttons and put the phone to his ear again, pulled it away just as fast, shaking his head. "Mason," he said. "But I only have his cell."

"Call information," Lizzie said. "Get Philip Roche's number. I think he lives on Charles Street."

"Good idea." Boomer dialed and waited, then spelled out Philip's name to the operator on the line, looking at us and nodding. "That's it," he said, then frowned. "Thanks anyway." He clicked off the phone. "It's unlisted."

"Do we know his address?" Lizzie said. "We could just go there."

No one answered. No one knew.

Lizzie put her fingers over her face. "We have to call her dad, you guys. We have to." She looked at me. "Anna, *you* have to."

I gaped at her. "Why me?"

"Lizzie's right," Tom said. "She's too emotional. If she calls, she'll just make it worse. And Willow's dad hates Milo." Tom glanced at him. "No offense, dude."

Milo shrugged—*whatever*—and took a slug from his beer bottle.

"He doesn't even know me or Boomer. You have to, Anna. You're the only one."

Your father was still an enigma to me. I only knew what he *gave* you: the department store perfume, the art books and supplies, the clothes and jewelry, the darkroom equipment. He paid your nine-hundred-dollar rent, a hundred more a month than I paid so you could have the bigger room, the better one, the quiet one that overlooked the small plot of land the landlord described as his garden but seemed to grow only weeds and rusty nails and trash. I'd been to your place in Chicago—I knew what those lake views meant, I knew how nice the furniture was. You had goddamned *staff*.

"Fine," I said.

Boomer handed me the phone.

I stood, reluctantly. "Someone give me the number."

"Here." Lizzie did something on her cell and handed it to me. "It's saved here."

I took both phones to the top of the stairs and rested my head against a wood baluster—*think, think*. But the wrong image fell into my mind: you on the cement floor of that warehouse, white skin and red blood and pink-tailed rats. My eyes flew open. I had to stop this. I had to call. If he'd heard from you, I could go downstairs and tell everyone you were safe and selfish as always, and I could tell Milo that nothing had happened with Tyler, that your absence had nothing to do with us. And then, finally, we could stop talking about you.

Your dad picked up on the first ring. "Willow?"

I panicked. I felt as if I had just landed here, in this house, in this country, in this millennium, with this piece of plastic in my hand, shouting at me.

"Willow!"

"No, I'm sorry. It's just me. It's Anna," I said.

"Anna? I've been calling the apartment—"

"Our phone's broken. I'm calling from a friend's house."

"Is Willow with you?"

Shit. I rubbed my temple. "No. We haven't heard from her."

There was a pause. It stretched on too long and made me nervous. "All her friends from school are here, at Lizzie Stone's house, waiting for her. We tried to call the gallery, but no one's picking up."

"I've spoken to Phil," he said.

"Philip Roche? His number's unlisted—"

"He's an old friend of Willow's mother."

Willow's mother. I swallowed this, feeling it land heavy as a rock in my stomach.

"Willow wasn't at the gallery yesterday," your dad said. "None of his employees came in. It doesn't open until ten, so it— They never opened."

Fear cracked open in my chest. Wet, cold fear, oozing into my veins. You weren't at Philip Roche's apartment in the West Village. You weren't there, and you weren't here, and I knew what that meant. *The warehouse. Tyler.*

A shuffling on the other end of the line, then a new voice. "Anna, honey, it's Leanne. Hang on."

Leanne? I was confused. Why was your nanny there with your dad, even though you were in New York? It was strange, but everything about Leanne was strange, and I didn't have the brain space at the moment to question it.

"Okay, honey," she said. "I'm alone. What about that man she was seeing?"

My stomach dropped, and I didn't know why. "What man?"

"I don't know his name," she said. "She never told me. She

said she was dating an older man. An artist. She swore me to secrecy. I don't want her to think I'm tattling, and I haven't said anything to her father yet, but we've been going mad since yesterday. He's been calling everyone, Philip, the police, the fire department."

The police.

My voice trembled. "What did they say?"

"Nothing, unfortunately, honey. Half the city's still missing. They have calls into the hospitals—we've been calling them, too—but they say there's nothing else they can do. Bill's moved on to his lawyers."

I kept my voice even. "Did Mr. Roche say anything about a guy named Mason?"

A pause. "Not that I know of."

"He's an artist, a sculptor. They aren't dating or anything like that, but they're friends from the gallery. They've gotten close this summer. We've been calling him but can't get through."

"Okay," Leanne said. "Okay, honey, good."

I took a deep breath and let it out slowly. I needed more time. I needed to find out what Tyler had done to you before anyone really started looking for you.

"The phones are still pretty messed up," I said. "And the subways and stuff. I'm sure she's just stuck somewhere. I'm sure she's trying to call."

"Yes, honey," Leanne said. "I'm sure you're right."

That's the thing, Willow.

I knew how to lie, too.

Ten

THREE YEARS BEFORE

LEAVING CAMPUS that first summer was painful, like being pulled from sleep before sunrise. When her parents arrived, Anna cried silently into her T-shirt, not wanting to hurt their feelings or make waves. Together, the three of them lugged milk crates full of her books and CDs and bedding and canvases down the dorm stairs and into the waiting trunk. Mostly, in the two hours it took to drive back to Bexley, they were silent. Her parents did not ask questions. They didn't care how much Anna's art had changed in the last eight months. How much *she* had changed. They had no interest in the new techniques she'd learned. They had no idea that she'd *become* someone—someone important, someone people talked about.

But there she was again, back in the lonely yellow house where Henry waited with his home health aide, whom they called his babysitter, where nothing ever changed. The pale-blue walls in Anna's bedroom were the same. The sand-colored carpet was the same. The Jack and Jill bathroom she shared with Henry was the same, too. Anna had lived there for as long as she could remember. Her parents had purchased the house before Henry was born. It was supposed to be a bright and sunny home for a bright and sunny family.

No one could plan for a room like Henry's, what it looked like, what it required. There were typical boy things—posters of *Star Wars* and *Ace Ventura*, Choose Your Own Adventure books, and video games galore—but there was also a hospital bed attached to monitoring equipment, a pulse oximeter, a blood pressure cuff, neurostimulation devices. A cooling vest, a helmet. In the kitchen, a dedicated shelf for his meds—Keppra and Topamax and steroids.

Unpacking her room felt like returning to a prison cell, and Anna fought back the feeling that there was something that she hadn't gotten away with. Something that she still must face. Her mother called her for dinner, and she went, plodding down the carpeted stairs, bracing herself.

The dining table was set—plaid place mats and matching napkins, silverware, water glasses—and the whole house smelled of cooked meat. Anna's mouth felt sticky and her stomach already full, but she took a slice of the meatloaf anyway, and the green beans and the mashed potatoes. She put small portions of everything on her plate. It was automatic. At home, she kept clean, did what was expected of her, and never, ever made a spectacle of herself.

"Looks great, hon," her father said.

Her mother pressed her lips together and smoothed the napkin in her lap.

Across the table, Henry smiled at Anna, his lips stretching so wide, so happy. "I missed you," he said.

Anna felt her heart crack. "I missed you more."

"All right." Anna's mother leaned over Henry's plate. "Let's cut this up."

"Mom," Anna started. Her mother always did too much, cooking food the texture of applesauce, treating him like an invalid. He could do more, Anna believed, if they let him. "He can't choke on meatloaf."

Her mother looked at Anna with eyes narrow as pencil tips, mouth pursed. "You don't know a thing about it."

"Hon," her father said, laying a calming hand on her mother's. They exchanged a look, and her mother went back to her task.

Anna cast her eyes to her own plate, the brown smudge of meatloaf there, and heard Willow's voice in her head. *We don't need that shit. We eat art.*

She set down her fork.

No one said a word.

Anna woke the next morning with a start. She sat up, eyes wide, listening to the quiet. *Too quiet*, she thought. Something was wrong. She flung off the quilt and jumped to the door, through the shared bathroom, and into Henry's room. His bed was empty. Her stomach bottomed out, and she spun back toward her own room, preparing herself for bad news—Henry had a seizure, he's back in the hospital, he's relapsed to that awful, awful vegetative state, hooked to machines and tubes and unable do anything, not even blink.

In her room, Anna stood still, a finger pressed hard to her lips, until she heard the rattle of a pan in the kitchen. The fear cracked open like an egg, slithering all through her. Someone was downstairs, making breakfast. That only happened on good days, she knew, which meant nothing had happened during the night. Henry was here. Henry was okay.

Anna crawled back into bed, pulling the quilt up over her chest and closing her eyes, though she would not be able to fall back asleep. Not now, not with her skin prickling and her heart battering inside her the way it was. That was life in the little yellow house—constantly alert, constantly careful. Everything felt as fragile as cobwebs, and Anna was afraid to breathe too hard lest she blow it all down.

When Willow called the last week of June and suggested Anna come to her house for a weekend, it felt like a door unlocking. Anna couldn't print out the MapQuest directions fast enough. The drive from Bexley to Chicago was almost six hours, longer than any trip Anna had taken on her own, but it would be worth it. She spent the majority of her time in her mother's old Acura avoiding intrusive thoughts about abandoning Henry. Instead, Anna imagined Willow's apartment. The urbaneness of it. She pictured what Willow's kitchen cabinets held. She wanted to meet Willow's father and talk about her mother. Mrs. Whitman, Anna knew, was the real link, the thing that connected the girls—even more than art. Anna had Henry, and Willow had her mother, and though the illnesses were not the same, the girls cradled them in the same way.

Anna crossed into Illinois, and immediately everything got bigger and more complicated. The smokestacks and factories of western Indiana gave way to huge billboards. Elevated trains snaked along their tracks. The highway splintered strangely, illogically, with express lanes and tunnels and underpasses and cars speeding past, honking and screeching and making Anna's neck prickle.

Willow's building was a skyscraper on Lake Shore Drive. The street itself was unlike anything Anna had ever seen, with the tall, loud city on one side, and the huge blue lake on the other. She slowed down, but there was no place to park on Lake Shore. Traffic whizzed by, and Anna pitched forward over the steering wheel, creeping around the block, then another block, and another and another, getting confused by the one-way streets, circling and circling, until she found a place to tuck the car.

She grabbed her purse and duffel bag from the backseat and retraced her way to Willow's building. She was sweating by the time she reached the lobby—large and grand, with gold sixties-era chandeliers and brocade couches, more like a hotel than a home. Anna felt oddly timid. She didn't have instructions; she didn't even know what floor Willow lived on.

A man in a uniform approached. "Can I help you, miss?"

Anna's self-consciousness stiffened her, armored her. She tightened her grip on the duffel and stuck out her chin. "I'm visiting my friend—Willow Whitman? She didn't tell me where to go."

The man smiled. "No problem. Let me ring up."

Anna watched as he went over to a podium and took up a phone. He glanced at her, the receiver crooked between his shoulder and ear, and frowned. Anna looked away. She had been invited here, she was certain of that, but still there was a nagging feeling that she was not welcome, that she had overstepped some crucial boundary. That if anyone knew who she really was, she'd be dragged out by the ear. She looked down at her short mall-bought sundress and military surplus store boots and wondered what the doorman saw. If some hem or label or mark betrayed her.

The man returned, and Anna held herself tight, chin still unnaturally high, as if ready to receive a punch. But his gloved hand gestured to the elevator bank. "Twenty-second floor, Ms. Vaughn."

Anna swallowed. He knew her name. It was okay—she had been recognized, deemed worthy. She belonged. She was meant to be here.

"Thank you."

He held open the elevator, eyes on the carpet. Anna walked past him, and the doors sucked shut.

"Jesus Christ," she said aloud, shaking the tingle from her arms, exhaling with relief. She scanned the numbers on the elevator—forty floors! A spasm of excitement passed through as she saw that the twenty-two button was already lit, and she began, quickly, to rise.

———

The elevator doors opened directly into the living room, and there Willow was, waiting, wearing a tank top and tiny shorts, the Hermès scarf over her short bleached hair. Her face cracked into a huge smile, and she ran to Anna, wrapping her in a bear hug.

"You're here!"

The smell of Willow's skin mixed with something muskier.

Something dirtier. Anna pulled back and looked around. The apartment was cold. Cold and white and squeaky, like a mall. It didn't look like an *apartment*. It didn't match the word. The living room was wide-open, a wall of windows glowing from beyond the cream-colored sofas.

The lake looked as grand as any ocean, but calm and soft. Everything was different here, Anna thought. Everything was tight together, tall and intimidating. Chicago was a fashion model of a city.

Willow came up next to her and took her hand. "That's Oak Street Beach. Wanna go?"

"Sure," Anna said, not sure exactly what Willow was pointing at.

"Bring your stuff," Willow said, turning. "We can change in my room."

Anna followed her down a hallway into a formal dining room with another wall of windows facing the lake and a long, glossy wood table. A middle-aged man in an Oxford shirt and reading glasses sat at the far head.

"Dad," Willow said.

The man looked up without moving his head—just a set of small, saurian eyes lifting over half-moon glasses. Anna's chest tightened. The hand that Willow was holding began to sweat.

Mr. Whitman made a crease in the center of his newspaper before laying it on the table. "This must be Anna." His smile was all lips, no teeth.

Anna shook off Willow's hand, took a step forward, and forced a smile. "Nice to meet you, Mr. Whitman."

He slipped the glasses off his face and settled back into the chair. "How was the drive from Cincinnati?"

"Columbus, Dad," Willow corrected.

That tight smile again. "Right, of course. Columbus."

Anna felt a need to raise his estimation of her. To raise her status. Maybe it was the doorman's frown earlier, or the forty floors, or the view from the windows behind Mr. Whitman, but Anna had an anxious, creeping sense of being an interloper. She didn't want Mr. Whitman to see it. She didn't want him to tell Willow that Anna wasn't good enough to be her friend.

"Bexley, actually," she said.

Despite Anna's middle-class house, Bexley was a wealthy suburb on par with Grosse Pointe or Lake Forest, and any well-off Midwesterner would know that.

Mr. Whitman frowned and nodded at the same time, an expression of acceptance. "Well, you are very welcome here. We are so pleased that Willow is making friends again."

Willow rolled her eyes. "That's enough, *Father*." She took Anna's hand again, pulling her from the room.

"'Making friends again'?" Anna said, laughing, when they were well into the hall. "What did you *do*?"

"Oh god." Willow smirked. "He thinks I'm friendless because I left the Catholic Youth Group."

"For real?"

Willow shrugged, pushed open another door.

Her bedroom had views, too. Not just of Lake Michigan, but a sliver of the city as well. Anna could imagine what it would look like at night, with the sky black and the buildings lit up, twinkling like a fairy-tale kingdom, and she couldn't wait to sleep there. The walls were painted a dark blue, with a plum fleur de lis trim and thick brocade draperies. It was a grown-up's room, Anna thought, fingering the stiff fabric, except for the glow-in-the-dark stars stuck to the ceiling and a string of Christmas lights pinned around the bed frame.

Anna had pulled off her dress and was wrestling into a new strappy bikini when there came two quick raps at the door. It cracked open without waiting for an answer. Anna froze, trying to cover herself.

A woman peeked her head in. "May I come in?"

Willow didn't turn. She was busy pulling books off her shelves, flipping through pages. "Sure."

The woman—tall and officious looking, in belted khakis and short brown hair—came straight toward Anna. "Finally!" she said. "The famous Anna." Her hand was out for Anna to shake, long yam-colored fingernails. "I'm Leanne."

"Hi," Anna said. If she took the woman's hand, part of her chest would be exposed. She did it anyway. The woman didn't seem to even register Anna's bare nipple, aimed right at her.

"We're going to the beach," Willow said.

"Great!" Leanne beamed, hands clasped in front of her. "Do you need anything?"

Willow dropped a thick white tome on her bed—Harrison and Wood's *Art in Theory*—and finally glanced up. "Actually, yeah. Could you pack us some towels and snacks?"

"You got it, girls."

Leanne closed the door behind her, a gentle snap, and Willow resumed her book browsing.

"Who was *that*?" Anna tried to make her voice gravelly and unaffected like Willow's, but it came out indignant. Almost bitter.

"My nanny," Willow said.

Anna laughed. They were nineteen. "No, for real," she said.

Willow didn't smile. "For real."

Leanne had one of those giant L.L.Bean tote bags, branded *WMW*, all loaded up in the kitchen.

"Towels, sunscreen, snacks, ice-cold Diet Cokes," she said.

"Cool, thanks," Willow said, grabbing the tote, stuffing in a couple books, her cigarettes, and a lighter, and heading for the door. She had a big yellow sweatshirt over her bikini, yellow flip-flops, too.

Downstairs, the same doorman ushered them outside. He actually tipped his hat. "Ladies."

Anna smiled at him, but Willow did not. Anna registered this and bit her lips, embarrassed, feeling she had given herself away. She followed Willow across Lake Shore Drive to the beach path, then onto the sand. It took less time than it did to cross North Lawn. Willow spread the towels—giant and thick, with green and white stripes—over the sand. Anna pulled her dress over her head, and Willow slipped off the sweatshirt. People turned to watch them, to ogle or glare, and they both noticed. They always noticed.

Willow made a visor with her hand. "God, you're so skinny," she said, scowling. "I'm so fucking jealous."

Pleased, Anna stretched flat on the towel, accentuating her ribs. In the weeks she'd been home, Anna had come to realize how little food she needed to survive. It was strangely powerful, to freeze a batch of Crystal Light in an ice cube tray overnight, letting those dozen cubes sustain her for twelve hours, then licking a spoonful of peanut butter and feeling full before sleep. She felt in control of herself, her body, in a way she had never been before.

"Well," Anna said, "you've got the best tits."

Willow laughed as she handed Anna a Diet Coke. "Touché."

"Why do you have a nanny? You don't even live here anymore."

Willow made a fuffing sound with her teeth. "I know. My dad hired her back for the summer."

"Why? To pack your beach bag?"

Willow smiled her lazy smile. "He doesn't trust me."

"Why not?"

"After my mom . . . after she got sick, I went a little wild. My dad thought I needed a 'positive female role model.'"

Anna thought about the first time she'd seen Willow, walking into the Highsmith studio. The crazy hair, the weird clothes and piercings. *Wild.*

"Seriously—what did you do?"

Willow didn't answer. She tossed a book onto Anna's towel. A catalogue for the Cartier Foundation for Contemporary Art's exhibition of Francesca Woodman's photographs. Anna knew this work; she'd read about the show in *Artforum* and knew Woodman had become famous soon after she jumped from a window and died at twenty-two.

Willow offered her face to the sky. "The MCA is close by. They have some of her stuff. We should go tomorrow."

Anna flipped pages. The work was mainly self-portraits Woodman had taken with long shutter speeds, giving her body a translucence, like she was on the verge of disappearing. Woodman was often nude in her photos, blurry, preyed upon by shadows. She merged into furniture, into walls. She was a ghost, Anna thought with a chill, even when she was still alive.

She closed the book, folded her hands over it, and used it

as a pillow as she watched Willow dig around in the kangaroo pocket of her sweatshirt.

"Aha," Willow said, pulling out her hand. She opened her palm to reveal a small, tightly rolled joint. "*This* is why my dad hired Leanne."

"Are you serious?" Anna said. "Here?" The beach was full of people, and they were beautiful young women in bikinis, conspicuous as fire alarms.

Willow shrugged. "I do it all the time. Just hold your hand around it. No one can tell where the smell is coming from."

"What if someone sees?" Anna had a flash of getting arrested in her bikini, and that strange, perky woman in khaki pants—Willow's *nanny*—coming to bail her out. She'd never be able to explain it to her parents. They would never let her come back here.

Willow cupped her hands and lit the joint. She was so brave, so unaffected by anyone or anything. Anna wanted to be like her. She was trying all the time.

Willow coughed a little, then handed it to Anna, who took it.

Anna's mouth was dry. Her stomach was empty. She only remembered taking two hits of the joint, but she felt small inside her body, like she'd shrunk down to a single, powerless molecule. She had small piles of green towel in each fist, and she was holding tight. If she let go, she might float to the sky.

"Shit," she said. This was not a normal high.

Willow turned and smiled slowly. "I know, right? It's special."

"Special?"

Willow's voice was low. "Special K."

Anna's stomach bottomed out, even though she was flat on her back. What the hell was Special K, she wanted to know, and what the hell was it doing to her? She could barely move. The sky was pressing down on her. Her heart raced in her chest. All she could do was creep her head around and look questioningly at Willow.

Beautiful Willow in the sun, lush and dappled as a Renoir.

Anna thought she'd been here before. Trapped on this beach. Unable to move. Time spread and oozed. The sky was azure and so low she could touch it. She lifted her hands, but they didn't move. Maybe she had fallen asleep. The beach was a dream. She lifted her head and looked down at her body, ribs poking against her skin like angry fingers. *What did you do? What the hell did you do?*

Panic fireworked in her chest. She moved her arm to Willow's back. She needed help. Willow rolled over. Her arms folded like a pillow, her cheek down. The sun had moved. It was low and slanting, spilling yellow light, Anna had no idea how long they'd been lying there. Hours, most likely.

"What the fuck was that?"

"I got it from Boomer," Willow said, froggy, like she was holding in a laugh. "In Indy last weekend. Met some of his high school friends."

The butterflies in Anna's stomach went angry and nervous. Not butterflies. Bees. Her fists tightened as another memory surfaced: Boomer's flaccid, disinterested dick. Anna's humiliation. They had pretended it hadn't happened, ignoring each other as best they could. Anna had to pretend so hard. She squeezed her eyes to dislodge the feelings.

"I want to try something," Willow said. "Can we?"

Anna blinked open her eyes but couldn't otherwise move. She was still high. The air felt liquid, ebbing and flowing like the ocean, tugging at her. Willow rolled herself closer, perched up on an elbow. Her hair glowed. The sun was liquid yellow. Paint dripping from the sky.

"My dad is basically a Nazi," Willow said, reaching a hand down to graze Anna's cheek.

"What?"

"He doesn't believe in bisexuality."

Willow leaned down and put her lips on Anna's lips. The sensation was unlike anything Anna had ever experienced: an explosion of softness and warmth. Her whole body fizzed. Willow's tongue was gentle and curious, and her hands were on Anna's skin, fingers grazing her stomach and tiptoeing under her bikini top. Something new grew inside Anna now—a want so delicious and so surprising she had no name for it. Anna opened her hands, letting go of the towel. She fell upward, until she met Willow's body. Until skin grazed skin, and Lycra grazed Lycra, and everything was alert and alive and yearning.

Willow pulled away as quickly as she'd landed there. Her chin went high to the sky as she let out a laugh, then she stood and brushed sand from her legs, which pricked against Anna's lips.

"*Psych,*" Willow said and ran to the water, leaving Anna a puddle on the towel.

WEDNESDAY AFTERNOON

"**HE HASN'T HEARD** from her," I said, handing the phone back to Lizzie.

"Oh god." She shrunk into the sofa. "This is bad. This is so, so bad."

"He talked to Philip Roche, though. *None* of the gallery people were at work yesterday. Not Willow, and not Mason."

"So they could be together." Tom handed me a glass pipe and a tiny orange lighter. "They could be partying or something."

Lizzie scowled at him. "Are you serious?"

I gestured around: the weed, the booze. This is what we did, this was how we coped. "Would you really be surprised?"

Tom touched Lizzie's hand. "She does this. You know she does."

"Leanne said she was seeing someone," I told them. "An older guy—an artist. Do you think they could be thinking about Mason?"

"Who's Leanne?" Tom said.

"Her housekeeper," Lizzie said at the same time I blurted, "Her nanny."

"Her what?" Tom repeated.

"Her nanny." I looked at Lizzie. "That's what she told me, at least."

Lizzie puffed out a laugh. "Why would she need a nanny?"

"Why would her housekeeper come to graduation?"

Lizzie looked at Milo. "What did she tell you?"

Milo was looking at the wall, biting the skin on his thumb. "She didn't tell me shit, apparently."

"It doesn't matter," Tom said. "You just said this Leanne chick doesn't know where she is. So the question now is—" He glanced at Milo. "The question is, was Willow hooking up with anyone? Someone that she could be with right now?"

"I wasn't going to say anything." Lizzie made an exaggerated sad-clown face at Milo, whose jaw moved like he was chewing something hard. You two had been broken up for a month, since that night in Chinatown, but it didn't mean he was over you. He would never be over you, no matter what I did to persuade him.

"I don't have any details," Lizzie went on. "But she told me she was after that photographer—the German guy with the solo show at Roche this summer."

My mind rewound to June, to the first opening reception you worked at the gallery. Those huge color photographs, that naked girl under the bright lights. *Another muse.* Another image of girl as prey, supine and silent. Your favorite thing.

"Jürgen Frosh?"

Lizzie nodded. "I don't know if anything happened between them, but yeah."

The pipe was still in my hand. I lit it, sucked down the smoke. I was chasing something. Chasing oblivion. Things began to soften. The Nina Simone record had ended, but no one bothered to flip it. The bowl was packed again, and it went round and round, blue-brown smoke veining the air. I let my mind wander, away from here, away from you. I thought about entropy, destruction, how things fade. Rauschenberg's de Kooning, Rotella's double décollage, afterimages, the way one thing can superimpose another, like a projection on wallpaper, like a memory and the current moment. Maybe I could work this into a painting, make it beautiful and smart for the AFYAA. I closed my eyes to let the images come to me. I was going inside myself. I was on the edge of a revelation. I could feel it. Something big and bold and groundbreaking. My masterpiece.

"We should call Jon Potts, too," Boomer said. "He's been couch surfing in the Village since he got booted from Yale."

My eyes flipped open. *Jon Potts.*

"I didn't know they were still friends," Lizzie said.

Boomer fixed his gaze on me. "They aren't."

Boomer knew too much. He knew all my secrets—all *our* secrets, Willow—and I didn't want them to come out. Not then. Not ever. I glanced at Milo, but he wasn't even looking at me.

"Why would we call him if they aren't friends?" Lizzie asked.

I finished what was left of my beer then stood. "Anyone want anything?" I needed to change the subject. I needed to escape.

"Wait." Boomer grabbed my wrist. My heart plummeted into my stomach. "Potts and Willow, they aren't friends—but they *do* have a history."

"So?" Lizzie said, arms crossed tightly. "What's your point?"

Boomer kept his eyes on me. He wanted backup, but I couldn't give it to him.

"He really, *really* dislikes her," Boomer said.

My heart tumbled. *Shut up, shut up, shut up.* I tried to pull away, but Boomer held fast.

"Why?" Tom said.

I tried to telepath my thoughts—*Don't say it, please don't say it.* I couldn't stand everyone going over what had happened at graduation. It was too humiliating.

"She's the one who got him kicked out of Yale," Boomer said.

Fuck. I yanked out of his grip.

"I thought it was because of that photo?" Lizzie said.

"Exactly."

Lizzie stared at him. "What are you saying?"

"She took it." It was Milo. He'd broken his silence to cross me.

The room went quiet. Everyone turned from Milo to me. They all knew I was the girl in that photo—of course they did—but no one had been brave or callous enough to talk about it. Until now.

"Why would she do that?" Tom said, and when I didn't respond, he turned to Milo and asked again. "Why would she do that?"

Milo shook his head. He wasn't going to say more. Neither was I.

"Ugh." Lizzie flung out her arms. "This is so stupid. People are dead. Thousands of people. This is not about Balwin, okay? This is not about Jon fucking Potts."

"She does do this, baby," Tom said, placating. "She does disappear."

"She did this *once.* At *college,* when everything was safe."

"You didn't think so at the time," Tom said.

"And not just once," I said. "She did it this summer, too."

"Jesus Christ, are you two serious?"

Tom turned to Milo. "What do you think, man?"

Milo let out a loud, bizarre laugh, then threw himself over his knees, like a child having a fit. Lizzie and Tom looked at each other. Lizzie gestured silently toward Milo, and Tom shrugged.

Boomer put a hand on Milo's back. "You all right?"

Lizzie jumped up, arms high and splayed. "We have to do something!"

She was right. I couldn't just sit there. I had to know if anything had happened with Tyler before my thoughts ran away from me completely. I started toward the door. "I'm going home. I'll wait for her and let you know if I hear anything."

Milo lifted his head. He had such an odd expression on his face. Pale skin, eyes sunken, mouth loose like he'd been slapped. "I'll come with you," he said.

I almost objected—the way he looked made me uncomfortable, like he was a stranger, an old man. I almost told him to stay, but Lizzie was already yelling at us.

"You *do that*, you two." She strode from the room, barking back over her shoulder. "I'm calling the fucking police."

***

Milo followed me outside, and I gave him an unsteady shove. "What's the matter with you? I told you the Jon Potts thing in confidence."

He didn't move, and fear fizzed inside me, a million little bubbles, all popping at the same time.

I pushed his shoulder. "Talk to me!"

"Lizzie's calling the police, Anna." He spoke robotically, not even opening his eyes. "She is *really* fucking missing."

I put my hands over my face. We couldn't push it away anymore. There was a real possibility that Tyler had hurt you, and now we had no choice. We had to be sure that you weren't lying there, hurt, dead. Then we could move on to Jon Potts or Mason or whatever *lark* you had tucked up your sleeve.

"We have to go to the warehouse," I said. "We have to see if she's there."

Milo's eyes flashed open.

"You didn't look yesterday, did you?"

He shook his head.

"Right," I said, waiting until he looked at me. "You know it as well as I do. Tyler took our money. Think about it. He can't be *that* innocent."

Milo's face hung loose like Play-Doh. Like I could stick my thumbs into his skin and mangle him.

"It doesn't make any fucking sense," he said.

"Don't be naive." We'd seen plenty of violence from normal-seeming men, hadn't we? Hadn't our entire lives been full of it? "Even if someone went in there and found her—what? They're going to report it? You think the police would even listen? They are a little *busy* right now." I gestured to the sky, the city, the fumes lacing the air, then pulled my shoulders back. "And don't forget. He could have her wallet, Milo. Her *ID*."

I didn't have to finish my thought. He knew what I meant. Dead body. No ID. Another Jane Doe stuck in a drawer at the world's busiest morgue. I jammed a knuckle into my cheek and bit down until I tasted blood. It seemed impossible that we were talking about you like this—like a victim. *Our* victim, I thought.

Milo spun a circle, hands on the sides of his face. "Fuck. Fuck, fuck, *fuck*."

My heart was tight in my chest. Most of the subways were running again, diverted around *it*. The rubble, the death. I shuddered, wrapped my arms around myself, and kept walking. I would take the F to 23rd Street, make my way west on foot. To Chelsea, to the warehouse.

To be sure.

Milo trailed after me, then clapped my shoulder from behind and spun me around. "A, wait." He was too hard, too rough. A couple stepped warily around us. I tried to smile, to seem normal, but they didn't meet my eye.

"No, Milo," I said. "I can't just leave her fucking *body* there."

"Jesus," he said, looking around.

But the couple had already turned a corner. We were alone. I couldn't think straight. I would never be able to think straight until I knew for sure what we had done.

"I'm going. Come or don't. I don't care anymore."

I forced myself to walk away from him. I forced myself forward. To turn the block onto Smith Street and move my feet until I reached the glowing orbs at the subway entrance. I had my purse, my cell phone, my wallet, my MetroCard. The subway always put me on guard, sobered me up.

It would do me good right now.

Twelve

THREE YEARS BEFORE

ANNA RETURNED TO CAMPUS on a Wednesday in late August, the summer heat weighing down tree branches, making clothing stick to skin. Her family had helped her reload packed milk crates and cardboard boxes and laundry baskets into the Acura, and her father had driven her away from the yellow house, leaving Henry and her mother to wave goodbye from the driveway. The two hours from Bexley to Balwin were strained and quiet, but Anna knew better than to attempt conversation. Her father was not a talker, not someone who knew how to respond to *feelings* or ask about friendships or classes or plans. His job was to work—to drive and to carry boxes—and that was all.

Each door on the second floor of Rector Hall had been decorated with construction paper cutouts of its occupant's name. *Like the first day of kindergarten,* Anna thought as she bumped hers open with her hip. She dropped the stuffed hatboxes she was carrying, wiped her face with her T-shirt, and took stock. Ancient, slatted wood floors. Walls thick and bubbly from countless layers of industrial white paint. A wood desk, a metal bed, a small dresser. One window, already open.

This was the Independent Floor, two rows of fifteen single rooms, boys on one end and girls on the other, each side with its own communal bathroom, and a staircase to separate them. This was the floor saved for the few sophomores and juniors who'd chosen not to go Greek, and it would be Anna's new home. She was glad for it, because it would be home to Willow and Lizzie and Milo and Tom, too.

Anna had gotten there early; she'd planned it that way. She wanted her father, in his rimless glasses and off-brand khakis and social awkwardness, gone when Willow arrived. Her timing was perfect—Anna had just finished making her bed when Willow swung open the door, Lizzie trailing behind.

"Babe!" Willow said, and they wrapped their arms around each other. What had happened on Oak Street Beach didn't matter; Anna had packed it away in her mind as soon as it was over, never to be looked at again. Lizzie's presence didn't matter, either, because here was Willow now—cool, dry Willow—hugging her. She hadn't forgotten.

Lizzie stepped between them, smiling wide, hugging Anna. "I missed you so much!"

Anna shoved her shoulder playfully. "Have less plans without us, then."

"My parents made me! You know I'd rather have been with you guys."

Willow took Anna's hand. "Come. We have to show you what we did."

They held hands and strode down the hall to Willow's room.

"Ta-da," Lizzie said as Willow opened the door. Anna was not surprised when she stepped into the room and saw the whole far wall had been papered with black-and-white photos.

"Damn," she said, looking around. They were all Willow's photographs, hundreds of them, but that wasn't what Anna was thinking about. She was thinking how long it must have taken for them to do this—and why they hadn't included her. They hadn't even stopped by her room. They hadn't looked for her.

"What d'you think?" Willow said.

Anna sucked down her jealousy, her worry. "It looks awesome."

"Look." Willow pointed to a spot near her bed, already made up with the same monographed duvet and fat goose-feather pillows as last year. It was a series of photos of Anna walking across North Lawn, taken a year ago. Four Annas lined up right where Willow would rest her head at night.

"I love it," Anna said. And she did.

———

Anna enrolled in Intermediate Drawing, where she endured Boomer's presence twice a week, and Printmaking I with Lizzie and Tom, where she learned to use a lino cutter. It was an interesting experiment—having to draw backward was tricky, but rolling her cutter into the gray blocks of linoleum, tracing her lines and making depth and shadow and shape with her blade, soothed some anxiety inside her. Anna felt free to make landscapes and faces again, beautiful but basic, because she was able to print her images onto interesting things. She rolled over her cut blocks with ink, then printed them onto cloth and rough wood and glass rather than canvas and paper like the rest of the class.

Willow, alone in the basement darkroom of Highsmith with the bulky photo equipment and pungent metallic smell of developer, had immersed herself in photography and film-making. Milo was the only sophomore in Kape's 2D class, but he soon became the favorite, painting rough expressionist canvases that everyone thought were deft and precocious, considering he hadn't ever taken a proper art class before.

Still, the group found their way together for every meal and every weekend and every night at the Bar Car, and despite being single, Anna didn't feel like she was hanging on. She felt connected to her friends and to her work. She felt her plans coming together. She felt her *life* coming together.

February, though, struck campus like a natural disaster—clouds heavy and gray as stones, a layer of ice on the sidewalks so thick and trodden on that it seemed permanent, like the surface of some other desolate planet. Everything seemed more difficult, classes and relationships and just getting around. Winter dragged on and on, splintering nerves. Boring them. Making them fussy and tired and snappish.

A bitter cold Thursday. Anna and Willow alone together in the sophomore studio at Highsmith, Anna entranced with her latest project for Materials—layers of incandescent paint over an old metal street sign she'd found abandoned by the truck stop—and Willow's nose in a Nan Goldin monograph.

When Willow said she was going to the gas station for Parliaments and Diet Coke, Anna barely noticed. A few hours passed before her trance broke and she realized that Willow hadn't come back. She didn't think much of it. She cleaned her brushes and tidied their spaces and made her way back to the dorms.

She phoned Willow to check the night's plans. No answer. It wasn't strange. Not yet. She called Lizzie next.

"Let's meet at the Car," Lizzie said. "Is Wills still with you?"

"She went to the gas station, like hours ago."

Lizzie paused. "Maybe she went to Goodwill or something."

Anna bit her lip. "Maybe."

That night at the Bar Car they all threw out places Willow could have gone. Back home to Chicago for the weekend? To the mall in Columbus? Abducted by a psycho killer while taking pictures someplace insane? And the thing that no one said: Had Willow finally tired of them? Had she only wanted to get away?

They were all nervous, but no one was ready to admit it. They one-upped each other with smiles, shots, and bad jokes, but all the while, they kept their eyes on the door. Willow was the reason they were all together, that night and every night. Willow had chosen them. She had assembled them. *Curated* them. They tried to play their parts without her, but nothing felt right. It was like being in a club with all the lights on—everything was too bright, too ugly, the sludge in the dark corners suddenly all you can see.

The next morning, Lizzie sweet-talked the RA into opening Willow's room. They looked through her things but found no hint of where she'd gone. Her computer was there, and all her supplies. Her camera on her desk, still loaded with film. Anna scanned Willow's calendar for a clue—a doctor's appointment, a meeting, a symbol—but found nothing.

The RA popped his head in the door, little glasses perched on the tip of his nose. "All good, girls?"

Lizzie glanced at Anna and made her voice chipper, all Southern sweetness despite the panic in her eyes. "Yes, siree. All good."

The RA closed the door again.

"Dude," Lizzie said, twisting her hair into points, staring at Anna.

Anna sat on Willow's bed, smoothing her duvet, thinking.

"Should we do something?" Lizzie said. "Call someone?"

Anna shook her head. "I don't think she would like that."

Lizzie tapped her lips with her fingers. "Yeah, okay. But if she doesn't show up by tonight, we have to get help."

Anna wrote a note—*Call us immediately*—and they both smudged on Willow's red lipstick, kissed the paper, and tacked it to her mirror.

Willow didn't call.

At some point late in the afternoon, at their usual table in the dining hall, Lizzie started to panic. "This is crazy, right? What is she doing? Where is she?"

Anna wadded her napkin and dropped it onto her tray, food uneaten, deciding. "We should look for her car."

Lizzie's eyes flashed. "Totally."

They dumped their trays and got into Lizzie's Range Rover, heat and music blasting. Beastie Boys, Willow's favorite. A siren song. Lizzie chain-smoked with fingerless gloves, blowing smoke out the cracked window, and Anna let the seat warmer get so hot her cords felt like they might catch fire. They checked the student lot where Willow usually parked, but her Mercedes wasn't there. They drove all the way down Wabash, circled the lake, then went off campus, to the town square, the coffee shop, and the Bar Car, out past Walmart to the cornfields that surrounded campus. Everything around them was flat, sepia-tinged, the sun casting a veil of light, thinner and thinner as the hours went on. They drove across an ancient, covered bridge, then another, then out to the highway entrance, through the Salvation Army parking lot and the truck stop's twenty-four-hour diner. They got out of the car, shivering, looking for Willow in the restaurant and the bathrooms, even behind the building where they kept the dumpsters.

There was no sign of her, or her car.

Lizzie pulled over at a gas station to refill the tank and bought them big Styrofoam cups of vending machine coffee and a bag of Hershey's Kisses that Anna wouldn't touch. They switched the CD to Mazzy Star, then Portishead, then silence. Back down Ash, up Asbury, checking the street parking near Highsmith.

A flash in Anna's mind: *multiple sclerosis*. Maybe something happened to her mother, and Willow went to see her. But she couldn't say anything about Mrs. Whitman to Lizzie. It was a secret. A connection. Far too precious to play with.

"Check the infirmary," Anna said instead, and Lizzie drove straight there. Anna leaned toward the windshield as they approached, peering through the dusky light. Nothing.

Night was coming. The second night.

"She wouldn't go to the frat houses, would she?" Lizzie said.

Anna looked at her—her scrunched brow, profile limned with white streetlight. Lizzie was grasping. Willow detested the Greek system, called it regressive and antiquated. But what was left? *Where* was left?

"Let's check," Anna said.

Back through campus, past the brick dormitories, another quick run through the student lots and the gym and the vast quad, deserted in the dark and cold. They turned onto the tree-lined side streets, so many knotty brown branches pointing down like arthritic fingers, the street so narrow Lizzie had to pull over twice when a car came the opposite way. They drove at a walking pace, surveying the rows of huge, Victorian houses that had been built when the railroads were still the best way to travel. The houses had been appropriated by the university in the early 1920s, transformed into fraternities and sororities, faculty housing, and the dean's mansion.

"Ha," Lizzie said, pointing down Maple Street. "Look." It was after five o'clock, and the sun was gone, the street lit only by their headlights. "Isn't that a Benz?"

"Pull up."

Anna leaned forward, squinting to get a better look, and

when Lizzie brought her SUV in line and flipped her brights on the small black coupe parked with a front wheel up on the curb—*yes*—Anna saw that it was a Mercedes. It was Willow's car.

Lizzie shoved the Range Rover into park, popped open her door, and slid out, lights and ignition on, alerts chiming. She made a tunnel with her hands and pressed her face against the Mercedes's driver-side window, then tried to open the door. She turned to Anna, her breath clouding out as she spoke. "Locked."

Anna flapped her hand for Lizzie to come back, and she did, slamming her door but keeping the car in park. She lit a cigarette with the car lighter. "What should we do?"

Anna shrugged. "What *can* we do?"

Lizzie blew smoke out the crack in the window, then pointed to a ramshackle old Victorian with all its lights on, five-foot-tall Greek letters on the roof. Sigma Alpha Epsilon. SAE.

"Let's go in. See if we can find her." Lizzie flicked her cigarette out the window. "Come on."

A frat boy opened the door. He was nice, almost fawning, introducing himself as Zack and inviting the girls in. The house was exactly what Anna had pictured from the outside: dirty and overbright, threadbare couches and a pool table in the living room, empty cans and bottles stacked in a pyramid in front of a dead fireplace. Everything smelled sharp, like old beer and urine. She looked questioningly at Lizzie, the idea that Willow would be *here* too absurd for words.

This Zack person was watching them, feet planted apart, arms folded, in front of the giant Victorian staircase.

"Do you know Willow Whitman?" Lizzie asked.

His eyebrows shot up at the question, stance firming. "Art school, right? Blond?"

Anna and Lizzie exchanged a glance. *She's been here.*

"Right," Lizzie said.

Zack turned toward the staircase and the girls followed, but he turned and shot out an arm to stop them from going farther. Zack yelled up the stairs, "Hey! Is Potts up there?"

Some noise—footsteps, a door slamming, then a single gruff, male voice. "Nope. Not up here. Check the basement."

The basement. The word alone made Anna's stomach swoop.

Zack pointed past the beer pyramid. "That way."

Anna didn't move from her spot on the bottom step. Lizzie didn't, either.

"Who's *Potts*?" Anna said.

"Jon. He's a TA in the art school," Zack said. "He knows everyone." He was guiding them, too quickly, down the hall, toward a big wooden door. He yanked it open and called down. "Potts!"

No answer. At the staircase, the smell was even stronger. *A public toilet,* Anna thought, putting her sleeve over her nose. *They must piss on the carpet.*

Zack called again, then turned to them, smiling. "Not sure anyone's down there, but be my guest."

Anna did not want to step foot on the sludgy carpet that covered those stairs. She did not want to see what was in that basement. But she had no choice. They had to find Willow. She put a hand on the railing and started down.

Exactly as she suspected, the basement was cavernous, with cement walls and sticky floors and exposed pipes. Several ancient couches strewn around. A row of trash cans lined up like a hedge, tops off, reeking.

"Hello?" Anna said, but there was no answer. Lizzie took her arm and held tight. Together, they walked from room to ransacked room. Empty. Empty. Empty. They pulled open a final door and found a bare, stained mattress on the floor.

"Gross," Lizzie said. "Do you think someone actually sleeps there?"

Anna flashed back to Boomer's bed. His awkward thrusting. She shivered, not wanting to imagine what went on in that room.

"She's not here," she said, pulling Lizzie back. "Let's go."

They clomped quickly back up the stairs to where Zack was waiting.

"Are you sure you haven't seen her?" Anna gestured toward the window. "Her car is parked outside."

Zack shrugged. "Lots of houses on Maple. I'll spread the word that you're looking for her, and if anyone sees her, we'll call you." He dug around his pocket and pulled out a matchbook, handed it to them. "Here, write on this."

Anna took it. "Pen?"

He felt around on the fireplace mantel and handed her a stubby pencil. Anna wrote down her own dorm number, and Lizzie's, and handed the matchbook back to Zack. She tugged Lizzie's hand. She wanted badly to leave.

Back in the car, Lizzie slammed the door, turned on the heat, and lit another cigarette, blowing smoke against the windshield. "Was that guy lying?"

"I doubt it." Anna stared at SAE's glowing windows. "Why would he?"

"What the hell is she up to?"

"Who knows." There was another frat house on the corner. Anna pointed at it. "She could be at Phi Psi," she said, then fluttered her fingers. "Or anywhere."

Lizzie pressed her hands into the steering wheel.

"Come on," Anna said. "We can go back and call all the frats if you want—the sororities too, who knows? At least we know she's still on campus."

Lizzie flicked her cigarette out the window, staring at the SAE house for a moment before cutting her eyes back to Anna's.

"Just 'cause she's on campus doesn't mean she's safe, babe."

Anna closed her mouth. She knew Lizzie was right.

They called all the frat houses, all the sororities. No one claimed Willow. No one knew where she was. They went to all the parties that night—frat keggers and smoky, off-campus salons—walking around and opening random doors like PIs. They watched Willow's car, which never moved from its spot on Maple Street. After midnight, they camped out in Willow's room—Lizzie, Tom, Milo, Boomer, and Anna—passing around a joint and a bottle of Maker's Mark.

Milo lurched from her bed and grabbed the phone.

"Who are you calling?" Boomer's voice was combative.

"Campus police."

Anna grimaced. "You sure?"

"If they call her dad," Lizzie said, "she'll kill us."

But it was too late. Milo was already talking, already telling whoever had picked up the phone the story: Willow, leaving Anna at the studio the day before, not showing up for meals, missing classes, not calling anyone, not responding to notes they'd left in her room. Her car on Maple Street, the strange way Zack had behaved.

When Milo hung up, he put his head into his hands, stretching his dark hair like taffy. "They are going to go by the frats. Make sure. They want us to come to the station to file a report, too."

"A *missing persons report*?" Anna pressed her hands against her face.

Lizzie stood, pacing circles around the room. "This is bad."

Milo was already gone, stomping down the corridor, Willow's door yawning open. Anna looked around the room—pacing Lizzie, stupid Tom, disgusting Boomer—and popped up, grabbed her coat, and went after Milo.

"Hey!" she said. "Wait!"

He was already in the stairwell, between the first and second floors, and glanced up. "Hurry," he said, barely slowing.

"You don't have to run."

His lips were pressed together, his eyes narrow and his brow furrowed as he clanged open the doors and they stepped out onto the quad. It was dark, frigid. Anna dug her warm beanie out of her pocket and yanked it over her head without breaking her stride.

"Someone was leaving her notes in her room and at the studio," Milo said. His breath was white as clouds.

Anna wrinkled her nose. She did not like to be told things about Willow. She did not like to think that Willow told other people things that she did not tell Anna. Not even her boyfriend.

"What kind of notes?"

Milo dug into the pocket of his big gray ski coat, pulled out a piece of folded paper, and handed it to her. Anna opened it to see a small sketch—a landscape, maybe—and a few lines of handwritten text, tiny and tight, almost like a computer font. Anna desperately wanted to stop and find a light to read it, to know what it said and why Willow had given it to Milo and not to her. But she knew Milo wouldn't wait for her if she stopped. She had to keep up.

"There are more," he said.

"I can't see." Anna matched his pace, walking fast over the icy sidewalk in the direction of the campus police. "What does it say?"

Milo glanced at her, not slowing. "Weird stuff, about the things they have in common, how much she *gets* him."

Anna stuffed the paper into her pocket. "And she really doesn't know who wrote them?"

"She says not."

Anna's thoughts were jumping around in her mind, from Willow's room, her dad, and the studio to the frats, Zack blocking them from going upstairs. That mattress, hidden in the basement like a crime scene.

Everything snagged.

Willow had always seemed impervious to danger. Something about the way she moved through the world, her confidence, her poise, her power. Until that moment, Anna never actually believed that anything bad could happen to her.

At the campus police station, Milo repeated the story about the notes while Anna unfolded the paper again. In the light, she could see the picture was indeed a small landscape, sketched in blue ballpoint, with a river running through the middle and a girl sitting on a rock, looking backward.

DEAR WILLOW, YOU KNOW ME. YOU'RE THE ONLY ONE WHO DOES.

Anna read the words over and over, looking for a threat or a clue, but it didn't click. Nothing was clicking.

"Anna."

Milo and the cop were telling her something. Anna crumpled the paper and stuffed it in her coat, looking up.

"Officers have been dispatched to the fraternity house," the cop said. "Go home now. We will let you know if we find anything."

Anna stood and followed Milo out of the station, back out into the bitter dark. She did not want to go back to her own room, or to Willow's, where Lizzie and Tom and Boomer were probably still waiting, so she followed Milo to his. Anna wanted to ask him more about the note, what he thought of it, where exactly in the studio Willow had found it, and why Willow had kept it from her—but something in the way Milo was walking, one pace ahead of her, not glancing in her direction, warned her not to speak.

———

Anna was dozing on Milo's pillow when the phone rang.

Milo snatched it from the wall and cut his eyes to Anna as he listened. She knew it was the cops by the expression on his face. He made some noises, some exhales and *okays*, and slammed the phone back on the hook.

"They arrested that Zack guy," he said.

Anna sat up. "They found her?"

He shook his head, fingers back in his hair, pulling the strands straight up. "They found ecstasy at SAE and arrested a few of them. She wasn't there."

Anna's stomach lurched. "Jesus Christ, Milo."

He sank his hands into his jean pockets, shoulders perked high to his ears, and he bounced on his heels. "They are canvassing. That's actually what he said. *Canvassing*."

He sat and bounced his leg, jittering the whole bed. Anna's mom did this when she was nervous. In hospital rooms, in doctor's offices, in cars and airports. Anytime she had to wait for bad news. Anna put her hand on Milo's leg. She only meant to stop him. To calm him. And he did stop. He stopped to look at Anna, his expression loose with surprise. No—with *disgust*. He picked up Anna's hand and slipped it off his knee.

"I think you should go wait in your own room," he said.

"Oh no, I didn't mean—"

But he was already standing, walking to the door, opening it for her. "I'll call you if I hear anything."

Anna flushed with humiliation. She wanted to protest, but the door had already clicked shut behind her.

The next day it was all over campus, starting with the front page of the school newspaper, which Lizzie brought to Anna's door. Three SAEs, including Zack Beyers, had been arrested for possession of a Schedule 1 drug.

"She's fine," Lizzie said, slapping the paper into Anna's hands. "She's back at the dorm."

A blaze of relief. Then something else, another emotion Anna had been pushing away, surged through her. Anger. "Was she there?"

"No, Milo caught her this morning doing the walk of shame," Lizzie said. "She confessed everything."

"Where was she?"

"With that guy, Jon Potts. At some off-campus party."

Anna sat on her bed, staring at the school photos of the frat brothers on the front of the newspaper. "It doesn't make sense."

Lizzie shrugged. "I guess she was on X."

Anna unfolded the paper. "It doesn't make sense," she said again.

At their table in the dining hall the next day, with the gloomy morning peeking through the windows, Anna found Willow in the black faux-fur hat she'd found at the Chicago Goodwill, picking little pieces of dough from her bagel and rolling them into small white balls.

"Girl, what the hell," Anna said, putting her tray down. She was going for humor, but Willow didn't smile.

"Don't start." Willow lifted her head, and Anna saw the puffy, purple bruise under her eye. A gash in her swollen lower lip.

"Jesus," Anna said. "What happened to you?"

Willow picked at her bagel. The hat and her sullen expression made her look like she was performing a Chekhov play.

"I fell on the ice," she said. "I was really fucked up."

"At the party?"

A little laugh escaped Willow's lips. "Yeah. Sure. At the party."

Anna caught something in her tone. Willow was holding back. Anna stared at her friend, the purple bruise under her eye, her gossamer skin, translucent eyes. She looked so fragile. She looked . . . *broken*.

Lizzie arrived, slipping her tray next to Willow's. "Milo's in the dean's office," she said. "Tom just told me."

"What?" Anna blinked, trying to absorb what Lizzie had said. "Why?"

Lizzie peeled the lid off her Styrofoam cup and sipped. "He went over to SAE and threatened Jon. The school is talking about kicking them both out."

"Seriously?" Anna said, looking from Lizzie to Willow. "Threatened him for what?"

"You know." Lizzie popped a Tater Tot into her mouth. "Typical 'don't fuck with my girl' bullshit."

"Screw this." Willow kicked back her chair and stood, taking her tray to the garbage and stalking out.

There was a lump of dread in Anna's gut. "What happened to her face?"

"She says she slipped," Lizzie deadpanned.

Anna stared. "Do you believe her?"

Lizzie stopped chewing. "Do you?"

"I don't know. Are we supposed to?"

Lizzie laughed, a strangled, high-pitched noise. "Good question."

Thirteen

WEDNESDAY AFTERNOON

THE SUBWAY WAS EERIE, nearly abandoned. I found a car with an older lady nodding off, plastic grocery bags twisted in her fingers. I sat near her, just close enough that if a man came, or a bomb exploded, we could latch on to each other. Not necessarily for security, but for comfort.

We rattled underground, air-conditioning blasting, everything flashing from light to dark, from Brooklyn to Manhattan. When the light returned, I realized I was shivering. I held my arms and tried to rub away the chill. At each stop I pictured you. East Broadway in Chinatown: Boomer's place. A stupid thought. He couldn't have lied that well, and why would he be hiding you? Delancey Street, the Lower East Side. Maybe Mason lived there—I could picture him in a rehabbed tenement. Leanne's voice popped into my head: *She said she was dating an older man.* Was Lizzie right—could it have been Jürgen? I tightened my face, concentrating, going through everything that had changed over the summer. The only older men I'd seen you with were Mason and Philip Roche, and they both had male partners.

But there were those other nights, nights when you didn't come home, when you weren't with Milo, and you weren't with me.

Second Avenue, Arcadia Café. It was probably open, probably packed as always. Tyler might even be there, tending bar. I pictured him smiling, handsome, dark hair and big dimples, except he had blood in his teeth.

Don't be crazy. I wasn't being crazy, though. Part of what kept me on that train that day was knowing that you'd agree with me. You and I knew exactly what *handsome smiling men* were capable of.

I closed my eyes until the train rumbled out of the station. On to Broadway-Lafayette, my stop for work— Shit, I was supposed to work the next night, and doubles all weekend. It seemed absurd, in that moment, on my way to find you, that I would ever be able to wait tables again. That I could take orders and listen to the food proclivities of strangers with any shred of sincerity when the city was crumbling beneath us and you were missing. But I'd have to, if the AFYAA meant anything to me. If my career meant anything.

West Fourth Street, the Village, where Philip Roche was and you were not. Jon Potts was staying somewhere off Bleecker Street, right above me. Boomer's voice played in my head then. *He really, really dislikes her.* Jon must have figured out who was behind that picture—who had ruined his relationship and gotten him kicked out of Yale. After what he'd done to you—my stomach knotted—it was possible that he'd always known. Our phone number was unlisted, but it was possible he'd found out where we lived through a mutual friend or the alumni association. We hadn't thought to block it, had we? We hadn't thought to protect ourselves.

I thought of Jon's body, deadweight on top of me, and shivered.

At Twenty-Third Street, I forced myself to my feet. The woman next to me turned, seeming to see me for the first time. A small smile slid across her face before she closed her eyes again.

I took the stairs by twos. The smell was worse here than in Brooklyn—heavier, thick in my lungs. I could actually see it, a cataclysmic haze. I breathed it in. I turned down Sixth Avenue, facing south, where just yesterday morning those huge, gleaming towers had been. Gone now, a gap, a missing tooth in someone's smile, bleeding smoke. There were people there at that very moment, snuffing out fires and digging through phosphorescent rubble for other people—survivors, or the opposite of survivors: people, regular people, who had families and careers and aspirations before the ground under their feet fell away.

Guilt churned sour in my gut. *What have you done, Anna? What have you done?*

It was overwhelming, being there. Different from looking at a screen. I forced myself to inhale the toxic air, to pull the stench of metal and death deep into my lungs, because this was *my* city now. Its breath was my breath, its sickness, too. I had made it so.

I knew my way now. I took off, speed walking west toward the Hudson. By the time I got to Tenth Avenue I was coughing and too warm. Breathless. I slowed and walked north in the shadows and orange streetlights, the abandoned warehouse pulling me closer. Then I was there. The recessed metal door, hidden in its dirty, dark alcove. This was the place where Tyler had stood yesterday morning, waiting for you.

The building was a squat rectangle with boarded-up windows and broken doors, set to be knocked down and turned into condos and galleries like the rest of the outdated industrial spaces in Chelsea. The chain on the door hung loose, broken, not protecting anything from anyone. All I had to do was push.

Inside, there were echoes and soaring ceilings, nothing more. No people. No cops. No homeless encampments. No construction workers. Not even daylight. Nothing moved or breathed in that place except me.

I looked around, trying to picture how yesterday had unfolded. It wouldn't have been hard for Tyler to drag you in here, small as you were. A hand over your mouth, a knife to the neck, and a few backward steps. A kick against the door. Then—*what?*

I spun a circle, then put my hand on a wall and looked up and around.

There was an elevator on the other side of the space, far enough from the sidewalk that if you'd screamed, it would have sounded like more street noise. I pushed myself forward, soundless as possible. Step by step. Terrified I would find you. Terrified to see the whiteness of your eyes, the emptiness of your judgment.

A scuttle ahead, and a yelp flew out of me, a sound I'd never heard myself make before. *Shit.* I clamped a hand over my mouth as I saw a long pink tail slither into the darkness. *Ugh.* I was right about the rats, at least.

I made it to the elevator, heart thumping. It was dark, but

enough light came through the slatted walls that I'd be able to see something if it were there. If *you* were there. But there was nothing. I pressed the grimy call button, then wiped my finger on my jeans. Nothing happened. I pressed again and again. No lights, no sounds, no movements. Even the elevator was dead.

There was another door near it, though, cracked and glinting. I gripped its metal latch, held my breath, and yanked it open. A staircase. It was darker than the rest of the warehouse, but I could see well enough to know you weren't there, either. I leaned in as far as I could go while keeping my boot on the door, holding it open. There was no blood, no Prada slides, no dropped cappuccino cup or bandanna—nothing at all to indicate that you or Tyler had been there.

Still, my fear was *alive*. I didn't want to let go of the door. I didn't want to be trapped in that lightless stairwell with the dust and the spiderwebs. But I couldn't stop now. However unlikely it was that Tyler was able to carry you upstairs, I needed to look. To be certain. I inched forward slowly, letting the door close without latching it all the way. I stepped to the first stair, then the next and the next. I touched the wall and cement crumbled down, a soft rain, and my fear thundered in my ears. This place wasn't safe. There was a reason it was being torn down. There was a reason for the caution tape and the chain and the Warning signs.

Still, I kept going. I had to. Up to the landing, a hard box of shadow, no light, then turning to the second run of stairs. I looked to the top. It seemed like more light was there, and I clung to that hope, forcing my feet onward.

As soon as I got to the final step, a light flew into my face like a giant yellow moth. I let out a strange, strangled shout and thrashed my hands in front of my face like I could wave it away.

But it wasn't a moth. It was a man, and he was shouting.

"Hey!"

My skin went cold. The fear that oozed through me was like being injected with something icy, numbing. He walked toward me, his bright light in my eyes, turning him into a silhouette. His clothes made noise, like he was wearing keys.

"Hey," he said again. "What're you doing in here?"

That was enough. I fled back down the stairs, boots thumping, shoulder checking the wall, cobwebs on my lips, but getting out. On the street again, lonely Tenth Avenue, I was running, running, not looking back, four long city blocks to Sixth Avenue, the orbs again, the subway, safety. I stopped and looked behind me. No one was following. No cops, no bad guys. I felt tears rush to my eyes. Everything pressing up against my walls, threatening to fall out, to give me away. I ran down the subway steps and waited near the manned booth, teeth chattering, until I heard a train approach, then stared at my reflection in the blackened windows the whole ride home.

Back in Brooklyn, all I wanted was a shower. The cobwebs and the smell and the rats and the light shining in my face. The horror at what I had been doing: looking for my best friend's murdered body. *Your murdered body.* I wanted to wash it all away. I hurried down Court Street, not running, but not just walking, either.

When I got to our stoop, I saw Milo, head in hands, waiting

for me. He looked up. Eyes big and sad and red. Asking me without asking me.

I shook my head.

He closed his eyes, lifted his face to the sky.

I sat next to him. He turned, put his nose near my ear. Every hair on my skin stood straight.

"Come up." I tried to make my voice calm, but I was desperate for him to follow me inside, up the stairs, into my bed.

I couldn't stomach another minute of being alone.

We stood in the living room, facing each other, not speaking. I had to break the tension. The silence.

"She's not there."

Milo shifted a little, biting his thumb. "So where is she?"

"I don't know, but—"

He blinked at me. "But what?"

At least we didn't kill her. At least it's not our fault.

We were quiet and still, watching each other, trying to read each other's minds. I couldn't take it. I stepped closer.

"She's okay. She has to be. She's just somewhere not thinking about us. Because she doesn't care about us, Milo. She never has."

His fingers grazed my cheek, almost mournfully, then he dropped his hand. I took it in mine and back to my face and held it there.

After that it was easy. I only had to tilt my chin upward an inch and his lips were on me. My cheek, my neck, my chest. His big hands pulled up my T-shirt until it was over my head, and I was bare. I led him into my room. Hospital corners on my frameless bed. Everything in its place. Everything as it should be. But him. Milo. Here. We left the door open. It was an invitation for you. A summoning. It was the only way any of this made sense.

When Milo pushed me onto the bed, I felt a release, like a water balloon popping, and I was liquid. My clothes were off and he tasted of ash and candy and every part of me went to him, every nerve and blood vessel, every thought, every sensation, all there, in the empty place inside me that for so long, I had saved for you.

Fourteen

TWO AND A HALF YEARS BEFORE

SOMETHING HAD HAPPENED to Willow on Maple Street, and Anna needed to know what it was. On Thursday morning, when neither of the girls had class until eleven, Anna got up early. She stopped at the cafeteria, bought two large French vanilla coffees to go, and brought them to Willow's dorm.

She kicked the door twice with her boot. "Babe, it's me. Open up."

"Hang on," Willow called from the other side, eventually cracking the door. She was wearing flannel pajama bottoms and a T-shirt, her face scrubbed clean as a newborn around the shiny black eye. It looked even worse that morning, a livid yellow-green. Her hair was matted to her head. She got back in her bed, pulling her thick duvet to her chin.

Anna closed the door behind her and set the coffees on Willow's nightstand.

"Are you okay?"

"Just tired."

Anna sat at the foot of Willow's bed. She had a plan. Sharing secrets had made them closer in the past, and she knew it could work again. She held Willow's foot beneath the blanket.

"I know something happened to you—something you don't want to talk about," Anna said. "And I want you to know that I understand. I have something I don't like talking about, too."

Willow blinked at her.

"Sit up," Anna said.

Willow sat up. Anna put a coffee in her hand and took the other. They both sipped.

"It's something I lived with every day until I came to school," Anna said. "I haven't told anyone because I loved that it didn't follow me here. No one knows. *No one.*"

"I won't say anything," Willow said, looking directly into Anna's eyes for the first time since she disappeared.

Anna stared back. Their matching gazes communicating something. Promising something. "You have to tell me what happened to you then, too, okay? Last weekend. It doesn't matter what it is. I will love you no matter what."

Willow took a sip of her coffee, then held it with both hands in her lap, never taking her eyes from Anna's. "Tell me."

"It's about Henry," Anna said. "My brother."

Willow sighed, her whole body sinking downward. She even dropped her gaze. "You already told me about him."

"Not everything."

Willow tilted her head up again, curious. Anna took a long, steadying breath, preparing to betray her own promise to herself.

"I told you that he lost consciousness once, right? That he had seizures and brain damage because of that?"

Willow nodded.

Anna fiddled with the lid on her cup. She had never told anyone this story. She thought she never would. "I did it."

"Did what?"

"We were on the beach, in Maine. We used to go every summer—before. I was seven and Henry was two, and everyone loved him so much. He was this perfect golden child, fat and blue-eyed like a Raphael cherub." Anna's memory of that day, of *before*, was distorted and choppy, but she clearly remembered Henry's chubby arms stuck into bright green floaties and his little blue swim trunks. When he ran on the beach, the trunks hung low enough to see the top of his round bum.

Her parents doted on him—talking, petting, holding, feeding, snapping pictures, bragging, cooing. They had never doted on Anna like that, not that she could remember. It was a constant struggle for her, trying to pull the attention away from him, doing cartwheels, talking, yelling—anything to make her parents look at her. But she only seemed to annoy them.

"My mother was taking pictures of him all day. Not of me at all. I get it now—Henry was so cute, he was still practically a baby, and I was this ugly, gangly second-grader."

"I doubt that," Willow said. "I'm sure you were a freaking adorable second-grader."

Anna gave her a joyless smile. "That's not how I felt at the time. I was jealous of him, all the attention he got from everyone. Strangers, but my parents especially, and when I saw my mom get down in the sand with her camera, I just—"

Anna paused. She took a sip of her coffee. This was it. The truth, right on the tip of her tongue. "I wasn't trying to *hurt* him. I never would have wanted to hurt him. I just wanted to get her attention."

"What did you do?"

"In Maine, the beaches are black sand and really rocky, and I ran and slid, I was trying to slide into the picture frame, I was smiling, I was playing, being silly, but the way I landed . . ." she said, shaking her head as if to erase the memory. "It was an accident."

Willow stared. "An accident?"

"I kicked his legs from under him. He went sideways. His head hit a rock. The back of his head." Anna put her hand to the base of her skull. She remembered the dull *thwack*, and her stomach churned.

Willow put her hand to her mouth.

"They called it a traumatic brain injury," Anna said. "A TBI. But when I ran at him, I had no idea. I was only *seven*. I didn't know . . ." Anna's voice cracked, and she had to look away from Willow's expression, the shocked hand over her mouth.

But Willow didn't let her stop. She put a hand on Anna's leg and squeezed. Anna looked up again.

"Tell me," Willow said.

"He . . ." Anna did not want to say more. She did not want to remember. But she needed to open Willow up. She needed to get it out. "He lost consciousness. His face swelled up. He stopped breathing."

The memory of Henry's face that day—the way it had inflated and turned blue and hard like a water balloon—had haunted Anna her whole life. The way her parents hopped around wildly, thrashing their arms and screaming, the way the people on the beach swarmed over her brother, the endless calls for help. And the accusations: *What did you do? What the hell did you do?* A stranger held her down, as if she were a psychopath and she'd go after Henry again, as if she had really been trying to hurt him. The stranger held Anna so tightly his arms felt like metal bars. Like a cage. She twisted in his grip, fearful as a bear in a trap.

"I didn't mean to hurt him," Anna told Willow now.

But she *had* hurt him, and she couldn't take it back. Her brother had been strapped to a gurney in front of her, rushed away in an ambulance with only enough room for their mother in the back. Anna's father, ashen-faced, speechless, was left with her, not touching her, not looking at her. It was the man with the cage-bar arms who took charge, driving them to meet the ambulance at the hospital. The stranger who looked at her as if she were a disease. As if she were *evil*.

When they arrived, her mother wouldn't let Anna see Henry. Her parents left her alone in the ER waiting room while Henry, her beautiful brother, was hooked up to a ventilator, partially paralyzed, and recovering from his first set of seizures.

Willow's fingers were still on Anna's leg when Anna stopped speaking.

"Shit," she said, and then she flung the comforter off her and threw herself onto Anna, wrapping her arms around her. "You were just a kid. It wasn't your fault, babe. How could you have known?"

Anna wiped her face with her palms. She wasn't crying. She was in shock, on the edge of dissociation. The thing that had kept her from having friends, the bad thing she'd done, the thing that made people watch her nervously and keep their distance, it was here now. She had told Willow. She had brought it here and laid it between them.

"I don't want everyone else to know." Anna's stomach soured

at the sound of her own desperation, but she knew exposing herself was the only way to get what she wanted.

Willow put a hand over her heart. "I won't tell anyone, I swear."

Anna had given Willow this information because she needed to. She needed answers, and now she would get them. "Who is writing you those notes?"

Willow's mouth fell open. "Milo told you?"

"Don't be mad," Anna said. "We were so worried. We were on our way to file a police report. He said you were scared. He said someone was harassing you. He told the police."

Willow didn't say anything.

"How did Jon Potts get you to go to a townie party?"

Willow didn't answer.

"Did he hurt you, Wills?"

To Anna's surprise, Willow began to cry. Fat tears rolling down her cheeks. Her skin went red and blotchy, face crumpled and wet. Anna was taken aback. She had never seen Willow look ugly before.

Anna reached out a hand. "What happened?"

Nothing.

"Willow," Anna said. "You need to tell me."

Willow lifted her face to the ceiling. "He raped me."

"*What?*"

Willow held up her quivering chin. Tears ran into her ears. She wiped her face and pushed back her white comforter. There was another bruise, lurid and purple, splattered across the inside of her thigh. She rolled up her sleeve; there was another on her upper arm. Like someone had gripped her there, like someone had held her down as he pulled her legs apart.

"We need to call the police," Anna said. "I have the guy's card—"

Willow shook her head. "No."

"We have to, Wills."

"I was on *drugs*!" Willow shouted, shutting Anna up. "I went to the lake with him because he said he had E. I was rolling, snorting coke. I was fucked up as hell, and I was someplace I should *not* have been in the middle of the night by myself, and I don't even *remember* everything that happened. You know how that would look. No one would believe me, not after . . ."

"After what?"

Willow shook her head. "Drinking," she said a moment later. "After taking drugs. You know how it goes for girls like us."

Girls like us. Anna didn't want to accept it, but she knew that Willow was right. Date rape was nearly impossible to prove, especially when the victim wasn't a model of virtue. Willow was wild. She wore strange clothes and got drunk and played by her own rules. She flirted with fire. She was asking to get burned.

Willow stopped crying. She wiped her face, roughly, and when she was finished, she had hardened.

"I will get him back, though," Willow said, "on *my* terms." She stared at Anna, her eyes like icicles, piercing. "And you won't tell a soul when I do."

THURSDAY MORNING

MY EYES FLIPPED OPEN, a dream lingering like a memory: a blank canvas, big as a church window and all mine, but whenever I tried to paint, all the bristles kept falling out of my brush. I sat up, remembering—the AFYAA, the World Trade Center, the abandoned warehouse, Milo in my bed.

I turned over. Milo was gone. I was alone again, and another day had passed. It was another day without you and another day closer to the deadline, and I was no closer to my goal. I flung myself out of bed. No more wasting time. I went to your door and pressed my ear against it. *Silence.* I cracked it open. The room was empty. Even the smell of you had faded.

Fine, I thought. *Good.* What I had told Milo the night before was true. You didn't care about us, and that's why you weren't here. There was nothing wrong. Nothing sinister had happened to you. You were being your thoughtless, self-centered, unavailable self. I felt determined again—righteously, selfishly determined. You were probably off partying somewhere, passed out in someone's bed or couch or— I thought about the bruises under your clothes at Balwin and shook it out of my head. *Whatever*. It didn't matter.

Wherever you were had nothing to do with me.

I crouched, peering under your bed, and saw a huge, heavy wooden box of Schmincke pastels. I clicked open the toggles, ran my fingers across four hundred sticks set carefully into tiered levels of foam like heirloom silver. They smelled of wet clay. You had the full set, untouched. I set it aside and dug some more—photo paper tied in thick black plastic, unused prefab frames, film canisters, the digital camera you'd gotten for graduation. A few sketchbooks, some calligraphy pens, mostly uncapped, tossed into a plastic bin. No premade canvases, though. Nothing for me to work on.

I went to your desk, pulled open the top drawer. It was empty; your mother's Hermès scarf was gone, the photo, too. I shoved it closed. Milo must have taken them before he left that morning. The thought of him pawing through your things, wearing your token like some kind of lovesick knight after fucking me, made my stomach roil. At least he took the photo of me, rather than any of your self-portraits. I pictured him thumbtacking it next to his bed, in a room I'd never even seen and probably never would. I went through the rest of your drawers. Nothing but junk: pens and empty cigarette boxes and bottle tops and random scraps of paper.

At some point, when everything settled down, when I was back at the restaurant getting tips, or, if I could get my shit together and make my masterpiece, after I won the ten thousand dollars from the Andrews Foundation, I'd go to Pearl Street and restock my materials. I'd be able to buy all the stretched canvases my heart desired. Right now, though, I had nothing to spare, no way to buy new paints if I wanted to pay October rent on time. I glanced at the Schmincke box and a tight net of anger came over me. *It wasn't fair.* Who gets a thousand-dollar set of pastels they will never even use?

Fuck it, I thought, bringing the box to the living room. When I became famous I'd pay you back.

From the safe spot near the coffee mugs, I grabbed the keys to the basement storage and ran down the stairs into the room of wide lockers. I inserted the key into number nine and pulled open the door. Mostly it was full of your photography equipment—the enlarger and the tubs and the chemicals that you'd stopped using since you went digital—but I had a box of stuff in here, too, along with some old work.

I rifled around for a blank canvas, something that wasn't trash, but found nothing salvageable. *Fuck it*, I thought again. *Fuck it, fuck it, fuck it.* I took my cardboard box, relocked the locker, and returned to the apartment.

I dug out a tub of gesso and a kite-shaped palette knife from my box and began to work—spreading the paste on my bedroom door, the only thing big enough in the apartment that I could eventually detach. Who cared if we lost the security deposit? Your dad had paid it, anyway. He probably wouldn't even notice. I scraped the gesso into a flat, perfect plane. As it dried, I picked pastels from your box—a few bright blues, some oranges, a red, a black, and a white—and used the palette knife to shave off slivers, then crushed the slivers into pigment powders.

I'd gotten about halfway through the black pastel when my cell phone rang. I froze. It had been two days since I'd heard it, but there it was, ringing. Working again. I ran to pick it up, palette knife still in hand.

"I finally got ahold of the cops," Lizzie said.

My heart juddered. "And?"

"They're sending someone to your apartment. The lady I talked to said a report had already been filed. I guess it was her dad. You said he called them too, right?"

She was talking too fast. I couldn't keep up. "The cops are coming *here*?"

"We called the hospitals, too. No one has any record of her. I told them about Jon Potts, that she'd run off with him at school. And about Mason and the gallery. They're going to talk to everyone."

I squeezed my fingers around the phone. A thought that had been lingering on the edge of my mind came screaming to the stage. The man with the flashlight. He had been patrolling the place—he could have found you, moved you from the warehouse in an ambulance or worse—and no one would know who you were because Tyler had your ID.

"I want to talk to the cops when they get there." Lizzie's voice quavered; she was trying not to cry.

"Lizzie—"

But she'd already hung up.

I slipped into a pair of terry-cloth sweatpants and a man's undershirt, my mind so unable to stop thinking that it made me *angry*. I pulled out the black pastel and started to scrape at it with my palette knife again. But I pressed too hard, too fast, and the knife slipped, digging into my cuticle hard enough to draw blood.

"Shit," I said, dropping the knife, putting my finger in my mouth and sucking.

Fucking Milo. He had abandoned me, and now I had to deal with Lizzie and the cops by myself. I paced the living room as the minutes ticked by, sucking the blood off my stupid finger, unable to think straight. I had to talk to Milo. We had to figure out what to say.

His phone rang and rang, and just when I was about to give up, he answered.

"Sorry I left," he said. "Forgot I had a job."

"The cops are coming," I said, bluntly. I didn't give a shit what he was doing. "You have to get ahold of Tyler. You have to find out if he saw her. We have to get our stories straight."

He was quiet.

"Do you understand me, Milo?"

"You don't need to say anything."

Rage surged up my throat—hot and bitter. It sounded like a laugh. "We are going to get caught. Do you get it? *Both* of us."

"We didn't do anything, A." His voice was too calm. Far too calm.

"Did you go through her stuff this morning?" I said. "Did you take her scarf?"

"What?"

"Her mom's Hermès scarf. It was in her drawer yesterday. There was a photo, too."

The buzzer rang, and my stomach wrenched.

"Shit." I squeezed the phone tight. "They're here."

"Don't say anything. Don't—"

I clapped shut the phone and ran to the kitchen window, expecting cop cars, sirens, lights, the works, but there was nothing outside but an old man walking a squat black Scottie dog in an American flag kerchief.

The buzzer sounded again. I pressed the button.

"Hey." Lizzie, not the cops. Not yet. "Let me up."

I buzzed her in, pacing until she pushed open the door and hugged me so tightly my heart felt strangled. She still smelled of beer and body odor and stale smoke, that sour, unwashed stink that had hung in the air around her yesterday. I pulled free, unable to stop myself from grimacing. A rash of pimples had popped up on her chin. Her eyes were hollowed and bloodshot, and her hair was pulled into two small, tense ponytails at the nape of her neck. I stared at the gold hoop in her nose, the tiny patch of peeling skin on her nostril. She looked hideous, I thought, more hideous than any person I had ever seen. I stepped farther back, looked down at myself. My stained sweatpants, my dirty feet.

What is happening to us?

Lizzie stood in front of the gessoed door, looking down at the crushed pastels. "What is all this?"

I shrugged. I didn't want her to know that I couldn't afford paint and canvases or that I'd gone through your things, taken your materials. "Channeling my anxiety, I guess."

She fell onto the couch, taking up so much space, staring at my little TV. It had been on, muted, for hours. The images were already burned into my brain. All of our brains.

"I didn't mean to yell at you yesterday," Lizzie said. "I'm just really freaked out." She lit a cigarette and flicked it with her thumb over and over. She was fighting her emotions, I could tell. *Flick, flick, flick.* She was trying not to cry. "I know you think I'm overreacting, but I can tell, A. Something's not right."

"Nothing's really *right* right now," I said.

She dug a big white envelope out of her messenger bag. She clamped her cigarette between her lips and opened it. Inside were photographs—they were all of you: smiling broadly in a T-shirt and shorts; doing a muscle pose at Coney Island; in a leotard and tights in your freshman dorm room; play-pouting in close-up; dressed for a party, your red lips split but unsmiling.

My jaw tightened, my stomach, too. It was too much. I wanted to tear the pictures to shreds. I wanted to rip them into confetti and toss them out the kitchen window.

"People have been making flyers for all the missing people," Lizzie said. "They're putting them up in the subways and near the hospitals and stuff. Just in case people are unconscious or can't remember their names. I think we should make one for Wills."

She stared at me, waiting, hopeful, until I had to look away. Lizzie still thought there was a chance that you could have been in the subway at the precise wrong moment, that you'd been crushed under Cortlandt Street by tons of fiery steel. She thought you were a victim of terrorism, and I had no reason to change her mind.

"You're right," I said. "It's a good idea."

I slushed through the photos again, plucked one out: you in three-quarters profile, smoking a cigarette in a truck stop restaurant, your white-blond hair piled atop your head, the blurry truckers and waitresses staring at you as if you were crazy, or famous, or both. I handed it to Lizzie.

"Let's use this one."

She took the picture and smiled. "Her favorite."

The picture was quintessential Willow Whitman. Everyone

at Balwin thought it was the best photo in your *MUSE* exhibition last year. I still didn't know who took it, and I know that was part of the reason you made these pictures, recruiting others to take your "self-portraits." I laid the photo on top of the glass coffee table, as if we were museum conservationists in white gloves working on a vintage Man Ray.

"It's perfect," Lizzie said. "She's so pretty."

A new picture flashed on the TV screen, almost like a painting: a brown bearded man in a white turban, shiny dark eyes, and a face that appeared to be on the verge of smiling. He looked peaceful, save for the machine gun leaning against the wall next to him. A banner with a name flashed underneath. Osama bin Laden.

I clenched my hands into fists. It felt like we were all trapped in an orbit around the news, around you. *Willow and the World Trade Center, Willow and the World Trade Center, Willow and the World Trade Center.* It felt like it would never stop, and I needed it to stop, or I felt I might actually lose my mind.

"Do you have a Sharpie?" Lizzie said.

"Can I turn this shit off?"

She shrugged. I clicked the power button on the remote, feeling an immediate wash of relief. I went to the kitchen and pulled open the junk drawer and rattled through the crap dumped inside—rubber bands, coins, batteries, receipts, dead pens, bottle caps, another palette knife. I spotted a thick black Sharpie and pulled it out. It was probably yours, probably dried out. I grabbed a scrap of paper from the drawer to test it.

Something was written on the paper. I flipped it over, and my breath caught.

YOU'RE BETTER THAN THIS, WILLS.

That handwriting. The tight, caps-lock print. I had seen that handwriting before. The last time we called the cops. A new note, and here, in New York. The notes had followed you, just like he had.

Shit, Willow.

It could only mean one thing—he had found you.

Jon Potts had found you.

Sixteen

TWO AND A HALF YEARS BEFORE

WILLOW STAYED CLOSE to the dorms the rest of that winter. She went to classes, but she didn't drink anymore, or get high, or go to the Bar Car with everyone else. Milo kept his distance, still aggrieved by Willow's disappearance and reticence, but not enough to break up with her. He loved her too much, worshipped her, so chose to believe that nothing had happened between her and Jon Potts.

Anna was the only one who knew what had been done to Willow, and she stayed close to her friend, feeling the need to protect her and comfort her, to make sure she felt safe. Anna brought her coffee and bagels from the cafeteria. She picked up magazines and monographs from the library. She walked her to class, waited for her on the bench outside Highsmith. All of this made Anna feel important and needed, and despite Willow's pain, Anna was happy.

But when spring broke, things shifted. Willow smiled again, asked about weekend plans, and started going out with the group, drinking and smoking and partying like nothing had happened. Soon enough, Milo was back in her life—sleeping in Willow's bed, eating meals with her, walking her to class—and Anna's calls began to go ignored. Willow "forgot" about planned meetups and studio dates.

It was like Willow had forgotten her.

Like Anna never even mattered.

The last Thursday before exams, they all smashed into a booth at the Bar Car, and Boomer put his arm around Anna's shoulder. She turned to him, her eyes full of something—anticipation, questions. It had been a year and a half since their bad hookup, and nothing had happened between them since. Anna hadn't kissed anyone else, unless you counted Willow at the beach. She didn't want to count that. She didn't want to think about that. She tried all the time not to.

Boomer moved his hand back into his lap.

It felt like another rejection, no matter how little she wanted him. The feeling expanded inside Anna, pushing against her edges. If it weren't for Willow, she'd leave. She'd never come back to the Bar Car.

Boomer sighed, then peeled the label off his beer bottle in one thin piece. He laid it flat on the table, smoothing it. Then he began ripping, twisting the edges, rolling pieces. Anna watched his hands work until she saw what he was making: a torso, arms, legs, a little head. He managed to make the scraps of the label stand up on wet paper feet. A delightful little homunculus.

"Hello, Anna," Boomer said in falsetto, pretending to be the little man. "Can I tell you a secret?"

But as soon as Anna smiled, Boomer dropped his paper man. He was on his feet, staring across the bar. Anna turned and saw what he saw: Willow splayed on the floor, unmoving on a carpet of peanut shells, her hair glowing in a puddle of mud-veined beer.

Boomer rushed toward her. Everyone did. Lizzie and Tom and the bartenders, and Anna, too. Her mind was a knot of possibilities. She was thinking about Henry. About the day on the beach when he turned blue. About his seizures afterward—their suddenness, the way they struck out of nowhere and dropped everyone to their knees. She thought about Willow's mother, too, and what Willow had told her. Multiple sclerosis. Anna had looked up the autoimmune disease at the library, wanting to understand what Willow was going through, how to talk to her, how to support her. Anna had studied the symptoms: blurred vision, muscle spasms, vertigo, rapidly changing movements. She had read about potential links in families.

Mother to daughter, Anna thought now.

Huddled around Willow, the friends pulled at each other, shouting, staring wide-eyed, everything disconnected and slow.

"Is she unconscious?" Anna's voice was pitched with fear.

"Call 911," someone said. Maybe it was Milo, or maybe it was the bartender, but it was Tom who ran behind the bar and picked up the phone.

"No!" Lizzie shouted, flinging herself across the bar. "Don't. We can't. We're underage. Oh my god, I have weed!"

Anna grabbed Lizzie's wrist. She didn't want to give Willow away, but she had to make it clear. This was a crisis. "We have to. She could have MS."

Lizzie shook her head fast, like she was trying to dislodge a fly. *"What?"*

"Her mom has multiple sclerosis. She could be really sick!"

Lizzie scowled in confusion. "Her mom's fine. She lives in Paris."

From the floor, there was a noise. It was Willow. She was laughing.

The huddle around her took a step back.

Willow sat up, looking at Lizzie first, that same half smile on her face. "Bitch. You'd let me die because you didn't want to get busted?"

They all stared at her, silent. It had only been a minute, less than a minute, but Willow had cut through everything. She had flipped on the lights and exposed them.

The bartender was there, a big man with a shaved head and a long mustache, like a Hells Angel.

"That wasn't funny," Milo said.

Anna's hands were still on her mouth.

"You're out of here," the bartender said, thrusting a thumb over his shoulder. "All of you."

Willow raised her hands, flittering her fingers. "Oh, stop, Robby. It was just a lark. Someone help me up."

"You better have ID," he said. "Or you're never coming back in here."

"Jesus," Willow said, rolling her eyes. "Relax."

Anna pulled Willow to stand, and Willow grabbed her purse off the bar. "Here," she said to the bartender, pulling out her wallet, handing him a little card. "Happy?"

He took it, studied it, handed it back. "Never do that again."

Willow gave him a beaming red smile, then hooked her arm in Anna's arm and led her away toward the bathroom.

Anna was still processing what had just happened. "When did you get a fake ID?"

"I don't need one," Willow said, and pushed open the bathroom door.

Anna had turned twenty in December, and Willow's birthday wasn't until August. "Why not?"

Willow dampened a paper towel and cleaned the dirt and beer from her arms and face. Anna watched Willow watch herself in the mirror and suddenly felt afraid. This person in front of her was a stranger. A changeling. Anna had no idea who she was. "How old are you?"

They locked eyes in the mirror. "I took a year break in high school. When my mom got really sick. I turned twenty-one last August."

"You took a year off?"

Willow whipped around. "I didn't tell anyone because I didn't want to explain my mom to all of them." She gestured to the door. "It'll be a thing. You know it will."

There was something thick in Anna's throat. Doubt. She thought about Leanne and Mr. Whitman and what Willow had said: *I went a little wild. He doesn't trust me.*

Willow turned back to the mirror. "Tell them you lied," she said. "About the MS."

Anna stared at her friend. "Why did you do that?"

Willow pulled a red lipstick from her pocket and smudged it on, kissing herself in the mirror. "I wanted to see what everyone would do."

"Lizzie said your mom lives in Paris." Anna's mind rewound

to the Eiffel Tower key chain that she had stolen freshman year. It was buried with old junk in her jewelry box.

"Lizzie doesn't know what she's talking about." Willow tossed the paper towels in the garbage and turned to face Anna again. "Paris," she said, laughing, and rolled her eyes. "Interesting way to describe McLean Assisted Living."

Anna took a steadying breath. She had a name, a real place.

"You're the only one who knows about my mom, Hollywood," Willow said. "You're the only one I trust."

She pulled Anna in and hugged her, and Anna let her.

She didn't want to believe that Willow had made it up.

She didn't want to believe that she had traded her darkest secret for a lie.

Seventeen

THURSDAY AFTERNOON

I DROPPED THE NOTE so fast it was like it had caught fire. I slammed the drawer closed, my mind reeling. A new one. It could only mean one thing.

Jon Potts really was back.

I took the Sharpie to the living room, handed it to Lizzie. I watched her work, unsure whether to tell her about what I'd just found. If I told her about the note, I'd have to tell her everything else, about what had *really* happened at Balwin with Jon, and even after everything, I couldn't break my promise to you.

Once Lizzie had finished the headline—*MISSING: WILLOW WHITMAN, AGE 22, 5 FEET 3 INCHES, 105 POUNDS*—she wrote our cell phone numbers across the bottom like a news ticker.

I licked my lips. My mouth was so dry. Lizzie didn't have your age right, but I didn't think to correct her, not then.

"Did Willow ever say anything about that weekend?" I asked. "The one with Jon Potts, I mean. The black eye."

"Just what she told everyone, that they were partying. Why?"

I swallowed hard.

"What's wrong?"

I turned away. *He really, really dislikes her.* Everything was tangled in my mind, a bunch of live wires—your bruises at Balwin, your lies, your face.

Lizzie touched my arm. "What are you thinking?"

Nothing made sense. I flashed back to Tuesday morning. My favorite coffee mug out on the counter. *World's Best Sister.* The crack, the handle. Your mess. Our fight. I had overlooked something: The milk was warm. It had gone sour. Not hours old, then—but *days.* The mug. You dropped it when we fought. I could see it on the floor. Was it possible that it had been sitting on the counter, unwashed, for a full week? Hadn't we made coffee since then? But you'd barely been home, and I didn't even like the taste. *Think.* Your mess. *No.* I would have noticed a mess like that. And your smell—your smell was everywhere. It was overwhelming.

Lizzie was watching me, eyes bloodshot, skin peaked. "You're freaking me out."

"When did you last talk to her?"

"We were supposed to meet up on Saturday," she said. "But she canceled. Last minute, she said a friend was coming to town."

Saturday. I'd taken extra shifts last weekend to get out of the apartment, to get away from you. I hadn't seen you at all.

"So when was the last time you saw her?" I said.

"At Happiness. On . . . the Tuesday before."

I felt a rush inside me, a drop, like an elevator losing a floor. *Last Tuesday.* A whole week longer than I thought. I pressed

161

the sides of my face together, as if I could mush my memories into one another, make it make sense.

I hadn't seen you since our fight—a full week ago. I popped up, went back into the kitchen for the note, and held it out for Lizzie. She took it, read it, then tossed up her hands.

"What?"

"It's him," I said, pointing at the note. *Jon Potts.*

"Boomer?" she said.

I blinked, confused, and the buzzer rang. "Boomer?"

Lizzie was staring at me. "What's wrong with you?"

"This is *Boomer's* handwriting?"

She nodded.

The buzzer rang again. *The cops.* It had to be. I couldn't make myself answer.

Lizzie stood and pushed by me to get to the intercom.

"It's me." Milo, his voice a crackle.

Lizzie raised a brow at me but buzzed open the building and let Milo in.

I gestured to the paper in her hand. "Did Willow tell you she had a stalker?"

Her nose crinkled. "Huh?"

"Back at school. Sophomore year. Milo told me. Someone had been leaving her notes. I saw one of them back then. One of the notes. In *that*"—I pointed to the paper in Lizzie's hand—"writing."

She studied the note. "This is Boomer's handwriting." She folded it into a little square and handed it back to me. "He wasn't stalking her."

I took the paper from her, thinking of Boomer, the way he never wanted me, the way he dismissed me. Those big white

162

teeth. Following us to the bathroom at graduation. He knew too much.

"Boomer's always had a thing for her," Lizzie said. "But he wasn't *stalking* her."

The floor wavered underneath me. *A thing for her.*

She spun down and picked up her bag and the flyer she'd made, your picture held tight under her thumb. "I'm gonna make copies. Leave you and Milo to do *whatever.*" She brushed by me, toward the kitchen.

I reached out and grabbed her wrist. "Wait." I was holding her wrist, my fingers on her skin. My fingernails. I knew how easy it would be to dig them into her skin, how easily I could hurt her. I dropped my hand. "Was something happening with Boomer and Wills? Did Milo know?"

She looked at me, both eyebrows high enough to draw deep furrows in her forehead, and shook her head. "I can't help you with this, Anna."

TWO YEARS BEFORE

AT THE START of junior year, Anna focused all her energy on getting accepted into Kape's Painting IV seminar the following year. She started saying no to Willow and Lizzie when they asked her to go to the Bar Car, spending time with her books and materials instead. She began to miss breakfast, heading to Highsmith as soon as the studios opened at seven. That's where Anna was, practicing some figurative work, spurred on by praise for her technical skill in Drawing III, when Willow jolted her with a loud, wet kiss on her cheek.

She slipped off her headphones, De La Soul now tinny and small on the table.

Willow smacked down a packet of photographs. "Check it out," she said, dragging a stool behind her.

Anna set down her paintbrush, irritated. She had been moving into another dimension, shifting the facts of geometry and light into something transcendent. She had been close to a revelation. To a breakthrough. It hummed inside her like a third eye, twitching, ready to open. But it was gone now. Willow had taken it away.

Anna sighed and opened Willow's packet—color photographs that had been developed at Walmart. They were all self-portraits—Willow, naked and slicked in mud and red paint, almost unrecognizable if it weren't for her white-blue eyes and her tiny hourglass figure. She was walking through a cornfield in one photograph, bathing in Wabash Lake in another. Small green plants seemed to grow from her body in some. In others, she was buried under stones.

Willow set her chin on Anna's shoulder so they were looking at the pictures together. Anna understood right away that they were lush and sexy—the late summer in Ohio transformed into an Eden, and Willow, the ultimate Eve. She was saying something about the female form, something about nature and life, even if Anna wasn't able to articulate *what* exactly Willow's message was.

"You like?" Willow's voice was right in Anna's ear.

"Who took them?"

Willow didn't answer, and in a way, Anna knew it didn't matter. Willow may have set up a timer or Milo or Lizzie could have trailed her to the lake and painted her with mud. These were Willow's photos, through and through.

"They're great," Anna said, but in truth, she thought the work was derivative. In the past two years, Anna had made a point to become a scholar of contemporary art, and now, the things that had evaded her for so long—theories, lineages, movements—had become a lens through which she viewed every piece of art she saw. As Anna flipped through Willow's photographs, Ana

Mendieta came to mind. The feminist Earth and performance artist was fifteen years dead, her life cut short at thirty-six after she and her much older and much more famous sculptor husband, Carl Andre, had been fighting and drinking, and she "fell" thirty-four stories from their bedroom window. Still, in 1999, people continued to use language that blamed Mendieta for the brutality committed against her. *She* had been the volatile one, despite Andre's notorious drinking and violence. *She* had been too ambitious, too argumentative, too drunk, too loud, too insecure. If Andre had done it, if he'd pushed her, killed her, she'd *driven* him to it.

Anna flipped the paper flap on the photo packet back and forth quickly with her thumb, understanding something. At its core, Mendieta's work was about violence against women, long before her husband murdered her. Anna turned back to Willow's photographs, the mud and the red paint like blood, the stones burying her body. It was about rape, Anna realized. Willow was trying to make work about what Jon Potts had done to her last winter.

"This could be important." Anna wanted to support her friend, however tacitly. There was no need to open her up anymore. They'd done enough of that. It had been half a year, and so far, they'd both kept each other's secrets. No one knew about Anna's brother or Willow's mom or what Jon had done to her. Anna was glad to see that Willow's anger had been channeled into her art, rather than something destructive.

"I think I'll do more of them," Willow said. "A performance piece, maybe, for my thesis. Something *big*."

"I can document it for you, if you want?"

"You know what?" Willow smiled. "I already have a plan for that."

Anna looked away, her feelings hurt. She hated being dismissed by Willow, even now, even in such a small way. She reached for her headphones. "I have to finish this painting today."

"Is that a hint?"

Anna smiled tightly. "Yep."

"Okay, okay. I'm leaving." Willow stood, leaving the stool where it was, a ghost lurking over Anna's shoulder. When Willow got to the door, she turned. "It's really good," she said. "Kape's totally going to want you."

Anna looked at her canvas. Technically it *was* good—Anna didn't need Willow to tell her that. The portrait was a hyper-real self-portrait à la Chuck Close, near perfect in execution, but something was missing. Some subtle shift that would change everything. The revelation that had been so close minutes ago—that bright, essential lightning bolt that would slash through everything—was far away again.

The door clanged shut. Willow was gone, and Anna was alone. The only sound was the whirring of the industrial fans. Anna frowned at her painting. Being *technically good* wasn't enough. It just wasn't enough.

She stood and paced the room, walking around her easel in circles, biting her lip and thinking. She'd burned through her destruction phase. She'd ripped and cut and torched as much as she could. That was done. Passé. She needed more. She needed to elevate. She looked around the studio. There were paints and tools and canvases—all the supplies she could possibly want. She gathered scissors and an X-Acto knife, some black paints, a thick brush. She put everything on her table and stared at it, disappointed.

Anna sat on the stool again, pondering her self-portrait, thinking of Duchamp and *L.H.O.O.Q.*, and considered defacing her painting the way Duchamp had *La Jaconde*. But even that wasn't right. The mustache Duchamp had drawn was about gender identity, which was not what Anna was thinking about. No—Anna was thinking about Willow, her fascination with muses of the past, how the women whose images lived on walls and in frames had been used up, squeezed out like a tube of paint. Warhol's Edie. Schiele's Wally. Rodin's Camille. Picasso's string of broken women. By now, Anna knew what the "master" had done to his young muses—he controlled them, locked them inside his house when he went out, cheated on them, belittled them, drove them to suicide or into mental institutions. Though Anna had never been a muse, had never even had a proper boyfriend, she identified with those girls. She was susceptible. Any man could overpower her, pin her down, break her apart. Just look at what had happened to Willow.

Without giving herself time to think, she picked up the X-Acto knife, slipped out its blade, and slashed it against the inside of her arm. It was hot but painless, and it began to bleed immediately. Anna lurched to her canvas, letting blood drip over her painted face. When there was enough blood on the canvas, she cleaned her cut gently at the sink, grabbed a few paper towels, and secured them on her arm with blue tape. The cut throbbed, but as Anna returned to her canvas, applying pressure, she saw that it was worth it.

She reached out her fingers and smeared the blood over her own smiling face.

THURSDAY AFTERNOON

MILO THUDDED into the living room and stopped at the sight of Lizzie. "What's going on?" he said, flicking his gaze to my gessoed door.

"Hi to you too," Lizzie said. She swept past him, holding up the flyer. "I'm taking this to Kinko's."

A tiny flinch shook Milo's face as he took it in. That word. *MISSING*.

"Hang on," I said, trailing after her. I still had questions: Boomer, Jon, the note.

"Call me when the cops show," Lizzie said, not slowing. "I'll come back."

Milo hooked his hand on my shoulder. I turned. He was covered in lavender paint—arms, corduroys, even a daub on his cheek. It seemed artificial somehow. Doubt churned in my stomach. I smacked Boomer's note into Milo's chest.

"It was *Boomer*?" I said. "All this time? Did you know?"

Milo glanced at the paper. "It doesn't matter," he said, holding it out for me to take.

I felt like hitting him, like digging my fingernails into his face. So much had hinged on Jon Potts—what he had done to you. I took the note back anyway, flicking my thumb against its worn corner.

Boomer, I thought. *Boomer?* I didn't understand what it meant. I thought back to that night in Chinatown—Boomer's arm around your shoulders, before I had sex with Milo for the first time. I cringed at the memory, that abrupt, almost hostile rupture in our lives. Why had we done it? You and Milo fighting in the rain. Milo, abandoned on Boomer's stoop. But it was Boomer who chased after you, when I was in the basement with Milo. You and Boomer. And then it made sense.

"You were using me?"

Milo didn't answer at first. He didn't have to. He had seen something that night that I hadn't. His girlfriend and his best friend, together. That night in Chinatown—that must have been what your fight had been about. God, how stupid I had been. I'd been nothing but a revenge fuck. Best friend for best friend. How mortifying for me.

Milo pulled cigarettes from his back pocket, finally speaking. "You used me, too." His voice was calm, but his hand was shaking as he lit up.

"I did not," I said. "I—"

"Listen, Anna," he said, stopping me. "We need to talk." He pulled out one of the kitchen chairs and sat down. Why were his hands shaking like that? Why wasn't he looking at me? He leaned back until the front legs lifted from the floor. The urge to swipe my foot against the chair came over me. I wanted to knock him down. I wanted to stop whatever was coming.

"Sit," he said.

A trap. He was trying to trap me. I wasn't going to fall into it, not again. I narrowed my eyes. "The phones are working again, Milo."

He set the chair legs down with a thud. "So?"

"Have you even *tried* to call Tyler? Have you even *tried* to find out if anything happened on Tuesday?"

"Jesus Christ with that." Milo stared at me. "Sit, Anna. Please."

I took a step backward. He was full of lies. No way I would sit. No way I'd do anything he told me to.

"Willow told Lizzie someone came into town last weekend," I said. "A visitor. Did you know that?"

"No. I didn't. But it doesn't matter—"

"You weren't answering your phone."

"Huh?" His lips pulled into a grimace. "I was painting a house last weekend. I was working."

"Were you with her?"

"Are you serious?"

He was smirking, and it occurred to me that he might be lying to me about more than just Boomer. Maybe I had been wrong from the beginning, worrying about the wrong people, the wrong things. Maybe the person I should have really been afraid of was right in front of me. Maybe Milo wasn't worried about Tyler because he knew Tyler hadn't had the chance to mug you. Milo would have known that if he knew where you were, if he had *put* you wherever you were. I stumbled backward. *Oh shit.*

His smirk faded. "Anna?"

I wasn't really hearing him. I wasn't listening. My heart was thudding in my chest, sending little explosions into my arms.

Milo was in love with you. Obsessed with you. He always let you walk all over him. He didn't care. He'd let you do anything, except leave him.

"The cops are on their way," I said.

He looked confused, maybe just surprised. But I didn't wait for him to figure it out. As soon as I sensed him about to stand, I fled into my bedroom. He was behind me, a shadow, trailing me, but I slammed the door between us.

He pounded on the door, cracking the gesso. "Anna!"

I fumbled with the lock. It finally clicked into place just as the knob rattled from the other side. *Oh god*, I thought. *How did I not see this before?*

"Anna," Milo said, and his voice was level again. Too level. "It's not what you think. None of this is what you think."

"I don't think anything." I could hear the tremble in my own voice. It was obvious what I thought. *Tyler never had a chance to hurt you, because Milo had already done it. I'd been afraid of the wrong man.* "The police are coming. They are on their way right now."

There was silence—until another thump came against the door, jolting me backward. "Jesus Christ!" Milo shouted. Another thump. "You have to listen to me."

Fear crept up my spine. "You're scaring me, Milo," I said. "You need to leave."

"Anna, come on—"

"Go!"

I pressed my ear to the door until I head his footsteps retreat and the outer door slam. He was gone. He was gone. But I stayed in my room, ear pressed to the door, for more than an hour, just to make sure.

TWO YEARS BEFORE

LIZZIE RETURNED from her semester abroad before Christmas, and she invited the group to Louisville for her family's annual New Year's Eve party. Willow picked up Anna on her way down from Chicago. Anna waited for her at the end of her driveway, a duffel bag at her feet, because she wasn't ready for Willow to meet Henry. Willow knew everything about him now. The whole truth. She would let Willow meet Henry when Anna was able to meet Mrs. Whitman.

Willow's Mercedes pulled up and Anna hopped in, stuffing her bag between them into the back.

"Let's dip," she said, and slammed the door.

Willow put the car in drive. "Where's the fire?"

"Ha," Anna said, and she slipped a Prince CD into the stereo. Willow flew around the cul-de-sac, one leg hitched up on her seat, and lit a Parliament, her eyes hidden behind small sunglasses.

"Have you been to Lizzie's house yet?"

"No," Anna said. "Why?"

Willow tutted, cigarette smoke funneling to the cracked window. "You'll see."

The flat middle-Ohio landscape rolled into hills as they drove south. Off the highway, they wound through empty fields and gas stations and strip malls. Louisville looked more or less like every place Anna knew—Columbus and Cincinnati and the rest of the Midwest in winter. Gray and brown and bare.

"I think it's here," Willow said.

"Here?" The middle of nowhere, it seemed to Anna—no mailbox or address marker, only a thin tar lane cutting through empty land. It wasn't what she expected, given Lizzie's legacy status at Balwin, the Range Rover, and study abroad. She had expected wealth, excess—something like Willow's condo in Chicago.

Willow took a turn too fast, and Anna reached for the handle to hold herself in place.

"Jesus, dude."

She didn't respond. Anna looked for signs of life between two red barns, the many mounds of dirt, a long raw-wood fence that looked handmade.

"Look!" Willow pointed out the driver's-side window. Three huge horses, dark chestnut brown, glossy as nail polish, swishing their tails.

The lane turned slightly, and between two giant evergreens, Anna glimpsed the house.

"Whoa," she said without meaning to. Part gray-stone

Victorian, part contemporary, it looked like a nineteenth-century museum with a new wing. Two masterpieces merged into something totally new, like the Louvre with its I. M. Pei pyramid.

They drove past the trees, and the whole building came into view: a cylindrical glass wing, wrought iron balconies, a black steel door with a simple evergreen-and-red-berry wreath. Hedges and hedges and hedges. Pines and cypresses and hollies and ivy. The house was stone and steel and glass, and absolutely enormous.

Willow pulled the Mercedes behind a cluster of bigger and newer and nicer cars. Anna wiped her damp hands on her jeans. She knew Lizzie was rich, but she had never imagined *this*. She was annoyed with herself, her naivete, dogging her even here. The clothes she'd stuffed in her backpack were all wrong: wrinkled, cheap thrift store shit, all of it. Jeans with torn hems. A camisole with spaghetti straps and cheap rhinestones. Lug-sole boots. She had been expecting a bonfire, parents in ugly holiday sweaters, not whatever *this* was. She should have known. She should have understood. She should have brought something else, something better, even if she needed to steal it.

Willow led Anna through the giant steel door. Inside—glass, Persian carpets, two stone fireplaces on either side of the front hall, both roaring. A pair of enormous Christmas trees, decorated in silver and gold. Anna looked up. A coffered ceiling, shimmering gold-green, the color of oxidized pennies.

Willow touched Anna's arm and pointed to a canvas, covered edge to edge with bright dots.

"Is that a *Hirst*?" Anna said.

Willow made a wide-eyed face, and Anna understood that it was real, a masterpiece in Lizzie's living room, close enough to touch.

"You know Lizzie's mom's maiden name, right?"

Anna frowned. "What?"

Willow leaned toward her and whispered. "Highsmith."

Just then, Lizzie sauntered in, wearing a long silk kimono, hair wet from a shower. *I'm a legacy.* Her voice rang through the room. "We gonna party like it's nineteen ... ninety ... nine."

Anna smelled her perfume, musky and deep like patchouli but not—this was something different, something refined. She welled with panic. "I don't think I brought the right clothes."

"Oh, god," Lizzie said, dismissing her. "Wear anything. Nobody cares."

Anna's nostrils flared in panic. It was the worst thing Lizzie could have said. Anna wanted people to take notice of her. She was desperate to be noticed and seen and accepted.

Willow threaded an arm through Anna's. "Oh, they'll care," she whispered. "Don't worry. We will make them care."

In an airy guest bedroom with floor-to-ceiling velvet draperies and carpet so thick and padded it was like stepping on a made bed, Willow pulled a long, silky black skirt from her bag. "Put this on."

Anna pinched the skirt, eyeing it and frowning.

"Just try it," Willow said. "It's better on."

Anna kicked her jeans into a corner and zipped up the skirt. It was bias-cut and low on her hips, deliciously soft. She stepped to the full-length mirror to examine herself. Willow was right about the fit. Anna looked thin and tall, like a statue. She pulled up her T-shirt, twisted to see her backside.

"No undies," Willow said.

Anna turned to her. "What?"

"I can see those granny panties from here. Take them off."

"And wear what instead?"

"Nothing, dummy." Willow's eyes flashed. She gave Anna a wicked smile. "Tonight, you get to be *free*."

Anna paired Willow's skirt with a flimsy black camisole from Express. She dusted her shoulders with glittery powder and pulled on her black combat boots. She looked elegant but felt oddly threatening, carrying a secret under that skirt. More than a secret. Her bareness was a loaded gun. It was power.

More than three hundred people came to the Stone house that night, adults and kids, friends of Lizzie's from private school. Three hundred people that didn't include the bartenders with their endless flutes of champagne and the waitstaff passing around trays of tiny salmon toasts, warm figs, goat cheese croquettes, lemon-and-sage panisses, bite-size feta-and-jam tarts. Anna's tongue tripped over the fancy words, the new flavors she was too nervous to taste. She repeated everything again and again inside her head until she'd feel comfortable saying them out loud if she needed to.

Lizzie's mother had newscaster-blond hair, swept back and sprayed into a chignon, and was wearing a low-cut navy silk suit with nothing underneath. Her chest was so thin and tan it looked like an armored breastplate. She held a champagne glass by the stem so loosely Anna had the urge to take it from her as Lizzie introduced them.

"Thanks so much for having me," Anna said. "Your home is beautiful."

"Thank you, dear," Mrs. Stone drawled, beckoning a waiter with a lift of a brow. The man approached, offering his tray to Anna and Willow. "Go ahead, girls, enjoy yourselves."

They each took a glass, clinked, and sipped.

Mrs. Stone caught sight of someone and flitted her fingers. "Most of your set is in the library," she said before floating away.

Willow and Anna followed down the hall. The library was in the "new wing," sprawling and white and lit like a museum, floor-to-ceiling glass shelves with built-in halogen lights displaying thousands of books.

Willow pulled out her camera and clicked. "Insane," she said.

They were buzzed, close to drunk, when Willow put her lips near Anna's ear. "Look," she whispered. "They're all here."

Willow was pointing to a little cabal in the corner, and Anna's arms prickled with goose bumps. Lizzie and her parents, Tom, and three Balwin art professors. Lizzie air-kissed Professor Kape like she was still in Florence.

"I think the dean is in the front hall," Willow said.

It was impressive, how Lizzie acted with those adults, how comfortable she was. Like they were equals. It was the name, Anna knew—Highsmith—but she wanted that ease and confidence for herself just the same.

"You should fuck him."

"What?" Anna pulled back to look at Willow. "Who?"

Anna followed Willow's gaze to the edge of the room. To Professor Kape, holding a crystal tumbler of something brown. She snorted. "Kape?"

Willow closed her eyes and moved her jaw from side to side with the beat of the drum. "He won the Hugo Boss Prize—did you know? He's going to have a solo show at the Guggenheim next year. He's so hot right now." Willow opened her eyes. "And you'd get into Painting IV for sure."

Anna sniffed, affronted. "I don't need to *fuck* someone to get into Painting IV, Wills."

Willow tucked her chin and looked at Anna with equal parts amusement and pity. "I forget how naive you are sometimes, Hollywood."

Anna frowned back at her. The feeling that she was missing some critical knowledge crept back under her skin—stodgy and tar-like, a specific kind of dread.

"You must know this, babe," Willow said. "All these big men, all these dudes in charge. They don't care about our work. Or what we can do. They're small-minded. They're *jealous* of our talent. Threatened by it. A beautiful girl who can paint like you?" Willow scoffed. "Old men are *afraid* of us. Kape won't help you. He'll never help you that way. He only helps the guys—haven't you noticed that yet?"

The dread stuck to Anna's ribs, to the lining of her stomach.

"You have to use their fear against them, babe. You have to wield your power."

"My power," Anna repeated.

"Exactly. You want to be somebody. I know you do. You want

it all. I know that because I do, too, and I'll do whatever it takes to get it." Willow gestured to Anna's skirt, the nakedness underneath. "We have what they want. And we can let them *think* they are using us, when *we* are really using *them*."

As if summoned, Kape looked up and smiled.

The band led the room in a countdown to midnight. People cheered and the musicians played "Auld Lang Syne." There was confetti in Anna's hair and champagne in her hand. She was buzzed and loose-limbed and free. The music changed, and Lizzie pulled her to the dance floor. The whole party watched them move. Boomer and Tom and Milo, parents and professors. Anna felt stage lit. She felt perfect.

Then Lizzie was gone, and Willow was there, pulling Anna close. Their soft fingers twisted together. Anna could smell Willow, salt and sugar, lemon drops and butter. Her mouth watered. She was hungry, but she didn't dare eat. The dance floor crowded around them. Willow pulled Anna closer and closer, and she felt herself light up. The night felt thick and electric, like thunder might crack the air at any moment, like lightning might flash. Willow led them closer to Kape. His black-and-white goatee formed a sharp vee on his chin, his hair poufed from his face, his shirt was unbuttoned far enough that Anna saw little sprouts of black-and-gray chest hair. She wondered if he was as old as her own father. For some reason, the thought made her toss her head back and laugh.

"Hello, Professor," Willow purred.

He looked at them, his eyes bouncing between their faces

so fast they were nearly vibrating. "Girls," he said, like it was a question.

Willow took his hand and set it on Anna's shoulder. His fingers were stubby and rough. Turpentine hands. Anna looked at Willow for confirmation, for affirmation. Willow pinched Anna's chin and turned it forward, to face Kape. He looked confused. Alarmed, even. Willow dropped her hand, she was gone. They were alone, just Kape and Anna. Her insides hummed. She was so hungry. The music changed again, sultry and up-tempo, and Anna felt herself on a stage, playing a role.

Kape buckled a little and let his arms drop. "I can't keep up with you." He looked away, all around the dance floor, anyplace but Anna's eyes.

Blood drained from Anna's face. He didn't think she was worth it. He didn't think she was good enough. Pretty enough. Talented enough. But Willow was back, dancing, taking Anna's hands, twisting her legs around Anna's thigh. Kape's face went slack. He moved toward them again, a few glances over his shoulder, like he was afraid he'd be seen. No one was watching. They were laughing. Anna's face tilted to the ceiling. She was buzzed and hot and deliciously drunk.

Willow was gone again, and Kape was leading Anna somewhere—a powder room, all marble and gold with peacocks on the wallpaper, and the water closet beyond—just a sink and a mirror and them. The door closed and clicked. Anna didn't actually want him—his musty-smelling skin, his puffed-up hair, his saggy jowls—but how could she say no to what he could offer her in exchange? *We have what they want. Wield your power.* Anna had to do it, she had to. Kape's tongue was already in her mouth, fat as a fish. He turned her around so she was against the wall, her palms flat on the peacocks. His hands were on her, under her camisole. He let out a moan as his mouth went to the nape of her neck. It was thrilling, what Anna was doing to him. The power she felt over him. Willow was right. Willow was always right.

Anna heard noises beyond the door, hollow footsteps and echoing voices. All those people, right there, and this, what they were doing, so illicit, so taboo. *He'll never help you that way.* Take the power. Anna understood so clearly now. It wasn't fair, the way the world worked, men always getting to be in charge. But Anna had something he wanted. Something *everyone* wanted. She had youth and beauty, and she could use those things like weapons. She wouldn't be passive anymore. Relying on goodwill and fairness. She would use what she had to get what she wanted.

"Oh god," Kape said, sloppy-voiced. "Should we?"

Anna moved his hand under her skirt. His finger slipped inside her. That was all it took. He was nothing but desire then—fumbling and grotesque. She had won. It was so easy. She looked over her shoulder as he tore open a condom wrapper with his teeth, that laughable, mournful look in his eyes, then spun her around again. Anna's cheek crushed against the wall as he put a hand on her head and licked her neck. A cat's tongue. Sandpaper. Anna was laughing. She couldn't help it. She heard the noises from the hallway and she didn't care. She didn't care how ugly and old and fat he was, how ridiculous and *alert* his penis was, sticking out between his shirttails, and he didn't care that she was laughing. He didn't care about anything other than getting inside her. *This is how it's done*, Anna thought. *This is how I will succeed.*

The next morning, in the room with the velvet curtains, the girls slouched against huge silk pillows in matching twin beds. Willow's mascara smudged a black line to her cheek and her lipstick was cracked, but she still looked pretty somehow. It was New Year's Day, the first morning of the new millennium, and they were hungover. Anna had been waiting for this moment—to have Willow alone, to tell her about Kape in the bathroom, the little towels and the peacock wallpaper and how he ripped open the condom wrapper with his teeth.

"I totally did it," Anna said.

Willow barely glanced at her. "Did what?"

Anna pulled the steel-blue comforter over her head, pretending to be ashamed. "I fucked Kape." It was almost harder to be so flip about it, using that word in that way, than it had been to actually do it.

"*What?*"

Anna flipped the comforter down. "Kape. We did it in the bathroom."

Willow's eyes went wide. She started to laugh.

Anna blinked fast, confused. Something heavy swung at her stomach. "What's funny?"

"You didn't really?"

Anna's heart fluttered wildly. She felt hollow. "You told me to. You convinced me. Painting IV—"

"I was joking." Willow leaned over the nightstand, piled with things—her camera, their wallets and jewelry, a Frida Kahlo biography, film canisters, gum wrappers. She shuffled it all around. "Where are my cigs?"

Anna stared at her for a moment, stomach churning.

She's changed, she thought. Ever since Jon Potts, Willow had been different. Colder, meaner, sneakier. Those weeks Willow spent in her room last February, cocooned in her bed, had metamorphized her into a new, wicked thing. Willow, oblivious to Anna's creeping dread, found her Parliaments and lit one, not even bothering to ask anyone in the house if it was okay.

Anna picked up the Kahlo book, staring at the cover. A self-portrait. A tortured woman, blood on her face. She did not want to be like her. She did not. Anger boiled in her chest, and her stomach roiled. *What had she done?* What had seemed like power last night felt like poison now. His sandpaper tongue. His absurd desire. She had let him fuck her in a bathroom. She had let him debase her. It was wrong, she knew now. She hadn't won. Kape was still in charge. He still held the keys to Anna's future. Everything hinged on him—and she had turned it into a joke, because Willow told her to.

Anna threw off the blanket—Kahlo book crashing, splayed, to the carpet—and ran into the bathroom to throw up.

Twenty-One

THURSDAY EVENING

I LOCKED THE DEAD BOLT in case Milo came back. It was already four p.m., and I was supposed to clock into La Soeurette in an hour. *Absurd.* There was no way I could leave the safety of my apartment to tie on my yellow apron and fake-smile at strangers. If the restaurant was even open, close at it was to the World Trade Center. But I couldn't lose my job. Once all this was over, I'd still need my tips to survive the city. I had no choice—I had to call. Regina, a Russian bartender with bright blue eyes, curly black hair, and a dagger tattooed on each wrist, answered.

"My roommate's missing," I told her. "She never made it to work on Tuesday. I'm on dinner tonight, but I can't do it. I just can't do it."

There was a pause. I pictured Regina as she was when we closed the restaurant together, curls falling loose from her ponytail, gold rings clinking as she poured me a glass of Sancerre.

"On Tuesday?" she said.

"Yeah."

"Was she— Could she have been down there?"

No. Impossible. "I don't know." *Milo is lying.* "Her train goes right under Cortlandt."

"Jesus, Anna."

I didn't know if I was lying. I only knew I wasn't telling the truth. It made my stomach sour, to be using the city's tragedy as an excuse. But the truth was too messy, too unclear for me to try to explain.

"Are you okay?"

"I don't know," I told her. "But I can't get fired. I need money."

"Don't worry about that. Don't worry. It's a skeleton staff here anyway. Everything's out of whack."

"I don't have to come in?"

"God, no," she said. "Not now."

In a great slump of relief, I leaned against the wall and knocked into a poster, a reproduction of Picasso's *Girl Before a Mirror* that you'd bought framed at MoMA at the beginning of the summer. It slid from the wall and crashed into the wood floor, the glass shattering.

"What was that?"

Glass glittered over the floor. I squatted to get a better look.

"Anna?"

"It's okay," I said. "I just dropped something."

Regina let out a small laugh. "Yeah," she said. "No serving tables for you tonight."

I smiled. The glass was so beautiful—pieces small as silt, and they were everywhere. I pressed my finger against them and brought it up near my eye. "Thanks."

"Take care, okay? Call us when you know more."

I hung up the phone. There were glass shards of all sizes and shapes, like sand on a beach but sharp enough to cut, all over the floor. I grabbed a small broom and dustpan from under the sink and swept them up, then poured the glass from the dustpan into a mug. I carried it into the living room and dumped the glass shards into a small pile next to the pigment powders I'd made the day before, lining everything up on the coffee table.

This was good. I was onto something.

In my bedroom, I slipped the glass from all my photo frames. My vanity mirror, too. I cleared off the kitchen table, laid down sheets of foil, and put all the glass on top. I put on a pair of sunglasses to protect my eyes and used a hammer to crush it all up. *Whap whap whap.* The sound was delicious, and the feeling of it—turning solid things to sand—filled my whole body with a kind of optimism I hadn't felt since art school.

When I'd amassed enough, I divided the glass into more cups and bowls and mugs and mixed a different pigment powder into each. I plucked a fat sable brush from the box under your bed and started with the red, pressing the bristles into the shimmery pigment. I made a long, curvilinear line on the gessoed door and stood back to take in the effect—the color looked alive and otherworldly, shimmering and smooth and loose, like nothing I'd ever seen before.

Yes, I thought, a sense of calm weighing down my shoulders. *I've done it.*

When the buzzer rang, I was in a trance, my brush tracing and retracing the same long, flowing lines. I didn't understand what I was making yet, but I understood that it had power.

I went to the kitchen window first, to see if I could get a good look at the stoop, make sure it wasn't Milo.

There was a police cruiser, double-parked in front of our building.

They were here. They'd actually come. I pressed the intercom.

"NYPD." The voice didn't sound gruff and harsh the way it did on TV. This voice was soft, almost apologetic. "I'm responding to reports of a missing person. Could I come up?"

I forced myself to buzz open the door, then set down my brush among the cups of colored glass on the floor next to my painting. My fingers felt numb and fat. The officer was at my door, knocking, and I pulled it open. Only one man, not too much older than me, in his uniform. The gun in his belt holster, the Taser and nightsticks; it all seemed incongruous in our space—a violation, as shocking and grotesque as a subway flasher.

He smiled softly. "Miss Vaughn?"

I didn't want to move. I didn't want him to see my work—I knew he wouldn't understand what I had done to a perfectly good door—but I had no choice. There was no place to run. I let him follow me to the living room. He blinked quickly at the door, at my swooping, glittering lines, but said nothing, only handed me a card. I stared at it. White and blue and gold, with an image of a badge. Officer Michael Tennison. New York Police Department. My hands were dirty with pastel dust. I'd already smudged the card.

The cop took out a small black notebook and a pen. He spoke softly but quickly. "I have some questions about Willow

Whitman. She's your roommate, is that correct? She lives here with you?"

I stuffed the card into the back pocket of my jeans and nodded. "Yes."

"And you know Elizabeth Stone?"

"Lizzie, yes. We all went to college together."

"And you know that Ms. Stone filed a missing persons report on Willow?"

It wasn't right, the way he said your name, too guttural, too heavy. "Yes, of course. I was there when she called."

Officer Tennison jotted something in his notebook. "Her father hasn't heard from her since last week."

I swallowed hard. *Milo is lying.*

"When did you last see Willow, Anna?"

I opened my mouth, but too much was kaleidoscoping in my mind to speak. I looked at my hands, my chewed fingernails, and shook my head. "I worked late on Monday. I was still sleeping when she left for work on Tuesday."

"Monday, then?"

I shook my head. "She doesn't work on Mondays. The galleries are all closed on Mondays. I thought she was just—out. I haven't actually seen her in eight days."

The cop wrote something. "Why didn't you call the police?"

"I didn't realize how long it had been." My voice quavered. "I thought it was only a day. She could have been anywhere for a day, any other day. She's done it before. I kept thinking she'd just come home."

"She's done this before?" He looked up, curious. "Left without telling anyone?"

"Yes."

"When?"

"A few nights this summer, and in college. She left for a weekend once and didn't tell anyone. She was with a guy." I waved my hands dismissively. Jon Potts was no longer relevant to me. *Milo* was the one who was lying now. "I think you need to talk to Milo Arvanitis. He's her ex-boyfriend."

The cop jotted it down. "She was with him when she disappeared?"

"No." I shook my head. "She was with another guy. Jon Potts. But I think—"

He looked at me, gaze hard and stabbing. "Does Jon Potts live in the city?"

I flinched. I knew what he was thinking; I'd thought the same thing just hours ago. "He was staying at a friend's place off Bleecker Street. I don't know if he's still there. I don't know him at all." But Jon Potts wasn't my problem right now. I needed this cop to find Milo before he came back. "Milo knows him, though," I said. "You should ask Milo where he is."

Tennison nodded. "Is there any reason you can think of that Willow would have been in the World Trade Center or around there on Tuesday morning? Any errands? A meeting? Anything like that?"

I shook my head. "We never go down there. I don't even really know what else is there, other than . . ." *the Twin Towers.*

He nodded. "Do you know Mason Montgomery?"

I looked up, surprised. "From Roche Gallery? Yes, he's a friend of Willow's."

The cop wrote something, then flipped his notebook shut. He was going to leave.

"Wait," I said. "What about Mason? Have you talked to him?"

"We'll keep you updated."

I clasped my arms across my chest, as if to keep my heart from jumping through my skin. The cop was turning away. He was heading to the door. I couldn't let him leave. I needed him to promise me that he would get Milo. That he would be the adult. That he would protect me.

I heard your voice in my head then. *You won't tell a soul.* I saw the bruises on your thighs, on your ribs. I could tell this cop what Jon Potts had done to you, if only to get him to ask Milo about what had happened.

I caught the edge of the cop's sleeve. "Sir!"

He turned, chin tucked, eyes narrowed. Waiting.

"They fought," I said. "In college, Milo and Jon fought over her. It was bad. Milo almost got kicked out of Balwin. He lives near the art museum." I paused, took a breath. "He's obsessed with her."

The cop flipped open his notebook again. "And the other man, Mr. Potts?"

I mustered all the good girl I had left in me, looking at the cop so earnestly I almost believed myself. "They didn't keep in touch," I said.

After all, Willow, I had promised to keep your secret.

So that's what I did.

Twenty-Two

ONE YEAR BEFORE

ALL WINTER, Anna worked on her portfolio, determined to forget her humiliation at the Stones' New Year's party. Sex didn't matter. Sex was nothing. Anna's art—her career—was too important to be trumped by one stupid night. So, like every other junior painting major, Anna submitted her résumé, a personal statement, and her portfolio. Like everyone else, she allowed Professor Kape to appraise her and decide her worthiness.

The acceptance came in a brief, ludicrously professional email that Anna read alone in her dorm room:

> Dear Ms. Anna Vaughn,
> I would be honored to serve as
> your senior thesis advisor
> for the 2000–2001 academic year.
> Be prepared to work hard in seminar!
> —Prof. Anthony Kape

Milo had been accepted, too, of course. Once Jon Potts had graduated, Milo was considered *the* painter on campus—and with Willow, the Class of 2001 art star, one half of a badass couple. Jackson and Lee. Diego and Frida. Björk and Matthew. Since sophomore year, Milo had worked in the studio in violent jags, slashing industrial brushes and throwing paint on huge, unprimed canvases, as if it were 1952 and everyone was meeting at the Cedar Tavern later instead of the Bar Car. Everyone loved him—the professors, the younger students, anyone who stopped in the gallery on the main floor of the art building where his work seemed to always be on view.

Anna didn't understand what was so great about *the artist's hand*—all that ego. To her, Milo's paintings were sloppy and trite, though she'd never say that out loud. And what did it matter? Anna had won, too. Anna, Milo, and four other guys.

Our woman-painter, Kape called her on the first day of senior seminar. No longer Miss Hollywood, but *Lee* (for Krasner) or *Elaine* (for de Kooning). It made Anna feel second-tier. It made her feel like somebody's wife.

Like Kape himself, the men in the class were all self-conscious grandsons of Abstract Expressionism, messy and predictable. Anna was so tired of Ab-Ex by then—the tedium of its masturbatory heroics. She had moved on. What she cared about now was intricacy and blood and fragility. She was inspired by Kusama and Bourgeois and Schneemann and, most of all, Ana Mendieta. In Kape's senior seminar, she began her magnum opus—mixing different shades of red, painting them on poster board, then punching out thousands of tiny dots and stitching each one onto sailcloth, creating the first undulating wave of what would come to be *Swell*. She worked without notice, without praise, without even eye contact from her advisor.

The first crit took place a month into the semester, and Anna pinned a two-foot-square portion of the project to the board. She had a bruise on her palm from the puncher. Some nights she dreamed only in red. She loved this work, the way it rolled and transformed, the way it signified beauty in violence. She had never made anything better.

Kape smoothed his goatee. "Very pretty."

The men in the room—these guys who all made the same giant altarpieces to their own machismo and privilege—sniggered.

"I see elements of craft," said one.

"Textile art, yeah," another said. "Like a quilt."

Someone snorted, and Anna's skin prickled. They didn't get it. Not at all. She stared at Kape, but he wouldn't meet her eye. She understood what was happening. Kape wanted to tear her down. He wanted to smash a wrecking ball into her ego. He wanted to scrape her ambition and skill and talent and put her into her place.

These men would never consider Anna an equal. To them, she would always be a girl making pretty pictures. A sideshow. It made her think, bitterly, that maybe Willow had been right, even if she had been joking that night at the Stones' party. Maybe the only reason she was in that room right then, one of the chosen six, was because of her body, and what she had allowed Kape to do to it that night.

Anna swallowed. Her heart went hard. Her face felt like chiseled stone. She would prove herself, one way or the other. She would catapult herself so far beyond these stupid boys, so far beyond the orbit of Kape and Balwin that she would pretend that they'd meant nothing to her. She would win. She would stop at nothing to win.

———

Kape hung a selection of his advisees' paintings in the Highsmith Gallery, which included so much of Milo's work that the kids in class joked it was his first solo show. The only thing of Anna's he included was the blood portrait she'd made the year before, which she'd called *Rosie*, after Duchamp's female alter ego, Rrose Sélavy.

Lizzie brought a joint over to Anna's room and they went to the opening giddy and stoned. That night, Highsmith was crowded and creepy and just off from what it was meant to be. Students wore neon and costumes and sipped wine from plastic cups. Teachers smoked out in the open, as if they were all peers.

Lizzie gazed at Milo's paintings—canvases as big as walls covered in jagged peach, ocher, and rust strokes, each with a not-so-subtle black *V* in its center.

"Are they *vaginas*?" Her voice was incredulous over the uneven din of the crowd. She'd slicked her hair back to show off the tiny hoops curling wormlike up her ear.

"Oh god." Anna rolled her eyes and caught someone familiar

walking into the room. She didn't recognize him at first—he'd buzzed off his hair after he graduated two years ago. He wasn't wearing glasses. But it was him—Jon Potts—and he was holding hands with a pretty blond Pi Phi in a dress and making his way toward Professor Kape.

"Listen." Lizzie, unaware, read from Milo's artist statement. "'They are called *Origins*.'" She giggled. "'The origin of our species'—Jesus Christ. He might as well have named it *Cunts*."

Anna flinched at the word; to disguise her reaction, she grabbed Lizzie's arm. "Jon Potts is here. Why would he come back here?"

Lizzie turned to look. "That's Poppy Ruel. They're together. Or he came for Kape—he was always Kape's pet."

Lizzie didn't seem very affected by his presence, but she didn't know the truth. She still thought Willow's disappearance sophomore year was a *lark*. They had all let Willow retell the story to suit her, except Anna. Because Anna was the only one who'd seen the bruises on Willow's arm and thigh. She was the only one who'd seen Willow's eyes that morning, the day after she returned, the hardness there that hadn't gone away. Anna was the only one who knew that Willow's black eye was just the start of it.

"Oh no," Lizzie said.

Willow was approaching Jon. She held a stack of papers to her chest. Anna froze, bracing for a confrontation. But Willow was smiling. It was Jon who took a step back. Jon who crossed his arms over his chest. Willow shook the Pi Phi's hand and gave them each a sheet of paper from her stack.

"What's she holding?" Anna asked. "What's she giving them?"

"Wills!" Lizzie shouted, and Willow looked over at them. She smiled at a stone-faced Jon, then walked toward her friends. She was so casual, so *normal*, and Anna had a flash of doubt: Had Willow lied to her? Anna saw Willow laughing on the floor at the Car, and Lizzie's face. *Her mom's fine. She lives in Paris.* She felt Willow's breath in her ear. *You should fuck him.* These things that Willow had done, the tricks and lies and larks—Anna believed they were Jon Potts's fault. That Jon Potts had done something so awful to Willow that it had changed her, made her mean. But now, watching Willow smile, watching Jon step back, she wondered where the lies actually began.

Willow was in front of her, still smiling, holding out a paper. "Save the date," she said.

The paper was in Anna's hand. She looked down:

HIGHSMITH ART GALLERY AT BALWIN UNIVERSITY PRESENTS
WILLOW WHITMAN: MUSE
DECEMBER 2, 2000

Willow's opening was on Anna's twenty-second birthday, in that strange, liminal time between Thanksgiving and Christmas, when everything slowed and nobody showed up where they were supposed to. Willow had been angry about the timing, afraid people wouldn't bother to come. She was wrong.

It was a mild night for December, almost balmy. Anna slipped on a gauzy black nightgown from the thrift store, her combat boots, and a men's duster and met up with Lizzie at Rector. They knew a bit about Willow's project—how she'd recruited different people to take photos of her in different places, sometimes allowing the *clicker* (as she called the person snapping the shutter) to dress and pose her. To put her exactly where they wanted.

Anna hadn't been allowed to see the pictures she had taken of Willow, smoking in the backseat of her Mercedes, before the opening that night. Anna wasn't even allowed to tell anyone which pictures she had shot. No one was. Anonymity was the whole point, Willow said, and she made all her clickers sign NDAs, like a professional.

———

When Lizzie pulled open the door to Highsmith Gallery, the noise was the first thing Anna noticed. Then the crowd. There were so many people milling about—students, professors, even some of the administration staff—and everyone was whispering, exclaiming, and pointing. So many more people had gathered for Willow's solo show than for the Kape advisees' group show.

It was a stroke of genius, Anna realized, getting other people invested in her work like this. *Including* them in the art.

All of Willow's photographs were small in scale, 5x7 or 8x10, and they were thumbtacked directly to the gallery walls. People stood in clusters, peering like they would into a dollhouse. Anna walked up to the first picture she saw. It was one of Willow's Mendieta prints: her body naked, her eyes closed, her face covered in dirt. The title was a date: *October 1, 1999.*

Anna walked around the gallery. Some of the pictures were captivating, some stark, some lurid and cringeworthy. Willow had her tongue out in one, giving the middle finger in another. There, she was topless. There, crawling. Anna saw her barefaced and made up like a clown. She could guess which ones were shot by frat guys, which by kiss-ass freshmen, which by professors, and friends, and strangers. Each title, like the first, was a date.

Anna understood that this was the culmination of Willow's work. All those years studying beautiful women in beautiful pictures—Dora Maar and Edie Sedgwick and Camille Claudel, Francesca Woodman and Ana Mendieta. That had always been Willow's goal: to be a muse, a flattened, perfected image—and she'd done it. Willow had done exactly what she set out to do, and it was disturbing. As Anna stepped from photograph to photograph, Willow's face seemed to distort and dematerialize. It was like seeing simulacra developing in real time—images of images. A set of features reproduced so many times that there was no *real self* left at all.

Willow had used one of the pictures Anna had taken—it was pinned in the center, a choice place. In it, Willow's face was pockmarked by shadows, her hair wild around her face, her head thrown back in laughter, her teeth so big and sharp she looked like a leopard. Anna shivered, pulled her coat tighter around her shoulders.

"Hey." Lizzie was back, speaking softly, as if they were in a library. "There's more."

Anna followed her, weaving in and out of little swarms of people into a narrow closet off the side of the main space. It was dark, lit only by the glow of an old TV, and empty except for a single folding chair set in front of the screen.

Anna stood back at first, taking in Willow's silent video of a sidewalk with black gum stains and flecks of broken glass, some shadows, an occasional set of feet walking through. Anna read the title—*2001*—stuck to the wall with vinyl lettering. She frowned. 2001? It was still a month away.

How sad, Anna thought, watching the sidewalk. *How lonely*. Willow had come into the space, silent as a deer, and was standing next to Anna now. Her hair smelled like perfume and smoke.

"I took this in New York over Thanksgiving," she said.

Anna didn't move her eyes from the screen. "I didn't even know you were there."

"I went with my dad. I had an interview."

Now Anna turned to her, brows up and questioning.

"At a gallery," Willow said. "And I got it. I got an internship at a real gallery in New York."

"What?" Anna said. "Starting when?"

"After graduation. And look, my dad is going to sign for an apartment, too. We are all going to go. Lizzie's parents agreed."

Anna's blood went cold. *They're leaving me*, she thought. *They're leaving me behind.*

Willow locked her arm into Anna's. "I want you to be my roommate."

"But I'm applying to Yale in January," Anna said, flooded with relief. "I didn't know. I've already asked for recommendations."

Willow rolled her eyes. "Grad school is child's play, Hollywood. Let's do this for real."

Anna turned back to the screen. The New York sidewalks.

She had already made her choice.

Twenty-Three

THURSDAY EVENING

I LEFT LIZZIE a message. *The cops came. They asked about Mason. Call me.* I turned back to my painting on the door, the swells of curves and shapes. I picked up the brush, but the spell had been broken. My mind was on the cop, and on Milo's lies. I straightened my materials into a small workstation on the floor by my door—powders, glass, brushes, knife—then washed my hands. I had to find out the truth before I could work.

I didn't even bother changing clothes. On the subway on my way to Arcadia, covered in paint dust, I thought about the questions I needed to ask, and whether or not Tyler would answer me. I'd never been properly introduced to him, but I'd ordered drinks from him at Arcadia many times. He was our age, maybe a couple years older, dark skin, a broad smile, and chin-length dark hair parted in the center. I wondered if he would recognize me. If he ever even noticed me.

The train pulled into the Second Avenue station, and I hurried through the drizzle, past twenty-four-hour diners and head shops and the huge new Starbucks and NYU dorms, toward Tompkins Square Park. Finally I was there, damp in front of Arcadia's cement façade, battered with graffiti: LOVE, LOVE, LOVE, it said, bright new peace signs thick as fists, American flags, the kind of red bubble hearts I used to paint as a child. I pulled open the door. Yeasty beer and old cigarettes hit me immediately. The place was quiet, nearly empty, save for a few East Village old-timers at the corner table, long, scraggly hair and faded blue tattoos peeking out from their sleeves, smoking and drinking and minding their own business.

I approached the bar, determined. I'd wait at Arcadia all night if I had to. I had to know once and for all what had happened that morning. What, if anything, Tyler knew.

The bartender turned. *Tyler.* I wouldn't have to wait at all, because he was right here, right in front of me. Stocky and handsome, his thick, wavy black hair tucked behind his ears. He wore a hemp necklace with two yellow beads around his neck and a Grateful Dead T-shirt, the bear smiling at me. Tyler smiled, too—wide, easy. White teeth, dimples, soft little crags around his dark eyes. He slung a paper coaster toward me. "What can I get you?"

I felt weightless for a moment. I stumbled over my thoughts.

"Hey," he said, smile going lopsided. "Is that blood?"

He was looking at my cheek, and I brushed my fingers there. "Just paint," I said.

"Oh right." He took me in. "I recognize you. You hang around Lizzie and them."

His voice was like an echo, repeating in my head: *Lizzie and them. Lizzie and them.* I took a breath to steady myself, to hold my thoughts in place, and clenched my fingers around the bar.

"Tyler, right?"

He smiled. "At your service. Red Stripe?"

"Sure," I said, though I didn't want a goddamned beer. His back turned, and I blurted it out. "Do you know where Willow is?"

Tyler swung back, beer in hand. "Willow?"

I searched his face for a hint that he was lying. "Friend of ours. The blond. The one who always has a camera?"

"Oh, yeah. You meeting her?"

I shook my head, clenched my fingers around the cold bottle. "Did you see her on Tuesday?"

He looked at me sideways. "Tuesday?"

"Milo told me you were meeting up with her." I took a sip of the beer, trying to look normal. Fearless.

But Tyler crossed his arms over his chest. He was frowning at me. "I'm sorry—who?"

I felt like a kid trapped in some kind of trippy fun house. I started to speak, but the air felt too thick to get all the way into my lungs. My hands were wet, my armpits too, but a coldness tingled down the back of my neck. I was right.

"Milo," I repeated, uselessly. "He said he made a deal with you?"

"I think you have the wrong person." Tyler had a small smile on his face but held my gaze unflinchingly, and I felt my heart drop. He was telling the truth. He didn't know Milo. Milo was lying about everything. Milo was nothing but lies.

"Sorry for bothering you," I said, fear thrumming through my body. "It's just . . . I can't find her."

"Oh shit," Tyler said. "Really?"

I nodded and slipped off the barstool. "Sorry," I said again.

"Hey, wait." Tyler set a pen and a napkin on the bar. "Leave your number. I'll ask around."

I wrote down my cell and pushed it across the bar. My hands were shaky. I had to get out of there.

Outside, it was drizzling. A soft, warm rain. Nothing made sense. Milo had been lying, all this time. It could only mean one thing—that he was behind this. As I walked back toward Second Avenue, toward the subway, I tried to picture how it would have happened. Not Tyler, but Milo. At his apartment, his roommate gone. He'd enticed you back there. But you didn't want to stay. You were sick of him. You were bored of him. And you knew about me. Maybe you tried to leave, and he wouldn't let you. He couldn't let you go. He loved you too much. He was obsessed with you. That was how these things usually went.

Down Avenue A, dodging bodies on Houston, walking fast. I thought of Milo's fist on my door. The broken gesso. How he'd nearly gotten kicked out sophomore year for threatening Jon Potts. I shook my head, trying to detangle the thoughts. It just didn't fit. Milo could have done worse to me today. He could have hurt me. He never touched Jon Potts.

The street was sticky and wet and smelled like the Arcadia bathrooms at two a.m. Your face tumbled around in my head. Your *MUSE* show—the way you'd flattened yourself. Over and over again, so many images of you that the real you seemed no longer to exist. *You'll never tell a soul.* I shoulder-checked a middle-aged man in a newsboy cap. I heard his apology as if it were underwater, turned my head, and stopped as suddenly as if I'd walked into glass.

Just across First Avenue, headed to the F train, a flash of

white-blond hair—*your hair*. A flash of a face. The girl turned away, and my heart started again. The yellow-and-blue Hermès scarf around your neck. The scarf from the drawer. My heart lifted. Milo hadn't taken it. You were wearing it right now.

"Willow!"

But you were already halfway down the subway steps, disappearing underground.

I ran into the street, only slightly aware of the taxi that screeched its brakes, the cyclist swerving away from me. People shouted. I held up my hand—to stop them, to apologize, I didn't know. I bolted across the street, sandals splashing water up my calves, making my jeans stick nauseatingly to my skin.

I made it to the other side. I ran down the subway steps, tripping on my wet shoes at the bottom. I landed hard on my knees and palms, but I didn't feel a thing. Only the loudness in my ears, the aching inside my head. The subway station felt like a video game—an enormous tiled chamber with so many different entrances and exits and hallways and stairwells and turnstiles and gates. I was on the wet, dirty ground, groping through the crowd with my eyes.

You were gone.

"Willow!" I shouted. *"Goddamn it!"*

People stared at me. Stepped away.

The subway walls were plastered with flyers of missing people. So many faces. I remained for a moment on hands and knees, facing those faces. So many eyes on me, so many people. It had been you—*hadn't* it? That hair, that scarf. No one else looked like that.

I got back to my feet, convincing myself. *It was you.*

It had to be you.

Twenty-Four

FOUR MONTHS BEFORE

DURING THEIR FINAL DAYS at Balwin, life was full. Exams and final projects were finished, with graduation still a week away. Parties took place every day and night, all over campus. The wind blew crab apple and redbud and cherry blossom petals over the grass like confetti, and everything felt like a celebration.

Despite Professor Kape's contempt for Anna in class, he'd given her an A in seminar. *Swell* had ballooned to ten feet in length, with thousands of red circles sewn into the shape of the sea. *Swell* wasn't sexy like Willow's photographs or Milo's paintings. It wasn't political like Lizzie's comic book or commercial like Boomer's designs. It wouldn't land her a job in corporate America. But it undulated and throbbed and bled, and it was special. She knew that, even if no one else did.

Anna ended her college career with a near-perfect GPA, which made her happy but ultimately didn't matter. She hadn't even bothered to finish her Yale application, which was probably a good thing, since Kape had never finished his recommendation letter. In a month, she was moving to New York City. They were all going. Boomer had been recruited by an advertising company, Milo and Tom would do house painting, and Lizzie didn't need a job. Everyone told Anna she could be a restaurant hostess—all she needed was her pretty face. Willow had found the apartment and her father had acted as guarantor, so Anna didn't need to ask her parents for anything. She had signed her name on the lease. It was more than she could afford, but it didn't matter. It would only be a matter of time before she caught up to her potential and got a gallery and shows and the fame and wealth she deserved.

Anna was unpinning a poster of Cindy Sherman's *Untitled Film Stills* from her dorm wall when Willow swung open the door, padded over to Anna's bed, and lit a cigarette.

"I can't wait to get out of here," Willow said. "Eat my dust, Balwin."

Anna frowned as she rolled the poster into a tight tube. Her room already looked empty. "I'm going to miss it."

"Ha." Willow tutted. "Just wait till you get to the city. You'll never look back."

Anna stuffed the tube into a milk crate. "I know," she said, but she didn't believe it. She was nostalgic for Balwin already.

"Hey, can you meet me by the lake tonight?" Willow said.

"Aren't you going to the faculty party?"

Every year before graduation, the Highsmith professors held a gathering for the seniors, with grown-up drinks and grown-up cheese-and-fruit plates, a way to usher them into adulthood. This year it would take place at the dean's house on Maple Street.

"Yeah, yeah," Willow said. "But I want to do a few last-minute portraits of you first."

Over the past three and a half years, Willow had asked Anna to pose for her a number of times. Anna enjoyed it. She liked to have Willow tell her what to wear and how to arrange her face and body and where to stand and what to look at. Sometimes Willow showed her the results, but mostly she kept them to herself. Anna was curious, but she figured Willow would show her eventually. Willow always had a plan.

"Can you?" she asked again.

"Sure, of course," Anna said. "What should I wear?"

Willow looked her up and down slowly. "Doesn't matter," she said after a moment. "I'll dress you there."

Anna moved to her bookshelf, started pulling paperbacks off the shelf and dividing them into two piles—sell back to the bookstore or keep. Most of them she would sell back. She needed as much money as she could get for New York.

"Nine o'clock, okay?" Willow said. "It won't take long. We'll go to the party right after."

Anna nodded. "Is anyone else coming?"

Willow winked. "Just us chickens."

Anna prepared herself: short skirt, tight cap-sleeved T-shirt, combat boots, black eyeliner, and red lipstick. Mostly her group had moved on from the thrift store wares, but the boots Anna couldn't give up. She stuffed her keys and ID into her wristlet and headed out to Wabash Lake. It was a mile from the dorm, and she left as the sun began to set, about eight thirty.

It was a nice walk, warm and windy, the air full of pollen. By the time she made it to the edge of the lake, things were quiet. All the students would be converging on the Maple Street frats, starting their nights with keg stands and shots and bong hits. Wabash Lake was small and man-made, a forty-acre hole dug in the 1950s so Balwin could recruit a crew team. Now it was mostly used for sorority sunbathing and as a place for frat boys to show off. Anna had come out a few times in the past four years, but only when the weather was ideal and she had nothing better to do. She'd almost always rather be at the Bar Car, drinking, or at Highsmith, working.

Twilight was fading. The sky was a deep, unnatural blue, the color of a kyanite stone, with high, thin clouds. The trees around her were sketches, silhouettes. A breeze caught, and Anna shivered. She looked around, but Willow had not yet arrived. She sat on a large rock and tilted her face upward to watch the sky darken.

A rustling behind her—then a fumbling, laughing sound. A male voice—deep and slurring to incomprehension. Anna turned quickly, fear rousing her, sharpening her. There was no one else at the lake. No one to help her.

But then—Willow's voice, a hoarse whisper: "Hollywood!"

Anna turned and saw them. Willow, dragging a stumbling, disoriented Jon Potts.

Willow's eyes looked strange in the dimness. Dull and colorless.

"Help me," she said, panting.

Anna hopped from the rock. "What are you doing? Why is he here?"

"Take his arm," Willow said, and Anna did. She pulled his arm over her shoulder, and they carried him to the rocks together.

Anna's heart pounded in her chest. She thought of Willow's icicle eyes and her hard voice. *I will get him back. And you won't tell a soul when I do.*

And now, Jon Potts was lying on the ground in front of them, nearly passed out, a lazy smile lingering on his lips. There were rocks everywhere. Rocks big enough to smash a skull.

"Why is he here?" Anna asked again.

"Pi Phi formal," Willow said. "It's tomorrow night."

Anna's hands tingled and she shook them, but the feeling wouldn't come back. "Willow . . ."

But Willow wasn't looking at her. She was arranging Jon on the ground. She was, Anna saw with a wave of panic, pulling down his shorts.

"What did you do to him?" Anna asked, but she already knew. She could tell by the way he flopped about. His blissful lethargy. The way he braced his hands on the dirt. Anna knew, because she had felt that way once, too. The day that Willow had given her the joint laced with ketamine on the beach.

Willow pulled her camera from her messenger bag and began attaching a lens.

"Did you—" Anna was breathing hard, trying to get the words out. "Did you *drug* him?"

Willow looked at Anna. "Are you going to help me or not?"

Anna stared at Jon, prone and splayed, his shorts and boxers clumped around his ankles. His penis was small and limp, and it was true that she hated him. He'd changed Willow. He'd hurt her. Violated her. She thought of Boomer and of Kape, and of herself. She thought of Edie Sedgwick and Dora Maar and Camille Claudel—muses of the past, all ground to dust by the men who idolized them. She thought of Willow's exhibition. Her disintegrated face.

"You know he's at Yale now, right?" Willow said.

Anna's breath caught. "The MFA program?"

"Yeah. That stupid chick, Poppy, is following him after graduation. Going to New Haven." Willow said, her voice bitter. "She thinks she landed such a *winner*."

Anna and Willow stood together, looking down at the man on the ground. They understood the deep unfairness that he epitomized, and they knew its trajectory. He would continue to take and take and take from the women in his life, to bleed them dry. He didn't deserve to have a girlfriend, or to go to Yale and become a professor, only to prey on young women. He didn't deserve his life at all.

"What do you want me to do?" Anna asked.

Willow smiled, barely. "Take off your clothes."

Anna stiffened. "What? Why?"

"I won't get your face, I promise," Willow said. "This is about him."

"Are you crazy?"

Willow's eyes flashed. "Am *I* crazy? Are you serious? He *raped* me, Anna."

"I know, but—"

"I told you I was going to get him back. You said you'd help me."

"Not like this, Wills," Anna said. "Come on."

"No." Willow's face was stone. "Aren't you sick of this? Don't you get tired of being belittled? Ignored? Girls like us, Anna, it's up to us. We need to fight back."

Anna bit her lip. *Girls like us.* She had felt it in so many ways.

The push-pull of attention. Of scrutiny. They were pretty girls. They existed to be looked at, touched, stripped, prodded—and to enjoy it, to feel *grateful* for it.

"If you don't help me, you're just as complicit as he is."

That's not fair, Anna thought, but she recognized a kernel of truth in what Willow was saying. The light cut across her friend's face, and for a moment she looked like glass. *Girls like us.* There were so many of them—women with bruises and broken faces, dead women, women in institutions—all because they'd won the desire of a master, a man who circled their bodies like a lion going in for a kill, ripping them apart, not with teeth and claws, but with eyes and paintbrushes.

Men got away with so much, calling themselves masters.

Calling women muses.

"He doesn't deserve a thing from you," Willow said. "Not one ounce of pity."

"I'm not thinking about him right now. I'm thinking about me."

"What do you want? I'll give you anything."

What *did* Anna want? Success and admiration, not for her sexuality or the way she looked, but for her skill. For her *work*. She wanted forgiveness and true love. She wanted what men like Jon Potts got for just existing.

"Power," Anna said. "I want power."

Willow smiled a closed-mouth smile. "Exactly. You help me now, and I promise I'll make it up to you. When the time comes."

Anna's breath was shallow. She had to believe Willow. She untied her boots, peeled off her shirt, unzipped her jeans.

"Not all the way," Willow said.

Anna stopped, shirt off, bra on. The air was cold. She was shivering. She did what Willow told her. She lay on the ground, flat on her back. She let Willow tug her jeans over her hips. She closed her eyes. She was slipping through time. She felt feral, like an infant or an animal. She pulled her arms over her head, let her legs splay. She let Willow roll Jon's unconscious body on top of her own, let her wrap his limp hands around her wrists. She knew what it would look like from above, through the god's eye of a camera lens.

She had to trust Willow now.

That's all she could do.

Twenty-Five

THURSDAY NIGHT

I PULLED OPEN the door to Happiness and walked into a wall of smoke, dim lights, and lazy, throbbing music, heading for our usual booth in the back. Lizzie and Tom sat at the table with bottles of Red Stripe in front of them, the plastic ashtray full of wasted hours.

"I saw her." I was out of breath, my lungs starving for air, my voice unnatural. "I saw Willow."

Lizzie's eyes snapped, pupils shifting like an aperture into focus. "What?"

"She was in the city," I said. "I went to Arcadia."

"Wills was at Arcadia?"

"No," I said, too loudly. "I saw her in the subway. Getting on the F train in the East Village. I tried to catch her, but she ran away."

Tom lifted his eyebrows, eyes wide. "You talked to her?"

"Jesus Christ." I rubbed my palms all over my face. "No. You're not listening. She ran away."

Lizzie and Tom glanced at each other.

"Are you sure it was her?" Tom said.

"She's messing with me—with us," I said, because as soon as I saw you, Willow, I *knew*. I understood what was happening. "I think Milo is in on it, too."

"Hey." Tom pulled out a chair. "Sit down."

"No!" I didn't want to *sit*. I didn't want to drink and dally and pretend anymore. "Can't you see what's happening?"

Lizzie and Tom went goggle-eyed. I had the urge to smash bottles against the wall, to make a scene. I held my fists at my sides, my knees bobbing, but I held it together.

"Babe." Lizzie took one of my hands in hers, pulling me gently to the chair. She was trying to placate me, but it only made me more furious. Why couldn't they see who you were—who you *really* were?

"No one has seen Willow in over a week," Lizzie said. "She hasn't called her dad. The police are looking for her. You really think she would do that to everyone, just to mess with you?"

I opened my mouth—*Willow is capable of anything*—but I couldn't get myself to speak.

Lizzie fumbled around trying to light another cigarette. She was pale, even in the reddish light of the bar. She looked unwell. She looked *terrified*. Tom took the Zippo and lit her Parliament for her. She exhaled toward the ceiling and spoke without looking at me.

"Milo's worried about you."

My mouth contorted. "What? Worried about what?"

"He's been saying some stuff."

"About me?"

Lizzie and Tom were quiet. It was only a moment, but it was too long.

"What?" I demanded. "What did he say?"

Tom's mouth stretched downward in a grimace. "He told me you tried to hire someone—that you wanted to have Willow jumped."

The bottom of my stomach dropped out. *He told them.*

"It's insane, actually," Lizzie said, looking at me cautiously. "You wouldn't do that. Would you?"

"I wouldn't—" My hands were flat on my chest. "I didn't do that."

"I didn't think so." Lizzie flicked her gaze to Tom. He was watching me, studying me, as if he wasn't as sure.

"I don't understand," I said, but I did understand. I understood completely. It was you, Willow. You were telling Milo what to say, what to do. The whole situation *stunk* of one of your larks. My hands were still on my chest, like I was protecting myself from what was coming.

Twenty-Six

FOUR MONTHS BEFORE

ANNA'S FAMILY was somewhere on campus, but she didn't look for them; there would be plenty of time for that after the ceremony. In her cap and gown, a disposable plastic thing that felt more like wearing a Halloween costume than an actual robe, she walked to North Lawn to meet her friends. The sun was stark and hot, but everything smelled of lilac and freshly mown grass, and it was beautiful. Anna surveyed the crowd, and the tension in her bones softened. She saw Willow's father, and all the professors she'd had over the past four years, and she was happy. There were so many people, and they would all see her graduate.

She meandered around the lawn, looking for Willow or Lizzie, someone to stand with until the music began and everyone had to take their seats. Students clumped in little packs, groups of friends, but she wasn't jealous anymore. She didn't need to be. She had that now; she was on her way to having everything.

A bulky figure in robes came rushing up—Boomer. She smiled at him as she always did, to hide the hard pit of humiliation she'd swallowed years ago. But Boomer wasn't smiling back. His brows were high on his face, lips pulled down.

"What's wrong?" Anna said.

"You haven't seen?"

"Seen what?"

A bead of sweat slid down Anna's spine. Bad news. She could sense it.

Boomer rubbed his lips and pulled a crumpled paper from inside his sleeve. It was a Xerox copy of something. Black and white. A photograph.

Anna didn't want to take it. She didn't want to see. "What is it?"

Boomer stretched out his hand, rustling the paper in front of her. "I think it's you."

She grabbed it then, because she had no choice, and her heart dove into her stomach. Boomer was right—it was her, her shirt hiked over her bra, her jeans around her ankles, her body prone on the shore of Wabash Lake. It was Anna, her face—*her face*—torqued to the side and scrunched as if in pain. Jon Potts was on top of her, his hands appearing to pin down her arms.

Underneath, there was a message: *JON POTTS IS A RAPIST.*

"It looks like—"

Anna stopped Boomer from saying more. "Where did you find this?"

He shifted on his feet.

"Where?" she asked again. "Where the fuck was it?"

He looked hopeless. "They're everywhere, Anna."

That bitch. That fucking bitch.

Willow had used her. She'd manipulated Anna into taking off her clothes. Into letting her pose Jon's body on top of her own. Absolutely exposed except for her own hair covering her face. Willow had promised no one would see it. And Anna, stupid, stupid Anna, had believed her.

Jon Potts had violated Willow. But in return, Willow had violated Anna.

Betrayed her.

I'll kill her, Anna thought as she ripped the Xerox into pieces. *I'll fucking kill her.*

She stomped across the lawn in her gown, pushing her hair and sweat out of her face. She felt people watching her. Eyes like thumbs in an orange peel, prying her open.

They know. They all fucking know.

"Anna, wait!"

Boomer was following her. She didn't turn around. How could she? She had to find all the pictures and destroy them before her parents and—*oh god*—before Henry saw them. Anna was running now, across North Lawn, because she knew exactly where to go.

Maple Street. The frat houses. She was panting. Her face was wet. The plastic gown was sticking to her skin. There was SAE. She ran up to the front door and saw herself. All over the door. All over the ramshackle porch. Her body. Her face. She bent down and started to pick up the papers. Then she heard laughter—female laughter. She heard *Willow*.

She turned, but no—it was just some random girls. They were on the sidewalk in robes, arms linked, headed to the ceremony. They weren't even looking at her. Anna felt the sting of tears. She knew it was useless, trying to get rid of all these pictures. There were too many. She'd never get them all. She sank to the ground and started to cry.

"Hey."

It was Boomer. He'd followed her all the way here.

"Come on," he said. "Get up. I'll help you."

Anna could barely look at him. Her humiliation was happening all over again. "Where's Willow?" Her voice was hoarse. She was so angry.

"Willow?" Boomer said. He didn't understand. He didn't know.

Anna's carefully applied makeup was smeared on her face. She glanced at him, her expression grim.

He rolled back on his heels. "Why would she do that to you?"

"I need to find her," Anna said. *"Now."*

Boomer dropped his hand to her, a rope, a lifeline. She took it, and he pulled her up. "I think she's at Highsmith."

They found Willow in the hallway near the faculty offices, still hanging up her pictures. Anna raced toward her, fingers clenched into fists to keep herself from reaching out and tightening her hands around her best friend's neck.

"No one knows it's you, Hollywood, chill," Willow said.

Anna clenched her teeth. "Everyone knows!"

Willow pulled Anna into the girls' bathroom and stood

against the door, blocking anyone from coming in. She unstuck one of the Xerox copies from the wall.

"Look," she said, thrusting it at Anna. "You can barely see your face."

Anna batted it away. "My family is here!"

"I didn't put them on the lawn, Jesus Christ. I did SAE and Pi Phi and Highsmith, where that stupid Poppy girl would find them. Your family will never see them."

"How could you do this?" Anna was shouting. Her hands were on her chest. "To *me*, Wills, after everything?"

Willow turned icy. She stepped closer. She pointed a finger in Anna's face. "It's not about you, Anna. For once, it's not about you."

Anna remembered how Willow had looked that day on her bed: eyes as sharp and cold as icicles, face so hard, so determined. *You won't tell a soul.*

"You're such a liar, Willow. You lie about everything." Anna was spitting. "You're a goddamn *psychopath*."

"You know what happened to me," Willow said, her finger jabbing into Anna's chest. "You know what he did."

"That doesn't give you the right—"

"I told you what I was going to do."

"No," Anna said, shaking her head. "You said you were going to ruin *his* life. Not *mine*."

Willow was silent for a moment. She crossed her arms over her chest and looked at her nails, painted red. "I actually thought you'd like it."

"What?"

"The attention." Willow's eyes had emptied. Her face was different. "You know, the thing you're so fucking desperate for."

Anna's mouth opened. But Willow stopped her from speaking. She was smirking.

"So desperate that you'd almost kill your baby brother for it."

Anna felt the air go out of her. She reached out a hand to steady herself against the wall.

A banging on the door. "It's three o'clock," Boomer said from the other side. "Everyone's lining up. You guys are going to need to work out whatever this is later."

One last look at Anna, and Willow pulled open the door and walked out.

Anna let the door close. Her hands clenched into fists. She squeezed her face and let out a silent scream and jumped in place. Then she picked up all the crumpled papers and shoved them into the trash can. She felt electric. There were hundreds of these pictures all over campus. She had to get each one. She had to stop whatever was happening.

She crashed down the metal steps at Highsmith, grabbing papers off the wall, every footfall an explosion, and pressed her way back outside. Sticky with sweat, she cut across campus the same way she'd come, back down Maple Street, past SAE and Pi Phi, picking up and ripping down every page she found along the way. By the time she got back to North Lawn, her face was flushed, her makeup had gone sticky, and her cap was missing. She had a stack of xeroxed pages in her hands, and she spotted her parents waiting for her.

Her father shifted uncomfortably in his suit, the thin hair around his ears damp, his face pink. Her mother's sundress, a full size too large, gave her the flimsy look of a ghost; one sinewy arm was hooked around Henry's shoulders. Anna's blood ran cold at the sight of her family. She wadded the papers into a basketball-size black-and-white clump and looked around North Lawn for a garbage can.

"We were looking for you," her father said.

Anna searched his face for some hint that he'd seen—the photograph, or the dark thing inside her. There was nothing beyond his usual apathy.

"I was at the studios," she said. "Something came up."

Henry pointed at the wad of paper in her hands. "What's that?"

"Nothing," she said quickly. "Trash."

Anna gestured behind her to where her classmates were taking their places, standing excitedly in alphabetical order, like preschoolers, waiting for the procession.

Her father leaned in, kissed her cheek. "We are so proud of you, honey."

Anna smiled, relieved, then looked at her mother. Her eyes were cold and hard. She did not blink. She took Anna's arm and pinched the skin under her gown until it hurt. "We'll talk later."

She knows, Anna thought. *She saw.* She tightened her grip on the wad of papers, a sour cramp of dread in her stomach.

Anna had nowhere to put the papers. She couldn't just drop them on the ground where anyone could pick them up. She had to hold them; she had to keep them close. She kept her eyes on the grass and found her place in line. She would not turn her head. She would not look at Willow, just seven people over. But she could feel her. Willow's gaze was hot. The other gazes, too. Anna looked ahead, the wad crooked in her arm like a baby, and kept face straight. Chin high. Eyes dry.

She would not break. Not for Willow. Not now. Not ever.

"Pomp and Circumstance" swelled, and the seniors settled, quieting, readying for the spectacle of themselves. They began to walk.

⎯

The hot sun. Metal chairs in the grass. The dean came to the dais, a giant man, fat and white with dyed black hair and a face like a blister—bulging eyes and a swollen, lopsided mouth. Anna couldn't hear a thing he said. She held her paper ball with both hands and felt like she was someplace else, like she was floating over her hot metal chair. This man looked exactly like Diego Rivera, she thought, and pictured him rutting atop Frieda Kahlo's broken body. She tasted bile.

⎯

Applause. Anna blinked and saw Anthony Kape rise in the dean's place, his gown matching Anna's, his tassels gold. He took the stage and breathed into the microphone. Anna felt that she might ignite. She gripped the sides of the chair. Why had she done it? Why had she let Willow destroy her?

"Hollywood."

Anna turned and saw Willow's perfect profile—her fat lips and small, sloped nose, her expression beatific as she listened to Kape's speech. Willow hadn't been the one calling to her. Anna looked down the line of students and saw Ryan Zimmerman, ringlets wild and free under her cap, watching her. Anna could tell by the look on her face that Ryan had seen. She had seen everything, from the start.

They were graduating now. The rows of students ahead of her had all stood and walked across the stage. It was her turn. She still held the wad of papers in her hands. She wouldn't set it down. She'd rather die than leave those papers in the grass. As she stood, as she walked toward the stage, she pulled the wad apart and stuffed the pages down the sleeves of her gown. She was sure she looked ridiculous. Stuffed like a turkey. She had no choice.

Anna watched the students ahead climb the steps to the stage, as if through the wrong end of a telescope. Willow was behind her. Ryan too. She felt like they were marching her down a wooden plank. To a guillotine. To a rope. Anna became very small, sunken inside herself. The hoots and applause of the crowd was revolting. Her name would come. She was already moving forward. She would walk onstage and accept her diploma, her honors, her reward, but it didn't mean anything now.

That part of her life was over.

Twenty-Seven

THURSDAY NIGHT

I STUMBLED DOWN Court Street like I was drunk, past the bodega and the laundromat, not thinking, just pushing forward, toward home. Toward the truth. Toward *you*. As I turned onto Congress Street, I spotted a black town car double-parked in front of our building, idling with its lights on. My stomach did a somersault.

"Anna!" The voice was loud, authoritative, more like the cops on television than the man who had come to the apartment. I fumbled with my key, trying to get it into the lock quickly, quickly, but my hands were shaking so badly the key ring tumbled right out of my grasp.

The car door slammed behind me. The voice again. Louder. "Anna! Wait!"

I was unwilling to face whatever was coming out of that car. I bent down to retrieve the keys, but I was too slow. Footsteps, up the stoop. The key went in. Nothing had ever felt so urgent—I needed to be inside—I needed to close the door behind me. I needed to get away. A hand landed on my shoulder. I didn't want to turn around. I couldn't, I wouldn't. I dipped my shoulder and pushed open the door.

"Anna, please."

I reared back. *Your father.* Clean in a crisp white shirt and pressed black slacks, hooded eyes, cropped hair. My legs twitched. I wanted to flee. I wanted to collapse into him.

"Please," he said. "We need to talk."

I don't remember answering him, but we were inside the building, together, and I was leading him up the stairs. When I opened the door and stepped inside our apartment, I smelled the fresh cigarette smoke first—*Willow's back!* But then I saw the place.

Trashed. The kitchen junk drawer had been overturned. Dead batteries and pen caps and bottle tops and paper-wrapped chopsticks and take-out menus were scattered over the floor. The oven door hung open. A chair was overturned.

"What the—" your dad said. "Were you robbed?"

I walked, stunned, into the living room. "I don't know. . . ." Pillows were ripped off the couch. Papers scattered. My neat piles of smashed glass and pigment powder spilled onto the floor like dust. Our home had been ransacked. I ran into my bedroom. The painted door was still there, intact. My paintings were still on the walls, my drawers tucked in tight. My room was untouched.

Your dad stood in the midst of the wreckage of your room—books torn from their shelves, magazines and papers littered across the floor. Your photographs had been knocked out of their frames. Your clothes ripped from the closet and cast off like candy wrappers. Trash and paper and fabric strewn all over.

"Who would do this?" Your father's blue eyes were as bright as yours but bulging uncomfortably. His cheeks were puffed like Henry's after a steroid treatment. A fear seized my heart, a fear that your father might be on the verge of some grand medical crisis.

"Who?" he asked again, his voice tissue-paper thin.

"I don't know." Nothing about this made sense. Why would anyone do something like this? *Why* now? And *how*?

Your father rolled open a desk drawer, and something clicked.

"Her scarf," I said.

Your dad turned. "Her scarf?"

"It was here." I pointed. "Her mom's Hermès scarf. She loved it. She wore it all the time. It was in that drawer on Tuesday morning, but it's gone now."

"I don't understand." Your dad stepped closer to me, voice rising. "What does that mean?"

You had been wearing the scarf when I chased you underground. But I couldn't tell your dad that—not yet, not until I knew for sure what you were doing. I held up my hands, trying to think. It was like my mind had clouded over. I kicked your pictures on the floor. Whoever had done this was *trying* to draw attention to themselves, trying to throw us all off.

Who would do that, Willow?

Who would destroy so much—

Other than you?

Twenty-Eight

THREE MONTHS BEFORE

ANNA HAD BEEN HUMILIATED. A hundred people had seen her naked. Her mother had seen it. Boomer and Lizzie and Kape had seen it. The dean and the administration had seen it. Jon Potts and his girlfriend had seen it. Poppy Ruel didn't attend her own graduation ceremony. Anna heard that she'd spent the day in a huddle in her parents' hotel room, devastated. Poor Poppy, who had done nothing wrong. Poor Poppy, who was, like Anna, an innocent bystander in Willow's war.

The picture traveled, too. It made its way to New Haven, where Jon Potts had just finished his first year of grad school. He was a TA at Yale, as he had been at Balwin, on track to get an MFA, then a professorship. At Yale, he was teaching freshmen, grading their papers, holding office hours. The implications were clear and immediate. A person like Jon Potts should not be in charge of anything, of anyone. He was kicked out of the program, investigation pending, but no one thought he would return.

Willow called, but for two weeks, Anna refused to come to the phone. She didn't know how to go forward. Her choices were impossible, thanks to Willow. Anna had given up her dream of an MFA but couldn't stay in Bexley under the aggrieved eye of her mother. Nor could she just forget what happened and go to New York with Willow.

Anna holed up in her childhood bedroom but left her belongings packed up. She painted. She read. She thought about who she was and what she wanted. What she was capable of. She thought about her future, hanging on the walls at MoMA. She made her way downstairs to dinner every night, and every night, she had to face her mother's distain.

"Set the table, please," her mother said, when Anna had been home for almost a week.

"Mom," Anna started. She knew that her mother had seen the picture. Her mother, who had bathed her and fed her and raised her, despite the awful thing that she had done—her mother would recognize her blindfolded. Her mother *knew* her. "Mom, I—"

"No." Her mother's eyes flashed. A warning. They were in the kitchen, and she was holding a stack of plates.

"It's not what you think," Anna said.

"I don't want to hear it."

"But it didn't even have to do with me. I was—"

Her mother lifted her hands and smashed the plates to the floor. They shattered on the tiles, loudly, dangerously, and Anna jumped back, hands to her mouth.

Her mother spoke through clenched teeth. "I said I don't want to hear it."

Henry appeared in the doorway, eyes wide. "What happened?"

"It's okay, honey," Anna's mother said, voice almost normal again. "I just dropped the plates." She pulled a stack of napkins from a drawer and put them in Henry's hands. "Put these on the table, please."

Henry took them, but he didn't move. He was looking at Anna.

"What happened?" he said again.

Anna fetched a hand broom and a small dustpan from under the sink. "It's okay, Henry. I'll clean it up, then I'll help you set the table."

That night, Anna couldn't swallow one more bite of her family's tasteless food.

———

She couldn't stay there. She couldn't. And she had an apartment in New York waiting for her. MoMA was waiting. Her whole future. She could not give up on herself because of what Willow had done. She wouldn't lose. Not now. She'd come so far. She wouldn't forgive Willow—but she wouldn't let her win, either.

She never did unpack her boxes and crates after graduation; instead, she lugged them to the driveway on a Wednesday in June, as planned, and waited for the U-Haul to pick her up.

Tom and Lizzie helped her load the truck, and they sat three across the front seat as they drove nine hours to New York.

They said nothing about the photograph, nothing about graduation, and Anna wondered if it was possible that they really didn't know. Willow hadn't told them about her rape, and Anna's face in the picture *was* blurry enough, cut through with her hair, that it didn't *have* to be her. It could have been another girl with long dark hair. Another girl splayed on the rocks.

During the drive, Anna felt her confidence return.

She would start over. She would forget the photos. She would forget Balwin.

She would find her own way in New York. One way or another, she would succeed. She didn't need Willow for that.

Willow had furnished the apartment on Congress Street—a couch, curtains, coffee machine, silverware. She'd bought groceries and stocked the fridge with Diet Coke and Blue Moon and oranges.

"I'm sorry," Willow said when Anna arrived. "I really am."

Anna hadn't expected that. She didn't know how to respond.

"I was so caught up with my own anger, I didn't see how it would hurt you. And I shouldn't have said what I said—about your brother. It was cruel, and I'm sorry."

Willow circled Anna's wrists with her soft hands, pulled her in for a hug.

Anna let it happen. In that moment, she made the decision to believe Willow, because she didn't know where to go without her. She didn't know how to live, what to wear, what to paint. She had been wrong, she realized. She *did* need Willow. She would always need Willow.

And after a few days, it felt right. The ugliness that had come over Willow since Jon's assault seemed to slough off her in the city. She was her old self. *They* were their old selves—best friends again, though sometimes Anna smiled through gritted teeth. In all, it was like Jon Potts getting kicked out of Yale had fixed what had been broken. Like it had all been worth it. There were moments when Anna wondered if she had been wrong to be upset in the first place. Surely, punishing a rapist should be worth it? Her mother despised her, but it didn't matter. Her mother had despised her for fifteen years. Nothing had changed.

But there were small moments, when Willow left her mess all over the kitchen, when she lied and withheld and disappeared, when she was careless with things that didn't belong to her—and in those moments, Anna hated her again.

She hated her with a laser-hot rage.

Twenty-Nine

THURSDAY NIGHT

I SAT ON YOUR BED, silent, as your father called the police to report the break-in. How could I explain to him, of all people, what I was thinking?

Milo might have been lying about Tyler and about the plan, but that didn't make him a murderer. You *made* him do it—implicating me to Lizzie and Milo, making me feel crazy. Milo was following your orders, Willow, just like he always did—like we *all* did—with no regard for his own well-being, or mine.

While your father paced on his cell phone in the living room, I picked up your books from where they lay scattered on your bedroom floor. Mostly they were museum catalogues and artists' monographs—Francesca Woodman and Ana Mendieta and Diane Arbus, your dead-women idols. There were tomes on feminist theory, too, performance art and photography, and biographies of your favorite muses. Your favorite broken women. The faces we gazed upon, the bodies we assessed. I

lined the books on your shelf again, spines straight and resolute, and when I finished, I saw it: a gap. The place that had
held your binders of developed negatives, all organized in their
plastic sleeves, *your* place, was empty.

You'd done it, Willow. You'd finally made yourself into one of
them. A spectacle, and nothing more.

Your father stomped back into the room. "They're on the
way. They want us to catalogue everything that's missing. Can
you help me with that?"

I sucked in a breath. I couldn't tell him what I knew, not yet.
I needed proof first. Solid proof. I began pulling things out from
under your bed. The same junk I'd found there earlier in the
week—broken frames and discarded materials, bins of photo
paper and unexposed film. I laid it all out, touching everything.

"Her camera," I said, realizing. "Her digital camera is missing, the one you got her for graduation." It had been there on
Tuesday morning. I'd seen it myself.

Your father nodded. "Anything else?"

"Not that I can tell," I lied. "But I don't know what to look
for."

He rustled through your jewelry box. My stomach tensed
with certainty. Your camera and your negatives and your
mother's silk scarf—the only things you'd ever really cared
about—all gone. It was validation that you had been here. You
were pulling our strings. And I knew why.

"Do you need me to stay until the police get here?"

Your father looked at me, brows raised.

"Actually." I turned. "I need to go."

I was already halfway out of your room when he spoke.

"Anna—"

I pretended not to hear him.

I grabbed my purse and bolted down the stairs.

———

No way I could sit on the subway feeling as pent-up as I did at that moment. It was late, dark, and I was alone, but I needed to walk. Over to Union Street, then deeper and deeper into Brooklyn. I couldn't see the smoke and fire of the World Trade Center, but I felt them, looming behind me, and the smell, still, the stench of smoldering metal hung heavy in the air. Between Third and Sixth Avenues the street traffic loosened, and I walked as fast and loud as my boots would carry me. I made eye contact with no one. I responded to no sounds. The storefronts darkened and I felt like a ghost, hovering over the old sidewalks. In Park Slope, everything perked up again—people, lights, dogs on leashes. I kept going. For nearly an hour, I walked, until finally I wound around Grand Army Plaza and into Prospect Heights—where Milo lived.

I'd never been inside his building, but I knew the beige mid-rise on Eastern Parkway by sight. I'd assumed it would be a hovel on the inside, that he kept us all away because it wasn't as nice as what the rest of us had in Carroll Gardens. But as I approached the building, I saw that it wasn't made of dingy cement, as it had seemed from the taxi, but rather painted brick. There were no bars on the windows, not even on the first floor. We were just a handful of blocks away from glorious Prospect Park. A middle-aged couple came out the front door, holding hands and walking a freckled cocker spaniel. I grabbed the door from them with as calm a smile as I could muster.

I stood for a moment in the vestibule, locked between two glass doors, until I spotted the intercom on the other side and hoped that Milo had listed his full name. Finger on the bubble-typed list, I ran down the names until I saw it: ARVANITIS, P. APT 6F.

Milo Arvanitis. The *P* had to be a typo.

I didn't want to give him any time to hide you, so I pressed the button underneath his.

After a moment, a warbly, elderly voice responded. "Yes?"

"I have a delivery for 5F," I said.

"What is it?"

I looked down at my paint-stained jeans and took a chance. "Artwork."

Silence first. Then the door buzzed open, and I was inside Milo's building. In the same place you were, I was sure of it. *Right under you.* The lobby was clean and bright, and there was an elevator bank on the opposite wall. *An elevator building.* I wasn't expecting that. I wasn't expecting Milo's place to be better than ours. I barely let myself consider it before I ran to the elevator and punched the button three emphatic times.

The doors sucked shut, and I was in a vacuum. My heart loud in my ears, beating out a mantra—*you, you, you.* My accusation. *You did this.* I was finally going to confront you. The doors chimed open on the sixth floor, beige wallpaper and clean carpet and brass door knockers. I scanned the long hallway.

6F.

I hammered the door with my fist. Determined to find you.

I waited.

I hammered again.

Finally, the door flew open, and Milo blinked at me.

"What are you doing here?"

"Where is she?" I pushed past him, barely registering that the furniture was all covered with tarps and plastic. Barely noticing the lavender walls. "Willow!"

He grabbed my arm, spun me around. "Jesus, be quiet!"

I jerked free and called out again. "Willow!"

"She's not here, Anna! Please."

"Bullshit."

He grabbed my arms again. Both hands, clamping my shoulders. "Anna, stop!"

A noise from the hallway. Someone was there. Milo let go of my shoulders and closed his eyes. Someone was here, in his apartment, and *I was right—*

"Mi," came the voice. My heart crashed into my stomach. It was not your voice.

A figure appeared in the doorway, and all the blood in my body rushed downward as I saw her—a large woman with short silver hair, glasses, and a velour robe.

"Who's this?" the woman said.

"This is my friend Anna, Gram."

Milo put out his arm, presenting her to me.

"Anna, this is my grandmother, Philomena."

TWO MONTHS BEFORE

A MONTH AFTER they'd moved in and made up, Anna went to Chelsea for the first opening Willow worked at Roche Gallery. She climbed the subway steps at Twenty-Fourth Street, twisting her neck surreptitiously, trying to get her bearings. She wasn't certain which way to walk but hated to look like a tourist, unfolding the laminated street map she kept in her purse. New York was her home now; she believed its logic should already be inside her, intrinsic and complete. She twisted her head from side to side as if she could see to the end of the avenue if she only tried hard enough.

All around her were huge, high billboards and warehouses with padlocked metal gates. Entrances to elevated train tracks chained off, abandoned. Halfway down a long avenue block she became disoriented, the sun hitting her at such a strange, hot angle, she felt like an ant being burned under a magnifying glass. Her clothes grew damp. Everything seemed empty, and New York never seemed empty. No people over here, little traffic. Anna walked by an abandoned warehouse near Tenth

Avenue—a cement cave chained with a padlock and Warning signs—and a hot gust of air hit her legs. She jumped, frightened and disgusted. She knew exactly what could happen to a girl in a place like that.

Finally, she caught the scent of cigarette smoke, then spied a small coterie down the sidewalk, smoking and talking, with their black clothes and bold eyeglasses and hats. She'd made it. Roche Gallery's giant glass doors were propped open, and she hurried inside.

———

Another beginning: The gallery was cement and white paint, with church-high ceilings and an enormous metal door that rolled up and down like a classroom map. People clustered here and there, leaning against the mammoth front desk or gazing at the oversize color prints in austere black frames. This was the place.

Anna stopped in front of one of the photographs, a woman or a girl, but young—skinny and naked and hunched, long black hair covering half her face. She was bestial, her head turned sharply, her one visible eye as sharp and sad as prey. It unsettled Anna. It seemed perverse—its placement in that stark room, under the hot spotlight, with these people in their clothes like armor, sipping wine and looking at her. This woman, once whole, was rendered flat and immobile. Anna knew exactly what that felt like.

She spotted Willow in the back of the gallery, behind a folding table full of wine bottles and little plastic glasses. Willow's white hair was ironed straight, and she was wearing a pastel slip dress with big pearl earrings that Anna hadn't seen before. Willow's brand-new Prada platforms looked so perfect here. *She* looked so perfect here, and that made Anna angry.

She took a plastic cup of wine. "Hey."

Willow smiled. "You're here!" She gave Anna a hug. "Can you do me a favor?"

"Depends." Anna would always be wary of Willow's favors now.

"Can you just stand here for a minute and hand out wine? I really have to pee."

"I don't work here," Anna said, but she felt a small rush. She *could* work there. She *wanted* to work there.

"You're a waitress, babe." Willow smiled. "You know how to pour wine."

Anna rolled her eyes. "I don't even know who the photographer is. What if someone asks?"

"Jürgen Frosh," Willow said. "Just two minutes."

"Jürgen Frosh," Anna repeated carefully, pronouncing the word with a soft *J*, *YUR-gen*, as Willow had. They were already trading places. "Jürgen Frosh."

"I owe you," Willow said before she disappeared into the crowd.

Anna poured small portions of wine into plastic glasses and set them on the table. People did not speak to her, just took what they wanted and wandered off. Her feet started to pinch in her new kitten heels. The cement was hard. She wished she'd worn her combat boots. Minutes passed, an hour. The small crowd had grown large. Anna scanned the room. She wanted to be out there, talking, mingling, being part of the party. Where the hell was Willow? Where was *anyone*?

She could have walked away. It wasn't her bar, or her job, or her responsibility. It wasn't fair that she was stuck, with Willow who knows where, probably laughing, drinking, chatting with some famous artist. *Goddamn her*. Anna tried to work up the nerve to leave, but she couldn't do it. Some strange obligation held her in place—some *promise*. There was a chance that Philip Roche would see her, working hard. That he would notice how well she managed, how naturally she fit in, and he would want to talk to her, hire her, mentor her, change her life.

At some point she saw Milo and Tom, both in suits like they were at a job interview or a funeral, their hair slicked back with gel. Milo wrote something in a Moleskine notebook with a ridiculous fountain pen. A man trailed behind them, gesturing in well-tailored clothes and small black glasses—someone from the gallery. *Oh shit*. Anna smiled. They were pretending to be collectors or critics.

A man was at the bar. He was speaking to Anna.

"I'm sorry," she said, flustered. "What did you say?"

The man edged closer to Anna behind the table. He was too close, all pointy and birdlike, with shaggy blond hair and black pants with seams pressed sharp as knives. He was taking the wine bottle from her hand.

"I said, did Philip hire someone new without telling me?"

Anna laughed weakly. "Oh, no. I'm Willow's friend. Willow Whitman? She asked me to pour wine while she used the restroom."

The man smiled. His mouth was narrow, and his teeth were sharp. "Oh, perfect."

Anna blinked at him, unsure how to respond to that.

"I'm Mason," the man said. He stretched out his hand. His fingernails were painted black. "I work with Will."

Anna took his hand. Mason had a stiff, lined face. He was skinny, with a chain belt on his pants and tattoos peeking from under his sleeves. He was unlike the grown-ups Anna had come across so far. "I'm Anna."

His face lit up. "The roommate! I should have known. You're as pretty as she said."

Anna's cheeks bloomed red, the compliment doing more for her than she would have admitted.

"She said you were her biggest competition."

"Did she?" Anna thought she understood, and she smiled, because that, too, was a compliment.

"Yeah," Mason said. "She said no one in the city could best her except you."

Anna tilted her head. It felt like he was trying to tell her something. "Best her?"

"Oh yeah." He picked up a glass of wine. "She's been working so hard to get ready."

"Ready for what?"

He held the plastic glass to his lips. "The AFYAA." He said it like it was a secret, and it must have been obvious to him that Anna had no idea what he was talking about, because he lifted his brows. "Oops."

"What is that—the AYF . . . ?"

"The Andrews Foundation Young Artist Award. There

are brochures at the front desk, honey. Deadline to apply is December." He smirked. "Don't tell Will I told you."

"What does the winner get?"

"Ten grand and a show."

"A *show*?" she said. "At the Andrews Foundation?"

He nodded. "Last year's winner got a capsule review in *Artforum*. She's going to be in the next Whitney Biennial."

Anna felt a burning in her chest. Willow knew Anna needed the money. She knew what a solo exhibition could do for her. At that moment, Anna understood something very clearly. Everything that Willow had done, from the lies about Milo to the photo with Jon Potts, was to control her. To hold her back. To make sure that Anna didn't surpass her.

Anna clenched her jaw and resisted the urge to swipe her arm across the table and knock all the wine bottles to the ground.

She found Lizzie first. "Have you seen Willow?"

"She's outside with a bunch of people."

Bitch, Anna thought, pushing her way toward the door. *You selfish little bitch.*

The gallery lights blinked off and on, off and on, and everyone knew it was time to leave. Anna spotted Milo and Willow in an empty corner. She could tell they were arguing. They weren't looking in Anna's direction, and she inched closer. Close enough to hear them.

"Philip cares, okay? You just can't mess with my job like that."

Milo snorted and leaned back, crossing his arms over his chest. "It's not a *job*, baby."

Anna bit back a smile. *Good*, she thought. *Let them fight.*

Willow started to walk away. "Fuck off."

He grabbed her arm. "Baby."

"You have no idea what I'm doing here." She shook him off. "You have no idea what this is about."

He grabbed her arm again. "You're not some *salesperson*. You're an artist."

Willow looked at Milo's hand on her arm, and something in the atmosphere changed. Anna held her fingers to the heartbeat in her neck.

"Get off me," Willow said slowly. He must have squeezed harder then, because she shouted. "Stop it, Milo!"

He towered over her, leaning like he might fall, like he might crush her.

"You stop it," he said.

Willow didn't back down. Willow never backed down. "Let. Me. Go."

Milo dropped his arm and held up his hands.

The cracks in their relationship were beginning to show.

Anna sucked herself into a shadow until they were both gone.

Outside, the sky was pink and blue and melting into darkness, but the air was still thick and hot. In the middle of a small crowd on the sidewalk Anna spotted Willow, smiling now, her red lipstick perfect, her face radiant, with Mason's arm around her shoulder. Lizzie and Tom stood nearby, smoking. Anna scanned the crowd—Milo was gone.

Anna stepped toward them. She wanted to grab Willow's shoulders and shake her. She wanted to yell in her face. She'd left Anna to do her work for two full hours. It would be the last time Anna believed a word out of Willow's jealous, mean mouth.

"The bathroom, Wills?"

Willow went wide-eyed. "I totally forgot!" She pulled Anna in, close to her body, close to Mason. "Come with us, Hollywood," she said. "Mason has a plan."

Anna liked Mason. He had given her a secret. He had been nice to her. No one had been nice to her in such a long time. That was why she let him hook his arm in hers, let him lead her down the steps of the C train. That was why she didn't leave Willow right then.

———

They changed to the L, exited someplace in Brooklyn, and walked into a rehabbed loft building. The elevator was as large as the ones in Henry's hospital, but old-fashioned, with a chain gate and hard black buttons. Techno music grew louder and louder. Mason pulled the gates open on the fifth floor. It was crowded, hot, and so dark that Anna had trouble seeing in front of her.

"Hey!" someone shouted. Anna turned. *Fucking Boomer.*

He hugged Willow, kissing both her cheeks. Anna faked it, forcing her lips to stretch, but her shell was cracking. The anger inside was just too alive.

Boomer put a cup in her hand, clear plastic, clear liquid. He seemed different here, lighter, happier, more confident. Anna sipped tentatively. It seemed like plain vodka, safe enough.

Mason and Boomer disappeared into the mess of bodies, and Anna tried hard to ignore Willow. Willow, dancing. Willow, laughing. Willow, in the light, as always.

When Mason reemerged, he was sweaty and smiling. He held a tiny metal spoon in front of Anna's face. It was like something from a dollhouse, except holding a small pile of white powder.

Anna pulled back.

"It's *cocaine*, sweetie!" Mason shouted.

Willow let out a laugh. "You snort it, babe."

Anna was teetering on the edge of something—a cliff, a chasm—she couldn't fall into. She thought of that day on the beach, the joint laced with Special K; she remembered the way time shifted without her awareness. She remembered how terrifying it felt to lose control like that. No—Anna had too much to do, too far to go. She shook her head.

Boomer steered Mason's hand to his own face, plugged a nostril, and leaned forward, inhaling the powder. He popped up and nodded at Willow. Mason refilled the spoon. Willow leaned over, smooth and unaffected as always. Mason held out the spoon, and she snorted easily. Anna knew right away that hadn't been the first time, and she looked at Willow with fresh eyes, trying to see what, exactly, Willow had been up to that summer without her.

Willow was laughing and spinning around, the way she had when she was in an especially happy mood. She pulled Anna toward her, to the center of the party. At first Anna held back, not wanting to give Willow anything after the way Willow had treated her at the gallery. But the vodka was warming her up, making the music more interesting. And the people, too, mostly men, all bouncing around her, shaking off sweat like dogs after a bath, smiling beatific white smiles. Willow looked ecstatic, happy and fresh and beautiful, her arms raised high, her eyes closed, her body rolling in the sea of bodies. Willow danced like a snake, her thin pale dress like a skin she was trying to escape. The men watched her. They cheered her on and moved closer to her. It was different from the men ogling and catcalling on the street, because those men saw Anna, too. These people didn't. Anna was being edged aside. She tried to keep up, swaying her hips and reaching up her arms. She closed her eyes to feel the music, to absorb attention the way Willow did. She wanted what Willow had. Even the mean parts of her. She wanted it all so much.

Thirty-One

THURSDAY NIGHT

MILO AND I stood facing each other on Grand Army Plaza.

"What the hell is going on?" I said.

He dug a pack of cigarettes from his pocket. *Buying time.* My jaw was clenched, and I was so tired. I couldn't just sit here and watch him smoke. I swatted the pack of cigarettes out of his hands.

He stared at me, unmoving, shocked.

"Tell me," I said. "Tell me everything right now or I'm telling the cops you did something to her."

He puffed out a laugh, bent down to get his cigarettes.

"You think this is fucking *funny*?" I shoved his shoulder.

"No." He faltered, then pulled himself up. "Anna—"

"Don't do that," I said. "Don't try to placate me. I need to know what the fuck is going on. Where is she? Where is she?"

"I've been trying to tell you."

"Tell me what, Milo? What?" I smacked his arm again. *"What?"*

"About the prank. About everything." He sat on a worn green

bench, slipped a cigarette from his pack, and gestured next to him. "Sit," he said. "Please."

I crossed my arms over my chest, watching him light up, unwilling to move from my spot on the sidewalk. "Spill it, Milo." I said. *"Now."*

He lifted his eyes to the sky. "I didn't think she'd take me back. I never thought she'd take me back. But then, I saw her at Happiness. You were working. She was mad at you, but she didn't seem mad at me. She told me she still loved me. She said she understood why I'd done it. Why I'd slept with you."

My stomach hardened. He was talking about the night before we fought. The night I knew I had to destroy you.

"I already know this part," I said. "I saw you in our apartment. I saw you with her."

A look of surprise crossed his face, then he carried on. "Well, it didn't matter. She was stringing me along. She said she was seeing someone else."

"Who?"

Milo shrugged. "I don't even know if it was true. I don't know if any of it is true."

"Did you tell her about Tyler, Milo? Did she know what we'd planned?"

He nodded, flicked his cigarette. "She thought the whole thing was hilarious. She knew just how to use it. To make you feel crazy. She was going to disappear for a few days, after the mugging, to make you think that your plan had gone sideways. She told me to play along. Then the World Trade Center happened. When she didn't come home—I figured she just went on with it, even with everything going on. I didn't know what to do.

I kept thinking she would call. I kept playing my part. I thought if I did, she'd come back to me."

I *had* felt crazy. I *still* felt crazy.

"When you talked to her dad yesterday," he went on. "I thought it would be over. I thought he would say *oh she's fine she's with so and so,* or something. But then he didn't know where she was. We were off script. I didn't know what I was supposed to do. I wasn't sure. I thought maybe *you* knew where she was. I thought maybe you were both fucking with *me*." He put the cigarette between his lips.

"So where is she, Milo?"

He shook his head, exhaled to the sky. "I have no fucking idea."

Thirty-Two

TWO MONTHS BEFORE

IN JULY, New York broke open—outdoor tables on the sidewalks, exposed skin everywhere, happy noise blasting from wide windows. Anna had worked the lunch shift at La Soeurette, then stayed late for extra cash, serving heaping piles of vinegary greens, rare steaks, crisp potatoes, and endless glasses of wine. The smell of goose fat and char and blood was everywhere.

Just after eight o'clock, Anna splurged on a taxi to Arcadia Café, tucked on a gritty corner of Tompkins Square Park. Spoken word was Lizzie's thing now, and Arcadia held poetry slams on weekends and was famous, she said, for making poets famous. Anna rolled the window down and let the overripe smell of the city blow hot against her face, feeling all the promise of the night.

Arcadia was the best kind of dive—girl bartenders with sleeve tattoos and Bettie Page hair, lips as red as stop signs; saloon doors to the bathrooms, always with a serpentine line of bodies in front of them, girls and boys bouncing and anxious to pee or snort a line or both; layers of graffiti on the brick walls like ancient runes; carvings deep in the wobbly wood tables; sticky, disgusting floors; and in the back, a dingy, cavernous room with folding chairs facing a small stage and a single microphone.

Anna's friends sat at a low sofa in the corner, Willow in the middle as usual. Anna went to the bar first. It was easier for her to be around Willow when she wasn't sober.

"Hey."

Anna turned. It was Milo, sidling up.

"Hey," Anna said.

The bartender put down her Jameson on the rocks. "Six bucks," she said.

"Can I get one of those?" Milo said.

"That all?"

Anna and Milo nodded, and Anna bent into her purse for her wallet. Milo put a hand on her hand and tapped a finger. "I got this."

It was only a touch, but the sensation of his skin on Anna's—the size of his hand and the warmth of it, the calluses and rough spots making the smooth parts even smoother—sparked something. An idea. Willow always had more than Anna, and still, she took and stole and protected her resources as if she might go starving. Now, in Milo, in this tiny gesture, his hand on her hand, Anna had found a way to take something back.

"Twelve together," the bartender said, setting his glass next to Anna's, still untouched on the bar.

Milo leaned forward to pull his wallet from his back pocket. He smacked down a twenty but didn't make a move off the stool. Instead, he flicked open his pack of Marlboro Reds, pulled one out, put it between his lips, and lit it with a match. Anna looked past him, over to the couch. Willow was watching, staring directly at them, her face as still as ice and just as unreadable. Anna's stomach flooded with pleasure. She lifted her whiskey to her lips.

At ten o'clock, Lizzie coaxed everyone into the back room to get seats for the poetry slam. A cold Red Stripe was sweating in Anna's hand before she'd even asked for it. Willow had an arm in Anna's arm and her digital camera holstered around her shoulder. Anna still felt Milo's hand on hers, something blooming deep and warm low in her gut. Willow sat in a chair in front, pulling Anna down with her. Willow snapped a picture, all flash, even in the light.

"Hey," Anna said, annoyed. "Wait." She turned her head, chin to shoulder, smiling for Willow's lens, but gazing backward at the crowd behind her. She saw Milo. He was coming toward them.

A man with long locs appeared onstage and howled into the microphone. The crowd quieted. A few people howled back at him. Others snapped their fingers. Milo settled himself between Willow and Anna. Boomer slipped in, too, and sat on the other side of Willow. They smelled musky, like they had just finished a joint somewhere.

The man onstage leaned into the microphone. "She's an Arcadia virgin, people," he said. "Give it up for Lizzie Stone!"

The audience clapped and hooted and snapped as Lizzie walked onstage. She looked like the superhero she used to draw:

slicked-back hair, purple-stained lips, eyelids painted black, clunky gold bracelets, cinched black corset top over low jeans.

She chanted into the microphone, "I am an artist."

A shout from the audience: "Yes, girl!"

"And I make *myself.*"

The room grew quiet again, listening, pensive, hungry for meaning. Willow's fingers were twisted into Milo's, and Anna watched him rub his thumb on hers.

"I build myself with wax and paint," Lizzie shouted. "I make myself beautiful for you."

More hollering from the audience. Behind the microphone Lizzie held her notebook with two hands, but she looked straight ahead at her audience, her gold septum ring glinting under the bare bulb above her head.

"I carve myself. I winnow down for you," Lizzie said. "I use my hands to dig through my wax, my flesh, my paint, my skin."

The audience murmured encouragement.

Lizzie dropped her notebook. It slapped the floor. She held out her hands. "I dig with these fingernails."

"Yes, girl!"

"To reach bone!"

Milo let go of Willow's hand and began to snap his fingers.

"And further and further," Lizzie said. "I rend my own bones."

"Oh Jesus," Willow said, too loudly. She covered her eyes with her fingers, a wicked smile on her face. "This is so embarrassing."

Lizzie whispered into the microphone. "I smash them into powder."

"Whoooo!" Milo cheered.

Willow twisted toward Anna and smiled. Anna understood. They were connected again. This wasn't art. Lizzie wasn't an artist, not really, but *they* were. Anna smiled back.

"For you," Lizzie said. She was pointing at someone in the audience. "Powder I bleed on, red, and mix into paint. Because *I* . . . am an artist."

The audience leapt up, snapping and cheering. Milo was the loudest among them, standing, clapping his hands above his head, howling.

Willow turned to Anna, camera over her eye.

She clicked a photo.

Later, after the slam dispersed and people went back to their drinks, Anna found Milo alone at the bar.

"Where's Willow?" she asked.

He turned, heavy-lidded, and swept his gaze around the room. He shrugged and hung his head. He was so drunk Anna was afraid he'd fall right off his barstool.

"No fuckin' clue."

"Did she leave?"

His elbow slipped, and his whole body followed. Anna put her hand against his arm, steadying him, a fresh rush of fear: *Did Willow drug him, too?*

Milo looked at Anna's hand on his arm, smiling with half his mouth. "She always fuckin' leaves."

Anna waited up that night, flipping channels on the TV and slowly sobering up, but Willow didn't come home. Anna fell asleep sometime before dawn, and when she awoke, it was Saturday afternoon, hot and bright. She was sweating under her quilt on their ratty blue couch, and she could sense Willow's absence even before she sat up.

Anna called Willow's cell phone. No answer. She made coffee in case Willow came home, showered off her hangover, and called again. Still nothing. Saturday was a workday in the art world, and no one had called looking for her, which meant either she'd made an excuse or she was at Roche. Anna opened her laptop and signed onto the internet as she sipped her coffee. She found the phone number for the gallery on its website. She dialed the numbers, trembling, not knowing what she was afraid of. She wanted to laugh but couldn't.

The phone rang only once. "Good morning, Roche Gallery."

It was Willow. Her voice was the same as always, cooing and bored. Anna pulled the phone from her ear and hung up, hoping the gallery didn't have Caller ID. She set the receiver silently on the table and stared at it, wondering what Willow was up to now, what kind of bomb Willow was building—and whether Anna would get hurt when it detonated.

Thirty-Three

THURSDAY NIGHT

I BORROWED Milo's hoodie, left him on the bench, and walked the two miles back to Congress Street, only to find your father pacing the sidewalk in front of our stoop.

"They haven't come." He spoke as if he couldn't believe his own words. As if this was the first time in his life that he didn't get what he asked for as soon as he asked for it. Which, I understood, it probably was. I felt like shouting at him—*Look around, dummy*. The city is in crisis. New York needed all its resources for itself, not for his daughter's selfish performance.

New York owed him nothing.

I couldn't say it, though. Not when he looked as broken as he did. Instead, I sat on the stoop, watching him pace and mutter, as I considered everything I knew about you.

"Where is your wife?" I asked.

Your dad stopped pacing. "Excuse me?"

"Your wife," I repeated. "Willow's mother. Where is she?"

He looked at me blankly.

"Is she sick?"

"What?" he said, and I *knew*. You'd been lying. Your mother didn't have multiple sclerosis. She wasn't in an assisted living facility.

"No." His face twitched. "Elodie moved abroad when I married Leanne."

My chest flooded, cold. "*Leanne* is your wife?"

"Of course." Your dad blinked at me. "What did you think?"

Jesus Christ. Leanne was not your nanny *or* your housekeeper. Leanne was your mother's replacement in an entirely different way. I remembered then what you'd said at Oak Street Beach, after I met her for the first time. *After my mom got sick I went a little wild . . . My dad doesn't trust me.*

"Why did Willow graduate so late?"

Your dad hesitated. He stayed on the opposite side of the stoop and wrung his hands. I was agitating him, but I couldn't let it go. I was too close to understanding.

"What was she doing?"

"We tried to send her abroad, too," he said finally. "But it didn't work."

"*What* didn't work?"

He shook his head.

"Mr. Whitman, please," I said. "Tell me."

When he turned to me, his face was red and his eyes were wet. I felt a momentary sting of pity for him, for whatever you had put him through.

"She had an episode," he said. "After Leanne and I told her we were together. Well, a series of episodes."

"What kind of episode?"

Your dad rubbed his face. "Hypomania. It is . . . a sort of delirium. She wasn't sleeping or eating. For weeks and weeks.

I'd find her drawing on the walls in the middle of the night. Breaking furniture. Now I wonder—" His voice got caught in his throat.

"Wonder *what*?"

He looked at me, eyes hooded and red. "I wonder if she's done this, too."

My arm went out automatically, gripping the iron banister for stability. Bracing myself. "What . . . what do you mean?"

"Upstairs." He raised both of his hands over his head, toward the kitchen window. "That mess. It looks like what happened before. It looks exactly like before."

"You think she did it?"

"I don't know. I don't know."

Funny how much I understood about you, Willow. Even before I had a name for it. I understood it when you'd chopped off your hair on a whim, when you wore a leotard to class, the way you worked in jags, sometimes for days, without sleeping or eating. The times you disappeared.

"What happened back then?"

Your dad shook his head. "She . . . she . . ." Whatever it was, he didn't want to say it. He didn't want to admit it. I think he was protecting you.

"You can tell me," I said softly, helping him along.

"She told us she was pregnant."

My mouth fell open. *A baby.* You had plenty of time to have a baby in that missing year of high school. I pictured you with a baby, and my mind spun fast. If what your dad was saying was true, your kid would be a toddler by now. I stopped breathing for a moment, pulling threads together. *You'd gone to find him,* I thought stupidly, *you'd been looking for your child—*

Your father must have understood the expression on my face, because he corrected himself quickly.

"She wasn't. It was a complete fabrication. But the father"—he shook his head—"the *man* she claimed was the father was a teacher at her high school. She said they were in love. She was acting completely delusional about what had happened between them."

"An older man." I thought of Leanne on the phone, of you in the Stones' mansion. Your lips on my ear. *You should fuck him.* "Oh my god," I said, sitting down on the cement step, absorbing this. "But you said she didn't run away?"

"No."

"Then where did she go?"

"McLean."

I shook my head, not understanding.

"It's a hospital," he said. "A psychological hospital."

"You *institutionalized* her?"

"I had to. I had to. She was a danger to herself. But . . ."

"But *what*?"

He turned to me then, eyes bloodshot, shoulders hunched, and I saw how badly a person could ruin himself, and it was terrifying.

"We found out later," he stammered. "We didn't know . . ."

He trailed off, and I felt my stomach twist.

"Didn't know what?"

"He," he said, "the teacher. He wasn't a good person. Last year . . ." Your dad hung his head. "He was arrested. For statutory rape. He'd done the same thing to another young woman. Another girl."

I sucked in a breath. "So Willow was telling the truth."

He nodded. "Yes. She was."

Hypomania. A new way to say *hysteria.* You only looked crazy because no one believed you.

Your dad took my hands in his. His sad, red eyes seemed to beg me for something. "I think we ruined her, not believing her," he said. "I think she's ruined, Anna."

Thirty-Four

ONE MONTH BEFORE

WILLOW WAS UP to something, and although Anna didn't know what it was, she knew that when Willow was up to something, Anna got hurt. She wasn't going to let it happen this time. She wasn't going to let Willow take one more goddamned thing from her. Anna dressed for another night at Arcadia in her own armor: short pleated skirt; black corset top; army boots; high, gleaming ponytail. The men at the bar stared at her, even more than they stared at Willow.

See? Anna thought, absorbing it all. *See what I can do?*

Boomer, happy and drunk, pulled her off the barstool.

"Hey!" Anna said, protesting.

But Willow had shimmied off, too, and Anna saw the way forward. She let Boomer swing her and wrap his fingers around her arm and dip her so hard and fast she thought she might smack her head on the ground. She ignored Boomer's meaty hands, the memory of him, and tried to look at him like a stranger might. He looked better than ever—healthy and tall and tan. Even his clothes had changed. New York suited him. He let Anna go and spun Willow like a ballerina in a jewelry box. Anna swayed along in time with the music, in time with Willow's hips.

"Who wants a line?" Boomer was wild-eyed and smiling with his big white teeth.

Willow raised her hand. "Oh me, oh me, oh me!" she said, eager as a fourth-grader, and everyone laughed as she followed him into the bathroom.

The perfect opportunity. Anna nestled in next to Milo on a low sofa. She still felt his touch on her hand. His eyes on hers. She put out her fingers, testing the air between them. Milo was watching. He didn't flinch. Anna let her hand fall to his thigh—high enough to be conspicuous. He was watching. He moved his hand, and for a moment, Anna thought he would cast her off again. Throw her away. But he didn't. He put his big hand on hers and squeezed.

Then Willow was back, and they pulled apart.

"Move, toots," Willow said to Milo, and he inched himself closer to Anna.

"More," Willow said, shaking a hand. "Scoot."

Milo was touching Anna again, the edge of him matching up to the edge of her and pushing, and Anna glanced at Milo and saw that Milo was looking at her, hard. She knew then that she had won. It was only a matter of time before he was hers. She drank her vodka and Milo had his whiskey, and she stopped paying attention to anyone else. His hand gripped Anna's leg, fingers inching up Anna's bare skin. Anna kept looking over at Willow, waiting for her to see, to rebuke them, but she seemed so unconcerned, blowing smoke rings at the ceiling.

She would need to do more. *More.* Anna moved Milo's hand

farther and farther up, until his fingers were under the hem of her skirt and his body felt like fire.

———

It was raining when they left Arcadia, sometime after last call. No umbrellas or jackets or cabs. At first, they loved it. Lizzie and Tom led the way. Milo had one arm around Willow, the other around Anna, and they hung back from everyone else as they trudged down Canal Street into Chinatown. Then the night shifted again, and Anna was walking with Milo, laughing at nothing, kicking the steam on the sidewalk. Willow was ahead of them, an arm through Boomer's arm, all of them stopping and gathering at Boomer's stoop as he fumbled for his keys, dropping them and laughing, dropping them and laughing again.

Milo leaned toward Willow, but she pushed him away.

Anna's mouth went dry. She couldn't stop feeling his touch, pleasure churning inside her. It was the delight of being desired, but it was more than that. She would have Milo because Milo was Willow's. It was the promise of besting Willow. Of having revenge—finally.

Boomer got the door open, and they pushed into the vestibule—everyone but Willow and Milo, who stood facing each other in the rain, beginning to fight.

Anna watched them through a window in Boomer's second-floor living room. She couldn't hear the words but understood the gestures, their stuttering bodies and arms waving—Milo would have perceived a slight, some transgression against their sacred coupledom, maybe he'd seen Willow flirting with another man, or she'd refused to take his hand or share some part of herself that Milo desperately needed. Whatever he was saying to her was a mistake—Willow was rolling her eyes at him. Pulling away. Didn't Milo know how much Willow detested being hemmed in—told what to do or how to behave?

As Anna watched from her perch, Willow heel turned and flew away from Milo, down the sidewalk, into the wet night. Milo stood completely still, watching the spot where Willow had been, then finally dropped onto Boomer's stoop, head in his hands.

Delight spread though Anna's chest. The tension that had been building between her and Willow since graduation—*no*, since freshman year, since that moment in Anna's dorm room when Willow first accused her of wanting Milo—was coming to a head. She could feel it as surely as she could feel the thick air before a storm. Here was the opportunity to change their trajectory, flip the dynamic of their friendship, regain the control over herself that she had long ceded to Willow. Finally.

She grabbed two Red Stripes from the fridge and went outside. Milo was on Boomer's stoop. She handed him a beer. She was conscious of how she must have looked in that moment: her hair slicked with rain, her thin camisole stuck like tissue to her body, her arms tanned and bare, her face and nipples turned up to him. "What happened?"

"It's over." He sucked on his cigarette and stared at the sidewalk. "It's really over this time. She's done with me."

"I'm sorry." Anna put her hand on the stoop, not touching him, not yet, but so near his body she could feel the heat coming off him. Milo moved his hand on top of hers, weaving fingers with fingers. He brought their hands to his lips.

Anna had him, she knew. She just had to play along.

The rain started again, and they ducked inside. They could have gone up to Boomer's apartment, but they didn't. They locked eyes, and Milo leaned forward until he was kissing her, lips soft and full, and a bolt of something hot ripped through her abdomen. Anna led him down the stairs by his fingertips. It could have been anywhere. She would have fucked him on top of garbage bags. She would have let him take her clothes off in Times Square. But they were there, in a Chinatown storage room, with a heavy metal door that didn't latch all the way. He grabbed her neck and pulled her toward him, then lifted her on his hips. Anna was as easy to pick up as a doll. She had made herself that way. She was no longer flesh, but hard and light as a plastic toy.

He slid her panties off and pressed her into the wall again, her back grinding against the bumpy plaster. Milo was inside her. His face nuzzled against her neck. She thought about Willow's lips on the Lake Michigan beach. She thought about Willow's mouth. Her cruel smile. Her perfect, tiny waist. Anna knew what she was doing with Milo, and she didn't care. She knew that Milo was Willow's. Milo was a part of Willow. That was why Anna was there.

De La Soul blasted from the cube speakers near Boomer's window, and Anna smelled the oceanic smell of sex on her skin.

More people had arrived in the time that they had been in the basement. A clump of strangers, maybe twelve in all. A small mirror lay on the coffee table, and Anna watched a guy in a green mesh tank top and locs lick his finger and drag it across the mirror, then rub the finger across his teeth like he was brushing them.

She saw Lizzie near the fridge and went over, feeling conspicuously sticky and sore. It was dangerous, she knew, to stand so close that Lizzie need only lean in and smell her. A part of her wished Lizzie would.

"Who are these people?" Anna asked.

"Boomer's new friends, apparently."

Anna took a bottle of Red Stripe and leaned back on the windowsill to sip. Milo stood in an opposite corner, nodding along with the music.

A guy in a Gucci bucket hat tapped a few more lines onto the mirror, used his nose and a tightly rolled dollar bill to vacuum one up, then handed the bill to another guy, a gallery type wearing a fedora and jeans despite the heat. Anna watched the bill go round and stop at stranger after stranger. They all seemed so content, so safe, so caught in their own perfect happiness.

Anna realized who was missing. "Where's Boomer?"

Lizzie shrugged. "He was worried about Wills. He, like, chased after her."

Anna swallowed. "Why?"

"He said she'd been telling him stuff."

"What kind of stuff?"

Lizzie shrugged. "Who knows. He's been drinking since like three. He wasn't making that much sense."

Anna thought back to Arcadia, the four of them squeezed

into that couch, Anna next to Milo next to Willow next to Boomer. She thought of the walk back to Boomer's place, the way the night shifted.

Lizzie set her beer on the windowsill and took Anna's hand. "I'm gonna do a line. Want?"

Anna considered it. She imagined what it would be like to follow Lizzie to the coffee table, hold her hair back so that it wouldn't brush away the powder. She could pretend to know exactly what she was doing. A part of her wanted to do it, knowing it could ruin her and doing it anyway.

Anna pulled her fingers free. "It's okay."

Lizzie shrugged and walked away. Anna leaned against the windowsill, knuckle jammed into her cheek. She stared at the door, waiting for some kind of fallout. Waiting and hoping for Milo, for Willow, for *something* that would never come, something big and permanent to crash through that door and blow them all to pieces.

Thirty-Five

THURSDAY NIGHT

YOUR DAD TOLD ME EVERYTHING—all the lies you'd told, all the secrets you'd kept. He was sorry, Willow. He was so sorry he hadn't believed you about your pedophile teacher. I pretended to be sorry, too, but I was thinking about Kape, how you'd tricked me that night at the Stones' party. It made less sense now than ever before. You had been manhandled and mistreated by a man just like Kape, and still you pushed me into him. It felt so personal, an attack on *me*—you wanted me to feel as humiliated as you were. But *why*? I had done everything for you, Willow, every single thing you had asked of me. So why did you want to destroy me? Why did you want to destroy everything we'd created?

Your dad smacked his thighs and stood, startling me.

"Where *are* they?" He meant the cops, I knew.

I eyed him. I wasn't afraid anymore. You were a force of destruction, and I was more convinced than ever that you were doing this. "I'll stay here," I said softly. "If you want to go talk to them."

For a few moments he said nothing, then, finally, he nodded.

"You're right. I'll go to the station." He wiped his face with his palms. "You'll call me, won't you? If they get here before I return?"

"Of course," I said. "I'll make sure they wait."

He nodded, and then he was gone.

So was I.

As soon as your dad was out of my line of sight, I jumped from the stoop and ran in the opposite direction, flying down Court Street until I was standing in front of Happiness. I expected to find Lizzie and Tom in the same seats, with the same shell-shocked expressions on their faces, beer bottles and shot glasses stacked up, ashtray overflowing, but our booth was empty. Instead, I spotted Boomer. Alone. He had an elbow propped on the bar, talking to the tatted bartender, sipping from a beer bottle. He was *smiling*.

Before I could stop and think, I marched up to him and shoved his elbow off the bar.

He jerked—"The fuck?"—and turned and saw me. His smile faded.

So much was swirling in my head, confusing me, and I felt like lashing out. "What are you so happy about?"

The bartender's eyes goggled, and I gave him a ferocious glance. He backed away.

"Hello to you too, Anna," Boomer said.

"I know about you and Willow," I said. "I know you were leaving her little notes and following her around and freaking her out all through school."

He took a sip of his beer. "Is that what she told you?"

"She didn't have to. I know you were in love with her. Everyone knows."

He laughed, and my anger exploded. I narrowed my eyes at Boomer. "Do you know where she is?"

"No." He gave me a side-eyed look. "Do *you*?"

I screwed up my face. "Me?"

"Yeah, you." He turned to face me head-on. He was scrutinizing me. "Why didn't you tell anyone what she did to you? Why are you always protecting her?"

"She didn't *do* anything to me," I said. "I am not protecting her."

He laughed. "Honey, I was there, remember? At graduation. I saw the photos. I know what I saw. And what I heard. That was a low blow, what she said about your brother."

I clenched my eyes shut, bracing myself for what I knew would come next.

"She told me about Henry," he said. "How it happened."

A laugh burbled out of my mouth. *Of course you told him. Of course you betrayed me.*

"Sit down, Hollywood," Boomer said, kicking out the stool next to him. "Order something."

My breath went shallow. That was *your* nickname for me. No one else called me that.

He flagged the bartender, ordering himself another beer. I shook my head even as I sat down. I didn't want to drink. I couldn't. I needed to stay alert. I need to figure out what was happening.

"Where do you think she is?"

"I don't know," I said. I didn't trust Boomer—not at all—but what was the worst that could happen if I told him what I thought? I needed all the help I could get. I let out a long, steadying breath. "But my apartment was ransacked. Her dad's been at my place for hours, waiting for the police."

"What do you mean *ransacked*?"

"Just that," I said. "Trashed. Torn up. But only her half of the place."

His brow furrowed. "Is anything missing?"

I nodded. "Her negatives. That big binder with the negative sleeves. That's all her work from Balwin."

He stared at me. "You think she took them."

I tried to read his expression. "Why would you say that?"

The bartender slid a fresh beer bottle in front of Boomer and a glass of water in front of me.

"Thanks," I said, but I wasn't really seeing him. I was too caught up in what Boomer was about to tell me.

"Willow is tricky."

"You think she's up to something?"

He nodded.

"Me too."

He set his beer bottle on the bar. "Tell me."

"I don't know." It was the truth, I knew you were to blame, but I couldn't figure out how. "What are you thinking?"

He looked at me, hard. "I'm thinking about the *MUSE* show."

"What about it?"

"And all her idols. The other muses."

"Those beautiful tragedies."

"You know what's a beautiful tragedy, A?"

I waited.

"Everlasting youth."

I blinked slowly. "What do you mean?"

"Edie, Ana, Francesca—what do they all have in common?"

A drop of cold ran down my spine. "They're all dead."

He said nothing. He was waiting for me to figure it out.

"Died young," I said. "ODs and murder."

He held my gaze. "And suicide."

Thirty-Six

ONE WEEK BEFORE

FOR THREE WEEKS, Anna and Milo met up, only in secret, and only during the day when Willow was at work. They'd get high in Anna's apartment and have sex. In her bed, or on the floor, or on the sofa Willow had paid for. Always the same hard, resolute sex that they'd had in the stairwell. There was something performative about it, even though they were alone. They never went to Happiness, or to the coffee shop on Smith Street, or to any place Lizzie and Tom might see them. It had nothing to do with Lizzie and Tom. Or Anna and Milo, really.

Only Willow.

At the end of August, when the city's heat bore down like something biblical and Philip Roche closed the gallery to retreat to the Hamptons with the rest of the posh people, Anna came home from work and smelled Milo in her apartment.

She froze, confused at first. Then she spotted Milo's boots in the kitchen. His Marlboros in the ashtray. She pressed an ear to Willow's closed bedroom door. He was in there—she was sure of it—even though both Milo and Willow had said they'd broken up. Were they going to get back together? Smoosh themselves together again, leaving no room for Anna?

She clamped her molars together. Held her breath. The bedroom door opened with the smallest creak. She tiptoed, her heart thrumming in her ears, her feet almost floating above the floor. She felt like a bird, like something magical and inhuman.

Willow and Milo were a single shape in the bed, twisted like martyrs in the white sheet. Willow's arms lay above the sheet. One pink nipple. Milo's hand rested on Willow's hip. That was it. All she needed to see.

The next morning Willow looked so smug, making coffee in her white silk robe, her fingernails painted the color of pearls, her mussed hair falling so perfectly over her shoulders, her lips so red, even then, even in the infected light of the morning after.

Anna hadn't slept. All night she'd listened for the door to close and Milo to be gone. She'd never be able to sleep again until she had this out with Willow. This big moment, what she'd been waiting for. Her heart thumped in her stomach.

"I have to tell you something."

Willow splashed milk into her coffee and stirred, leaving the wet brown spoon on the counter. She took a sip, looking pointedly at Anna. She was using Anna's favorite mug. *World's Best Sister.* Anna knew she wouldn't bother washing it. She never did. Willow took everything Anna loved and never asked permission. Anna felt her resolve build.

"Milo was here last night?"

Willow raised her brows, as if to say *and?*

"We've been sleeping together." Anna's relief was immediate, like vomiting.

Willow's face barely moved, so Anna went on.

"Milo and me. We've been sleeping together."

Still nothing.

"We've been having sex."

Willow smiled then—the smallest, strangest smile.

"I—" Anna said, and stopped. This was not what she had expected. She wanted tears, or anger. Something to show that Anna had taken something back, finally. Something that mattered. "It started two weeks ago."

"You're so fucking stupid, Anna," Willow said. "You're so fucking *easy*."

Anna went hot. Her face burned. Her legs burned, too. "What?"

"You think I don't know? You think Milo didn't feel so guilty that he *had* to tell me?"

No. It was not supposed to happen like this. *Anna* was supposed to be the one to tell her. *She* was the one who was supposed to get revenge.

"Why do you think I even let him fuck me last night?" Willow snorted. "The boy needed a little reward for his loyalty."

She strode toward Anna then, the white silk of her robe billowing, her hair so soft—like she'd been cast as an angel in some old movie. Anna stopped breathing as she got closer.

"Pathetic." Willow held out the mug, and dropped it right at Anna's feet, splashing coffee everywhere. The mug lay on the floor, cracked. "Oops," Willow said, then walked right past Anna, toward her own room.

Everything stopped. The only sound was the hum of the fan on the floor and the heartbeat in Anna's ears. She felt lightweight, like a helium balloon, floating away. She was so close to Willow, she only had to reach out and her hands were on Willow's shoulders. Her fingers were hot. She needed Willow to care. She needed Willow to break. To be human.

"What is wrong with you?!" Anna yelled.

"With *me*?" Willow said, spinning around to face Anna. "Are you serious? It's you. It's always been you. You're so fucking transparent. It's embarrassing. I'm actually embarrassed for you."

No. Willow was trying to close the door, trying to stop Anna from coming in. But Anna was so strong. She was nothing but strength. She had to stop her. She pressed her palms on the door and jammed her foot sideways on the threshold.

"You're done." Willow smirked. "*We're* done."

But it was like Anna couldn't hear. Like she was controlled by something else. The air around her was electric. It was the rage of four years of being messed with and stepped on and tossed away. *No.* It was her whole life. Being blamed for everything that went wrong. And Willow, using that. Lying to manipulate her. Willow had taken the secret Anna had given her—*only her*—and twisted it between her fingers like a garrote. Electricity was all around Anna; it was surging through her. She was so goddamned tired of losing all the time. She wanted to scream.

And then she did. "*You don't get to tell me when we're done! You liar!* You've never been sorry for anything. You're an awful person, Willow. You're an awful, awful person."

"Look who's talking." Willow snickered, moving her hand

up and down at Anna's body. "You only got into Kape's seminar because you fucked him," she said. "That's all you are, you know. A place for men to stick their dicks. That's all you've ever been."

Willow let go of the door to push Anna out. Anna looked down. Two hands, white nails, pushing against her chest. But she barely felt it. She pressed forward, propelled robotically into Willow's room. She was full of energy—rage and electricity and fire.

"You did that to me," Anna said, bearing down on Willow. "You *made* me do that."

Willow was still smiling, but there was fear in her eyes now. "Am I that powerful, *Hollywood*?"

Anna's hands were on Willow's shoulders, squeezing. It wasn't enough. Anna pressed harder until they fell to the ground. Anna straddled Willow, splintered wood grinding into her knees, her knees splayed around Willow's body, thighs squeezing. Anna's hands were so close to her neck—that long, ballerina neck—so easily she could have wrapped her fingers around it. So easily she could have squeezed the breath out of her, taken back all the air that Willow had stolen from her. In Anna's mind, her hands were already there. Willow's white skin. Anna was muscle and breath and rage, and she squeezed.

A jolt came from underneath, and Anna flew backward.

Willow had bucked her off. Anna was on the floor, stunned, a hand to the back of her head.

Willow scrambled to her feet. "Get the fuck out of my room!"

Anna's hand came away from her throbbing head. She expected to see blood, but it was clean. She expected to stop breathing, but she didn't. Energy swooshed out of her. She was dazed. She was so tired.

"Get out!" Willow screamed again.

Anna stumbled to her feet. Her face was wet. She had lost. Again. Willow would always be stronger.

"Fucking psycho!" Willow shouted, and slammed the door in Anna's face.

Thirty-Seven

FRIDAY MORNING

I WOKE UP ravenous. A deep, painful hunger I hadn't felt in years. For a few hours I distracted myself by cleaning your mess—sweeping up glass and paint, replacing drawers and picture frames and couch cushions. I went into your room, too, but not to clean. I dug through the jacket pockets and discarded purses in your closet, collecting almost fifty dollars in loose bills and change.

There was a hardware store four blocks away on Court Street, and there, I picked out the cheapest set of screwdrivers I could find. I got some wood putty and a starter kit of enamel sign paint—six quarter pints for twenty-three dollars—and paid with your money. Guiltlessly. I deserved it, I felt, because of everything you had put me through. Next, I stopped at the bodega on the corner and got two disposable cameras, a bag of tortilla chips, a copy of the *Post*, and a bacon-egg-and-cheese on a roll. I devoured the sandwich right out of its warm foil before I even walked home. I couldn't remember the last time I'd eaten anything resembling a meal, and that felt like your fault, too. I had been hungry for years, Willow, and not just for fame. For real food, for nourishment, sustenance. As I tossed the trash and licked my fingers, I wondered if you'd wanted to keep me that way. If hunger was an easy way to keep me small.

In the apartment, I unpacked my materials and lined everything up. I took the biggest screwdriver to my bedroom door. Starting with the hinge on the bottom, I twisted all four screws loose until the door dangled from the top corner like a baby tooth; then I dragged a kitchen chair over, climbed up, and unscrewed the top hinge. The door was hollow-core pine, cheap and lightweight, and it fell to the ground easily. I set it on its side, removed both hinges completely, then the knobs. I used the wood putty to fill the hole and sat back to let it set.

My painting was better suited to this horizontal orientation. Through tracings and shimmering lines, I began to recognize body parts: elbows and hair and the curve of a waist, like a woman moving through a series of poses. The dent left from Milo's fist was a perfect shoulder. On the left side, her knees were splayed and her neck pitched backward. In the middle, she was standing, long hair waving, and in the last, she was curled into a ball. It was part *Les Demoiselles d'Avignon*, part *Nude Descending a Staircase*, but different, too. Picasso had had no empathy for the sex workers whose likenesses he'd blunted in 1907, and Duchamp had been interested only in capturing movement in paint, not his model's mind.

My muse deserved better.

Thirty-Eight

THREE DAYS BEFORE

ANNA PINCHED SAND between her fingers. It had been half a week since her fight with Willow in the apartment, half a week of Willow's door shut tight, of stubborn silence, of dread. Anna couldn't stand it anymore. She had to do something—*change* something. She'd called Milo; she'd brought him here, to Coney Island, because she knew he could help her. She wasn't sure he would come, wasn't sure if Willow had told him about their fight, but he was here, stripped to swim trunks, lying on her ratty, pink-flowered blanket in the sand.

Anna let the sand fall from her hand. "Are you back together?"

"Nah." Milo's eyes were closed to the sun. "She's not talking to me again."

Of course, Anna knew why Willow wasn't speaking to Milo. She knew Milo knew, too, but he didn't know that. Anna flattened the sand.

"Did they invite you?" she said.

"Invite me where?"

"The Hamptons."

Milo propped himself on his elbows to look at her. "The Hamptons?"

Anna nodded. "They're all going. Willow, Lizzie, Tom, Boomer. Willow got a house through Philip." Lizzie had told her yesterday, not understanding why Willow hadn't included her. But Lizzie hadn't known about Anna and Milo yet, or about Anna's fight with Willow—Willow hadn't told anyone. Anna knew what it meant to go to the Hamptons, the big houses and private beaches and exclusive parties, the place where the blue-chip gallerists and art stars spent their summers. She didn't care about riding bicycles and getting fucked up; she cared about what the Hamptons signified. It was the hobnobbing, the deal-making. Being invited in. Anna needed that, so much more than Willow did. She knew what it meant to be excluded, and it enraged her.

She had told Lizzie about her and Milo right then, out of spite and anger. *See how it feels, Willow? To be humiliated?*

"Boomer's going?" Milo said.

Anna nodded.

Milo lay back again, hand covering his eyes. "When?"

His chest was thin; Anna saw the vulnerable space below his ribs, the soft slope of skin. She stared off into the ocean. "The fourteenth."

There was time to stop her. There was time to correct this final insult. That's why she had brought Milo here.

"Unless . . ."

He turned. "Unless what?"

Anna shrugged, as if she didn't know. As if she hadn't already plotted it out—the abandoned warehouse near Tenth Avenue, its chains and the hot, empty darkness that rushed up her legs the night of Willow's opening.

"What if we do something?" she said. "Freak her out, or something."

Milo laughed.

She glared at him. "I'm serious."

"How?"

"We could take something from her." She picked up a pile of sand and let it run through her fingers. "We could mug her."

Milo blinked at Anna. *"What?"*

"Not for real. We could pretend to. Like one of her larks." Another pinch of sand. She let it fall onto Milo's belly this time. Goose bumps rose on his skin. He lay back down, a crooked smile on his face.

"Pretend to *mug* her?"

Anna pictured Willow walking by the warehouse, her route from subway to gallery. She ran a finger up Milo's neck and around his ear.

"We could hire someone. Not to hurt her. It's not about that. It's about scaring her. Stopping her."

"Why?" Milo said. "Who cares if she goes to the stupid Hamptons?"

Anna traced shapes and lines on his stomach, to his chest, his collarbones. "Because I'm sick of her getting to control everything."

He shrugged like it was nothing, and Anna tensed. He didn't know the half of it. He didn't know that Willow had been lying and manipulating them all for four years. From the moment Willow banged on Anna's door in her black tights and told her

Milo was into *her*, not Willow. To trick her, to trap her. It had started long before Jon hurt her. Willow had always been a liar.

Anna had to make Milo see. She worked herself up, pulling at her eyes until the tears came.

"Hey," he said. "Don't cry."

"She cheated on you." It was a lie, but Anna would do what she had to do. She would use the tricks that Willow had taught her. She would be the monster Willow created. "Back at school."

Milo shaded his face with his hand to look at her. He said nothing.

"She lied about Jon Potts. She was the one who put those pictures of me and him all over campus. She lied to me about it. She convinced me to do it by lying to me. She lied to you, too. She lied about everything."

Anna put a little sun oil on her hands, rubbed it on her arms.

"You're serious?" he said.

She leaned down and put her lips on his throat, and under her, she felt his whole body stiffen. "I'm sorry I didn't tell you before. She made me swear."

"I knew it." He clapped his hands, once. "I fucking *knew* it."

"Milo," Anna said. The sun blazed high above them, approvingly, turning the light behind her eyes orange as she spoke. "She deserves it. A taste of her own medicine. You know she does."

Milo's jaw was clenched tight, and Anna knew she'd said the right thing. She knew she'd won him.

"Yes," he said finally. "She really does."

Thirty-Nine

FRIDAY MORNING

WHEN THE WOOD PUTTY had dried, I spackled over it with gesso and picked up the *Post*. The cover featured a photo of the president, one arm wrapped around a fireman, the other holding a bullhorn. UNITED WE STAND, the headline proclaimed. The article said nothing—another puff piece about hope and resilience. I shook out the paper and flattened it on the coffee table and began to scrape pastels with my palette knife, making new piles of pigment powders and setting them aside.

From the cabinet under the bathroom sink, I pulled out your hair dryer and blasted heat onto the gesso until it was hard. I picked a few sable brushes from your stash, pulled down my melamine plate, then popped open the small cans of enamel paint—red, blue, yellow, black, and white.

With black I outlined my figure as she moved across the panel. I tapped silver powder into white paint and made highlights. Mixing blue into red and adding drops of black, I conjured a deep purple, the color of a bruise, and used it to build a face. I kept going. The power of the gaze—my figure took it back. She was looking at me as sure as I was looking at her, the way Manet's *Olympia* had confronted her Victorian viewers. I stepped back, pondering this. My figure deserved more. More, certainly, than Victorine Meurent, Manet's model, had received. Meurent hadn't been a prostitute as so many people assumed but an accomplished portrait painter, doing a favor for a man she considered a peer. Funny how no one remembered that part.

I kept my figure's joints sharp and loosened everything else. Playing with light, I captured movement and the shape of a woman. And then, outrageously, I gave her clothes.

After several hours, my painting was complete. I stood back and studied it. The face, in the style of photo-realism, was not your face, Willow, and it was not mine. It was both of us, merged into one. The figure's body was sketchier, looser; there was nothing outright titillating, and yet—and yet—the painting was alive. My figure held so much power.

I used the disposable camera to take shots of the painting. Long shots and details. Every possible angle. And when the film was used up, I dropped the camera into my bag, slipped on my shoes, and set off for Photoreal to have the pictures developed into slides to send with my AFYAA application.

As soon as I stepped out onto the stoop, though, I saw two men, waiting.

"Ms. Vaughn."

It was the cop from yesterday, Tennison, and behind him another man, holding a large, empty box. They were huge, towering and thick as elm trees, and it would be so easy for them to flip me around, put me in cuffs, shove me into the backseat, lock me into a cell for the rest of my life. Guilty, without having done anything.

"Hello," I said. My voice was vague, like a whisper.

"Just a few more questions for you, if you don't mind." The new cop didn't introduce himself. As he spoke, he looked over me, past me, at the building behind me, *our building*, as if appraising it.

Tennison leaned forward. "You said you had met Mason Montgomery?"

My heart hitched. "Yes," I said. "I met him at Willow's gallery. Why?"

Tennison cleared his throat. "Mason was at breakfast on Tuesday morning, celebrating a friend's birthday. A man named Jürgen Frosh."

"The artist," I said.

"You know him?" Tennison's voice was so soft. He was being delicate, as if I might explode if he jostled me in the wrong way. It made me even more nervous.

"Not personally." I didn't know what this was about, but I felt skeptical of them. Everything felt like a trap. "He had a show at Roche, where Willow works, and I saw his photographs. Willow didn't introduce me. I don't even know if he was there that night."

"He was there," Tennison said.

The new cop moved closer to the stoop. "Jürgen Frosh," he

said, pronouncing the name with a hard *J*, like the lotion, and I had to swallow the urge to correct him. How I had practiced his name that night. "His breakfast was at Windows on the World."

It took me several moments to solve the equation in my mind. I had never been to Windows on the World, but I had heard about it—the fancy curved booths, white tablecloths, old-school waiters, crystal glasses, tea service. I heard you could see all of Manhattan from its windows. You could see the Statue of Liberty, Ellis Island. Everything was visible from the one-hundred-sixth floor of the World Trade Center.

My voice croaked out a question. "Is he okay?" I was trying to make sense of what they were telling me, but I couldn't.

"I'm sorry," the officer said. "We believe both Mr. Frosh and Mr. Montgomery died in the attacks."

Blackness crept into the edges of my vision. *Mason*. With his black fingernails and pressed pants and the warehouse party. His little spoon of cocaine, dancing around. He'd told me about the AFYAA. He had been so generous. In this harsh city and the harsher art world, he'd been so *kind* to me.

"He's dead?"

The officers exchanged a glance. "Would it be okay for us to look in Willow's room?"

I made a flimsy gesture with my arm. I could barely feel it. I was trying to parse the situation, trying to understand what their message was. Mason and Jürgen were in the World Trade Center when it fell, which meant that they were dead, and now the police were looking for something in your room. Was it—*could it be*—that they had found a reason that you were with them?

My teeth began to chatter. I lurched to my feet and ran up the steps after them. The cops were hunched over your things like vultures, picking. Tennison's arm was behind your desk.

"What are you looking for?"

"We have her father's permission to take her computer," he said and straightened, wrapping the unplugged cord in his palm.

I blinked. "Why?"

He hefted the computer into the box, then the modem, but he didn't answer.

"What are you looking for?"

The other officer was coming toward me, and I shifted away. "What aren't you telling me?"

"Sit down, honey," he said. His hand was on my wrist.

I yanked it away. I didn't want to sit down. "Please—just tell me what you're doing here."

Tennison approached from the other direction, his hands out. I stumbled backward. Away.

"There is a chance," he said, slowly, softly, like he was talking to a skittish horse. "That Willow was at breakfast on Tuesday, with Jürgen and Mason."

"A chance?"

He nodded. "A chance. We don't know anything for certain. That's why we need her computer."

My mind spun. "But . . . her negatives are missing," I said.

He frowned. "Her negatives?"

"There were binders of them." I gestured to your bookshelves. "All her developed negatives, she kept them there, all organized. They're gone. Someone was here. *She* was here."

Tennison set his hand on my shoulder. A sandbag, weighing me down.

"No." I shook him off. "You don't understand. I *saw* her."

The other cop was too close. I smelled stale cigarettes on his breath.

"Sweetheart," he said. "I'm afraid you're imagining things."

ONE NIGHT BEFORE

EARLY SEPTEMBER had been exquisite, and Anna loved New York more than she'd thought possible. The lapis skies, the warm yellow sun, the city streets alive. But by the time Anna ended her shift at La Soeurette on Monday night, rain poured from the sky. She emerged from the subway onto Court Street, everything wet and chilly and deserted. Even the bodega had rolled down its gate. She rushed toward her building.

From the sidewalk she saw the kitchen lights on. Willow was home. Anna stumbled a little, slowed her pace, preparing for a new battle, when an uneasy feeling that she was being watched hit her. She turned her head. The street was empty. She looked back up to the glowing window, thinking maybe she'd see a flash of white hair, Willow glaring down on her, but there was nothing.

Every bone in Anna's body felt tired. Tomorrow was the day. Milo had made the arrangements with Tyler, given him three hundred of Anna's hard-earned tip dollars. All month she would go without food, without drinks at the bar, without fresh art supplies. It was the only way to keep Willow in check. To keep her from going to the Hamptons, pulling even farther ahead of Anna.

She clomped hatefully up the stairs, shoving down the memory of Willow's bruises sophomore year. It didn't matter to Anna at that moment that Willow had been violated. It didn't matter because Willow was a monster. Willow was Anna's monster. For the past four years, she had made Anna sick with hunger. She had humiliated her. Used her body. Destroyed her confidence. Taken away what mattered to her. So, no, Anna thought, stomping her feet up the stairs, making as much racket as she could, she wouldn't feel guilty for hurting her. Not even a little bit.

She stomped harder on the stairs, wishing she could wake the whole city from its precious sleep.

The apartment door was unlocked. Anna pushed it open. Inside, it was way too bright for two in the morning, and she felt a clenching rage at Willow for leaving the lights on. She knew Anna was struggling with extra shifts to get by, saving her tips, but she didn't care about the electric bill. Anna meant nothing to her. She never had.

Anna flipped off the lights in the kitchen, ignoring Willow's mess, and went into the living room, turning off those lights, too. A soft glow emanated from the gaps around Willow's door. Anna approached, stood close and put her ear to the wood, then pulled back as she caught a whiff of something—Willow's smoke and perfume, and something else, too, the yeasty smell of sex, the sticky metal-and-sugar smell of a man. Anna wrinkled her nose, taking it in. It was bracingly familiar.

She dropped her hand, panicked, and rushed back into the

kitchen. Milo's shoes weren't there. None of his Marlboros were in the ashtray. But it didn't matter. There was a man in there with Willow. She still had everything—Lizzie and the rest of their friends, men who lusted after her, a job in a gallery, a boss who let her use a Hamptons house. And Anna had nothing. Willow had done that. One by one, Willow had plucked away every single thing that had mattered to Anna. It felt finished, too. All the things she had lost—the MFA, control over her body, pride in her work, even the sacred relationship with her brother—all of it seemed to Anna to be gone forever. All because of the girl now snuggled in her monogrammed comforter, some man's arms wrapped around her, keeping her safe.

Fuck her.

Willow deserved everything that was coming.

Forty-One

SATURDAY AFTERNOON

I DIDN'T BELIEVE the police, not at first. After they left, I tried to go back to my painting, but I could only think about Mason, a real person I had met in flesh and blood, an innocent person, at the top of the World Trade Center. He was a real victim of what had happened to our city. My stomach roiled. My mouth was dry and pasty. I couldn't fucking paint. I couldn't do anything.

Something occurred to me then, and I dropped my brush and flipped open my laptop, tapping my fingers on my lips as it logged into AOL. I went to the Andrews Foundation website, and all the air gushed out of me as I read:

DUE TO THE TRAGEDY IN OUR CITY, THIS YEAR'S ANDREWS FOUNDATION YOUNG ARTIST AWARD HAS BEEN CANCELED. THIS INCREDIBLY DIFFICULT DECISION WAS MADE TO HONOR THE VICTIMS AND THE HEROES OF THE SEPTEMBER 11TH TERRORIST ATTACKS. WE AT THE AF SEND OUR GRATITUDE TO FIRST RESPONDERS AND OUR LOVE TO ALL THOSE SUFFERING.

I slumped over the keyboard. It was over. Really over. All the hope I'd felt when I moved to the city, all the expectations I had for my career and my life—it was gone. You had taken it all with you, wherever you had gone. I was trembling, my insides shaking, my head limp in my hands. I wanted to cry. To feel the relief of tears. I willed the dam inside me to break, but it wouldn't. I'd built it up too strong. Nothing came.

My cell phone rang. I couldn't turn it off, but I couldn't answer. I knew it wasn't you, and no one else mattered. No one else could bring back what I had lost. I pressed the flaps of cartilage over my ears as if they were mute buttons until voicemail picked up. I let out a breath. But within seconds, the ringing began again. I tried to block it out. I plugged my ears and hummed. But the ringing wouldn't stop. It wouldn't stop until I faced it. I forced myself to pick up the call.

"Anna?" A pause. Then Lizzie's voice again, shrill, piercing. "Anna?"

"Yeah."

"Jesus, thank god." Shrill and hoarse at the same time. Her voice made me feel seasick. "I've been calling and calling you. Where the fuck have you been?"

"Here," I said. "I haven't gone anywhere."

"She's gone, A. The police told us. She's, she's..." Lizzie sniffed. "She *died*."

I sat on the floor in front of the painting on my door, staring at our two faces merged into one.

"She was there," Lizzie went on. "At the World Trade Center. She was with Mason and Jürgen Frosh. I was right about that, too. Jürgen *was* the guy Leanne was talking about. There were emails between them. They were going to see each other in the Hamptons, too. They think it's enough."

"I know. The police were here, too."

"Her dad is here, and he—"

I couldn't listen to another word. Nothing Lizzie said would change anything, would bring anything back to me. I pulled the phone from my ear and snapped it shut.

PART
2
AFTER

Forty-Two

THERE WAS NO place to park. My father sat at the wheel of the Subaru, cursing under his breath, my mother stony beside him. In the backseat, I bent the corners of an old photograph of you and me, the two of us smiling, almost innocent. An email had circulated a week ago, after the funeral plans had been announced, asking your friends to bring something to put inside the casket. Something to bury instead of your body.

My father sighed and rounded the corner again—turn, turn, turn, just like I had done the first time I visited you in Chicago. He rolled the car toward the tall wood doors of the church and stopped the car.

"You ladies get out here. Henry and I'll meet you inside."

I glanced at my brother, gazing out the window. Staring at the traffic. The people. The colorless sun. The skeletal, looming buildings. He shouldn't be here, I thought. He should be at home, playing games, reading his Choose Your Own Adventure books, safe from these gawkers and vultures. I slipped from the car reluctantly, rickety in my heels and tights. It was too hot for late October, and I was not supposed to be there, at your funeral. The sun felt hostile, and I was mushy and rotten, a piece of fruit no one had bothered to eat.

The church was crowded. I peered past the bodies to the casket, open and hungry at the altar like a busker's guitar case. I pushed my way through elbows and eyes, not bothering with apologies, not looking back for my mother, just pressing forward. Then my hands were on the lacquered wood of the coffin. I set the picture of us inside and ran my fingers along the cold metal clasps and the butter-yellow satin, the letters and tokens and pictures that people had left.

I had my own token for you—the Eiffel Tower key chain I'd stolen all those years ago. I had it in my hand as I stared at all the letters people had written to you, the notes, the sentiments: *Willow, we love you. Beautiful girl. Our angel. 9/11. Never forget.* Picture after picture after picture. You, glamorous in New York. Bohemian in college. Surrounded by smiling girls in your high school uniforms. Small, almost awkward in middle school. In all these pictures, there was a *look* about you. That smile, those teeth and eyes—some aura of specialness that had marked you from the start. You were destined for such a spectacular end, weren't you?

A twenty-four-inch photograph was propped on a wire easel next to the casket. It should have been a black-and-white self-portrait from the truck stop, or a long-exposure print from your Francesca Woodman phase, or a full-body shot in your mod Edie Sedgwick leotard. But it wasn't any of those. It was the same one from your high school yearbook five years before that you had pinned to the board in Professor's Kape's class. Pride and sloth.

I put the key chain back in my pocket and turned away.

A lot of Balwin kids were in the church, splintered between rows and pews. Boomer stood with a group of overgrown frat guys at the back. I saw Tom and Lizzie with Lizzie's parents and averted my eyes. I'd been avoiding our friends to protect myself from my own bitterness. After all this with you, *they* got to stay in New York, and I was already packing my apartment.

Your father held Leanne's arm. I caught his eye, and he smiled at me—quickly, falsely—before turning away. He had dealt with our landlord—paid our entire October rent, out of guilt, probably—but that was it. He wanted nothing more to do with me. I was a reminder to him, of all that he had done wrong, all that he had confessed. I watched as he clasped hands with a man in a gray suit jacket. A shiver passed through me. I knew it was Professor Kape before I even saw his face. Kape turned to a small blond woman on the other side of the apse, almost bowing, his reverence that profound.

I froze. *You.* But it wasn't; it couldn't be. You were dead. The woman turned. She was older. Perfectly coiffed, perfectly made-up, not you. *Your mother.* Your beautiful, healthy mother.

Someone bumped me from behind. No apology. No acknowledgment. All these people, whispering, crying, smiling, hands touching arms, heads tilted toward each other, nodding. Everybody wanting to touch the big, famous tragedy. In my pocket, I squeezed your key chain until it bit my hand. The church grew louder around me, everyone talking over each other, desperate to share their own connection to it, to you: *I knew her I knew her I knew her.*

My mother leaned toward me. "Do you see your friends?"

I shook my head. Without you, I had no friends. I had nothing. "We can sit anywhere."

She put an arm around me after we found a spot. It felt awkward and wrong. She never did this for me. My father and brother arrived and squeezed next to me in the pew. I was hot, itchy with claustrophobia. I sank into the hard wood bench, letting gravity grind down on me, until finally, the organ sounded mournful and loud from someplace behind me and Henry took my hand in his, and the long Catholic service began.

Back outside, I felt fingertips on my arm. Milo. He'd cut his hair. He looked clean. It had been over a month since I'd seen him outside his grandmother's apartment.

"Are you coming to the hotel?"

"What hotel?"

"Lizzie's been trying to call you." Milo fidgeted. "She has a suite at the Drake. We're meeting there later. I think some of Willow's friends from high school are coming."

I could imagine it—people gathered to talk about you, how perfect you were, how talented, how *tragic.* My lips curled.

"Please come." Milo took my hand. "Please."

"I'm with my family."

"After you're finished with them. Please. It's close by, on Walton Place."

I didn't say anything. Milo dropped his hand.

"I'll wait for you at the bar."

I could still feel his fingertips; I could still feel him holding on.

Forty-Three

AFTER LUNCH with my family, I asked them to drop me off at the Drake Hotel.

"You're sure?" my father said, glancing at me in the rearview mirror.

I nodded. "I'll get a ride back home tomorrow. My flight isn't until Tuesday."

"You're leaving?" Henry whined.

I couldn't look at him—I already felt the frisson of tears behind my eyelids. If I saw Henry's face, I knew there would be no stopping them. I took his hand and kept my eyes low. "I have to go back to New York."

"Not for long, though, Henry," my father said. "She'll be back before Thanksgiving."

"And for good this time," my mother added.

Henry's hand was tight in mine. I felt his eyes on me. I still couldn't turn my head. The tears were waiting for me to slip up.

The Drake was right off Lakeshore Drive, sprawling, old and ornate, with a brass-and-gold awning, whipping flags, and its name lit up in an old English font, like the *New York Times*. I said goodbye and slipped from the backseat—a temporary reprieve. I stepped inside the hotel, noting the little historical plaques celebrating its importance, letting its guests imagine sleeping in the same rooms as Marilyn Monroe, Charles Lindbergh, and Walt Disney, as if *we* were all the same.

In the lobby bar I sat at a glossy table, wishing I had a sketchbook, something to do with my hands, but I didn't have to wait. Milo was already there, holding out his hand.

"Come on," he said. "Everyone's upstairs."

Lizzie's suite was on the seventeenth floor and overlooked Lake Michigan, just like your bedroom had. As soon as we walked in, she was there, bear-hugging me. She smelled clean again, like vanilla and lavender. I didn't pull away this time.

"God, are you okay?" she asked me. "I know we are all struggling, but I've been so worried about you."

"I went home."

Lizzie nodded. "I did, too. But I'm back now."

I couldn't tell her how deeply that wounded me. I was only going back to the city to finish packing our apartment. "I'll be back on Tuesday."

"Willow would want us to keep going," Lizzie said, smiling blithely. "*America* needs us to all to keep going. Otherwise they win, right?"

"I need a drink," I said.

Lizzie pointed to a wood desk that had been transformed into a bar. "Help yourself."

—

I was pouring Grey Goose over ice cubes when someone said my name. I turned. It was the girl with curly hair from 2D who had a boy's name. *Ryan.* I could almost hear her voice, the criticisms she'd lobbed at both of us. I could picture her life as it was at Balwin, pretty and boring, probably a Theta or a Phi Pi, maybe a friend of Poppy Ruel's, going to keg parties and getting pawed on ratty couches. I could picture her life now, too, working one of those endless entry-level jobs that required faxing and cardigans, relegating her palettes and brushes to the weekends, slowly picking them up less and less, until eventually she would never paint again.

"I just wanted to say," she stammered. "You know. I'm sorry. About Willow."

I screwed the top back on the vodka and shook the drink in my glass. "Yeah, me too."

She wrapped a curl around her finger. "You were living with her, right? In Brooklyn?" After I nodded, she went on. "I thought we could do something for her."

I frowned, immediately suspicious. "Like what?"

"Her pictures were so good," she said. "The ones from *MUSE* especially, and I wondered—do you have any of them?"

All of your things were still at the apartment on Congress Street, in your bedroom or the basement storage room, but not for long. Everything was going. That apartment would be empty next month.

"Why?"

Ryan shifted. "We could have a show for her. I got an internship at the Andrews Foundation. It's a—"

I cut her off. "I know it." I hadn't exactly given up on my career, but since the canceling of the AFYAA, I hadn't been working. My door painting was collecting dust in our living room. I hadn't even developed the photographs I'd taken of it. I hadn't even given it a name.

"I was thinking we could have a show for her there." Ryan was looking at me, waiting for a response. Her face was wide. Her eyes were dark and set deep, casting shadows, and made her look older than she was.

"I don't understand," I said. "The AFYAA was canceled."

She shook her head. "No, something else. It was actually the director's idea. I told her about Willow, about how she died in the World Trade Center, and she's into it. She wants to see her pictures."

A blubbering sound slipped through my lips. I put my hands to my face. Ryan touched my shoulder. She thought I was *crying*, but I wasn't sad, Willow. This was rage. Somehow, even after death, you were managing to control everyone around you. Using us to get everything you wanted.

"It's a good thing, Anna," Ryan said. "Willow would want this."

It couldn't have been better if you'd set it up yourself. Another beautiful dead girl. Another photogenic tragedy. Another muse. I took a long slurp of vodka.

Ryan touched my hand. "You could show us what you've been working on, too."

I studied her. The rage inside me felt electric—the *need* I had to propel myself forward, even as you stayed static, trapped in your pictures. I remembered something then, from the night of the Stones' New Year's party. *Let them think they are using us*, you'd told me, *when* we *are really using* them.

I wasn't powerless. I had something someone else wanted—but it wasn't sex this time. It was *you*.

"You'd have to talk to her family," I said finally. "Get permission and everything."

Ryan's lips twisted into a small smile. "Of course."

Forty-Four

MILO GOT ME a ride home the next day with a Sigma Chi named Clay who was driving them back to Cincinnati. Clay was nice enough and had an old BMW station wagon with peeling tan seats. I curled into the backseat for six slow hours, my head lolling against the cool window. I closed my eyes and pretended to sleep until the BMW rolled into my half-moon driveway and came to a stop. Clay didn't bother to turn off the ignition.

"See you in the city," Milo said as I got out. "Tomorrow, right?"

"Yeah." I closed the car door too gently and had to pop it with my hip to hear it latch. It was late, and my house was quiet. I hoped my parents were asleep. I slipped through the back door, into the kitchen, into that small world so familiar to me—the plastic-clean smell, the round breakfast table, the big yellow artificially happy tiles.

Unheimlich. The word dropped into my head. I knew it from studying surrealism at Balwin—those guys loved the Freudian notion of the uncanny, the eerie, the ever so slightly *off*. The house felt like stepping inside a Joseph Cornell box.

I slipped off my heels and tiptoed up the carpeted stairs to the bathroom I shared with Henry. I cracked open his door, gently, not wanting to wake him. It was empty. A little spasm of fear ricocheted through my chest. I dashed into my parents' room, also empty.

I stood on the carpet with my palms to my cheeks, letting the little house spin around me. I dug my cell phone out of my purse, flipped it open. Dead. Of course. I plugged it into an outlet and stood there, waiting for something to happen. And then, when the power returned, the voicemail chimed. I pushed a knuckle into my cheek and bit down. I already knew. I knew by the silence in the house. It had happened again.

Henry was in the hospital.

Three voicemails. I pushed my knuckle harder into my teeth until the skin inside my mouth broke. I pressed play.

There was no point in returning my parents' calls. While my phone charged, I packed things for Henry I knew my parents hadn't thought of: his Game Boy and Walkman and a bunch of CDs. I stuffed a bag full of oranges and apples, two overripe bananas. My mother always complained about hospital food, but she never left Henry's bedside to indulge herself in anything fresh.

I loaded everything into the Acura. How strange to drive this car again, after five months of living in New York, the same cherry-candy smell. I knew how to get to the hospital; I knew my way around the trippy white maze of the place, with all its unmarked doors and elevator banks and locked closets and wings and turns and hallways. I went straight to the restricted unit on the third floor. A nurse buzzed me in and gave me the room number with a smile.

"Anna." My mother barreled down the hallway toward me. "I've been calling all night."

She looked terrible: dark circles, skin mottled and creased.

"I know. I'm sorry. My phone died." I held up the grocery bags. "I brought some stuff."

She led me a few doors down into Henry's room. I felt my muscles slowing, the bones in my legs growing heavy. I didn't want to go any farther. I didn't want to face what was on the other side of that door. My biggest shame.

I stood at the door, unable to open it. I had to brace myself. "Is he awake?"

My mother put her fingers to her temple, nodding. "He's doing a twenty-four-hour EEG."

I exhaled as she pushed open the door. Henry was propped up in the bed watching a wall-mounted TV, a crown of wires on his head, all held together with a stretchy white net. A camera pointed down at him—twenty-four-hour observation, the neurologists watching the screens in their own offices for any signs of seizure activity.

Henry looked up, pupils as big and dark as craters. He smiled when he saw me. It had been years since I'd had to face him like this. He'd had seizures when I was at Balwin, and I knew he'd had to come in for observation a few times, but I had tried so hard to mix my paints and go into my trance and not think about his illness and this world I had left behind. Now I was back—the wires and the monitors and the tubes pushing oxygen and the doctors in their white coats—and I was deep into my childhood again, inside my guilt and rage and shame.

"I brought your Game Boy," I said, pulling the little computer out of a bag. I didn't know how much he knew about what had happened to him. We never talked about it. No one in the family did. He went back to watching *SpongeBob SquarePants*.

My mother walked over to him and touched his hand.

"What happened?" I asked.

"He had another cluster, probably from all the time in the car, the stimulation." Her face flashed fast and hostile, and I knew she still hated me, still blamed me. I knew she was remembering everything I was remembering, everything we always remembered in the hospital but never spoke of. She recovered her expression, returning to calm.

I knew what they were looking for, what they were always looking for, le grand mal, or worse. Catastrophic damage. *The end.*

I set the Game Boy and the rest of the bags on the floor and leaned my face into Henry's face, gave him a big, loud kiss.

"Gross," he said, wiping his cheek.

I bit my lip to keep from crying. The tubes, the cameras, the wires—I'd done all that to him, whether I meant to or not. I sat on his bed, looked him in the eyes. "You okay?"

"Yep," he said.

My mother held up the bag. "Are you going to be here a minute?" she asked me. "Long enough for me to put these in the fridge?"

I nodded and watched her slide the door closed. Henry and I were alone.

"Hey," I said, and he broke his gaze from the TV to look at me. "Do you know what happened to you?"

"I had a seizure."

"Did it hurt?"

He wrinkled his nose. "It feels like being asleep."

"And when you wake up? Are you in pain?"

"No, only tired." He smiled. "Except that time I hit my shoulder and got that big bruise that looked like a dog."

I smiled back at him, relieved, and in a way stupefied that I had never asked him these basic questions. I held up a clump of wires and snuck underneath them, cozying up to him. I put a finger to my lips. "Don't tell Mom."

His grin grew wider. "I won't."

We lay together for a moment, breathing, looking at the cartoon blobs dance around.

"Anna?"

"Yeah?"

"Are you leaving again?"

"Yeah."

"Back to New York?"

"Yeah."

"Mom says you're not doing anything there."

"She does, huh?" I lifted myself to an elbow and looked at him. "What do you think?"

"I think you're an artist. I think that's why you left."

My breath caught in my throat, and I sucked in a stream of air, pushing against the swell of emotion in my chest. "Yes, Henry. That's exactly why."

"It's okay, then."

"What is?"

"That you're leaving again." He turned his head and the wires went with him, rustling. "But Anna?"

"Yeah?"

"Will you email me more?" he said. "I have my own email address now."

"Of course I will, Henry."

"And will you send me pictures of your pictures?"

"I would love to," I said, which was the most honest thing I'd said to him since the accident. "And I think, once I get settled again, you should come visit me. Without Mom and Dad."

"Really?"

The door slid open, and my mother was there again. "Oh, no, Anna," she said, seeing me in Henry's bed. "You can't be in there."

"It's fine, Mom," I said.

"No, it's not." She marched toward us. "Get up."

I pressed the red call button on the remote attached to Henry's bed.

"What are you doing?" my mother said.

The nurse popped her head in. "You rang?"

I hadn't moved. I was still snuggled in next to Henry. "Is it okay for me to be here, in bed with him?"

The nurse looked from me to my mom, who had her arms crossed over her chest and said nothing.

"Henry?" the nurse said. "You comfy?"

He smiled. "Yes. Anna is my sister."

The nurse smiled back, then looked at our mother.

"I think it's fine, Mom," she said. "I think it's good for them both."

Forty-Five

BACK IN NEW YORK, it was impossible to forget what had happened. The fires downtown still smoldered. The air still stank, even in mid-October.

I clomped up the four flights of stairs to the Congress Street apartment, my small suitcase bumping behind me. I went to your bedroom first. It was still a mess, a month after the break-in. I'd been so sure it had been you, but now I understood that it was chance. Like everything else. After your dad filed the police report, the landlord changed the locks, chagrined. It was good enough for now, but I couldn't stay in our apartment forever.

There were other places, though. A million apartments to sublet, a million girls looking for a roommate. My conversation with Ryan made me realize that I didn't have to give up. There was still a way for me to get what I wanted.

I picked up broken frames, clothes, and books. I swept up glass and threw away used-up materials and broken pens. I organized everything. I even tucked the sheets into your bed, though I didn't bother looking for your comforter. I fluffed your pillows and stacked your CDs. I gingerly lifted your photographs out of the debris and set them aside.

There were more, though. Many more. I took the key to the storage room from the kitchen cabinet where we kept it tucked between the coffee mugs and ran down to the basement.

Locker #9. Nothing had changed. Flat file boxes made of thick black cardboard, stacked three feet high, each with little silver latches that reminded me of my old diaries. I flipped open the top of the first box. Inside were dozens of your black-and-white photographs, various sizes, various finishes, various degrees of abstraction. I clamped the box closed. There were eight of them, and it took me two trips to get them all upstairs. When I was finished, I went back down again for the only thing left of mine in the storage room: *Swell*.

The piece's handmade, plywood frame was on its side—ten feet long and thick as a Bible. Too big for any of our apartment walls. I shimmied it out of the closet and leaned it against the door. The light down there was too hot, blasting white circles on the Plexiglas. Even so, I could see how good it was—thousands of meticulously hand-painted red dots sewn together like a hybrid of pointillist painting and Byzantine mosaic. My eyes grazed from corner to corner, taking in the undulating wave of red. I had blended each shade from cheap acrylic tubes. Just a year ago it had been, though that was hard to believe. I rubbed my hands together, as if I could bring my fingers alive. As if I could will myself to keep fighting, to create again.

I put the frame face flat on the floor and started peeling back the tape. I pulled out an X-Acto knife from the pocket of my jeans and cut the cardboard bracing. I lifted and flattened the hooks that kept the frame together, then pulled the backing off and slowly pulled out the sailcloth. It lay in front of me, across the dirty cement floor, like a prayer carpet.

All the work I had done. All the hours, the blistered fingers, the cramped wrists. And this work had still gotten me nothing. No awards or gallery representation. No money. No career. I had nothing but this worthless *thing*. I clenched my fists to stop myself from ripping the whole thing apart.

Because Kape and his minions were wrong. It wasn't worthless. It was powerful. It was blood and pride and effort, broken and rebuilt. It was my life. I knelt in front of it, then started on the far end, slowly rolling it up to keep it safe. I kicked the empty frame back into the closet, carried the picture upstairs, and pinned it to the living room wall, next to the door piece I'd made last month.

I turned on a classical music station and made myself a cityscape of your black boxes and began. I flipped through stark Mapplethorpe-esque still lifes and half-candid shots of friends and blurry landscapes and botanical details. Then the street shots. All your pictures were well-captured and well-framed, but they weren't what would interest the art world. I needed the ones that would stop the director of the Andrews Foundation in her tracks.

I needed your self-portraits.

I moved on to the next box and felt sick. They were all of me and Jon Potts at the lake. I turned them over and set them aside. I'd destroy them. I'd never let anyone see those.

The next box. Right away, you were everywhere—posing at the truck stop, smoking a cigarette, drinking coffee, gazing out a window. Sometimes parts of you were blurry—a moving hand, a bouncing foot, a turning face—smudging the picture like an eraser might.

I dug deeper. Box after box, opened and inspected and set aside. So many images of you, your face in every expression, your skin and eyes aglow with confidence, your fat lips and the gap between your teeth so suggestive of sensation, of actual wet touch, that my skin prickled.

I set aside the best photos, making a small stack on the coffee table.

There were images of our friends: Boomer shooting pool; Tom's ringed, ink-stained fingers holding a cigarette; Lizzie smiling wide; me, too, painting or smirking or drinking a beer. I spent some moments gazing at the images of myself, looking at myself the way you had seen me. There was a hardness in my face I never realized I had before. I put them back in the box.

There must have been a hundred pictures of Milo—his face over and over, shot fast like movie stills, or close-ups of his arms and his feet and his big, paint-flecked hands. There were pictures of Milo painting and pictures of Milo laughing and Milo drinking beer and Milo sleeping.

I kept going. At this moment I was a curator. I had white gloves on my hands, a chic outfit, bold glasses. *This*, I thought about a shot of the jukebox at the Bar Car, Milo's hand reaching for a button. *This*: an extreme close-up of the top of a Christmas tree, an old-fashioned ceramic angel with a gold-tipped but broken wing. *Definitely this*: a crop of a round and naked haunch, covered in gooseflesh, tiny hairs perked up. I held this picture a long time, staring at it until I knew exactly what it was that thrilled me about it. That soft, impossibly feminine thigh was my own.

Color photos. Digital prints from your new camera. I recognized the blanket we took to Coney Island on our first NYC weekend. I recognized our hands, and the plastic cups, and the pink wine, the gingham napkins. Strangers eating ice cream and hot dogs. Suntanned children in flip-flops. The Cyclone. Your hand. Your face. You and Boomer, smiling broadly, your arms around each other.

At the bottom of the box, there was a large manila folder. I slipped out the first photograph: a stunning ten-inch-square photo, high-contrast black and white with a thin white border. In it, you stared directly into your own lens, gorgeous in that wood-creature way—high cheekbones and freckle constellations and otherworldly eyes—with your hair slicked back like you'd been swimming. You were expressionless, exposed, completely unadorned, except for a bruise under your left eye.

I peered at the photograph. I gently touched my fingertip to the bruise, as if it were a mote of dust I could wipe away. It didn't budge. Of course it didn't. This was from the weekend sophomore year when you disappeared. When Jon Potts raped you.

I slipped the rest of the photos out of the envelope. I flipped through several of the Ana Mendieta types. You were naked, covered in mud, or grass, or stones. I had seen these pictures before. I set them aside and moved on, expecting to see the young me, freshman year, walking toward you on North Lawn. My hands froze. That wasn't what I found at all. What I found was much, much worse.

Professor Kape.

He was shirtless, in bed, smiling at the camera. In *your* bed, on the Independent Floor at Balwin—the thick white duvet, *WMW* embroidered at the top, the wall of photographs behind him. My stomach loosened. It took several stunned seconds for me to understand what I was seeing. I flipped through more pictures and spread them out over the floor. Kape's lascivious mouth. His empty, bullet-hole eyes. Several pictures of him dressed, also covered in mud. He must have taken the Mendieta pictures, I realized, painting you with mud and grass and clicking the camera shutter when you told him to.

My hands disconnected from my body. I scattered the pictures, my heart thumping inside my chest. I jumped to my feet and stared, wide-eyed, my hands over my mouth. I wasn't breathing.

Click.

It was like a wall falling down. A great rumbling release.

You and Kape—all this time.

I hadn't known. I hadn't known anything.

More. I squinted, then bent down, my heart hammering around like it was trying to climb up my throat. I nudged a photo out from under the others with my toe.

The peacock wallpaper.

The gold faucet.

The Stones' powder room.

And me, pressed against the wall, cheek to wallpaper, skirt hiked up, legs splayed. Kape hunched behind me. I immediately thought of the etchings in Picasso's *Vollard Suite*: The artist depicted a hulking minotaur, raping and devouring his young mistress Marie-Thérèse Walter.

A sound left my mouth, small and sharp.

You'd pushed me so hard into him that New Year's Eve. I had always assumed it was to humiliate me, nothing more than a stupid *lark*, another way to keep me down. But this—this was something more than humiliation. This was something I did not understand. Something I did not *want* to understand.

I swept all the pictures into a pile.

Forty-Six

I CONSIDERED CALLING Lizzie. I could have shown her the pictures of Kape in Willow's bed, Kape with me in the bathroom. But what would it prove? Other than telling the world that he was worse than Picasso when it came to preying on young women. That you and I had both fallen for the same act. No one would care. No one ever cared. Picasso was still in every museum. His paintings sold for millions. He was a legend, a king, an icon. No one cared that Marie-Thérèse had committed suicide. No one cared that Dora Maar had had a breakdown.

I opened my laptop and drafted an email.

Hey Ryan, I typed. *I'm back in New York and I would love to show you a few prints I found in Willow's things. I'm working on something new, too. Can't wait for you to see! Let me know when you can come over.*

I pressed send and jammed a knuckle into my cheek. I had to do something with the pictures of me and Kape, me and Jon Potts. It seemed risky to put the photos in the trash—even the bins outside. Anyone could find them. *No.* I'd have to destroy them properly. I'd have to burn them. I looked around the apartment—*Where?* I thought. *How?*

My cell phone rang. I stuffed the pictures back into the manila envelope, except the one of you with a black eye that I would give to Ryan, and snatched it.

"Tell me about them," Ryan said.

I was taken aback by her tone, flat and practical, no chatter, no small talk. The nervous girl twisting her hair at the hotel in Chicago had been replaced by a Manhattan professional. My confidence faltered. I held the envelope in my hands, proof of my stupidity. My gullibility.

"I found a lot of cool self-portraits." I hated the halting, idiotic way I spoke.

"Can you bring them here?"

It was already five o'clock. I looked down at my terry-cloth sweats. "Tomorrow?"

"Yeah, great. I'll email you a time."

I bit my lip. I still hadn't dropped off my film at Photoreal. If I ran over there tonight, they might be able to have the slides by tomorrow. "Should I bring anything of mine to show her?"

Ryan was quiet for a moment. "Let's focus on Willow now. You can bring your stuff next time. Maybe we can even set up a studio visit with Helen."

A studio visit. Something waved through me. Excitement, embarrassment. I didn't have a studio, of course, but maybe I could use your room. I could clean out all your things, set up my easel and supplies, push the bed to the wall to use as a sofa when I needed a break. Maybe this was how it was all supposed to work.

I clicked off the phone and stood biting my cheek. Then I

stashed the manila envelope in my underwear drawer to deal with later. I would go to Photoreal anyway.

—

The next day, Ryan led me into a room that looked like a storage facility. I unclipped the clasps on the black box and carefully laid thirty of your photographs across two folding tables.

"You want gloves?"

"I'm being careful," I said. How infuriating that these pictures, taken by an almost-teenager and printed in that ugly cement building in Ohio, would wind up here, in this church, this shrine, deserving the respect of art-handling gloves. I took a deep breath to calm myself. *A studio visit.* I wasn't here for you, but for *me*. For my own future. For a chance.

Ryan leaned over the pictures, picked up the black-eye photo by its edges, and placed it in the center of the table. She closed in on it, frowning. "There are no dates, no signatures."

I pointed toward the black-eye photo. "This is from February '98."

She glanced at me, giving no clue as to whether she was happy with the work or not, and pulled a pencil from her curls. "Did you document them?"

My cheeks grew warm. I didn't know how any of this worked. I didn't know what I was supposed to do. "Not yet."

"Okay," Ryan said. "We can do it now."

She stepped over to a metal desk and pulled out a ruler, two pairs of white gloves, a small digital camera, a notebook, and several pencils.

"Let's get to work."

She showed me how to inventory the prints: Each needed to be measured, examined for marks, photographed, and given a special number. The numbers were then penciled in tiny block letters on the verso. I told her as much as I could about each print—approximate date, location, media. Most were silver gelatin prints, and yes, the negatives were gone. None could be reprinted. That made them unique, and especially valuable.

Some of the prints had tiny scratches on the surface, creased corners, notations. Anything that you'd signed was set aside, worth more money. Ryan wrote it all down on her notepad. Later, she told me, it would be entered into the computer system that all the foundation employees had access to. Despite the fact that they were your pictures, I found myself enjoying the process. The details, the precision, the sharp pencils, the neat little inventory numbers.

Ryan loved your truck-stop pictures, but she agreed with me that the black eye was the best.

"I can't wait to show Helen," she said, holding the photograph gingerly with her white-gloved index fingers. "I can totally see this one on all our press materials."

I could see it, too. I could see your face on postcards and in advertising, on the cover of *Artforum*. I stood and tried to make my breath move soundlessly around the fat lump in my throat. I reminded myself I wasn't doing this for you. I was doing it for *me*.

"I'll grab her," Ryan said. "I'll be right back."

Alone in the room, I pulled out one of the rolling desk chairs to sit. I stared at your photographs. I had to stop my fingers from raking across the table and sloshing them all to the floor. I gripped both sides of the chair and breathed.

—

Ryan held open the door for Helen. I shot up to my feet.

"Hello, Anna," she said. She was nearly as tall as Boomer with chin-length gray hair and wore a short black dress with knee-high boots and round black glasses. "Thanks for bringing these in for us."

I shook her hand. "So nice to meet you. Ryan has said so much about you."

But Helen had already moved on. She was leaning over your pictures, nose down, examining each. "Oh, yes. Extraordinary." She took a step, still bent over. "I see it, Ryan. I do quite see it."

I stood off to the side.

Ryan pointed, and Helen murmured. They rattled off numbers and framing ideas and titles. I was too nervous to speak. I realized I wouldn't mind a job like Ryan's, in a place like this, a place to start, a place to learn, cooing over art, reading and writing and thinking about it all day. I could do this, and I could use what I learned to better my own work. I consciously mirrored Helen and Ryan—their erect posture and slightly pursed lips, their hands folded behind their bodies, all their purpose.

I could do that, I thought. I could talk like them and dress like them and work like them. I could mold myself. I could transform into them if I focused hard enough. It might take some time, but I would make them see me. I would make them pay attention to my work.

I left the Andrews Foundation with a signed document in my bag. Insurance values were placed on each of the twenty-nine pictures I left there—values that I could not believe. Five thousand, three thousand, seven thousand dollars. Ryan said she'd send the paperwork to your dad for the signature. I found a seat on the C train and pulled out the consignment agreement and a pencil. Jesus, the black eye was marked at twelve. I added all the numbers together: *fifty-two thousand dollars.*

And none of it mine.

Before I could stop myself, the papers were crumpled in my hands. I wanted to throw them at the wall. I closed my eyes as the train lurched forward. Black washed over my vision. I sat still, only breathing, until the train stopped again, and I opened my eyes and uncrumpled the papers, smoothed them out against my thigh.

Forty-Seven

YOUR OPENING at the Andrews Foundation was set for the week after Thanksgiving.

"Helen had to push the Saul Leiter show to January," Ryan said when we met for lunch in a bistro just north of SoHo. She was wearing a gray pencil skirt and pressed white blouse with collars large as envelopes. Her hair was a mess of curls—wild, almost distracting.

"She was so excited about Willow's pictures. She didn't want to miss the momentum of 9/11."

I stopped twisting the pencil through my fingers to write the name Saul Leiter. Still, even after studying art for this many years, I felt so far beneath everyone else, always grasping for the names they rattled off so easily. I couldn't bring myself to write *the momentum of 9/11*, to see the vulgarity of those words in my own handwriting.

"I think the checklist is done," Ryan said. "At least for now. Her mom helped with the dates and bio and stuff. All the pictures in inventory are at the framers."

I looked up from my notebook. "Her mom?"

Ryan's brows knitted as she took a bite of her thin yellow omelet. "Yeah, she's running Willow's estate now. You know she's like a big-deal art advisor in the Marais?"

I nodded, but inside, I was screaming. The Marais, the gallery district in Paris.

Ryan dabbed her lips with a linen napkin, which she held near her face as she spoke. "Elodie thinks she can broker a deal with a gallery here, though. In New York, considering..."

I put my pencil down. I hadn't been back to La Soeurette since the terrorist attacks and I could barely afford this bowl of tomato soup, and the Andrews Foundation had a five-hundred-dollar-a-frame budget. It was bullshit. I picked up my spoon and ran it around the edge of my bowl. I hadn't had a chance to show them my own work yet, and they had said nothing about a studio visit. I had something else in mind.

"Ryan?"

My palms were damp, and I set the spoon on the saucer, placed my hands in my lap. The casket had been buried. The boxes of your photographs were at the Andrews Foundation, getting catalogued and photographed and framed. Everyone would get something out of this show, and it was clear to me now by their diversions and delays that Helen had no intention of coming to see my work. I deserved something, too. I had steeled myself for this moment, this question I was about to ask. Everything hinged on the answer. My apartment, New York City, my career, the rest of my life. Everything.

Ryan set her tiny espresso cup off to the side of her saucer. I stared at it, wondering briefly if it was a faux pas or a *thing*. She was staring at me, waiting.

TELL THEM YOU LIED

"Do you think maybe there's something for me at the foundation?" I said.

"Helen is so busy with Willow's show—"

I shook my head. "I don't mean that. I've actually always wanted to work in a museum."

"Let me talk to Helen. I don't know about the Foundation, but she might have a lead on something."

I nodded. I couldn't give up. I still wanted to be an artist. I *needed* to be. I needed to win.

———

The meeting left me feeling buzzed and hopeful. I walked over to Prince Street, deeper into SoHo, looking into shop windows at the merchandise I couldn't afford. I stared at my own reflection superimposed on the outside. I imagined what you would say if you were watching me now. I felt sure I was doing the right thing.

La Soeurette was just ahead, the blue-and-yellow awning flapping gently in the breeze. I hadn't stepped inside since September 10, almost two months ago, and I had never called to explain what had happened to you after that first call.

The door chimed as I pushed it open. The place was bustling with a late lunch service. Regina was standing behind the bar, busily mixing and icing and crushing and pouring, but it only took a moment for me to catch her eye. She glanced back at me—a double take—her face tanned and flushed at the same time, her eyes bright as coins.

She lifted her chin in greeting and nodded around the side

of the bar. I slipped past the empty hostess stand and moved toward the bar. Regina's hands never stopped moving.

"Hey," she said, opening a beer tap over a pint glass.

I sat on a stool. "Hey."

"You disappeared."

I knew what I had to say. "My roommate, the one I told you about—she died."

She closed the tap and brought her hands to her apron and wiped them dry. "Holy shit."

"Windows on the World," I said, glanced down at my own hands. I couldn't look at her. I was using you and the city's tragedy, and guilt waved through me, sour and mean. I shook it off. It was only fair. You had used me so many times, Willow.

"Shit. Wow." Regina's hands were on her slim hips. "Are you okay?"

I looked at her. I didn't know why I was there, not really, but something was pulling me. Her shirtsleeves were rolled up and damp at the edges. I could see the dagger tattoos on her wrists. I ran my eyes back up to her face. Her eyes were intent on me, and her concern looked so real. "Not really."

"I'm so sorry," she said, then found the bottle of Sancerre. She had turned me on to the wine that summer, so different from the shots and car bombs we drank in college. Such a relief. Regina poured a glass and pushed it toward me. When had anyone been so nice to me? I took the glass by the stem, heavy with gratitude. Just for this—a simple glass of wine.

When I thanked her, my voice came out warbly.

She watched me take a sip. "Do you think you want to come back? To work, I mean?"

"Would they let me? The way I left ..."

She looked over her shoulder at the kitchen, then back at me, and nodded. "I'll tell everyone what happened. I'm sure they'll put you back on the schedule if you want."

I took another sip. "Thanks, Regina."

She gave me a small smile and tapped the bar, making her way to another customer, leaving me to my glass of wine.

The light on my phone blinked. A voicemail.

"Hey," Ryan purred. "Helen says there's a new space in Chelsea that needs someone to run the front desk. They want a face. She loves your look and thinks he will, too. I think it's a salary."

A face, I thought. *A salary.*

Ryan spelled out an email address and told me to send my résumé. I spent several frantic minutes tweaking the thing I'd had on my laptop since graduation. I still had no art-world experience, so I settled for buzzwords—*restaurant attendant, staff liaison*—and added anything I could think might help me: *3.9 GPA, thesis honors, mentee of Anthony Kape, Balwin College.*

I held my breath and pressed send.

A gallery job, and salaried. One of those huge industrial spaces in West Chelsea like the Philip Roche Gallery, where glamorous people sold the work of the famous to the rich. I logged out of the internet in a kind of dream state and shut my computer.

I could pour wine at openings, sure, but I'd do more than that. I wouldn't even be an intern, but a proper employee. I'd hobnob with clients, go to parties, pick out frames. I'd meet the right people, make the right connections. I'd *work*. I'd have a *career*.

I went into your room. Your closet was huge and full. I ran a hand along the hangers, a finger up and down the stack of folded clothes. I stopped at a soft black sweater—cashmere—pulled it off the shelf, unfolded it. It was slim-fitted, with an asymmetrical cowl neck and tiny pearl buttons around the wrists. I wasn't sure if I had ever even seen you wear it. I put it to my nose and inhaled your lemon-and-smoke smell. Yes, you'd definitely worn it. Warmth cocooned me.

I slipped off my own clothes—the jeans and blouse I'd worn to meet Ryan—and tossed them on the ground. I slipped on your sweater. It was *so soft*. Like an animal, mammalian and protective. I dug deeper into the closet and found a pair of your favorite Theory pants. I pulled them on. They sat low on my hips, even lower than they had on yours, but they were a stretchy knit, and they hugged me perfectly. The sweater cinched my waist, the pearls on my wrists glowed with their white-blue shimmer.

I turned to look into your full-length mirror. Even you would have admitted that I looked perfect—a *face*. A gallery girl.

I knew I would get the job.

I walked back to your closet and stood in front of it, staring at the clothes the same way I had stared into that huge Frankenthaler painting at MoMA when I was sixteen. The collection here, too, was mesmerizing, calming in the same way. Almost as if it were telling me what to do.

So many black pants, all my size—with kick pleats, darts, wide legs, flare bottoms, or skinny hips. Sweaters in all shades of black and gray and cream and white. Plunging V-necks, scooped ballet tops, austere high turtlenecks. Belts of all kinds: silver studs and gold grommets, fringe and embroidery and tassels. I touched it all, imagining myself inside each piece.

Over at your dresser drawers, I pulled through your things: lacy camisoles, thong underwear, all the things I could use. When the pile looked big enough, I carried it all into my own room and shut the door.

Forty-Eight

I WAS READY. I had blown out my hair, parted it in the middle, and pulled it into a sleek ponytail. I had on your cashmere sweater and the Theory pants and a green wool coat with brass buttons, like a relic from a long-ago war. My own black platforms were knock-offs of the Prada shoes that you had worn the day you died. My new shoes were cheap, on sale at Aldo, but they were black and thick-soled and the right size, and they would have to do.

I spotted my face with foundation and blended everything into the perfect shade of nude. A little mascara, a little blush, a swipe of your red lipstick. Nothing dramatic. A blank slate. *A face.* You'd taught me how to do that, too, hadn't you? The first time you took my picture, walking across North Lawn. *Make your face blank*, you told me. *Go . . . empty.* I blinked at my reflection—a moment's disappointment. I was making myself a muse now, too.

Chelsea. The whole world. I pushed through the turnstile at West Twenty-Third Street, passing the tattered Missing posters, and flew up the steps. It was overcast, and much colder than it had seemed in Brooklyn. I pulled your coat tightly around me and marched west, the blisters on my feet screaming at me. I knew my way. I wouldn't stop for anything. As I crossed Tenth Avenue I turned my face away from the abandoned warehouse.

The city was awake again, despite the rubble, despite the stink. Everything felt *turned on*, electric, almost frenzied. Like we had to prove that the terrorists hadn't gotten the best of us. As I walked farther west, that feeling got more tenuous. There were smatterings of galleries, art people smoking cigarettes on the sidewalks, a coffee shop and restaurant here and there—but this neighborhood, with its wide avenues and giant billboards and old warehouses, had a stark feeling: black and gray and glass, windswept, cold, distant.

It wasn't that long ago when I had been here at your opening, propped up behind the card table, pouring wine, but it felt like years. I felt so much older now. I had changed. I was hard, fierce, and wise, and I could handle pain.

I pulled open the huge glass door to Markson Gallery. Inside was cavernous and quiet. Cement floors, an enormous black desk, white plaster walls. Empty. Nothing at all hanging on the walls, and for one electric moment, I felt I had walked into a trap. A hot bolt of fear struck through me as I pictured your wide red smile. I stood in the middle of the space, silent, stock-still, terrified of what was to come.

And then a man emerged, a regular man, a man like every other I had ever seen in Chelsea. Middle-aged, dark hair, beard, black glasses. A suit with no tie, collar open. Everything about him was ironed flat. He was coming toward me, and I forced myself not to cower. I pulled myself up straight and smiled with my neat soldier teeth.

The man stuck out his hand. "Daniel," he said, introducing himself.

I stuck out my own hand and shook as firmly as he did. "Anna Vaughn."

He stepped back, looking me up and down, rubbing a hand over his beard.

"Did you bring your résumé?"

I slipped your leather bag from my shoulder and removed a folder. Daniel took it and turned. He barely glanced back at me, waving his fingers over his shoulder. "This way."

Inside an office, small and white. A potted orchid on the desk. Daniel motioned toward an office chair opposite him. I sat, relieved, set my bag on the floor and smoothed the knit pants. Should I take off my coat? I glanced around the tiny room—no hooks, no hangers. Daniel had on his sport coat. I pulled my own tighter around me and waited.

"Well." He dropped the résumé on the desk and leaned back in his chair. "How do you know Helen?"

I bit back surprise. I thought he would ask about artists or art history or my own work, but I found myself telling him the story of you and your photographs, and Ryan and Helen and the opening at the Andrews Foundation in a few weeks. I told him everything haltingly, omitting pieces here and there, pushing from my mind the fear that you were watching me, even here, even now.

"Helen told me about her," Daniel said. "Said she's going to be big. *Willow Whitman.*"

Something about the way he said your name. . . . You were a stranger. A star.

Daniel leaned back in his chair. "Answer the phone."

No phone was ringing.

Daniel made the rudimentary hand sign for a phone and held it up to his ear, like a man playing with a toddler. "Ring, ring."

I hesitated. Was he making fun of me? I turned my fingers into a phone and held it to my ear.

"Hello?" I said softly.

Daniel burst out laughing, and I felt my heart sink. Again, the prickly cheeks. The fire inside. My hands were sweating.

He dropped himself forward and put his elbows on the desk. "Is *that* how you would answer for me?"

"Oh," I said, and as the pieces clicked together, a sense of relief flooded me. "This is, like, an audition."

Daniel nodded, a strange smirk on his face. "Yes. Good. An audition."

Again, I waited.

"Action," he said, and clapped.

I picked up the phone on his desk. Something about his smirk, about this whole situation, was revolting. It triggered memories of Kape, his goatee, his nicknames. Ripping the condom wrapper open with his teeth, the peacocks watching us. The pictures you had taken of us. But this man was separate from everything that had happened at Balwin. This was no longer about you. This was about my future.

The dial tone buzzed in my ear like a gnat, and a voice came out of my mouth—soft, stern, pleasant. "Good afternoon, Markson Gallery."

I never knew I could sound so professional. I looked at Daniel with eyebrows raised for an appraisal.

"Again," he said.

In my ear, the buzz morphed into a crank. "Markson Gallery."

"Again."

My heart was beating fast. I didn't know what was happening. "Markson Gallery, may I help you?"

"Again."

I remembered the flat, almost bored way you'd answered the phone at Roche and tried it out. "Good afternoon, Markson Gallery."

Daniel leaned back and clasped his hands at the base of his skull. "Just like that."

I held the phone away from my ear. He nodded for me to hang it up, and I did.

"Well," he said, still leaning back. "You've certainly got the look."

I wiped my hands on your pants. I was so hot. God how I wished I had taken off the coat, draped it on the chair or over my lap, anything.

Daniel pulled away and took a packet of papers from a drawer in his desk and handed it to me. I looked at the papers in my hands—black-and-white thumbnail images, about an inch square. I had to squint to make sure I was seeing correctly. But yes, they were your pictures, the same ones I had delivered to the Andrews Foundation a few days before. Fear shot through me again.

"Helen's offered them to me first," Daniel said. "Phil Roche wants them, too. He knows Willow's mother from somewhere, I gather. But Helen and I are old friends."

I tried to hand the papers back to him.

"No, no," he said, shaking his hands at me. "I want you to tell me which ones are the best."

"The best?"

"I haven't seen them. They'll be at the framer until the opening. I need to know the condition, which ones have scratches or bent corners. I need to know which are, compositionally"—he paused to cock his eyebrow and smirk—"the most arresting. So I can buy them."

He was asking the same thing everyone asked about you. It wasn't about condition reporting. It was about sex. And it was a test.

I slipped a pen from the desk, not bothering to look at Daniel. I circled one of the truck-stop pictures on the first page—your eyes looking sleepy, almost drugged, smoke hovering between your fat lips. Next, another self-portrait, you in a slip up against a brick wall—one of the smudged and disappearing pictures from your Woodman phase. There was your bruised face, too, miniaturized, in black and white. I hesitated—a sudden, unsettling compassion welling in my chest. You had been hurt in a way I hadn't understood before your father told me about your hypomanic breakdown. You had been used by men, then locked up because of it, and here I was, circling images of the pain they caused you, rating them—the more pain, the better. I was selling you back to them.

It almost made me sad. We could have been a team, Willow. I would have done anything for you. We could have worked together and broken them. Beaten them. But that's not what you did. You used me to get your revenge. You used me the way those men used you. It didn't have to be that way, but it was. That was where we were, and it was my turn to use you. You taught me that.

I circled the picture and kept going.

When I was finished, I slid the sheets back over to Daniel. His chest rose and fell dramatically as he flipped through them. I didn't need to ask. I knew he was pleased.

"I can start you at twenty," he said.

"Twenty?"

"Twenty a year."

I swallowed. A salary, but a paltry one. I'd need to keep some shifts at La Soeurette.

"Okay."

He cocked an eyebrow. "Okay?"

"Yes," I said. "Thank you."

"Good." Daniel stood and stretched out his hand for a shake. "Start Tuesday. Ten a.m."

I was standing then, too, my feet already under me, my hand already in his.

Forty-Nine

I HAD TAKEN only a few things from your closet—blouses, a pencil skirt, ballet tops, a few pairs of pants, some sexy seamed stockings and underthings. It was a small percentage of a huge whole, really, hardly anything at all. Leanne was coming at the end of the month to get your things, but she would never notice what was missing. She'd probably donate it all to Goodwill, I thought, amused by the circular nature of things. I'd hung the clothes in my own closet last night and closed the door to your room firmly, resolutely, telling myself I was finished in there.

I had to get ready. I blew out my hair with a diffuser, crunching it as I went along, but stopped before I was finished. My hair would never curl the way Ryan's did—those springy, wild spirals so unique, such a *trait*. Like your white hair. I needed something like that.

I ran a brush under the faucet and wetted my hair with it, redrying it stick straight. I stood in front of the bathroom mirror, studying myself, trying to put myself in line. The women at the Andrews Foundation, clacking around in their stilettos, the thick glasses I'd seen at the galleries that summer, Ryan's wild curls, Helen's sleek silver bob.

I took the side of my hair between two fingers, bending the brown locks right at my chin. I turned and turned and stared. A bob would change everything.

There was a pair of scissors in the junk drawer. I pulled my hair into low pigtails. I snipped and snipped and took the rubber bands out and snipped some more. It wasn't perfect, but it was good enough, even and straight—I'd always had a steady hand. I smiled at my reflection. I looked like a different person.

You were right; I did look like Edie Sedgwick.

Then, the outfit: a pressed white blouse, sleek black pants, and my Aldo platforms, despite the blisters they gave me. I gathered essentials for my first day at the gallery—red lipstick, wallet, subway card, keys, Eva Hesse book—and put everything into your black leather satchel. I tossed the army coat over my shoulders and took another glance at myself in the mirror.

I looked like nothing had ever happened.

———

Gloomily overcast, wetly cold, but I didn't mind the weather—I felt so good climbing out of the Twenty-Third Street subway station. I had given myself extra time to stop at the hole-in-the-wall that you had loved for take-out coffee. Inside the shop, people looked at me. I felt confident under their gazes. No one here had known you, no one had known what I had done. No one knew anything about my past. All these people were looking at me for me: appraising my face, my body, my clothes, and slotting me into my status. *Must be a gallery girl*, I knew they were thinking. *She must belong.*

I paid for the coffee and took it outside and walked farther west toward Markson Gallery, toward my new life. As I crossed over Tenth Avenue and passed the abandoned warehouse, I reminded myself that none of that had happened. You hadn't been mugged. I had done nothing wrong.

When I turned my head, I stopped as hard and violently as if I'd run into a wall.

You—the black-eye photograph—floating above the city.

Your face was stark in black and white, as big as the sky. You stared down at me, gorgeous in that opaque, otherworldly way I knew so well. Cheekbones and freckles and eyes and lips, unadorned, bruised, so blissfully smug.

My coffee cup slid from my hand, splattering on the sidewalk, on my pants and shoes and the lady walking by. I stumbled backward, staring so hard at your face that I almost missed the billboard's text.

THE ANDREWS FOUNDATION PRESENTS
WILLOW WHITMAN: VANISHING ACT

I had fallen down. My palms were pocked and dirty. I must have used my hands to catch myself. This was not how it was supposed to happen. Today was not about you.

Vanishing Act, I thought. *Vanishing Act. Vanishing Act.*

That day last year, at the studio. The day I slit my skin and bled onto my painting. You had those self-portraits in the style of Ana Mendieta. I remember what you said to me.

A performance piece . . . Something big.

Of course. It hadn't even been a year since your video, *2001,* the empty sidewalks, the only piece in your *MUSE* show that didn't include an image of you. A blank sidewalk, an empty sidewalk. Your *vanishing act.*

Coat bunched awkwardly around my middle, ass wet from old rain and coffee, palms were bleeding, I was a mess on the sidewalk, unable to move my eyes from your face, looking down at me. Those huge white letters. There was a quote from you, printed in white. *My mother always told me, my work is my future.*

Your mother? Your healthy, art-advisor mother who had fled to Paris after your father's marriage and set up shop in the Marais. Your mother was in charge of your estate now. Your mother was in charge of *everything.* It wasn't Milo hiding you, as I had suspected before, but you weren't dead, either.

In that moment on the sidewalk, with your face, beatific, above the city, I understood. You and your mother had been planning this for months. All of it. You made yourself disappear because you knew what we would do for you. What *I* would do. I fell right into your trap—taking your prints to the Andrews Foundation, making sure you got this solo show. Who needed a stupid young artist award when you could fake your own death and get a billboard in Chelsea?

Fifty

I DIDN'T CALL Daniel Markson before picking myself off the sidewalk and running away—from the billboard, from your eyes and the voice in my head—all the way back to the Eighth Avenue subway, underground, on the train, wiping my skinned palms on my pants and biting my lip until my mouth flooded with the taste of metal.

The billboard had cut through the effigy in my mind. You *had* made this happen. You'd planned your own vanishing act, and now I knew exactly how you'd done it.

I had to find your mother.

Your mother, her connections, her art-world savvy. She was already establishing your estate. Pulling strings, making connections, doing everything she could to establish your place in the canon. It was so obvious to me then.

She was hiding you.

I found myself in Carroll Gardens again, half running down Court Street, muttering to myself—"She did this, she's alive"—my mouth full of bile. Arms crossed, chin tucked, barreling down the sidewalk, I was barely conscious of people crossing the street to avoid me. I didn't care what they thought. I didn't care what anyone thought anymore.

Congress Street was just ahead, and I started to sprint—my lungs light as balloons, my feet barely registering the blisters. I ran and ran and turned the corner and ran even faster, feeling like I could take off. Like I could actually take flight if I pushed myself hard enough.

On the stoop, in our stairwell, going up—I heard the door above me bang shut. I stopped. Looked up. There was only one apartment on the fifth floor. Ours.

You were back.

My heart hammered in my chest. I took the rest of the stairs two at a time. Our apartment door was cracked open. I pushed it with both hands, like shoving a person down the stairs.

"Willow!"

I bounded into the kitchen.

Nothing.

The door shut behind me.

I turned, face full of triumph, expecting to see you, to *catch* you. But it wasn't you at all.

It was Professor Kape.

His voice was calm as he nodded to my painted door. "Very nice work," he said. "You've matured."

I wasn't frightened yet, only confused. "What are you doing here?"

He leaned his back against the door, arms crossed. So calm, except his face. His face was red and hard. He stared at me. "I need your help, Anna."

"With what?" I glanced at the deadbolt over his shoulder. He'd locked it. Fear prickled down my spine.

He kicked off the wall and stepped toward me. Those same old work boots on our floor. My blood whooshed from my chest, a shock of cold down my arms. *His eyes.* A simple thought crystallized: *I am in danger.* My feet and hands tingled. My bones turned leaden. My skin was wet and too thin to hold me together.

Kape planted his boots wide, blocking the door. "I didn't mean to scare you. I really just need your help."

"How did you get in here?"

He rubbed his face with his palms. His skin was red and bloated and pocked. His hair was greasy and disheveled. He was a stranger. In our apartment.

I stepped backward, away from him, but he came closer.

"I need her pictures, Anna."

His hands landed on my shoulders, and I glanced toward your room. *Oh.* That smell, the sticky sweet smell of sex, the acrid stench of turpentine and clay. *Oh, of course.* He'd been in your bed at Balwin—I'd seen the pictures. But there was more. Of course there was. There was always more with you. He'd been *here*, too. In this apartment. The weekend before you disappeared. It hadn't been Milo in your room that night. The smell was familiar because it was *him*. It was Kape.

"I—I don't know what you mean," I said.

He shook me—once, hard. He shook me as if I were sleepwalking, and he needed to wake me. And it did. My mind had been thick and slow, playing tricks. But when he shook me, I was awake again. My attention snapped to his eyes.

"She told me about the photos, Anna. I need to know now—did you show them to anyone?"

I shook my head. The pictures of us in the Stones' bathroom were just over there, on the other side of that wall, tucked in my underwear drawer. I should have torn them up. Burned them. *Something*.

Kape shook me again, hard, then closed his eyes and inhaled through his teeth like he was in pain. "She told me, Anna. She said she left them for you. Honey, please. Please. I don't want to hurt you. I just need those pictures."

Your lips. Your voice. *He won the Hugo Boss Prize.*

"The Guggenheim show," I said. Of course. Kape had been in New York. He must have been in the city on and off all summer to prep for the Guggenheim show.

"You have to understand, Anna. My life was at stake. My *career.*"

The pieces were coming together. The photo of me in your desk drawer—it had been Kape you'd been focused on, not Jon Potts. And that night, in the Stones' bathroom—I knew you'd played me, but I didn't understand why. Not even after I saw the photos of Kape in your bed. I didn't understand until that moment.

"She threatened you?" I said.

"She *manipulated* me. She'd been manipulating me from the start. We were all part of it. I know you know that. We can help each other now. Let me help you."

"How?"

He dropped his hands from my shoulders and looked

toward the ceiling. My gaze roamed around the room for something—anything—I could use as a weapon or a shield. But I was in an empty corner, and Kape was blocking me. There was nothing for me to grab on to.

I steadied myself, palm flat on a wall. "What did she do to you?"

Kape dropped his head, leaned toward me, nearly whispering. "She sank her *fangs* into me the moment she stepped on campus, Anna. She took pictures. She thought she was so smart. She thought she was a fucking genius."

His arms lifted. A gesture of despair, of pleading. "What could I do? She had me by the balls. She had me, and I couldn't let her." He looked back at me. "She had *ideas*. About herself. She was crazy—she was fucking *crazy*."

"I—I don't understand."

"She wanted me to do it, Anna. She . . . she *made* me do it."

"Do what?" I asked, but I already knew.

"Don't you see?" Kape's eyes darkened. Everything about him was red except his eyes. His eyes were black. He held his hands in fists near his shoulders, defensive, even as he closed in on me. "Don't you see?"

I shook my head no, stepped back until I felt the wall against my back.

"She's a monster!" Spittle landed on my face. "I had no choice. She planned the whole thing like a goddamn *performance piece*!"

I didn't dare wipe the spit from my cheek. I didn't dare move. My hands were out in front of me, keeping him away.

"Concocted by her—*manipulated, disgraced*!" He grabbed my wrists in a hot, tight grip. "And there was nothing—there was nothing I could do to change her mind. I like girls—it's not a *crime*. I am not a *murderer*. I tried to tell her, but she wouldn't listen."

He hunched over me, glaring, jaw tight. My head thumped against the wall. His breath was hot, rancid. "They would have taken the show away from me. She knew it. She *used* that against me."

"The Guggenheim?"

"Yes, the *Guggenheim*." His eyes were closed, face tilted upward, jaw tight. "Please just give me the pictures, Anna."

He'd been the one. He had broken in and stolen your negatives, but he didn't know about the storage room. He didn't know you'd stashed prints down there, but now he did. He'd seen the billboard in Chelsea. *Vanishing Act.*

I had to lie. I had no choice. "I don't have them."

He was on me again then, in one lumbering move, breathing through his teeth, hands squeezing my shoulders. "Don't *lie* to me."

My chest felt as if it would explode. My vision blurred with tears. "I gave everything to Ryan Zimmerman," I said at last. "All the prints are there, at the Andrews Foundation."

Kape's nostrils flared. I had never felt my bones like this, like dry twigs, like kindling under his hands. His face was so red, his teeth clenched, skin slick with sweat. He was feral. He was going to kill me, too. No matter what I did next. No matter what I said.

He shook me again, harder. "You stupid, stupid little *girl*."

It felt like being in a car accident, my neck unable to support my skull. I twisted and felt tears break over my eyes.

"Wait!" I couldn't get the rest of my words out because his

hands had gone to my neck. I toppled over. My head throbbed. My vision was blurred, but I saw my door painting above me. Right over there. Kape was on top of me, all his bulk, a giant, a monster. Squeezing. I squirmed under him, trying to free myself, to slip away. I couldn't breathe. I felt so small, so broken. I couldn't make a sound.

A ringing in my head, growing louder. Ears popping. I pushed against the floor, moving toward my painting. Toward the glass and pigment powders I'd made. I did not want to die. My work wasn't ready. There would be no show, no billboard, no monograph for me. Not yet. I squirmed, bucked, kicked limply. I'd made so many mistakes. I had done everything wrong. I tried to tell him so, but nothing came out of my mouth.

A flash of light. I stretched my arms like angel wings—out, out, then up over my head. I touched my powders. I felt my brushes, laid out, waiting. And then I felt what I was reaching for—the cold metal of my palette knife. It was in my hand. I gripped tightly, feeling for the sharp top edge, and brought my arm up.

Use your power.

I rammed the blade into his neck. He grunted; his bulk shifted on top of me. I didn't know if it would be enough, but I had no choice. I pressed hard and twisted and twisted. He let out a choking sound. I could almost breathe. I yanked out the knife. My hand was wet with blood. I squeezed it tighter and plunged it into him, again and again, until there was so much blood the knife slipped from my hand.

Kape was still on top of me, but I was coughing. *I was breathing.* His grip was gone. I heaved his body up and off of me. A grunt. A wail. I was flat on the ground again, flashes of light in my eyes.

I twisted myself into sitting and clutched my throat with my bloody hand. There was blood everywhere. I had to get up. Kape was a lump. Unmoving. I had to do something. I maneuvered to my hands and knees, a pain ripping through my chest. My purse. Your purse. I crawled across the floor until I felt the strap in my fingers, tugged it toward me. I dug around inside for my phone. I flipped it open and dialed 911. When the operator answered, I said the only words that I could muster.

"Willow's dead. Please. Four ten Congress Street."

Fifty-One

MEN POUNDED DOWN the door. Kape was flat and blue and swollen on the floor, blood pooled under him. The men were shouting things at each other. They strapped Kape to a gurney. I had sunk myself into a corner of the living room, shivering. I willed myself small, to disappear. I covered my eyes, and when I looked again, Kape was gone but his blood puddle was expanding across the wood floor, like it was trying to get to me. The smell, too: thick and rotten and metal. I retched, but I was empty. Nothing came out. My hands felt glued to the sides of my face. Someone was shouting at me, but I couldn't answer. I couldn't understand anything. An EMT gathered me in a swoop. I couldn't resist him, there was no point. He was too strong. I was shivering, small and weak and insubstantial.

He carried me down the steps and outside and into an ambulance. Someone put a blanket around my shoulders. My teeth chattered. They cut off my shirt. I tried to stop them. *No bra.* I didn't want to be exposed. But they held me down.

"We have to check for injuries," a woman said calmly. "There's so much blood."

―

I opened my eyes in the emergency room. I was in a hospital gown. My hand was wrapped in bandages. My throat was raw. Someone was holding a Styrofoam cup of water, straw bent to my lips. I blinked.

Boomer.

"Drink," he said.

I took the straw in my lips and sucked, then let it fall. "How did you get here?" I asked, voice croaking.

Boomer set the water on the little tray. "We've been taking turns."

"We who?"

"Everyone."

"How long has it been?"

"Not that long. Six hours or so. Your parents are on their way."

Maybe the EMTs had given me something to sleep. I didn't remember changing clothes or being bandaged. Everything was dim, foggy.

"What happened?"

"You killed him, Anna," he said. "You cut his jugular. You saved yourself."

Things were coming together again. I put a hand on my throat. "He killed her."

Boomer nodded. His eyes were misty.

"And you," I said. "You were in love with her."

Boomer smiled, smoothed my hair back. "No."

I didn't flinch at his touch. It was soothing, gentle, but I was still confused. "Those notes, though. Milo—"

Boomer laughed, the sound small. It turned into a long sob. He dropped his head forward into his chest. "I tried to tell you. So many times. I wanted to tell you. I knew you would understand. I wasn't stalking her. Nothing like that. I was begging her to leave me alone. To give me time." He wiped his face, then looked at me again. "She knew something about me I wasn't ready to tell you all about."

I waited.

"All my life," he said. "I tried with girls. I tried so hard. With you, too, Anna. I just wanted to be like everyone else. All my football buddies. But I was lying. I don't want to lie anymore."

I leaned forward then, toward Boomer, because it did make sense. The changes in him, his freedom, his joy, Mason, that bartender at Happiness. They were more than friends. I just couldn't see it, because I was too obsessed with *you*.

"I had a relationship at school," he said. "We kept it a secret."

"Who?"

He shook his head. "A football player. He's why I quit the team."

I understood. Oh how I understood. Boomer was living with secrets, buried deep inside, just like I was. "How did she find out?"

He laughed then, tears in his eyes. "She saw us in Indy. She took pictures of us." His shoulders shook. "She held it over my head for three years. She made me buy her drugs. She made me do her dirty work—dosing Jon Potts with Special K."

"You knew?"

He didn't look up.

"Hey," I said. "Hey. It's okay. I understand."

The curtain around my bed zipped open, and Officer Tennison walked in.

Boomer stood. "I'm sorry for all the secrets." He shook his head. "It was so stupid. So fucking pointless."

He was gone, and Tennison was waiting.

It was time to tell the truth.

Fifty-Two

I WISH YOU could have seen it, Willow.

After the story broke, it wasn't just the art world that cared about you. It was everyone. Everywhere. The *New York Times* reprinted your black-eye photograph on the front page of the Art & Design section. One of your Mendieta prints got *Artforum*'s December cover. Susan Sontag published a four-thousand-word opinion piece in the *New Yorker* on the intersection of photography and violence, after being oh so affected by your show.

Your value ballooned, too. Kape had destroyed the negatives he'd stolen from our apartment—police had found the remnants in his Midtown hotel room, along with your Hermès scarf—which meant your photographs were one of a kind. Daniel Markson, now your gallerist, bumped up the prices until each print was worth more than a little yellow house in Ohio. Nobody questioned it. We all knew what was for sale—and it wasn't just photography. It was the *frenzy* you'd made. The sensation. You were a phenomenon, Willow. Beautiful and perfectly tragic, desired to death.

They wanted me, too, for a while. A stark black-and-white portrait you'd taken of me on the subway wound up in the *Post*, next to one of you and Kape together. The headline read DARK ARTISTS, and the story underneath was salacious. Reporters called me for quotes. Photographers followed me for weeks. It made sense—I was the only one left alive—but you'd be proud of me, Willow. I held back. I gave them nothing.

It was the landlord who found you—out in that overgrown plot that he called his garden, wrapped in your monogrammed comforter, no longer pristine. Your body, in a shallow grave, three months dead, was bloated, leaking, and torn. Your skin had turned from blue to green to ocher and had just recently begun to liquefy. Your gums had lost their hold on your teeth, and your pearly nails had loosened from the sludge of you.

Beautiful Willow Whitman, no longer beautiful.

We knew all that because before he called the police, the landlord used a whole roll of film to capture you out there. I heard he sold the negatives for half a million dollars—but I never asked him myself. I never saw him again.

I cried, though, because the truth was inescapable. You had worked your whole life to fit yourself into a frame, and you got it, Willow—your image was everywhere. Your pictures would live forever. But your *life* was over.

It wasn't a fair trade.

Vanishing Act covered two full floors at the Andrews Foundation. The opening was packed. Your dad was there, as misty-eyed as a father of the bride, with Leanne on his arm. Your mother, the director of your estate. Ryan, and Helen, and Philip Roche, and Daniel Markson, wearing a fucking cravat. Representatives from all the auction houses and art museums, including two curators from MoMA, came by to bless your canonization. I only know because I saw Patrick McMullan's photo spread of the event in *Interview*.

I stayed home. Not at our place—I haven't walked down Congress Street a single time in all the years since your death—but in Boomer's Chinatown apartment, where I stayed for six months while I pulled myself together. I went back to work when I could, letting Regina pour me glasses of Sancerre and pull me out of myself until I realized who I was, and who you were. It was Regina who helped me pick apart my feelings for you—how I had conflated envy with desire and love, making something close to hate.

That January, I submitted my MFA application to Yale under a fake name, as to not be associated with the spectacle of you. I didn't use the painting of us I made, either. I left the door in the apartment, and never bothered to pick up the slides from Photoreal. I sent Yale *Swell* instead.

In New Haven, I began a series of fabric paintings—old garments sourced from Goodwill, painted and cut into tiny squares and sewn onto sailcloth like tiles in a mosaic. My new works were monumental, as large and spooling as quilts, and they were all city scenes: three brownstones in a neat row; a skyscraper; a crowd at Central Park.

Maybe I could have used them to land a gallery and launch my career, but I didn't. Because when Henry saw them, his eyes flicked brighter than I'd seen them in years. And when I asked if he wanted them for his room, he nodded once, emphatically, and rushed over to hug me.

You were wrong about one thing, Willow. You believed your only power was in your youth and beauty. I don't blame you. I really don't. All the men who used you, who violated you—that's what they wanted you to believe. They wanted all of us girls to believe that's where our worth was. Your father was right. They *had* broken you. They had made a monster out of you.

Because there's one thing I never told anyone. The thing that Kape said that day in our apartment—the thing that has echoed in my mind all these years: *Like a goddamn performance piece.*

I didn't tell the police, but he was right.

Kape was the weapon you used on yourself. You'd tested all of us, like trying out new media, to see how far we would go for you. Kape was the one who had passed. He was the one who had too much to lose. He was the one who would take your life for you. The rest of us just played our parts.

You got everything you wanted, Willow.

But it's okay.

I promise not to tell.

Acknowledgments

Huge thanks (bouquets of flowers, boxes of brigadeiros, gallons of champagne) to my agent, CeCe Lyra—getting your first email in May of 2021 was the best thing that happened to my writing career. I am forever indebted to you for seeing the potential in my work and helping me navigate the crazy world of publishing. Thank you also for the book and podcast recommendations—I know I can count on you to match my freak when it comes to stories!

To Cassidy Leyendecker for taking this book on, and to Adam Wilson for seeing it through. I was so lucky to have *two* brilliant editors who understood what I was trying to do. Both of you helped me crystallize my ideas into an actual story. Adam, I will never see the word *muse* without thinking *m(is)use*.

This book would not exist without Francesca King's keen eye, Caitlin Kunkel's genius for plotting, and Melissa Elliotte's enthusiasm, care, and thoughtfulness. You three are the best writing friends a person could have.

Thank you to my early readers: Jennifer Close and the writers at Catapult, Arkadia Delay, Jen Evans and the twisted sisters, all the supersmart interns at P.S. Literary who gave me the Gen Z take. To the brilliant women who indulged my waffling panic along the way: Bianca Marais, Andrea Bartz, Amanda Pellegrino, and Caitlin Barasch. Emily Lowe Mailaender, I'm sorry you got mugged in 2001, but thank you for letting me steal that nugget for my story. I'm so glad you are okay!

My children, Hugo, Juliet, and Cyrus—thank you for leaving me alone for *several minutes* at a time. You really taught me time-management skills! My parents, you guys are crazy but I love you. Your generosity has helped me accomplish all that I have, and I appreciate it every day. My siblings, Lizabeth, Leigh, and Johnny—we've really been through it! You have been my rocks, and I will always be there for you, too. I love you.

And Jordan—the optimist. You've believed in me more than anyone in my life (even before you read a word I'd written), and you gave me the space and time I needed to make my dream come true. Thank you.

Author's Note

Among the fictional characters in this book, I've mentioned some very real people, too. Camille Claudel, François Gilot, Dora Maar, Ana Mendieta, Wally Neuzil, Edie Sedgwick, Marie-Thérèse Walter, and Francesca Woodman are among so many other women whose art I admire and whose lives I find compelling and haunting.

In the history of art, there exists a specific deadpan scrutiny of *female as object*—and a dangerous dismissal of the trauma such scrutiny can cause. I believe that it is impossible for women to exist within the art world's fun house of reflections without absorbing some of its cold and critical eye. So often that eye turns inward, especially with young women. Young women begin to see themselves as objects to be examined, images to be beheld. They will be gazed upon. Judged. Worshipped or ridiculed, depending.

And so, to any such young woman reading this, I have a message: You are more than *thing* and more than *image*. Don't let anyone flatten you.